PRAISE FOR CHANDLER KLANG SMITH

"Chandler Klang Smith is one of the most exciting new novelists I have read in some time. Her precise, lyrical voice should enchant a good many readers. *Goldenland Past Dark* is an impressive debut that signals the beginning of a long and fruitful career."

—**Nicholas Christopher,**
author of *Veronica* and *The Bestiary*

"Like a Max Fleischer cartoon or a Charlie Chaplin film, *Goldenland Past Dark* sneaks in real, unsettling weirdness and lingering melancholy behind a facade of zany fun. In this vivid, highly original debut, Chandler Klang Smith proves herself to be an imaginative force to be reckoned with. Step inside this circus tent: you'll be glad you did."

—**Christopher Miller,**
author of *The Cardboard Universe*
and *Sudden Noises from Inanimate Objects*

"Chandler Klang Smith's debut is filled with fascinating freaks and language that evokes the magic of a night under the big top."

—**Lev AC Rosen,**
author of *All Men of Genius*

GOLDENLAND PAST DARK

BY CHANDLER KLANG SMITH

ChiZine Publications

FIRST EDITION

Goldenland Past Dark © 2013 by Chandler Klang Smith
Cover artwork © 2013 by Erik Mohr
Cover design © 2013 by Samantha Beiko
Interior design and divider image © 2013 by Danny Evarts

Lyrics to "Nickelodeon," on pages 246–248, by David Crellin, aka Armitage Shanks, The Carny Preacher (*www.thecarnypreacher.com*), reprinted with permission. With thanks to Pinky d'Ambrosia and Circus Contraption.

Distributed in Canada by
HarperCollins Canada Ltd.
1995 Markham Road
Scarborough, ON M1B 5M8
Toll Free: 1-800-387-0117
e-mail: hcorder@harpercollins.com

Distributed in the U.S. by
Diamond Book Distributors
1966 Greenspring Drive
Timonium, MD 21093
Phone: 1-410-560-7100 x826
e-mail: books@diamondbookdistributors.com

Library and Archives Canada Cataloguing in Publication Data

Smith, Chandler Klang, 1984-
    Goldenland past dark / by Chandler Klang Smith.

Issued also in electronic format.
ISBN 978-1-927469-35-4

    I. Title.

PS3619.M58G64 2013   813'.6   C2013-900091-7

CHIZINE PUBLICATIONS
Toronto, Canada
www.chizinepub.com
info@chizinepub.com

Edited by Samantha Beiko
Copyedited and proofread by Kate Moore

Canada Council   Conseil des arts
for the Arts   du Canada

We acknowledge the support of the Canada Council for the Arts which last year invested $20.1 million in writing and publishing throughout Canada.

ONTARIO ARTS COUNCIL
CONSEIL DES ARTS DE L'ONTARIO
50 YEARS OF ONTARIO GOVERNMENT SUPPORT OF THE ARTS
50 ANS DE SOUTIEN DU GOUVERNEMENT DE L'ONTARIO AUX ARTS

Published with the generous assistance of the Ontario Arts Council.

Printed in Canada

For Eric Taxier, my first and best reader, always.

"They'll never find me, behind this nose."
—Jimmy Stewart, *The Greatest Show on Earth*

GOLDENLAND PAST DARK

PART ONE

KING
OF THE
CLOWNS

1962

CHAPTER ONE

THE CLOWN IS PUTTING ON HIS FACE. Light bulbs ring his dressing room mirror, and on his vanity a dozen glossy photographs show him posed atop a saddled ostrich—he's autographed about half of them, so far. Watching his reflection, he uses a delicate brush to paint dark diamonds around his eyes, then adds a dab of red to the tip of his nose. He draws surprised commas for eyebrows. Just as he's finishing, a bejewelled acrobat appears at his door. She knocks shyly.

"Mr. Bell," she says, "they're waiting."

Meanwhile, under the big top, the crowd rustles and fidgets in anticipation—until the ringmaster steps into the spotlight. His black shadow spills out behind him. Around his neck he wears a red bow tie, which spins slowly, like a tiny propeller.

"Ladies and gentlemen, boys and girls," he intones. "I give you the one—the only—king of the clowns!"

Deafening applause. Men lift their sons and daughters onto their shoulders to see. Women fan themselves excitedly. Some swoon.

Three burly men carry a life-sized painting of the clown in his harlequin suit out into the ring. The crowd groans with disappointment; they laugh sheepishly behind the backs of their hands. But even though it is only a painting, they feel strangely drawn to it. It's a perfect likeness: the clown sits carelessly on a throne, surrounded by peacock feathers, bunches of grapes, and velvet curtains. He wears a tiny gold crown slightly askew and holds a sceptre topped with a jester's head. His harlequin suit, checkered black and white, swirls like a dream of chessboards. He looks content, affable, with a guileless, almost childlike grin. He has a hunchback, is a bit on the small side, true, but these flaws just add to his quirky charm, like Charlie Chaplin's moustache or baggy pants. In some inexplicable way, he looks familiar.

Gazing out on the crowd with hooded eyes, the ringmaster announces that he will now cast a spell, even though he retired from magic—"that dark art"—long ago. The three burly men prop up the painting on a giant easel, then cover it with a tarp. The ringmaster pulls on a pair of white gloves and draws a slender wand from his sleeve. It is black as ink, with an inch of white at its tip, like ash on a cigarette.

"Abeo, novo, exorior!" he thunders, slashing the wand through the air.

Smoke billows everywhere. As it clears, the three men remove the tarp from the painting. The crowd gasps. Though the painting is as beautiful as ever—the grapes, feathers, and curtains remain brilliant and unchanged—the clown is now standing outside the frame, crown, sceptre, and all.

Applause roars all around him, but the clown ignores it. He's intent on getting back inside the painting. Much laughter as he shakes his jingling sceptre in annoyance, pushing and kicking the picture. He goes around behind it, climbs the easel and looks over the top of the frame. He walks away, then comes back with a running start and flings his body at the canvas. But it's like running into a wall. He falls flat on his back. The crowd is in stitches. The ringmaster comes to help him up, but the angry clown just shakes his fist. You got me into this mess, he seems to be thinking. You get me out.

The clown limps around a little, scowls, and stomps his foot. Then he holds a finger in the air, struck by an idea. He hurries off stage left and returns with—a cannon! The crowd is now torn—some still howl with laughter, but many others shout warnings, shriek, cover their eyes. The clown ignores it all. He puts on a helmet and goggles, lights the long rope fuse with a gigantic match, and climbs into the barrel. He waves the three burly men over, and obediently, they aim him at the painting. The fuse burns, burns, burns, leaving a snail trail of ash, until, in a flash of sparks, he hurtles out.

He flies, and for a second as he hangs in the air, it seems like his plan might actually work. Then he tears straight through the canvas, leaving a clown-shaped hole.

Webern Bell woke up face down on the dirt floor of his tent, arms and legs splayed, as if he'd just been thrown a great distance. All around him, the canvas walls rippled in the wind, hitting the tent poles in dull slaps. He had the same queasy sensation he always did when he woke up too suddenly: that he wasn't alone, that an intruder was too close for comfort, not just in the room with him, but a little ways inside his mind. Webern tried to ignore the feeling. He tried to pull the blanket up over his head, but someone else yanked it away first.

"We have to go," insisted the blurred figure. Webern rubbed the hump that rose from the left side of his back, and squinting, reached for his glasses. It was just Explorer Hank, the animal tamer, crawling around the floor of the tent. Hank was busy stuffing the many pockets of his khaki shorts and safari jacket with everything he could grab: a rubber chicken, a set of red juggling balls, a slide whistle, a comic book.

"Hank, it's still dark out."

"It'll get a lot darker if we don't hurry." Hank found Webern's suitcase under a red wig and a pair of inflatable pants. He popped it open and started to throw things in. "A man like that sleeps for nobody."

"Who, Dr. Show?" Sometimes, the ringmaster delivered Shake-spearean curses and threatened them with the kinds of torture that hadn't been around since the Middle Ages, but Webern knew better than to take him seriously.

"It'll be us, next!"

"What in the hell are you talking about?" Webern pulled on a pair of dirty jeans. The roof of the tent was low—four feet high—but he was able to stand without stooping any more than usual. He glanced around, looking for his sneakers.

"Mars Boulder." In his haste, Hank pulled a tent stake loose, and a flap of canvas whipped through the air. He said something else that Webern couldn't hear. Needles of rain flew into the tent.

"Who?" Webern yelled over the roaring wind.

"Out there! Look!"

Webern peered out into the storm. In the middle of the campground, a meagre bonfire was still spitting. A lone figure circled it. He moved heavily but with terrifying force, like a tree tearing itself up by the roots. Silhouetted against the sky, his face looked smashed in, as though his nose had been broken several times. For a moment, as he gestured against the pale flames, Webern thought he was trying to conduct the storm. Then he saw that it was a sword he held in his hands.

"Meow?"

Webern looked down. Ginger, the tiger cub, was rubbing her face on his legs.

"Give her to me." Explorer Hank crawled over to Webern, shoved the suitcase at him, and scooped up the bedraggled animal. "Shh, shh. Daddy's here."

Webern glanced around the tent. The only shoes still unpacked were a pair of green frogman flippers, so he stepped into those.

"I feel like a freak," he said, looking down at his feet.

"No one's gonna stab this kitty," Explorer Hank murmured to Ginger. "Not if Daddy can help it, oh no." He covered the tiger's ears with his hands. "Stop upsetting her!" he hissed. "Just grab your shit so we can get out of here!"

Except for some empty Moxie cans and a sock or two, the dirt floor looked bare. Webern didn't notice the circus's travelling schedule left crumpled up in one corner. He hefted his suitcase and followed Explorer Hank out into the rain.

Cold drops stung Webern's naked hunchback, and he hugged the suitcase to his chest self-consciously. Most of the other performers' tents were already gone; Hank must have woken them sooner, when there was still time left for packing up. Leaving his bed behind in such cruel weather gave Webern a lightheaded feeling, and as he snuck along behind Hank, he thought vaguely of children in bedtime stories, who floated out their windows into the cold blue night.

Once they were far enough away from the campsite, Hank began to run across the empty field without looking back. Webern scrambled to catch up. Behind them, he thought he could hear blades clashing. Maybe it was only the wind.

"Hank," he whispered, "c'mon, wait up. That guy does look nuts. Should we really just leave Dr. Show like this?" His arms ached under the weight of the suitcase.

Hank glanced over his shoulder, barely slowing down. "If you want to stay, it's your funeral." Ginger meowed and pulled herself up onto his shoulder. Her wide eyes reflected the distant fire. Hank kissed the top of her head, hushing her.

Webern's flippers slapped the ground. A few yards away, a pair of headlights switched on. The white light blinded him. Hank hurried around to the side of the car, and Webern followed him.

The yellow Cadillac was packed with other circus performers. Webern sat with his suitcase on his knees, crushed between Hank and Brunhilde, the bearded lady. In front of him sat the giant, Al, who had the seat pushed all the way back.

"We leave now?" asked Vlad, who, along with his Siamese twin Fydor, sat in the driver's seat. They were joined at the chest, in a pose that suggested they were always just on the verge of breaking off a brotherly embrace.

"Yeah, and step on it." Hank slammed the car door and the Cadillac sped off down the muddy road.

Webern leaned forward to look around Brunhilde and out the window, but all he could see were raindrops racing across the glass. "Where's everybody else? Where's Nepenthe?"

"Schoenberg has brought this fate upon us all—foolish man." Brunhilde swung her thick golden braid over one shoulder. She was a tall warrior goddess of a woman, with hips the breadth of reindeer antlers, and right now she was taking up half of Webern's seat. "I warned him he must never cross a Klingenschmiede. They strike a devil's bargain, and they never forget what they are owed."

"Beats me how Dr. Show even found that Clinging Swede in the first place." Hank tapped his riding crop against his knee; Ginger batted at it with her paws. "It's some kind of curse. Riffraff and flimflam after us everywhere we go."

"Like attracts like," quipped Fydor. Vlad snickered.

"Enrique played his part too, though, didn't he?" Hank leaned back in his seat. Enrique was the sword swallower, but he'd gambled away his blades in a cockfight two towns earlier, and since then had been putting decidedly less glamorous objects down his throat instead, like the handle of a shovel.

"Enrique's just an excuse," Al grumbled. "Dr. Show's been saying for months he knew a guy out east with some antique sword for sale. Woulda thought it was Excalibur the way he talked. Probably the reason we came this way in the first place."

"Can't you all shut up for *one minute*?" Webern hated it when his voice squeaked. He tried to keep his breath steady. "I asked a simple—"

"Shh. Calm down, little buddy." Hank ruffled Webern's hair like he was another baby tiger. "She's with Eng and Enrique, in the truck. They're right behind us."

Webern half turned to look. Sure enough, the jalopy followed them at a distance, tent poles strapped to its roof, dragging the rusty red trailer behind it. Its headlights flickered dimly as they strained against the night.

Webern Bell hadn't been traveling with the circus long—he'd joined up in March and it was now only August—but already he couldn't imagine going home again. He had grown up in Dolphin River, Illinois, a suburban town where the trees were skinny and the houses brand-new or (often as not) still under construction. The air there smelled like overturned dirt. Supermarkets announced grand openings every weekend. Jackhammers ripped through underground cables and put all the stoplights on the fritz, while the smokestacks of the light bulb factory poured endless clouds into the sky. Sometimes, walking through his neighbourhood, Webern would find a street full of nails, or discarded lumber cut into unusable chunks, like enormous jigsaw puzzle pieces. He didn't know why he bothered exploring. Every road ended in a cul-de-sac.

Before Dr. Schoenberg discovered him, Webern lived with his father, a silent man who spent his evenings in an easy chair with a bottle of gin and a box full of war medals, which he often fell asleep clutching to his chest. Sometimes he rattled the box when Webern got too close. Webern had a mother once, and sisters too, but they were all gone. He hoped his sisters wouldn't come back; he knew his mother never would. His high school was built right next to a garbage dump, but when he biked there in the mornings, he always felt like the vultures were circling him, not the mounds of steaming trash.

Dr. Schoenberg discovered Webern one spring evening when the trees were full of songbirds returning from long journeys. Webern was riding his unicycle outside in the rain-damp street, and Schoenberg, driving his yellow Cadillac, spotted the boy a moment too late.

"Hands on the handlebars, hands on the handlebars, my boy!" he had exclaimed as Webern slid off the hood of his car.

Webern limped to his 'cycle, which had rolled some yards away, and hefted it upright. He checked its chrome for signs of damage. "Sorry, mister. But there's nothing to hold onto, see?"

Fortunately, the Cadillac's fender hadn't hurt Webern much, nor did it wreck his unicycle. But nevertheless, Schoenberg insisted he wanted to "atone." He took Webern out to an all-night diner and, over pancakes, explained the enormous undertaking that had distracted him, that was, in fact, consuming his life: the creation of a new travelling show, destined to be unlike anything the world had ever seen.

"It is not all glory and fire, I am afraid," Dr. Schoenberg intoned, his dark eyes flashing. "I, my boy, am but the humblest of circus servants. I know not of the tightrope, nor the trapeze; I venture into the mouths of neither cannons nor cats. I cannot juggle, I do not throw knives. And I ride bareback only when necessity demands it."

"So, what do you do, then?" Webern asked.

"Why, good sir—" Schoenberg leaned toward Webern across the sticky table. "—I am the ringmaster."

If Dr. Schoenberg had grinned or snapped his fingers, if he had talked about fun times or money or even fame, Webern would have seen through the trick. In his fifteen years, he had come to distrust winks and handshakes, guarantees and hearty laughs. But the man's solemnity, verging on sadness, and the odd, antiquated way he spoke— the pallor of his face under the diner's fluorescent lights, and the gently shaking fingers with which he held his cigarette—these things drew Webern in, mesmerized him, even. In Dr. Schoenberg's blue-black hooded eyes, Webern saw something strange and yet familiar. Maybe it was a particular madness they both shared, a longing for escape that filled their veins like slow poison. Maybe it was a peculiar melancholy that shaped itself into visions of weird and freakish acts. But, though he doubted Schoenberg's promises of gorgeous tightrope walkers and fabulous silk-lined tents, Webern knew he would follow him anywhere. He left that night, taking nothing more than the clothes on his back and his unicycle, stowed in the Cadillac's trunk.

The unicycle was there now. Webern could almost hear its wheel spinning, *tick tick tick*, in the compartment just behind where he sat. As the Cadillac splashed down the muddy lane, he wished he could pedal along outside for a little bit—it would calm him down. They'd been driving for more than two hours, and right now, with his legs falling asleep under his suitcase and Ginger batting playfully at his hands every time he moved, it was hard not to surrender to a sense of impending doom.

It didn't help that Brunhilde had taken out her suitcase and was now clucking somberly as she flipped back the lid. Webern resisted the urge to cover his eyes. The inside of Brunhilde's suitcase was shellacked with mementos of what she called "the forgotten atrocities," mostly snapshots she'd taken while wandering the wreckage of her burnt-out city during the war: steeples like black spikes—the Ihagee cameraworks, now a shattered mausoleum—a charred arm, lying in the street—and, most damning of all, a vast panorama taken from a distance, the great wooden skyline gazing out from the faded page with glass-less windows like haunted eyes.

"You know, we often had evacuations of this kind in the Fatherland." She stroked the loose corner of one photograph, which depicted a headless statue—Webern hoped it was a statue—lying in the ruined Frauenkirche cathedral. "Just before the bombing—"

Everyone groaned.

"Oh, give it a rest, Brunhilde," said Explorer Hank. "Not Dresden, again."

She hefted the suitcase onto her knees and swivelled it towards the front seat. "I believe Al still has much to learn from my little museum."

Al swatted the suitcase away with the huge paddle of his hand. "I'm good, lady."

"It is important that we remember, is it not, Webern?" Brunhilde nudged the suitcase toward him. Webern mimed a noose tightening around his neck, crossed his eyes, and stuck his tongue out one corner of his mouth. She clucked again, but this time allowed herself the faintest wisp of a smile.

Brunhilde was a little crazy, no doubt about that, but fortunately Webern was still more or less on her good side. When he joined the circus, she showed excitement (or hints of it, anyway—Brunhilde never got too excited about anything but Dresden) on hearing his name with the W pronounced as a V, and unlike the rest of the performers, she never shortened it to "Bernie." She even asked him if the name had been in his family long, to which he replied vaguely that he was sure he had German in him somewhere. He didn't dare tell her the truth: that his father had first heard the name while serving overseas during the war.

"Henry, I take it that you, too, cannot bear to face the truth."

"You know, I never enlisted," said Hank. "Flat feet. It's not my fault they burned down your house. So how come you want to torture me?"

Brunhilde stroked her beard. "Why should it be torture to understand?"

"Oh, come on. You wouldn't show us dead babies and exploded hospitals if this was a history lesson."

"You Americans act so tough, but underneath you are just like the ones you call the rubes. You want cotton candy, cotton candy that melts away to nothing and leaves only sweetness. You let the little man on the little stage show you tricks, and then you give him your wallet. Is that what you call a history lesson?"

Hank sighed. Ginger stood up in his lap and cleaned his chin with her rough pink tongue.

"You are the one who needs to learn a lesson from history, " Fydor retorted. "You and all of your people. Many stories could be told of the war. Many, many sad and monstrous stories. But you will listen to none. And yet the tale of your suffering you have told us a thousand times."

"A thousand and one," Vlad agreed dolefully.

Webern leaned back in his seat. A few drops of rain still pattered, here and there, on the Cadillac's windows, but it was slackening. The storm was almost over, and soon they'd be out of this car, somewhere warm and dry where Dr. Show would meet them—unless, of course, that Boulder guy hacked him to pieces first. Webern tried to keep from getting carsick. At least Nepenthe was safe. But thinking about her just made him feel anxious in a different way.

Along the shoulder of the highway, little red signs flashed like warnings: *She put a bullet / Thru his hat / But he's had closer / Shaves than that / Burma Shave.* Webern closed his eyes and leaned back. Maybe he could still sleep a little bit tonight.

"Whoa, there." Hank prodded the back of Vlad's neck with his riding crop. He pointed out the back window. "I think they're trying to tell us something."

Webern turned to look. Sure enough, the headlights of the jalopy were flashing behind them.

"We stop, you say?" Vlad asked. Up in the darkness ahead, pink neon letters flickered *EATS*. Without waiting for a response, Vlad jerked the wheel in the direction of the exit, and in moments the Cadillac was splashing into the parking lot of a desolate all-night greasy spoon.

Webern was relieved to climb out of the cramped back seat, away from Ginger's claws and Brunhilde's prodding hip bones. He was even more relieved to move the heavy suitcase off his legs. But as he leaned against the car door to stretch, he remembered he didn't have a shirt on. He started to duck, but it was too late: the beams of the truck's headlights had already caught him. He slipped one hand protectively over his hump. Back in middle school, some of the other kids had made a game of patting it—"for luck"—whenever he let his guard down, even for a second.

The truck crunched to a stop on the gravel, and Nepenthe hopped out the driver's side, swinging the keys around her gloved finger. She wasn't supposed to drive since she didn't have a license, but apparently tonight was an exception. In her black hat and veil, she looked like a rich widow.

"Dr. Show said he'd meet us here," she announced.

Some of the other performers exchanged doubtful glances, and Nepenthe snorted, as if she'd just delivered the punch line to a joke way over their heads. She jumped down from the running board, lifted her veil, and spat a peach pit into a puddle. Eng the contortionist climbed out the passenger side window, but Enrique stayed behind in the cab of the truck. No one said anything to him.

Webern was rattling the locked door of the Cadillac when Nepenthe came over to join him. She hopped up on the hood, crossed her legs, and pulled out her cigarette case, a little silver box that she sometimes claimed to have stolen from her psychoanalyst. According to Nepenthe, her life before the circus had been posh.

"Got a light?" She took out a green, hand-rolled clove.

"Sorry." Webern gave the door handle one last tug, then gave up and folded his arms to his chest.

"That's quite an outfit you have on there," she said. She looked from his bare hump down to the green frog flippers. Her face was all but invisible behind the veil's thick black mesh. "You look like an evolutionary leap."

"Yeah, well, that's Hank's fault. Did you see where Vlad and Fydor went? I need to get back in here for my shirt." Webern squinted across the parking lot, empty except for their two vehicles and a dented station wagon. The rain had dwindled to a stinging mist. The other circus players were filing into the diner, murmuring anxiously among themselves.

"No problemo." Nepenthe reached up under her hat, into the masses of dark curly hair she wore in a messy chignon. She extracted a bobby pin, hopped down from the car hood, and in seconds, jimmied the lock.

"Thanks," muttered Webern. He crawled into the car and dug through his suitcase till he found a T-shirt and shoes. Inside, he was cursing. She always had him at a disadvantage.

Webern had met Nepenthe, whom they called the Lizard Girl, the day after he joined the circus. She was his age, but she seemed different than the girls he'd known in high school, and not just in the obvious ways. Nepenthe called herself a poet, and she wore her loneliness proudly, the way other girls wore their dates' letter jackets. She carried a drawstring bag full of salted peach pits, which she sucked, then spat out in the street, and she constantly smelled of the spicy clove cigarettes that she rolled in green papers. She often called Webern "a chauvinist" and Dr. Schoenberg "a real megalomaniac," as if these were objective diagnoses, or even nicknames, but when she really got angry, she just opened a book and sat behind it fuming.

Webern thought about her skin, a dry shell, scaled over like his father's elbows. From a distance, it looked grey and rough as unpolished stone, riddled with cracks and imperfections; it was even flaking off in some places. The first time he'd seen her, he'd imagined cold blood moving like anti-freeze through her blue-green veins. He'd stared at her and she'd returned his look, raking her emerald eyes up and down him, from his smudgy eyeglasses to his tiny hands to the toes of his weathered All-Stars. Later, though, when he'd touched her wrist by accident, he'd been surprised by how warm it felt. It was at that moment, he knew now, that everything changed for him.

Sometimes he wondered if he'd ever get to touch her again. Even in hot weather, Nepenthe wore scarves and veils and gloves to hide her deformity, though she always stared out fiercely, as if daring people to look a little closer. The only time she showed her scales in public was during her nightly performances, when she lay on a plaster-of-Paris rock under a green light bulb like an iguana sunning itself. But Webern knew for a fact that she spent the hottest afternoons in her tent, up to her chest in a kiddy pool full of ice. She was warm blooded, boiling beneath her scales. Her skin couldn't breathe like a normal girl's. That was what Brunhilde had told him.

When he came back out again, fully clothed this time, Nepenthe was leaning against the Cadillac's back bumper with her veil flipped back. Loose tendrils of hair trailed across the scales of her face. She'd found a light without him: she was already deep in a cloud of clove smoke.

"Did you manage to pack up your tent?" she asked.

"Nope. And I'm guessing there's no chance of going back for it."

"Probably not. What a drag. I bet you'll wind up bunking with one of us till Dr. Show buys you a new one." She offered her clove to Webern. "Want the rest of this? It'll make your lips taste like honey."

"Sure." Webern took it and puffed a little. It felt like a sandstorm in his throat and he tried, unsuccessfully, to suppress a cough. "So, sounds like you know all about what happened tonight. Wanna fill me in?"

"I just know what Enrique told me." Nepenthe took her clove back from Webern. She blew out a smoke ring and contemplated it. "He was pretty shaken up, poor guy. Apparently, a few hours ago, Dr. Show came charging into his tent with a brand new sword and some delusional story about how he's been challenged to 'a duel.' We have to run, we're all going to be dismembered, etcetera, etcetera. Enrique wasn't too worried, because this is par for the course with Dr. Show, but then, while Show's giving him the directions to this random place, there's a ripping sound. Enrique turns around and sees another sword blade coming through the wall of his tent."

"Wow."

"Oh, but wait, it gets even better. Enrique runs outside, because, when he's not betting on chicken fights, he's a fairly rational guy. He hears some shouting, and then all of a sudden, his tent collapses—collapses to the ground. Mars Boulder wrestles his way out and starts pulling the canvas up, slashing at it with his sword like he's fighting a ghost or something. But Dr. Show isn't under the tent. He isn't anywhere." Nepenthe lowered her voice. "He's *vanished*."

"Jeez." Webern tucked in his shirt. Dr. Show didn't ply his illusions very often, but when he did, they were masterfully crafted and expertly timed. "That sounds like something to see."

"Um, right. It sounds to me like Dr. Show pissed off the wrong guy and then pulled some crazy stunt. Makes a good story, though." Nepenthe tapped ash on the fender. "Dueling. Jesus God, what an archaic custom. Leave it to Dr. Show to get killed like an eighteenth century nobleman. What do you think they were fighting about, anyway?"

"I don't know. Money or something, I guess."

"I bet they have some kind of sick history. Maybe Dr. Show kidnapped his legless sister and sold her to a sex fiend with a dungeon in his basement. Now the guy can't rest until Show's impaled on the blade of his sword. Freud'd love it."

Webern forced a smile. "You don't really think that'll happen, do you?"

"What, the impaling? I sure hope not. He owes us all two weeks back pay, doesn't he?" Nepenthe stubbed out her cigarette butt and, without another word, strode across the parking lot toward the diner. Webern watched her go. She walked like it was an inconvenience, like she might just fling herself down any second. Only once, when she reached the door of the restaurant, did she look back over her shoulder to see if he was following.

CHAPTER TWO

ACTUALLY, NEPENTHE WAS WRONG. Dr. Show didn't owe them two weeks back pay—he owed them three. Once a week, Dr. Show was supposed to give each of the performers—except for Vlad and Fydor, whom he compensated as if they were one and a half people—a small stipend out of the returns. Even when he paid up, it was hardly a living wage, but he also provided for their meals, supplies, gas for the vehicles, and all expenses for the show, which included costumes, props, makeup, and sets. From time to time, he even threw in a new case of Magic Pirate rum, or bourbon so cheap it burned like gasoline.

Most of the players, Brunhilde especially, grumbled about this set-up—they argued that they could buy their own tights and groceries, and better ones too, if Dr. Show would just fork over the cash. There was no denying that Dr. Show could be pretty chintzy about food and supplies. They ate a lot of hot dogs stamped "irregular" by the manufacturer, and Schoenberg mined the bargain bins of grocery stores for dented mystery cans whose labels had peeled off in the summer heat. What they grabbed at diners came out of their own pockets, but was worth the loss, compared to their reused coffee grounds and the enormous drums of fruit cocktail they consumed around the campfire to ward off scurvy. And they hadn't had toilet paper since June.

Even if he complained along with the rest of them, though, it was obvious to Webern the current arrangement was the best thing possible for the circus. It wasn't like Schoenberg was keeping the money for himself. Every dollar he saved went straight back into the show. Schoenberg bought velvet and gold braid for Brunhilde's costumes; he equipped the single spotlight with bulbs that glowed so brightly they sometimes burst like an explosion of stars. He paid for Al's barbells and supervised with a megaphone the afternoon they all assembled an elaborate mail-order obstacle course for the tiger cubs. When he couldn't find a muralist who satisfied him, Schoenberg bought vials of rare paint—ochre, cerulean, jade, magenta—stretched canvases, and lovingly painted the circus's posters himself. And every now and then, a few new packets of twisting balloons for Webern or a hooked cane for Vlad and Fydor's comedy routine turned up inexplicably in the Cadillac's trunk. Still, it was never enough. Props were always getting broken or lost or—like Enrique's swords—gambled away; costumes tore, and the tiger cubs never did learn to walk the A-beam or dive down the tunnel slide. No matter how much money Dr. Show spent, the circus was constantly vanishing around him.

And now he had vanished along with it. Empty coffee cups, crumpled-up napkins, bacon grease, and toast crumbs littered the tabletop in the diner, and still Dr. Schoenberg had not appeared. Webern glanced at the clock that hung askew on one wall, but the minute hand had hardly moved since he looked at it last. He took a deep breath and continued doodling in the ketchup on his empty plate, using a French fry for a pencil. So far he had drawn a top hat, a sword, and a tiny head with X's for eyes.

Across from Webern, Al sat slumped; his chin rested on one gigantic palm. He'd lost his appetite just halfway through his third stack of pancakes. Beside him, Vlad and Fydor argued in Russian, completing each other's sentences even as they disagreed. To ease his tension, Eng sat on the floor, legs twisted into a full lotus, and beside Webern, Hank brushed Ginger so hard that her orange fur fluffed out in all directions. Only Brunhilde, who sat at the head of the table, smoothing the long curls of her beard, appeared to have her mind on other things.

After picking out her tenth song on the jukebox, Nepenthe returned to the table. The waitress followed her, hanging back nervously.

"You guys are like a bunch of existentialists. Stop it with the moping, already." Nepenthe pulled out the chair next to Brunhilde and flung herself down onto it. "Jesus God."

The first strains of "Mack the Knife" filled the air. Several feet away, the waitress timidly waved a receipt.

"I have the check for y'all," she offered. Her voice raised an octave in forced levity. "Now, who gets it?"

"Give it here." Nepenthe turned around and reached toward her. Between the glove and her sleeve, an inch of flaky grey skin revealed itself. The waitress smiled, but the receipt trembled in her hand.

"All righty." The waitress continued to smile as she edged around the table.

"No, give it to me, I said." Nepenthe straightened her veil, but behind it her green eyes burned.

"Here you go." The waitress reached in and dropped the check. "Oops."

Nepenthe snatched it out of the air. Her tight grip crumpled the lower corner. She stared at the waitress, who grinned back, frozen with terror.

"Now, let's see, what's the damage." The waitress darted back into the kitchen. Nepenthe unfolded the bill against the table and peered through her veil at the list of charges. "Who ordered the tomato juice? That you, Eng?"

Since Webern had first met her, Nepenthe had come a long way in controlling her temper. Once, several towns back, a saleswoman in a department store had refused to let her try on a dress, and Nepenthe had thrown a tantrum, knocking over mannequins and screaming about "contagion" until two security guards dragged her out of the store, hissing like a snake. She hadn't talked to anyone for hours afterwards, hadn't even come out of her tent for dinner. When Webern brought her a plate of cold franks and beans, she would only say, "I wish to God that bitch knew who my father was. I just wish to God she knew that." Webern had nodded, not knowing quite how to respond. Even he didn't know who Nepenthe's father was. She'd never told anyone her last name.

"I can't make sense of this." Nepenthe shoved the check away and leaned back in her chair. "Somebody else divide it up, huh?"

"Maybe we shouldn't pay yet," said Webern.

Brunhilde reached over and picked up the check from the table. She removed her pince-nez from her pocket and carefully scrutinized the numbers.

"We have to keep waiting for Dr. Show. We should order another pot of coffee or something."

"Let us not be like little children. We cannot stay here all night." Brunhilde lifted her embroidered handbag up onto the table and reached inside for a handful of dimes. She stacked them deliberately beside her plate.

"Maybe not, but where are we supposed to go?" Explorer Hank scratched the white fur of Ginger's belly. "Bernie's right. Doesn't make sense to cut out just yet."

"I suggest we all check into a decent hotel. In the morning we will return here to retrieve Schoenberg, if he has arrived at all." She folded her hands and looked around the table at each face. Though she was probably only in her early forties, her beard made her look older at such moments—even presidential. Maybe part of it was the way she dressed, in watered silk evening gowns that draped like old opera curtains. She always wore nylons, even in muggy weather, and around her neck hung a locket, as heavy and round as an ancient gold coin, which she never took off. She fingered it thoughtfully now. "Tonight's events are his fault, are they not? He should be the one to wait."

Al snorted. "Hotel, sure. And how we gonna pay for that?" He shook a forkful of pancake in Brunhilde's direction. "I'm not gonna blow the last of my dough on room service."

"We have the cashbox. Schoenberg keeps it in the Cadillac's glove compartment. Have you not seen him put it there?"

"And the key?" asked Vlad.

"I believe Nepenthe could help us get it open."

Nepenthe sat up a little straighter. She cracked her knuckles inside her gloves.

"I believe our minds will be clearer in the morning. If Schoenberg has not arrived, we can discuss then what it is we should do." Brunhilde looked around the table. Most everyone seemed to agree. Here in the warm, dry diner, clashing swords and leaky tents seemed very far away.

Webern looked down at his plate. He rubbed the French fry into the little top hat he had drawn until it became an unrecognizable smear.

"I don't know if we should," he said. His voice sounded plaintive and whiny, even to him—a boy's voice, not a man's. "Dr. Show trusted us with that cashbox. It's not like he's dead. At least—I mean, he's coming back. He'll be pissed off if we go through his stuff, especially if we take his money."

"His money? *His* money?" Brunhilde exhaled sharply, the ghost of a laugh. "Webern, when was your last paycheque?"

"I dunno. Same as yours." Webern peeked up at the faces scrutinizing him from around the table. They gazed back, not hostile but not smiling either. Nepenthe flipped her veil back down; he couldn't read her expression. Brunhilde's arms were folded, and her eyes probed him.

He imagined her pulling his German name off like a mask, exposing the American underneath. "I just—listen, okay, it's not *his* money. But it's not ours either, not really. It's the circus's. If we just blow it all on a bunch of hotel rooms, that's it, we're sunk." Webern shaped his hands into an airplane and, with a low whistle, nose-dived it into the table.

"It's the circus's money, sure." Nepenthe shrugged. "But what if Dr. Show doesn't come back? How long are we supposed to wait, Bernie?"

"Longer than a couple of hours, anyway. You said he'd meet us here."

"He told Enrique that, yeah. But I'm not sure we can hold him to it, under the circumstances." Nepenthe lowered her voice. "Think about it, kiddo."

"Yes," said Brunhilde. "Schoenberg may not have had a chance to make his escape. But let us be honest with each other. Even in the best of times, when has he really kept his word?"

Vlad and Fydor exchanged a glance. Eng touched his forehead to the diner's floor. Hank sighed, and in his arms, Ginger mewed plaintively. Even Al gave a reluctant nod. Webern pushed his plate forward on the table. It was true, of course—Dr. Schoenberg certainly hadn't kept all of his promises, at least not lately. He baited them with luxuries he could never afford, fame that eluded them with every measly audience that half-filled the bleachers in their big top. And now he was getting himself killed over a sword he'd most likely stolen from a psycho named after another planet. But he still seemed inherently honest, despite it all. He'd rescued Webern from an empty life in a town filled with the skeletons of houses. Was that really enough, though? When *had* he kept his word?

"I can think of a few instances."

The circus performers turned in the direction of the voice. There, in the diner's doorway, stood Schoenberg. His top hat and tuxedo dripped with rain, and a fresh bloody slash marked his cheek. But he held a sword. His dark eyes blazed. Walking out of the kitchen with a coffee pot in her hand, the waitress saw him and shrieked.

A few hours later, the yellow Cadillac was climbing a twisting mountain road; the jalopy followed not far behind, slowly negotiating the rusty red trailer around the curves. Both cars still burned their headlights, but all around them, the world was waking up. In the dishwater grey of early morning, Webern, sitting shotgun, looked out the windshield at the clapboard stands that stood along the roadside, selling bullets and maple syrup, and at the houses that clung to the slope on rickety stilts. Lights winked on in kitchen windows.

The circus had been travelling through New England for only a few weeks, but now the leaves were starting to change—it was time to head south. Next stop was Paradise Beach, Delaware. The circus chased summer all year long, first south and then west. It was a practical decision, mostly—heating the tents would cost money, and who would go to a circus in the snow?—but to Webern it still seemed magical, a little arrogant even. It reminded him of the fairy tales he'd grown up reading, filled with men who outsmarted death with riddles and boys who brought home treasures from their dreams. The Boy Who Ran From Winter—yep, that was him.

Webern settled back and looked over at Dr. Schoenberg, who sat beside him in the driver's seat. Schoenberg had changed into dry clothes; he now wore the black and white checkered coat that made him resemble a deranged vaudevillian. Much to Webern's relief, the slash on his cheek, now bandaged with a fistful of paper napkins from the diner and several strips of Scotch tape, had proven to be only a shallow wound. As he drove, the pain didn't appear to bother him in the slightest; his dark eyes focused on the road ahead with steely intensity.

Webern looked into the back seat where Nepenthe, Brunhilde, and Explorer Hank sat side by side by side, all three fast asleep. Ginger the tiger cub had returned to her cage in the red trailer. In a low voice, trying not to wake anyone up, he whispered to Dr. Schoenberg, "So, you had a close call with that Boulder guy, huh, boss?"

"Close call—ha! I only wish my opponent had been worthier. Alas, pity required that I spare his life."

Webern glanced into the backseat again; Nepenthe's eyelids fluttered, but otherwise the sleepers didn't stir. "Brunhilde called him a Klingenschmiede. What's that? Some kind of sword-maker?"

"That brute was no craftsman, I'm afraid."

"Oh. Okay."

"He's a keeper of accounts."

"Like a bookie?"

"Nothing like that."

Webern nodded and looked out the window again. A passing sign predicted an avalanche of large, tumbling rocks. He yawned and was about to close his eyes when Show spoke again.

"I knew him long ago, in the Old Country."

"The Old Country? I thought you were from New Jersey."

"I travelled much in my youth. At any rate, some months ago, when he heard of my recent success, he wrote to me, offering to part with a few family heirlooms at a discounted price. Among these were his swords. Since this stop on our tour brought us near his home, I thought it would be worth my while to drop by and have a look."

"Makes sense. We could use a new sword, too. It was kind of lame when Enrique swallowed that yardstick."

Dr. Show sighed. "These swords, Bernie: they're no simple props. When I saw them mentioned in his letter—ah! I remembered them from those long ago days, so light, so elegant, endowed with the power and mystery of generations. Our little company has many things: talent, spectacle, brash originality, and singularity of vision. But such blades, touched by the ghosts of history, would lend us gravitas, a mooring in the ages." His tone darkened. "Little did I know that he meant to use them only as bait to draw me to his lair."

"Jeez. What did you do to make him so mad?"

"In his fevered imaginings, what didn't I do? I was a Casanova who defiled young women and drove them to suicide, an impresario who thought only of his own celebrity, a heartless charlatan whose mellifluous voice lured so many to destruction that his crimes cannot be numbered." Dr. Show's eyes strayed from the road. "Tell me, Bernie, am I as monstrous as all that?"

"Of course not. Maybe he has you mixed up with somebody else. How'd you meet him, anyway, back in the Old Country?"

"Oh, my dear boy, I won't bore you with any more details." Schoenberg trailed off as the bravado leaked out of his voice. "I'm not sure why you're asking so many questions, actually. It's a rather private matter, a dispute like that."

Webern stared down at his lap. "I was just curious, that's all."

Schoenberg cleared his throat.

"In the future," he said, "it might do you good to confine your curiosity to that which concerns you."

Webern felt the car accelerate slightly. He hugged a knee to his chest and remembered the inside of his tent back at the abandoned campsite, the way the wind had rippled the walls like sails at sea.

"But it does concern me, Dr. Show," he mumbled.

"Thank you, Bernie. I always knew you were a sensitive boy. But your worries were most unnecessary, I can assure you." A strange glint lingered in Schoenberg's dark eyes. "Don't look so glum. I didn't mean to snap at you. This evening has been draining for us all, I think."

"Do you need me to help keep you awake?" Webern offered. "While you're driving, I mean? We could start planning some new clown acts for the show. My notebook's in the back seat, and—"

"No, no." Dr. Schoenberg smiled faintly. "You needn't amuse me. I couldn't sleep if I tried."

Webern looked at Schoenberg carefully. His black moustache, usually waxed impeccably, drooped at the corners, and through his napkin bandage, small dots of blood were beginning to show. Webern wanted to say something more, but he didn't know what.

"I find," Dr. Schoenberg finally added, "that morning is often the best time for solitary contemplation."

"Okay." Webern kicked off his sneakers. "Think I'll take forty winks, boss."

"Sleep well."

As Webern leaned back in his seat and closed his eyes, he tried to look forward to the meal they'd make at the next campsite (powdered eggs with off-brand Tabasco and Spam cubes skewed on sticks), and he thought about the clown act he was performing in the next show (a turbaned snake charmer, unable to get his cobra out of the basket). But he drifted off unsettled, nevertheless.

High above the big top's dirt floor stretches a tightrope, trembling slightly, like the string of a guitar that has just been plucked. A single spotlight reveals the slow progress of a tiny figure moving hesitantly along it, now forward, now back again, surrounded by blackness on all sides.

It's the clown, wearing a Pierrot suit of simple silky white, and he's riding a unicycle. He's juggling too—three silver batons—but his movements are uncertain, and the crowd seems bored. They sit silently, rustling popcorn bags and letting their babies cry. Only when the clown lets his batons fall down into the dark space beneath him do they respond at all, and then with nasty laughs.

The clown struggles to concentrate on the thin rope beneath his unicycle's wheel. The spotlight seems to melt his silk costume on his skin, and he drips with sweat. Greasepaint rolls off his forehead in streaks. He pedals and pedals upon the high wire, but he barely seems to move at all.

It's as if something—or someone—is holding him in place. Wiping his brow with one sleeve, the clown looks down. He feels the dread before he even sees them. Two pairs of hands grip the unicycle's spokes, one pair pudgy and stub-fingered with dirt under the nails, the other pair bone white and knobby with brittle talons. The smell of burning leaves fills the clown's nostrils, and the crowd's cackles are high-pitched crow caws. The hands tighten their grip on the wheel, and two figures begin to pull themselves up. The clown squeezes his eyes shut. He cannot bear to see the masks they wear. He holds his breath and waits to fall.

Webern woke to the sound of snoring. Beside him in the driver's seat, Dr. Schoenberg—despite his predictions to the contrary—had dozed off with his arms crossed over his chest. It relieved Webern to notice the car wasn't still moving.

Neither was the jalopy. The two vehicles sat parked next to each other at a scenic overlook, near the top of the mountain they'd been climbing when Webern fell asleep. Through the windshield, he could see a wooden fence and a metal viewfinder mounted on a pole, though little of the actual view. He glanced into the backseat at Nepenthe, Brunhilde, and Hank. All three were still sleeping soundly; a strand of Brunhilde's beard hair had found its way into Hank's open mouth, and Nepenthe murmured softly beneath her veil. Webern quietly opened the car door and stepped outside.

Webern hugged himself as he approached the edge of the parking lot, but he didn't go back for a jacket. The cold air cleared his head. He climbed over the fence and sat down on the dewy grass that covered the steep slope on the other side. The valley opened out below him. A covered bridge, painted red, stretched over a brook beside a pasture dotted with grey ponies, haystacks, and a rusty abandoned school bus. Uneven rows of tombstones lined the yard behind a little stone church. Beyond that, patches of maple trees bloomed orange amid white wooden houses, and, even farther away, cars crept along the narrow road up into the Green Mountains on the other side.

Webern squinted into the distance. He couldn't shake the way the dream had made him feel. He ripped out a fistful of grass and tried to throw it, but most of the blades just stuck to his hand.

Whenever Webern remembered his sisters, he thought of the little boy from the funny pages who had a dark, smudgy rain cloud hovering over his head. While he still lay in his cradle, they towered over him, eclipsing the light, and when he grew older, he began to notice the dark streaks they left on every lovely thing they touched.

When Webern was six, the girls were twelve. They wore soiled white nightshirts to school, cinched at the waist with their father's leather belts. They played games Webern did not understand, games with headless dolls and trash can lids, black feathers and moths pinned to beds of gauze. Webern asked the girls to teach him their games, but in response they usually just offered him a bloated earthworm or a teacup full of dirt and watched, with glowering disgust, his frightened reaction. They spoke only in rhymes.

Willow and Billow had been born during a time in the family's history from which there remained only one photograph. In this picture, Webern's mother, Shirley Bell, stood on the front stoop of the house, wearing a large, shapeless coat that looked far too big for her. She held the twins out awkwardly, as if threatening the photographer with a pair of dangerous weapons. Willow was a stick of dynamite; Billow, a cannonball. Their mother's eyes looked haunted and bruised.

Webern knew bits and pieces of the history that swirled around the photograph like gritty black smoke, and he guessed the rest. When Willow and Billow were born, they left a deep empty place inside their mother. After she came home from the hospital, Webern imagined she had wandered the house, looking for what she had lost. She moved her hand over the shelves, the counters, the shiny surfaces of the appliances, but in all her searching, it never occurred to her to pick up the red, wrinkled infants, squalling and rollicking in their terrycloth straightjackets. Three times a day, she fed Willow and Billow condensed milk, tilting the bottles through the bars of their crib. Then she retreated to the living room, where the roaring vacuum she pushed almost drowned out their wretched, persistent wails.

One day, arriving home from work, Webern's father Raymond found Shirley slumped on the floor of the kitchen, her head resting on the open oven door. A greasy toothbrush dangled from her hand. Had she been out to hurt herself? Or to clean meatloaf drippings from the burner? After the paramedics resuscitated her, her answers flew out, frantic and contradictory, but in one general direction: she did not want to go home any more. So she went from the emergency room to a different kind of hospital—one with locked-up windows and plastic knives and a special machine that buzzed louder than any appliance, that crackled like lightning, that made all the hall lights dim.

Back home in their crib, Willow and Billow began to babble to each other. Their mother was a strange, unloving woman, whose hands smelled of cleaning fluids; their father was a blunt, strong man whose false, hearty laugh sent them into fits of crying. So, whom could they trust? Only each other, only each other. Their babbles were a pledge of loyalty to each other and no one else.

When their grandmother Bo-Bo flew in under the black bat wings of an umbrella, they vowed not to trust her, either. When she entered the room, grimly brandishing rattles or pacifiers, the twins fell silent; when she reached to pick them up, they lay stiffly in one another's arms, not allowing her to pry them apart. Their grandmother wondered how her daughter-in-law would handle the stubborn, unreachable girls; but when the young Mrs. Bell returned, twitchy and shivering but with a determined smile, the old woman had no choice but to shake the rain from her umbrella and take again to the skies.

Over the years, as Webern pieced together this story, inventing some parts, seeing glimpses of others in nightmares and in life, it became clear to him that his mother, despite her contrition and sack lunches, had never been able to penetrate the fortress the girls had built for themselves in those early days. They rejected every gift she gave. The twins had strung the backyard trees with imitation pearls; they had sunk an Easy Bake Oven in a ditch. And they had brought their wildness into her clean house. The crushed birds' eggs and dead fireflies, the cardboard box caves and the necklaces of dog teeth scattered around the girls' room all served one purpose for Willow and Billow: to shut their mother out. Webern had only realized later—too late—that inside those fortress walls, the girls were also plotting against him.

CHAPTER THREE

What's funny
is the way they laugh.
Maybe only I really see: you
tightrope walk, they knock

you down, you explode
out of a cannon's mouth,
you ask for help, they punch
you out, you tumble down

some makeshift stairs.
Sure, it's all an act this time,
but that doesn't mean you
don't feel the cuts

and scrapes from practicing—
your backbone bent
like an old man's. Dummy,
anyone should know
you had to learn to fall.

—September 13, 1962

NEPENTHE CLICKED HER BALLPOINT PEN, examined the last few words she'd written, and nodded with satisfaction. She tore the page out and folded it neatly, then dropped her notebook on the floor and sighed.

"Why am I such a goddamn genius?" she asked her empty tent.

Nepenthe lay in a blue-green inflatable kiddy pool, surrounded by ice cubes that floated in the water around her like tiny glaciers. Her hair hung in a limp, messy ponytail, and her grey skin glistened. She yawned and reached for a fashion magazine. Sandra Dee grinned up from the cover at her, an enormous sun hat encircling her head like a halo. Nepenthe snorted. She opened the magazine at random to a fall fashion spread, clicked her pen again, and began to draw scales on the exposed skin of all the models. After a moment, she spat a peach pit at the green canvas wall. It stuck.

Nepenthe was gouging holes in an article titled "The Girls I Go For" when she heard a sound outside: a sort of scrabbling, hesitant and sideways, like a crab through dune grass. Immediately, she hurled her magazine at the front flap of her tent.

"Go away, Bernie! I'm not decent!"

"Dr. Show sent me. They need you for a lighting check."

"Well, I'm not going."

"What?"

"Hang on a second."

Outside her tent, Webern shifted from one foot to the other. It wasn't even noon yet, and already he felt dazed and sweaty. They'd just finished putting the big top up, and his job had been driving tent stakes into the ground with a mallet. Now his hands were so mottled with bruises, they felt like tenderized meat. He'd have to wear gloves to cover them in the show tonight.

In front of him, the tent flap rapidly unzipped, opening to reveal Nepenthe in a ragged pink bathrobe. She'd combed her hair down over her face in a makeshift veil.

"Hi, Nepenthe," said Webern. He looked from his hands to hers. For once, she *wasn't* wearing gloves. Beneath the rough grey scales, her fingers curled inward. He glimpsed the deep lines that riddled her palms before she pulled her fists into her robe sleeves. "Oh, Dr. Show wanted me to give this to you." He pulled a crumpled envelope out of his back pocket. Her name was written on it in flourishing script.

"Finally!" Nepenthe ripped around the wax seal and quickly counted the bills inside. "This is it? You have to be kidding me. After two weeks?"

Webern shrugged. "Returns've been lousy. We're lucky to get that much."

"He tell you to say that?"

"So, anyway, we put a new gel on your light, and Dr. Show wanted . . ."

"Wanted me at his beck and call? Listen, you can tell Dr. Show something for me. You can tell him I don't get paid to do him favours in the middle of the afternoon. I don't get paid to help him install lights. Jesus God." She shook the envelope in his direction. "I mean, look at this. Lately, I barely get paid at all."

"Don't get all bent out of shape." Webern rubbed his hump; his back was killing him. "It'll take five minutes. What's the matter with you?"

"It's the principle of the thing. All morning, he had us running around, pitching tents, escaping doing God knows what. Now I'm finally getting some time to myself." Nepenthe softened a little. "Boy, you look spent. What does he have you doing over there? Running sprints?"

Webern wiped sweat off his forehead with the back of his hand.

"It's not so bad."

Nepenthe reached down and took the glasses off his face. She stood a foot and a half taller than him, and as she cleaned the lenses on her robe sleeve, Webern felt uncomfortably like a little boy on his way out the door to school.

"Give them back. Please?"

"Just a second." Nepenthe held the glasses up to the light, checking for smudges. The frames were round, brown tortoiseshell. Impulsively, she put them on her own face. Strands of hair caught between the lenses and her emerald eyes. "How do I look?"

"Beautiful," Webern said. "Now will you quit horsing around?"

Nepenthe seemed hurt. She pulled the glasses off and handed them back.

"See you later, Bernie." She disappeared into the tent, zipping the flap shut behind her.

Webern paused, shook his head, then started walking back across the beach toward where the orange big top stood high on the dunes. He always moved with an uneven gait, as if he were carrying an awkward load that threw him perpetually off balance. But today he walked even slower than usual. He'd begun to hate delivering the pay envelopes. And why did Nepenthe always act so cranky before the show? She almost sounded like Brunhilde sometimes, talking about the indignity of this and that, the "principle of the thing." Earlier that day, when they'd pitched the tents only to discover they had to move their campsite to another part of the beach, those two had been whining the whole time, talking about how any sane company would just check into a hotel. Always with the hotels. And before that, Nepenthe had hissed at two terrified sunbathers, who'd run away screaming. It had been funny, sure, but maybe not the best way to sell tickets. Didn't Nepenthe ever think about anyone besides herself?

Of course she did. He wasn't really being fair. He just wasn't in the best humour himself today. It was his birthday—his *sixteenth* birthday—and although he hadn't told anyone it was coming up, he still expected the day to seem special, somehow. Even when he'd been living at home with his dad, he'd always gotten some reminder of the occasion: a store-bought cake in the refrigerator; a new football on the living room floor; a ten dollar bill, left like a tip under an empty highball glass on the kitchen table. But today, everyone was just bossing him around. A piece of green glass by Webern's foot caught his eye, and he kicked it through the sand.

Webern arrived at the entrance to the big top, but before going inside, he turned around and looked back down the beach, toward the water. The sea shone blinding white. He looked at the campsite, clumsily thrown together near the shore—the patched-up, tilting tents, the hasty pile of driftwood for tonight's campfire, and some yards away, the big-finned Cadillac, trailed by the tracks it left in the sand. Brunhilde had placed her sitting pillow atop its yellow hood, and she posed there now, tatting lace with a pair of glinting needles. They had a permit for the big top, but not to camp here; still, it occurred to Webern that maybe they could pass the extra tents off as a sideshow if any authorities came prowling around. He'd have to mention that idea to Dr. Show.

On the other side of the big top lay the boardwalk, with its booths of penny games and its herky-jerk rides: Tilt-a-Whirl, bumper cars, the Inverter. An intricately wrought Ferris wheel stood silhouetted against the sky, slowly turning now, Webern noticed, with one or two baskets already laden with early riders. Before too long, it would be showtime.

He hurried back under the big top, where Al and Explorer Hank were hammering together the bleachers. Dr. Schoenberg stood on an enormous ladder in a corner of the tent, tightening a spotlight on its mount. He was in his shirtsleeves, an ascot knotted around his neck. Sunshine seeping through the canvas made his face glow orange, and beneath his curled moustache he was smiling—he hadn't looked this cheerful since before the swordfight. Webern grinned back up at him, but he couldn't help feeling suspicious. He wondered what Dr. Show had up his sleeve this time.

"Bernie!" Dr. Schoenberg waved exuberantly with the screwdriver in his hand. The ladder creaked. "Was our young lady indisposed?"

"Sort of."

"Ah, no matter—but perhaps you can lend some assistance."

"Sure."

"Just take her place on that rock. I need to see what this new lighting does to a complexion." He looked down at Webern critically. "You're not quite the right shade, of course, but you'll do."

Dr. Schoenberg gestured to the plaster-of-Paris rock that stood to the side of the tent's centre ring. Webern approached it. Though he'd seen Nepenthe on it dozens of times, he'd never really paid much attention to it before. Mounted on four wheeled legs, it now reminded him of the many examining tables he'd seen in the doctors' offices of his childhood, where he'd gone again and again for doomed procedures designed to straighten out his hunchback or help him grow. He hoisted himself up onto it and sat on the edge, remembering the backless robes he'd had to wear, the crinkle of butcher paper under his legs. He almost wished he was still driving in stakes with that mallet.

"This good, boss?"

"Recline, my boy, recline!"

Webern stretched out over the uncomfortable plaster-of-Paris crags. Once, a doctor had fitted him for a back brace, measuring every inch of him with steel instruments that opened like jaws. Now Webern could feel their cold points pressing into his skin all over again. At the top of the ladder, Dr. Schoenberg switched on the light, and suddenly, a warm emerald radiance enveloped Webern. He shut his eyes, but even inside his lids the world glowed green.

No wonder Nepenthe was always so out of sorts before the show; she had to lie here for nearly ten minutes while Dr. Schoenberg circled her, pointing with his cane and telling the tale of her unholy origins in the Great Dismal Swamp of Virginia, where he claimed to have rescued her from a giant python. It was one thing to go out in a clown suit, disguised in makeup and a false nose. . . but to lie here practically naked, with eyes all around, glittering in the darkness? She was right—she deserved a raise.

Dear Bo-Bo,

I bought this postcard back in Vermont, before we had to clear out in a big hurry. The place where I found it, they sell guns in the gas station and rabbit skins on a clothesline right outside.

It made me think of you. Say hi to Marzipan for me.

Love, Bernie

Webern licked the stamp and stuck it, upside down, onto the corner of the postcard. Then he flipped it over and looked at the image on the front. The sun-bleached paper showed a cartoon moose eating a platter of flapjacks; a tap in a nearby tree poured genuine maple syrup onto his breakfast. Over the last few months, Webern had become quite adept at writing postcards that conveyed as little information as possible; even though he didn't want his grandma to worry, he didn't exactly want her showing up at one of his performances, either. He carefully tucked the postcard inside the cover of his clown notebook, to protect it while he walked to town.

When Webern first joined the circus, he had expected to spend his days like a young man on vacation, wandering the sun-drenched boardwalks, gazing out at the world through the smoky haze of dime store plastic sunglasses, maybe even finding time to catch a movie matinee in the afternoons. That was before he learned exactly what kind of an operation Dr. Show was running – how much each and every one of them was expected to "pitch in."

"A company such as our own cannot afford to delegate even the simplest of tasks to the uninspired," Dr. Show had offered by way of explanation. "Our work is too important to entrust to roustabouts, those crude mercenaries of the arts." Which was why members of their circus pitched their own tents, raked their own sand, sold their own tickets, and, on those chilly mornings-after, picked up their own litter from the stake-scarred camping ground.

Webern didn't have it too tough—his size and shape prevented him from doing the heaviest labour, which fell mostly on the hands of Enrique, Hank, and Eng—but he still sometimes resented that, by default, he'd become everyone else's errand boy. Al had poor circulation and fell victim to fainting spells, Vlad and Fydor moved as slowly as children in a three-legged race (Webern noticed their coordination fell off sharply whenever he asked for their help), and of course Dr. Show couldn't be bothered with too many trivialities. When the ringmaster wasn't fussing over lights and costumes, he passed many hours in his director's chair under the big top, a red bullhorn dangling from his hand while his eyes grew soft with daydreams. Webern was less sure how Nepenthe and Brunhilde spent their time, but he'd figured out right from the start that he couldn't foist any of his chores—no matter how small—off onto them. It wasn't because they were women, not exactly; rather, they were ladies; the aristocrats of the circus. No matter how many locks Nepenthe picked or how many peach pits she spat, she still thought like the daughter of a tycoon.

So Webern's days overflowed with a million little tasks: stapling together makeshift sets, feeding the tiger cubs, washing clothes, tacking up posters, and gathering twigs and cardboard boxes to burn in the campfire. He didn't mind any of it too much, except for the shopping. Every two weeks or so, the entire crew would go into town to buy groceries and other supplies, then parade about the streets, their canned tomatoes and bottle of rum held aloft like trophies. At those moments Webern had no trouble laughing at the chumps they shouldered past, the open-mouthed rubes who gaped from the windows of slow-cruising cars or ogled them from behind the handlebars of zigzagging bicycles.

But in between these big trips, little disasters happened all the time—nylons snagged, cage latches snapped, salt spilled onto the ground—and Webern never felt quite the same walking into town by himself, especially not when he was going to buy a girdle for Brunhilde or a magazine of pistol blanks for Explorer Hank. Sometimes Webern suspected the others of sending him off on these errands out of spite, or using his trips into town as a means to scare up curiosity for their acts. Still, he always gritted his teeth and set off down the dusty road by himself.

Webern tried to practice his clown acts when he could, but it was a lucky day when he could get an hour or two to himself, let alone a whole afternoon. Sometimes he half-hid, riding his unicycle around the barnacled stilts of a deserted pier at low tide or practicing a bit of mime around the plywood back of a little-visited hot dog stand. Other times he stayed in his tent, trying to ignore all but the most urgent requests shouted in his direction. Every once in awhile, he lost himself in the rhythm of clowning, delighted himself with a new walk, a new face, a new way of holding himself, but other days he found himself knotted up, jumpy and agitated with frustration. If only he had more time! It was bad enough using the same costumes and makeup show after show—greasepaint and burnt cork could only do so much—but to hurry like this, that was the worst constraint.

Now and then, Webern found himself fantasizing about another kind of circus, one with money and a skeleton crew and doors that shut, a circus where he could have his own boxcar and an hour to paint his face. But every time he daydreamed about it, he felt a twinge of guilt. If it hadn't been for Dr. Show, Webern wouldn't have found the circus in the first place—he'd still be trapped at home. He took pains not to forget that. Whenever he noticed himself getting greedy, he squeezed his eyes shut and held his breath until the voices of his sisters chattered again in his ears.

The big top seated seventy, but in the time Webern had worked there they'd never had a full house. It didn't seem likely that they ever would, despite Dr. Schoenberg's best attempts to advertise. The ringmaster phoned in notices to print in the next town's pennysavers, and he always sent Webern out with a can of glue and a fistful of rolled-up posters the morning of their first show. Once, in New Hampshire, they had staged a parade of sorts, with tin cans clattering from the back of the Cadillac and Vlad and Fydor blowing kisses from the jalopy's roof, but the local sheriff had informed them that such displays after ten PM were considered a disturbance of the peace, then had ticketed their red trailer for double parking. They never attempted such a "spectacular" again.

Despite their efforts, though, the show only drew a middling crowd most evenings. Thirty-five to forty was the norm: mostly frazzled mothers, teens who necked in the back row, kids with fruit-punch moustaches, and a few screaming toddlers thrown in at a discounted ticketing price. That wasn't bad; the creaking bleachers could hardly support more weight, anyway. But lately, some shows had shrunk to a crowd of twenty-five, or once, even fifteen. Al, who'd been with the show the longest, sometimes waxed nostalgic for the early days, when Dr. Show had displayed him in a curtained box outside of flea markets and they'd turned a profit every time. But Hank, Eng, and most of the others—even Brunhilde in her better moods—still believed Dr. Show's prediction that things were just about to turn the corner with ticket sales. All it would take was one fantastic performance, and the word of mouth would be out there, the best form of advertising, free and invisible but real as talent itself.

That night in Paradise Beach, it almost seemed as if the prediction was coming true. Webern peeked around the flap at the back of the big top where the performers entered and exited. The bleachers were nearly packed—fifty-five at least. In the low lights of the pre-performance, they were mostly shadows, but a few figures toward the front were distinct: a tubby man in swimming trunks and a bowling shirt unbuttoned well down his hairy chest; a lanky girl with a hula hoop balanced on her knees; a busty blonde, babbling obliviously to her beau, who fiddled with the hearing aid in one ear.

"Get a load of this crowd," Nepenthe whispered. She leaned in close. She was in her show robe, floor-length satiny green with an oversize hood. "What a bunch of weirdos."

Webern thumped his bowler hat against one leg, then put it on, careful not to smudge the incredulous black eyebrows he'd painted in the greasepaint on his forehead. He pulled a long balloon out of his pocket and stretched it between his hands. He'd make a flower first—a daisy, green stem with a white bloom, kid's stuff—and give it to Miss Hula Hoop in the front row. Then he'd go straight into the sweeping routine, the one where he wound up dancing with the broomstick.

"Don't look so scared, little buddy." Hank patted Webern on the head. Hank was all decked out in his best safari whites; Freddy, the older tiger cub, trailed behind him on a leash. "You know what I always say: it's not the size of the lion in the fight, it's the size of the fight in the lion. You're going to do just fine."

"Cut it out, Hank. Course I am." Webern resisted the urge to kick Hank, hard, in the shins. He glanced back at Nepenthe. "It's you guys I'm worried about."

"Jerk." Nepenthe pinched his rubber nose. It squeaked. Out on the dunes behind them, Brunhilde practiced singing scales.

After that evening's show, the performers celebrated around the campfire, drinking warm rum from toy trumpets. Dr. Schoenberg had bought the trumpets for the shooting booth he'd set up a few towns back, but they'd made lousy prizes; now they were going to much better use. Webern thought so, anyway. He lay in the sand off to the side of the group, still wearing his hobo costume with its fingerless gloves and patched-up pants; he'd washed off the greasepaint, but that was all. The audience had applauded; nothing else mattered now. The beach undulated beneath him, and the stars turned above, orbiting too fast, like the speeded-up fake sky in the dome of a planetarium. His toy trumpet tilted up, empty, from his hand.

All around the fire, the other circus players talked and laughed, but their words blurred to incomprehension in Webern's ears. Al was playing Louis Armstrong on his portable record player, and Dr. Schoenberg accompanied the album on his concertina. Everyone else was trying to stop him, but Webern liked the combination: the concertina's yawns and sighs, melancholy and comic at the same time, twisted in and out of the singer's honeyed voice. *Sometimes wonder why I spend the lonely nights . . . dreaming of a song . . .*

"Bernie? You out for the count already?"

Webern opened his eyes. Nepenthe towered over him, dressed in the lime green bedsheet burka she usually put on after the show. At first she'd looked exotic, but now she just reminded him of a child in a Halloween costume.

"Hey, what's so funny?" Nepenthe glared down through the slit left for her eyes. She kicked sand at him.

Webern swatted at her foot. "Stop it, stop it."

"Get up, then. We're out of rum."

"Ugh." Webern pulled himself up onto his elbows, then sank back to the ground. "Why do I gotta go get it?"

"Because you drank most of the last bottle. Come on, come on."

It occurred to Webern that he ought to do a drunk act sometime. With a groan, he pulled himself to his feet. He swayed, first to the left, then to the right. He could get a big jug with a skull and crossbones on the side—the Demon Liquor. Maybe Eng could dress up as a devil and chase him across the stage on all fours, with his legs bent back over his head. Then again, that might scare the little kids.

"Bernie?" Nepenthe waved her hand into his field of vision. Her gloves were green too, but darker, the colour of leaves.

"I'm going, I'm going." Webern pushed past Nepenthe and stumbled off into the dark.

"Come back soon!" she called.

Webern walked carefully as the sand shifted under his feet. Behind him, the campfire crackled, and a chorus of cheers rose into the night as Al finally prized away Dr. Show's concertina. Webern was a ways away when the sound of waves crashing grew louder than the party around the bonfire.

Even at night, the big yellow Cadillac was not too difficult to find. It gleamed softly in the darkness like an oblong moon. Webern groped his way around to the back of the car and opened the trunk. Inside, batons, leotards, masks, wigs, and tins of greasepaint and rouge lay together in a jumbled heap. Webern saw a burnt skillet—a roll of canvas and Dr. Schoenberg's special set of paints—a yardstick and a record of klezmer music—and rummaged past a frayed whip, a beaded shawl, and a sombrero. At the very bottom he finally found a half-empty bottle of Jamaican dark, right next to Mars Boulder's sword.

Webern had never really gotten a good look at the sword, but now, seeing it under the moonlight, he began to understand what the fuss was all about. Jewels crusted over the hilt, an elaborate arrangement of what looked like rubies, sapphires, and diamonds. The blade itself was smooth and flat. Webern saw himself darkly reflected there. He leaned in closer. Even though he practiced funny expressions or made himself up almost every day, it had been a long time since he'd really looked at his face.

"That's me," he murmured. "That's me." It made less sense the more times he said it. He thought of a riddle he'd heard once: if that's me in the mirror, then who am I? He pulled off his glasses and peered again into the sword. "That's me. That's me." His features began to separate from each other. They were as much a part of the night as of him. "The person in the mirror is me."

Webern's trouble with mirrors had begun the day they cut off his body cast, when he was six and a half years old. The carpet had felt strange beneath his feet, uneven, and he'd wondered why he couldn't straighten up all the way, why he felt lopsided. He'd thought maybe he was just stiff from so much bed rest. He had tried to stretch. Then he had looked into the glass. For a second, before he saw his own face, his own body—stunted and crooked, terrifyingly unfamiliar, but his just the same—he had glimpsed someone entirely different on the other side of the mirror: another little boy, one he had no trouble recognizing.

"O!—Cruel fate! Horror of horrors!"

"Aah!" Webern grabbed the rum bottle and whirled around, brandishing it like a weapon. A spectre loomed a few feet away. It occurred to him that he should have picked up the sword instead. "Get away!"

The spectre moved closer, and Webern lowered the bottle.

"Sorry, Dr. Show. I couldn't really see you."

Schoenberg swept the top hat from his head and held it reverently to his chest.

"This wretched, vile duty! I cannot tell you—but I must. Bernie—

young Bernie—the dark horseman of fate has swung his cruel axe."
His hooded eyes lowered; one hand stretched out as if it held a skull.

Sometimes Dr. Show was tough to understand when he shifted into
full-on Shakespearean mode. Webern squinted at him.

"What do you mean?"

"O, torment me no longer!" Schoenberg turned away. "I cannot say.
But come quickly! There may still be time."

Dr. Show's black tuxedo jacket rippled in the breeze as Webern
followed him back to the campsite. Webern listened for his friends
above the plunging waves, but he couldn't hear them at all now—no
laughter, not even a note of Louis Armstrong. When he saw the other
performers standing in a tight circle around something he couldn't
see, he wanted to go running down the beach in another direction.
But he kept moving forward, drawn almost against his will. He saw his
feet plodding along the sand, tasted sea air spiced with woodsmoke,
and felt the heavy bottle in his suit coat pocket *bump bump bump*
against his thigh. In his mind, he saw his face again as he'd seen it in
that sword.

The hushed circus performers turned to look at Webern and
Schoenberg as they approached the campfire. Vlad and Fydor laced
their arms around each other, as if they were afraid of being separated.
Al held the concertina in one hand; the other covered his mouth,
hiding his expression. Brunhilde, fingering her locket, let it drop when
she saw Webern coming. Explorer Hank wore an exaggerated frown
and held onto his riding crop with two clenched fists. Eng sat on the
ground with his legs over his shoulders, rocking. And Enrique stepped
aside so Webern could see what so keenly held their attention.

Nepenthe lay on the ground, her burka shrouding her. A huge
reddish splotch spilled across its fabric, and a wooden knife handle
stuck up out of the centre of the stain, casting a small shadow like the
style of a sundial. Webern couldn't see Nepenthe's face beneath the
veil, but her eyes were closed. He felt lightheaded, dizzy; black stars
exploded in the periphery of his vision. He sank down to the sand and
found himself clutching one of Nepenthe's hands in his. Even through
both their gloves, he could tell she was still warm.

Webern tried to breathe. In his mind, he saw a kaleidoscope of
Nepenthe from the last few months: Nepenthe lighting a clove,
Nepenthe spitting; Nepenthe reading philosophy, psychiatry, a book
of poems; Nepenthe in a beekeeper's hat and a pair of oven mitts;
Nepenthe yelling, cursing, yawning; Nepenthe throwing a book,

a baton, a pail of water; Nepenthe playing pinball, punching the sides of the machine; Nepenthe lying on her lizard rock, dyed green from the lights. None of those images matched up with this one, none of them made any sense, until suddenly Nepenthe sat straight up and declared, "Surprise!"

CHAPTER FOUR

THE LITTLE CLOWN FALLS SLOWLY THROUGH THE DEEP GREEN WATER. He wears a black suit and a bowler hat; in his right hand he carries a cane. When he touches down on the sea floor, he uses it to steady himself.

Down here, the water is shadowy, but the sand reflects the light of the moon—a dim yellow, like the tail ends of fireflies. Fish-schools flicker, swimming in rippling formation. The clown cuts a lonely figure as he walks along. He pokes his cane at sea cucumbers and bottom feeders, who stare up at him with bulging eyes.

Just when he thinks he'll never see her, she appears, veiled in murky water that hangs like a mist between them. A starfish wraps around her left wrist, a living bracelet; above the glimmering scales of her tail, she wears a modest bathing suit of shells and woven seaweed. But dark currents blur her pale face. She could be monstrous or lovely, the age of the clown or old enough to be his mother.

The clown reaches up to tip his hat, but he notices too late that his bowler is floating away; he has to jump to snatch it and jam it back onto his head. Next he bends down to pluck a sea anemone from the bed of flowers that grows beside him. But as soon as he touches one blossom, they all snap shut in a burst of sand. The clown frowns, furrows his brow. Shamefacedly, he turns back to her empty-handed.

The mermaid laughs and shakes her head. Tossing the clown a kiss, she vanishes again into the dark waters.

Webern groaned and rolled over onto his back. He spat out a mouthful of wet, gritty, rum-flavoured sand. His head throbbed, and a whooshing sound filled his ears. He was freezing, too; his hobo suit clung to him like he'd just walked through a rainstorm. With an effort, he opened his eyes. Stars still flickered above; if anything, morning seemed farther away than it had when he passed out. Webern let his eyes drift shut again. Just then, another wave rolled in, engulfing him from head to toe.

Webern crawled away from the incoming tide. He pulled himself onto his hands and knees toward the drier sand. But before he could flop down and fall back asleep, he saw someone approaching, silhouetted against the lights of the boardwalk, which still burned in the distance.

"Aha! I suspected it was you." Dr. Schoenberg walked swiftly to Webern's side. He reached down to grasp Webern's hand and pull him to his feet, but when Webern moaned and collapsed, he reconsidered and sat down beside him instead.

"What am I doing here?" With some effort, Webern straightened his glasses. A strand of kelp hung against one lens.

Dr. Schoenberg gestured toward the empty rum bottle, which rolled in the surf near Webern's discarded hobo hat. "Continuing your festivities alone, it seems."

Webern remembered then: the smile leaving Nepenthe's eyes, his blurred escape into the garish maze of the boardwalk, the hour or so he'd spent staring into the dark waves, drinking and feeling sorry for himself.

"I'm such a fool," he murmured. He felt dead with shame. With great effort, he sat up. His insides rollicked. "Ohhh. I bet everybody hates me now."

"Don't be absurd, my boy. The fault was ours entirely." Dr. Schoenberg allowed himself a rueful smile. "In hindsight, I can see the prank had a rather macabre edge." "I'm sorry. I'm sorry. Everyone must think I'm crazy."

"No one thinks anything of the kind, I can assure you." Dr. Schoenberg removed a white monogrammed handkerchief from the pocket of his tuxedo jacket, unfurled it, and offered it to Webern. "But even if they did, it's none of their affair. Bernie, let me show you something." Dr. Schoenberg shucked off his tuxedo jacket and rolled up the sleeve of his shirt. "Do you see this mark?"

Webern stared at the inside of Dr. Schoenberg's arm. Faint pink lines—scar tissue—marked it from wrist to elbow. Dimly, Webern could see they were letters, spelling out a name. *Sebille.*

"Never feel ashamed of your passions, my boy. When I was your age, I thought I would die for love." He ran his finger over the scar gently. "Her name was actually Sybil, but I preferred the Arthurian spelling."

Webern imagined a young Dr. Schoenberg, holding a concertina, gazing up at a young girl's window with mournful eyes. He smiled a little; Dr. Show chuckled and shook his head. He rolled his sleeve back down.

"Most people joined my circus as a last resort," he said. "They came to me because they were ill-equipped for anything else. I know that. But I also knew from the first that you were different. You're a young man after my own heart, Bernie: too sensitive for your own good, perhaps, but with extraordinary talents."

Webern looked down at his hands. In the moonlight, they gave off a pale glow, and he imagined the rest of himself glowing too, greasepaint white, like the clown in his dreams. No one had ever said anything like that to him before.

"Thanks," he said.

Dr. Schoenberg rose, put his jacket back on, and shot his cuffs. "Now, shall we go assuage Nepenthe's fears? She's thoroughly convinced you've drowned."

Webern let Dr. Schoenberg drag him to his feet, but once he was standing up he felt even sicker. He took a step forward, and the ground rolled beneath his feet. Dr. Schoenberg caught him just in time.

"A little off balance? No matter—I came prepared."

Dr. Schoenberg reached into an inner pocket of his tuxedo jacket and removed a small black wand, about the length of a conductor's baton. He pressed a button on one end. *Click, click, click.* The wand telescoped out into a walking stick. Webern took it and tentatively leaned on it. It held under his weight.

"That's a boy!" Dr. Schoenberg strolled ahead. He sniffed the salty air. "What a splendid night."

It was. The beach glittered under their feet, and the dark ocean stretched out endlessly beside them, joining up at some invisible nexus with the rich velvety blue of the sky. Webern thought about his dream as he walked. It almost did seem like mermaids might swim in these waters. He looked down at the cane in his hand and again thought of those shimmering scales, flashing away where he couldn't follow.

Webern didn't like to think of his mother very often, but seeing Nepenthe tonight, laid out as if for burial, had stirred up his memories. He tightened his grip on the cane and tried to turn his mind away from the first image he saw—the car crash, with its broken windshield shining in rubied splinters on the pavement, his mother's dress, a bottomless pool of spilled green silk. He thought of Nepenthe's burka, with its red stain spreading, and of the swords that crashed like lightning around that spitting fire. Maybe he put a curse on everyone he loved. Maybe *he* was cursed.

"Watch yourself, my boy!" Dr. Schoenberg grasped Webern's arm just as he tripped over a hunk of driftwood. The cane tumbled into the sand.

"I'm sorry." Webern tried to hold perfectly still, but he could feel himself swaying. "Jeez, I'm so sorry."

"No matter, Bernie, no matter. Cruel Bacchus visits us all now and again." Dr. Schoenberg picked up the cane with his free hand and snapped it shut. Webern stepped more carefully, staring down at his feet. They seemed very far away. "Don't fret. We'll have you well in no time. Did you know, my boy, that in Haiti they would cure your ails by poking thirteen pins into the cork of the offending bottle? Left, right. There, you have it now. In Assyria, they quaff crushed swallows' beaks, mixed in a paste with myrrh. But back at camp, you may have to settle for strong coffee and an icepack. Whoa there!"

Webern narrowly avoided slipping on a beached jellyfish. Up ahead, the campsite was almost visible.

"We're nearly there now, my boy," Dr. Schoenberg said. He pointed with his wand. "The others will be so relieved. Hank was all for alerting the authorities, but I knew I could find you myself."

"You shouldn't have gone to all that trouble."

"Don't be absurd. Would you have me leave you tossing in the surf?"

When Webern had started going outside late at night to practice his unicycle, his father just sat around in his bathrobe, staring at the TV, his feet resting on the wooden crate his gin bottles had come in. He never came out to make sure Webern was all right. He probably didn't even notice that Webern was gone.

"Dr. Show, do you have any kids?"

"I'm afraid not, my boy." A shadow crossed Schoenberg's face, but just as quickly it disappeared. "I was not made for the pleasures of hearth and home. One must make sacrifices for one's art, you know. Besides, our little company is a family of sorts, isn't it? We look after one another."

Back at the campsite, Explorer Hank sat beside the fire, poking at the flames with a stick. Ginger and Freddy slept curled together in a cardboard box beside him. When he saw Webern, he leapt up.

"Bernie! Where the heck did you go? You had us worried sick. The cats've been shedding like crazy."

Webern shrugged. The warmth from the fire reminded him how soaked his clothes were. He moved a little closer to the blaze.

"Sorry," he muttered.

"Well, you should be! I was all set to call the Coast Guard—"

Dr. Schoenberg gave Hank a stern look, and Hank stopped himself.

"It's just a good thing you're safe," he finished. "But you should go see Nepenthe right away. She made me promise to wake her up when you got back."

Dr. Schoenberg stretched. "Well, I think I'll retire. Hank, will you prepare Webern some strong coffee? I think it would do his system good."

Hank nodded, and Dr. Schoenberg strode away into the darkness. He always pitched his tent a ways away from the others.

"I'll put the kettle on," Hank said.

"Okay." Webern took off his jacket, wrung it out, and put it back on. Hank kept standing there. "Thanks."

"But you should see Nepenthe first. She's in her tent."

Webern had never been in her tent. "I heard you the first time."

Hank chucked him under the chin. "Go get her, little lion."

Nepenthe's tent, a green half-egg, sat nearest to the campfire. Tonight, it looked dark and silent, but the canvas walls breathed in and out, in and out, as if it were a living creature. Webern reached to unzip the flap, then hesitated.

"Nepenthe?" he whispered. No one replied. But his voice came out so quiet, even he could hardly hear it. Webern sucked in his breath, then reached again for the zipper. If she was asleep, he'd leave right away.

Webern unzipped the flap as quietly as he could, then stepped inside. It took a moment for his eyes to adjust; the only light came from the moon, filtered through the green canvas walls. Webern looked around slowly.

On the floor, a half dozen fashion magazines lay open; from their moon-silver pages, models smiled up at him with a haunting desperation, their faces like unanswered love letters. Nepenthe's trunk sat beside one wall, its leathery top strewn with veils and gloves, but also with limp brassieres and tubs of skin cream with curious names: Aqua Velva, Satina Smooth, Extra Pearl. A teddy bear with one black, shiny eye half sat, half lay on the corner of a spiral notebook.

Nepenthe herself reclined in the tent's farthest corner, up to her elbows in the kiddy pool. Most of the ice cubes around her had melted; the few that remained had diminished into slivers of themselves. Nepenthe still wore her burka with its dark crimson stain, and the fabric floated around her like a lilypad, but her discarded veil lay draped over the side of the tub. In the dim light, her face, grey and rough though it was, looked oddly fragile, like the cracked faces of heroines painted on Italian frescoes. Her eyes were shut, and for a moment Webern thought she was asleep. But just as he began to back out through tent flap, she opened them.

"Bernie," she said. Something in the way she said it amounted to an apology, a confession, and a question all at once. The word hung in the air between them for a long time. Nepenthe blinked; her emerald eyes sparkled, and with a slosh, she sat up straighter in her kiddy pool. "Bernie, you're drenched."

Webern never got back to sleep that night. Nepenthe sent him to the tent he shared with Al to change into dry clothes. When he came back out to the campfire, he found her waiting for him, wrapped in a blue blanket, holding two mugs of coffee. She'd put on a set of white butcher boy pyjamas, but no veil or gloves; even her feet were bare. He sat down next to her, and she draped the veil around both their shoulders.

"Aren't you hot?" he asked, remembering what Brunhilde had said—*her skin can't breathe like a normal girl's.*

"Nah, I'm okay. You're freezing." She ran her hand over his. "Brr."

"I'll be fine. At least I've got dry clothes on, now." Webern thought of the melting ice cubes. "Do you always sleep in the water?"

"I try not to. It ends up drying me out even more." Nepenthe scratched the back of one hand. "But sometimes it's the only way I can doze off, you know? At school I had a bunch of electric fans, but there's no place to plug them in here."

Webern took a mug from her and sipped his coffee. "Did you go to a boarding school?"

"All girls, too. Don't remind me." Nepenthe lit a clove. "Want one?"

"I'm good." Webern watched her face in the flickering light. Fissures lined it like a palm. "Does it hurt when you smile?"

"Why all the questions, kiddo?" She wasn't smiling now. "Am I really so strange?"

"You can ask me stuff, too. I didn't mean it like an inquisition."

"Great. Does it hurt when I do this?" Nepenthe punched his hump, not that hard, but with a closed fist. Webern rubbed it.

"Yeah, it hurts. Thanks a lot, Nepenthe."

"You deserved it, you dope." She held her crackled hands out toward the fire. "I just hate how people do that—ask me questions about my skin. Like that's the 'real me.' Did you ever read that comic *Undetectable Girl*, Bernie?"

"Sounds familiar." Webern conjured up the image: a translucent ghost-girl in a cape, perched on the observation deck of a skyscraper. "I was more into Space Ace Grin McCase."

"Figures. Guys don't like comics about women unless they're tied to the railroad tracks or getting raped by Martian octopi—chauvinists. It's a degraded art form anyway. I don't know why we're even talking about it." Nepenthe stared down into her coffee cup, then took a drag from her clove instead. "But what I was going to say is, sometimes I pretend to be Undetectable Girl, when I'm out there in the ring. I look out at the audience, and I get this tingling feeling all over, like Marla Blaine does when she twists the jewel on her radiation pendant and starts disappearing. Because they can't see me, you know. It's just my skin." She blew smoke out her nose like a dragon. "What a cliché, right? Sometimes I don't even feel invisible. I feel like I'm not anywhere at all."

"Don't say that."

"Oh, come on. You never feel that way?"

Webern hesitated. "When I'm performing, it's not really me—I mean, I guess sometimes I pretend I'm someone else, too."

"Yeah? Who?"

"Someone I used to know when I was a kid. A friend. He was funnier than I was—crazy, almost. He did things I could never do. Nothing scared him."

"Whereas you're a paranoiac who flees at the first sign of danger?"

"Exactly. Nice of you to remind me."

"Why'd you run off like that anyway? Can't you take a joke?"

"You upset me."

"*You* upset *me*. Jesus God, Bernie." Nepenthe looked away. "I didn't mean to ruin your goddamn birthday."

"You didn't ruin it." Webern looked at the sand between them—just a few inches, but it might as well have been a whole desert. He sipped his coffee again and watched Nepenthe smoke. Her hair was down, and 55 now a chunk of it hung loose, covering the side of her face. Impulsively, he reached over and tucked it behind her ear. All of a sudden, there was no distance between them at all: Webern felt Nepenthe's warm, rough face brush against his, and then just as quickly, it was gone.

Webern remembered little of what they said after that. They sat for hours under the blanket, but the words they spoke seemed far less important than their interlaced fingers and the places where their knees touched. Nepenthe read Webern a poem she'd written in honour of his birthday, but later he could only recall the poem's shape, its hard sweetness like a green Jolly Rancher on her tongue. They talked about nothing, about the show and Webern's act and if he would get a driver's license now that he was sixteen. After a long time, they stopped talking at all. Nepenthe's head fell to rest on Webern's hump, and he left it there, feeling her breath come, slow and warm, in waves on his neck. It comforted him, but he wasn't even close to sleeping. The feeling that surged through him reminded him of the excitement he'd once felt on the mornings of his birthdays—the secret knowledge that now there was nothing between him and what he'd waited for. It was only as the sun came up over the ocean that it occurred to him: his birthday was already over.

CHAPTER FIVE

YEARS BEFORE WEBERN'S ACCIDENT, before he was even old enough to go to school, his mother read him picture books in the afternoons before she put him down for naps. Webern's mother could barely stand to let sleep separate her from her little boy, and the picture books were a kind of procrastination, a way to hold off the lonely quiet of his dreams. She read him stories about dwarves and pirates and goblins and grails while he leaned against her, lured by her voice into the depths of the illustrations. In one picture, a frail boy and girl crept hand in hand through a night forest. The forest gleamed with eyes. Every time Webern looked at this illustration, he tried to count all of the eyes before his mother turned the page. Every time he failed.

Webern Bell was a solemn, methodical little boy, with an old man's frown and a pale round face. Only his mother could coax him to grin, or tickle him into fits of giddy, toylike joy. Sometimes Webern even presented well-planned jokes for her approval.

"What did the cat say to the hammer, Mommy?"

"I don't know Bernie, what?"

"Me-*ow!*"

Webern's hair was slow to grow, so for the first three years of his life, his head was naked and shiny as a wigless china doll's. This suited him, since his mother dressed him like a doll anyway. Webern wore sailor suits and cowboy shirts, bow ties and silk pyjamas. Later, when he learned to ride his bicycle around the neighbourhood, he started to come home with black eyes and bloody noses. Given the choice between her son's face and his wardrobe, Webern's mother chose to protect the former, but they both cried when he tried on his first pair of dungarees.

But when Webern was still too small to go to school, he spent all his days in the company of his mother, with no scabby little boys or sticky little girls to knock him down and spoil his nice clothes. In the mornings, he peeled himself from his sun-ripened bed and padded through the house. By this time of day, his father and sisters had already left for work and school, and the rooms were silent and wondrous. In his red robe and slippers, he felt like a little king. His mother stood at the kitchen stove in a ruffled apron, wearing pink high heels even though they were inside, and sizzled breakfast in a coal-black skillet. She listened to his dreams with gentle amazement. When Webern finished telling of yellow stars trapped in jelly jars and squirrels who slept in hammocks, of cold blue palaces carved from ice and a circus on a sailboat, she always explained, with barely contained excitement, what they would do that day.

On Webern's fourth birthday, his mother took him downtown, to the toy store on the corner of Oak and Main. The store was part salesroom, part doll hospital, and Webern liked to look at the ceramic limbs, the coloured glass eyes, the tiny toupees and the vials of paints that the owner left scattered on his workbench, which resembled a messy operating table.

Webern and his mother jingled in the door. The toy doctor nodded to them from his perch behind the counter. With a pair of small, sharp scissors, he was amputating a cracked porcelain arm from a baby doll's overstuffed body.

"Lovely day we're having, eh, Mrs. Bell?" he said without raising his head. To help him with his work, he wore a miner's cap. A bright light beamed down from his forehead onto the ceramic limb. "How's sonny boy, there?"

"Oh, Bernie here's fine. He just turned four today."

"Well! You're a big boy now, aren'tcha?"

"Bernie, sing Mr. Saul the song I taught you. Go ahead, don't be shy."

The toy doctor looked up with interest, and the light from his miner's cap shone into Webern's eyes. Webern retreated behind his mother's legs. Today he wore a red beanie with a propeller on top, and he imagined it revolving faster and faster, carrying him up into the endless blue of the sky.

"M, 'n' N, O, P," he mumbled, reaching up for his mother's hand. She squeezed his and smiled down proudly.

"Bernie's learned the alphabet," she explained.

"He's a sly one, all right," observed the toy doctor. He lobbed the doll arm toward a trash can. It shattered on the floor. "But I say, how do you like this weather we've been having, Mrs. Bell? Hot enough for ya?"

"It is unseasonable," she agreed, fanning herself with one hand.

While the grown-ups talked, Webern slipped away to look at the toys. Most stores on Main Street had big picture windows and glaring overhead lights, but cobwebby shadows draped the doll hospital even in the middle of the day. Webern rolled a red fire truck back and forth on a dusty shelf. He played with the marionettes until their strings tangled into impossible snarls. He stacked the geometrical coloured blocks to build a rainbow castle, and he wound up all the wind-up toys. These little metal creatures held a peculiar fascination for him. The seal slapped its grey flippers together; the monkey pedaled a tricycle; the fat cat slapped a coin into its mouth with one greedy paw. They were the best toys, really; the same gears that turned the hands of clocks moved their insides with a kind of life. Webern watched them for a long time. Then he snuck back to his favourite part of the store.

The toy doctor kept his miniatures in glass cases that hung from the wall and glowed like magic aquariums. These cases looked like tiny rooms; some even had rugs and wallpaper and little closed curtains where the windows would be. In the first room, the toy doctor had arranged a shrunken feast. Webern stood there on his tiptoes to see the three-tier wedding cake, the stripey bags of popcorn, the fat hamburgers, the martini glasses, and, in the centre of it all, the roast pig, splayed on a silver plate with a gumdrop in his mouth. The second room looked like a museum. On the walls, paintings the size of postage stamps—*Whistler's Mother*, the *Mona Lisa*—hung beside a medieval tapestry, intricately woven to depict a unicorn and a satyr frolicking beside a well. But the third room was Webern's favourite. This room looked like a little boy's bedroom, and it was heaped with toys.

On the floor, an exploded jack-in-the-box craned his accordion neck over a battleground of tin soldiers, while nearby a wooden train derailed. Meanwhile, in a makeshift fort of blankets and pillows, teddy bears and rabbits conspired against a pair of arrogant robots, with stiff straight arms and orange light-bulb eyes. Tiddly-winks lay like confetti around an auto show of sleek race cars, and a rocking horse reared on its hind legs, eyes wild with excitement. On a disorderly shelf in the back of the room, picture books stacked and tilted upon each other, the titles on their spines already dimly familiar to Webern's illiterate eye: RUMPLESTILTSKIN, PETER PAN,

THE LONELY ISLAND. Above it all hung a painting of a clown balanced on a unicycle, spangled arms spread, harlequin suit sparkling and swirling like an impossible constellation.

Beneath this painting lay a bright blue bed, usually neatly made under a comforter dappled with rocket ships. But today, pressing his nose to the glass, Webern saw something in the miniature room that he'd never seen before. Tucked snugly under the covers lay a tiny boy with smooth gold hair and a face a lot like Webern's.

For a second, Webern thought that the little boy might be a doll. But, as Webern's mouth fell open in amazement, the little boy's mouth also opened wide, into a slow sleepy yawn. He stretched his arms out, then swung his legs over the edge of the bed. He put on a little leather cap with a feather in its brim and a pair of white knee socks. He was already wearing lederhosen.

Webern stood there, open-mouthed, unable even to gasp, as the little boy buckled on his heavy German shoes and reached down to touch his toes. But when the boy stood up straight, snapped the straps of his lederhosen, and clicked his heels together, Webern found his voice again.

"Knock knock, who's there?" Webern asked, bumping his finger clumsily against the glass.

"Dwayne," said the little golden boy.

"Dwayne who?"

"Dwayne the bathtub, I'm dwowning!"

The little golden boy danced a jig, and Webern clapped his hands.

"But what's really your name?"

"Wags, Wags Verder, at your service." Wags doffed his leather cap and bowed till his head touched the ground. Then he turned a somersault. Webern grinned.

"I'm Webern Bell."

"Well, what do ya know? I wouldn't have took you for a ding-a-ling."

"Bernie?"

Webern turned around. His mother and the toy doctor were standing there, looking at him. The bulb on the miner's cap shone right into his eyes.

"Bernie Bee, who're you talking to?" Webern's mother asked from inside the blinding light. Blinking away spots, Webern turned back around to the display case and started to point.

"I just met . . ."

But before Webern could show his mom and the toy doctor, Wags dove through the bedroom wall, leaving a boy-shaped hole.

He zipped through the museum so fast, Whistler's mother and the tapestry unicorn turned their heads to watch him go. Then he leap-frogged through the feast, stampeding over sandwiches, capsizing a cornucopia, and finally plunging into a pink punch bowl from which he did not emerge.

"Did you see him?" Webern cried. "Did you see how fast he ran?" His mother and the toy doctor exchanged a puzzled glance. Webern pounded on the glass case. "Hey, Wags! Wags, come back!" But the little boy in lederhosen would not return.

All the way home, Webern scowled out the car window. He sat with his arms folded over his chest and refused to play with the new toy—a ping-pong paddle with a red rubber ball attached—that his mother had bought when he refused to pick out any other present. He didn't talk. For the first time, he had seen something that his mother hadn't seen, that she hadn't even believed in. Something was gone from his life now. He felt the new empty place like the socket of a missing tooth.

When they got home, it was time for Webern's nap.

"Do you want me to read you a story?" his mother offered brightly. But Webern just shook his head and stomped up the stairs.

When she came up an hour later, she found him sitting cross-legged on his bed, looking at picture books. They lay open all around him. Webern was staring at the picture of the night forest from Hansel and Gretel when she sat down beside him.

"There are seventy-two eyes," he said glumly. "I don't think they'll ever get home."

Webern's mother stroked his hair. It was starting to grow in, thin and fuzzy and mousy brown, like the fluff on a baby chickadee.

"You don't believe me, that Wags was even there," Webern continued. "You didn't see him. You think I'm making him up."

She pecked the top of his head. "I didn't see him," she admitted, "but I certainly don't think you're making him up."

"How come I saw him and you didn't?"

"I don't know, Bernie. It's a doll hospital. Maybe Wags is the ghost of a little doll who's not born yet."

Webern rubbed a finger against the glossy page of the picture book. "I don't think so."

"Well, maybe he's your conscience."

"No, not that either."

"He could be your guardian angel, you know. And maybe he won't come back again until you really need him."

Webern stared again at the picture of the night forest, the starved children and the fingers of dark trees, grasping. Then his sisters arrived home from school.

The morning after Webern's sixteenth birthday began quietly enough. Webern watched the sunrise and saw the seagulls come to land on the beach. He looked at the boardwalk, which had finally shut down sometime in the very early morning, and the spiky, uneven skyline the rides made against the pale clouds. The spokes of the Ferris wheel looked delicate in the morning light, as faded as crosshatchings in a dime store comic book.

Webern was half nodding off at last, when around six thirty, he heard rustling in one of the circus tents. He nudged Nepenthe. She opened her eyes slowly, first one, then the other.

"They're waking up," he whispered.

"Jesus God. Thanks, Bernie." Nepenthe wrapped the blanket around her and pulled part of it up over her head like a cowl. She squeezed his hand quickly. Her bare feet shushed in the sand as she hurried back to her tent.

Nepenthe had barely zipped the front flap when Brunhilde came gliding out to what was left of the campfire. In a grey dressing gown and ancient brocade slippers, she looked well-rested—she was probably the only one without a hangover this morning, since she didn't drink. She looked disparagingly at the charred logs, then at Webern.

"Chilly, isn't it." Brunhilde had a way of saying a question so it wasn't a question at all. She tossed the pillow she'd brought onto the ground and lowered herself down upon it. Pointedly, she breathed on her hands to warm them, then extended her palms toward the few remaining flames. "I see you returned, Webern."

"Yeah. Dr. Show came and found me." Webern dutifully got up and started piling more driftwood on the fire.

"I knew you would return when you had your fill of our attention. But he, he wanted to be a hero. Your rescuer. The two of you share a taste for amateur theatrics, it seems."

The logs bumped, releasing a shower of sparks. Webern grimaced. Great. She was still mad about what happened at the diner. Well, if he had to choose sides between her and Dr. Show, he'd definitely made the right decision. He wasn't going to let Brunhilde ruin his morning now. He thought about Nepenthe instead: her tousled hair, her emerald eyes, the way her hard grey feet had looked, burrowed in the sand. Involuntarily, he glanced at her green tent, and Brunhilde followed his gaze.

"Poor girl," she said. "She was not bred for this kind of life."

Webern shrugged. "She seems to like it okay."

"Are you certain of that." Brunhilde smiled. "The day will come, and soon, I think, when our little *eidesche* returns to her rightful place."

"Well, I wouldn't know." Webern nudged the kettle toward the fire with a stick. Some coffee was still leftover from the night before, and once it started to bubble, he refilled his mug.

Brunhilde removed her pince-nez from one pocket of her dressing gown and pulled out a well-worn paperback from the other. *Die Deutsche Katastrophe*. It seemed appropriate to Webern that she spoke a language where they said "die" every other word. He sipped his coffee. Last night almost felt like a dream. Even his hangover was nearly gone, the headache just a dull echo of its former self. But somewhere inside him, the memory still glowed, warm and secret.

In a few minutes, most of the others had joined Webern and Brunhilde at the campfire. Explorer Hank cooked up sausages in a skillet, and Eng, a vegetarian, put his little pot of beans and rice on to boil. Eggs slid into sizzling fat as Vlad and Fydor bickered over who had slept worse, and Enrique mixed the powdered instant coffee with water before he put the kettle back near the flames. Explorer Hank handed Webern a plate of eggs and sausage. Webern hadn't realized how hungry he was, or how tired. He'd have to get a nap that afternoon before the show. He hoped no one would send him trekking into town.

Webern was about to nod off when Dr. Show came out, wearing his undershirt and suspenders but looking immaculately frightful just the same. His black moustache, glossily waxed, curled at the corners, and his hair, newly slicked back, drew parallel black lines on his scalp. Enrique poured him a mug of coffee as he unfolded his director's chair and exchanged good mornings with the other performers. Brunhilde gave him a nod, courteous but distant, as though glimpsing a half-forgotten acquaintance across a crowded room.

"You brought the kid back, boss." Al, who'd just arrived, helped himself to a skillet full of eggs. He jerked his head at Webern. "Good job."

Schoenberg smiled beatifically. "All in a day's work." He sipped his coffee and looked over at Webern. "Have you seen Nepenthe yet this morning, my boy? She was quite concerned, you know. You ought to tell her you've returned."

Webern's face grew hot. He felt like he should make an announcement, but what would he say? What had even happened last night anyway? Back at his high school, boys had "pinned" the girls they went steady with, but he couldn't imagine pinning Nepenthe. If they got into a fight, she'd pin him.

"I think she knows," he mumbled.

"Ah," said Dr. Schoenberg. Reflexively, he touched the inside of his forearm. He changed the subject: "How are the tigers this morning, Hank?"

"Oh, fine, fine, they're doing fine. I'm a little worried about that abscess in Freddy's paw, but other than that—well, and his ear mites . . ."

Dr. Schoenberg gazed down the beach as Hank droned on about the cats. At first, his expression looked content, languid even, but then his dark eyes fixed on something in the distance and he sat up straighter in his chair.

". . . and Ginger—well, this whole thing with the formula's been a nightmare, but now that I'm getting her onto solid foods, her constipation . . ." Hank speared another sausage on his fork; he was eating them right out of the skillet.

"Who is that?" Dr. Show interrupted. He pointed down the beach. "Do you know that man?"

Hank looked over his shoulder, and most of the others stood up to look, too. Some distance down the beach, a low-built tank of a man was rolling in their direction.

"He's back." Enrique's words were more like a punctuation mark.

Mars Boulder came into focus slowly, like a face forming in a dream: first his smashed-in nose, then his heavy brow, then the gargoyle grimace of his protruding lower jaw. Al ducked behind a tent—Enrique's—near the fire, and Brunhilde remained reclining on her pillow, but the others stood frozen. No one tried to run away. Webern felt turned to stone by those oily, heavy-lidded eyes, gazing at him from down the beach.

Mars Boulder stopped a few yards from Dr. Schoenberg, just beyond the tent that Al crouched behind. A sword hung from a scabbard on his right hip. He wore thick leather gloves.

"Why are you here?" Dr. Schoenberg, stepped behind his director's chair. He looked whiter than Webern had ever seen him—even his lips were pale. "What is your business with us?"

Mars Boulder said nothing.

"What do you want from me?" Dr. Schoenberg glanced around at the others, then added, "I paid for that sword."

Mars Boulder still didn't reply. He stepped closer.

"If you have no business here, I must demand you remove yourself from the premises," Schoenberg cried. He grasped the back of his chair. His moustache trembled. "Will you go? Answer me!"

Mars Boulder didn't budge. Above him, clouds moved soundlessly.

"I have asked you once." Dr. Show's voice, thunderous under the big top, sounded thinner with no walls to hold it. "I will not ask again." He lifted the chair and shook it threateningly. "Back. Back, I tell you. Back from whence you came!"

Dr. Show hefted the director's chair into the air and, with a roar, brought it crashing down on Mars Boulder's head.

Except it never crashed. With an almost inaudible "*shing*!" Boulder drew the sword from his scabbard and sliced through the chair's canvas seat. The wooden frame folded into jumbled sticks at his feet. Dr. Show leapt back. He glanced wildly at his performers.

"Traitors! Will none of you save me?"

Around the campfire, the circus players held their breath. Wood popped on the fire. Seagulls squabbled down the beach. Mars Boulder touched his blade's edge with one gloved finger. He tested its weight in his hands. In one graceful move, Brunhilde grasped the handle of Hank's sausage skillet and cracked it against Mars Boulder's skull.

Boulder thudded to the ground. He lay there face first, motionless.

"Is he dead?"

"Check his pulse."

"Should we call the cops?"

No one wanted to go anywhere near him. Brunhilde stood over Boulder and stared down. Finally, she knelt beside him and flipped him over on his back. A crumpled paper fell out of his pocket. For a long moment, they all listened with relief to the snuffled breaths the smashed-in nose made. Brunhilde mopped her brow with the cuff of her dressing gown. Then Hank reached down to pick up the piece of paper that lay beside the unconscious hulk. He held it up. It was their travelling schedule.

Nepenthe came out of her tent then, yawning, in a summer hat adorned with wooden cherries and a white veil. She still had on her butcher boy pyjamas, but she kept her hands hidden in the sleeves.

"What the hell's happening out here?" she demanded. "I'm trying to get some sleep."

Fortunately, the day before they'd already taken down the big top and lashed its orange canvas to the back of the jalopy; all that was left was the campsite, and the performers were getting used to tearing down their own tents in a hurry. Within a few clattering, scattershot moments, they were kicking out the fire and pulling the last of the poles from the yielding sand. It was like they'd never been there.

Al wanted to dig a pit and throw Mars Boulder into it before he came to—he figured leaving a knocked-out guy in the ruins of their campsite might draw suspicion. But getting away fast seemed more important to the others, especially Brunhilde.

"Leave him, leave him," she kept repeating as she circled the prone figure. "We have done damage enough."

In the end, they compromised: with fistfuls of sea-wet sand, the circus players built a mound over Boulder where he lay, then covered what still showed—his hands, his feet—with a striped beach blanket. When Webern stood over the body, though, something still looked wrong. With quivering fingers, he added a pair of sunglasses and swiped a streak of white greasepaint across the smashed-in nose in place of zinc oxide. It snuffled when he touched it. They left Mars Boulder there, a tourist asleep on the beach.

They also took his sword. Webern was never certain who peeled back those thick, leathery fingers from the jewelled hilt, but when they arrived at the next stop, it was lying in the trunk, alongside its shining twin. This sword was older-looking than the first, bevelled and opaque, its edge dulled by use. Schoenberg, out of bravado or fancy, took to hanging the two blades in his tent, crossed against each other like a coat of arms.

But that was all much later. That hot, sunny afternoon, the circus players sped down the Delaware highways, their bodies tense with acceleration. They didn't know where they were going, and Dr. Schoenberg, grim and silent behind the wheel, did not seem inclined to tell them. They were off the schedule now, and the world seemed as mapless as the open sea.

Webern sat between Brunhilde and Dr. Show in the Cadillac's front

seat. He hadn't slept in a day, but despite his exhaustion, or maybe because of it, his mind raced. *Traitors. Will none of you save me?* And Webern had just stood there. What a coward. Even his father had the guts to fight when he was called to. Webern let a bearded lady do his fighting for him. He had to be crazy to think any girl would put up with that, least of all Nepenthe. He thought of what he could do to toughen himself up—do pushups maybe, stub out cigarettes on his arms, take a job as a rodeo clown and wrestle bulls with his bare hands. He made a fist and stared at it there in his lap for a long time.

In the backseat, Vlad and Fydor played a chess match, using only a paper, a pencil, and coordinates they named in confident English— "Knight to b3," "King to d7"—interspersed with grumbled Russian. They draped their arms around each other's shoulders, twin icons of manly camaraderie that tapered to a single waist. Fydor was winning their game. Webern wondered what it would be like to face off with someone who was an extension of yourself, whose heart beat in your chest, whose blood quite literally flowed through your veins. He was glad he'd never have to find out. The only person he'd been so connected to was Wags, and he was long gone.

Eng meditated with his back to all of them; his hum filled the car along with the vibrations of the road. It had nearly lulled Webern to sleep when, at long last, Schoenberg finally cleared his throat and spoke.

"Brunhilde, my dear, I hope you know your sang-froid in this matter will not go unrewarded." He lowered his voice. "I understand our accommodations, of late, have been somewhat modest. Of course, for most of the players they present a marked improvement, but for someone of your valour—and upbringing—"

"Schoenberg," Brunhilde said stiffly, "I should not have needed to protect you from that man."

"Of course not, my dear! Of course not. He was a most unsavoury character, and I pray we shan't meet his like again. But when the danger presented itself—well! You rose to the occasion like the true Valkyrie you are."

"No." Brunhilde tugged on her gold locket. The chain pressed deep into the flesh of her neck. "Your quarrel with him is your own. I never should have intervened."

"Nevertheless." Dr. Show coughed. He plucked at his bow tie. "You must accept my gratitude."

Brunhilde drummed her fingers on the lid of her suitcase. When she finally spoke, her voice sounded flat, almost as if she were reciting words learned by rote.

"You Americans. Your memories are so short. To you, he is buried forever in the sand. But the sand will blow away, and still he will remain. His kind does not forget what they are owed, Schoenberg. If you do not come to understand that, he will destroy you."

Late that afternoon, they stopped at a diner, as usual. Nepenthe, still in pyjamas, grabbed Webern by the wrist before he'd even gotten out of the Cadillac door. Her hand felt hot, the scales crumbly. She'd been roasting in the red trailer.

"What happened, Bernie?" she whispered. "You look awful. I mean—are you okay?"

Webern shook his head. He was so tired his eyes felt like blisters. He stepped out onto the parking lot; Nepenthe caught him just as his knees started to buckle.

"Jesus God, kiddo, you're wrecked." She opened the car's back door and negotiated him inside, pushing down on his hump to make him sit. She pressed a hand to his forehead. "Lay down, will you? I'll get you something to eat."

Webern shut his eyes. Green clouds, burned there by sunlight, moved across the inside of his lids. Hours later, he woke up, his head pressed against Nepenthe's shoulder, a cold burger leaking grease in his lap. It was dark; shadowy trees blurred past the windows. Still, they were driving, driving, driving.

CHAPTER SIX

Dear Bo-Bo,
I've been looking out at the world through a windshield for so long,
I'm starting to feel like one of the little people inside the TV. Ha-ha.
Life on the road isn't all it's cracked up to be. You're probably smart
not to drive.

Love, Bernie

DR. SCHOENBERG'S CIRCUS FINALLY STOPPED in a town made of dead ends and chicken wire, where stray cats roamed the alleys and the street glistened wetly, as if it had just rained. Even though it was still September, something about this place reminded Webern of the day after Christmas. He found burnt-out firecrackers scattered in the street.

The town was Lynchville, West Virginia, and it was surrounded by forests that reached in toward it with creeping roots. The circus players set up camp in the one abandoned lot they could find, a field overgrown with long grey grasses under an ashen sky. When Webern walked through the field in the mornings, water filled his muddy footprints. They gathered sticks for the campfire, but the wood was damp. Their sausages tasted smoky and mushy on the inside.

The first day, the circus players pitched the big top, but their hearts weren't in the show, and the few townspeople who came, dressed in faded calico, sat silent and unimpressed. Out under the lights, pratfalling in his hobo suit, Webern noticed there were only three children in the audience, including one little girl who never removed her finger from her nose. He wondered if perhaps a bigger and better circus had swept through town just before they arrived, taking with it all the starry-eyed dreamers and leaving behind only those with regrets, bad memories, and impossibly high expectations. Either that or he was losing his touch. No one even wanted his balloon animals here.

After an abysmal second performance, they tore down the big top. But they left their own tents up, staying for a third night—a fourth— and then finally for a whole week, the longest they'd ever parked in one town. Dr. Show didn't send Webern around with the pay envelopes, and he didn't remind the players that their valiant self-sacrifice was in service of the show's glorious future. In fact, he barely spoke at all. He appeared briefly at breakfast one morning to tell the performers he was "getting his wits about him"—booking new venues and mapping a route to take them there, in other words replacing the schedule Boulder had stolen. But other than hitting Al up for pocket change to use in the local pay phone, Show did little to indicate that plans were really in the works. A light burned in his tent until late in the evenings, and when he emerged, always briefly, during the day, he came out in full costume, his moustache waxed, his bow tie straight, his tuxedo brushed, but his dark eyes haggard, red-rimmed, and depressed.

With no show to prepare for, the circus players spent long hours counting their meagre savings and speculating about how much worse their current situation would have to become before Schoenberg did something desperate and got himself arrested. The exact nature of his future crime was a matter of spirited debate. Vlad and Fydor contended he would pose as a purveyor of medicinal spirits, which would sicken one young woman and drive another insane. Hank prophesied that Schoenberg would attempt to harness the town's feral cats to pull a float in the show; he'd be busted for animal cruelty, if they didn't claw him to death first. Nepenthe spun the wildest stories, about Schoenberg seducing widows who resembled his mother only to dispatch with them during a symbolically charged "cut the lady in half" trick, but she generally trailed off just before the juiciest parts, when she saw the look on Webern's face.

It did give Webern an ache to hear them all laugh about the prospect of Schoenberg working on a West Virginian chain gang. But he consoled himself with thinking that, even if their suspicions were well-founded, none of them would betray their ringmaster to the authorities: they were all dead broke, entirely dependent on Dr. Show to get them out of this godforsaken place. Enrique got a temporary job as a soda jerk at the local malt shop, replacing a young man who'd gotten a girl in trouble and disappeared, but he was making peanuts, and besides him, the rest of the players stayed away from the locals, who regarded them warily, not as curiosities but as intruders.

During the afternoons, the performers found ways to pass the time. Vlad and Fydor played "the Fool" with a deck of dog-eared cards; they shielded their hands from each other to little avail and cursed dead ancestors under their breath. Eng practiced new stretches. Al strung up a makeshift hammock between a telephone pole and a hickory tree, but the mesh fabric sagged to the ground as soon as he fit his jumbo lanky frame inside. Perhaps inspired by his own tales of animal cruelty, Explorer Hank fashioned elaborate, jingling collars for Fred and Ginger, and Brunhilde clipped pictures from an ancient pile of Life magazines, no doubt assembling materials for a Dresden attaché case. She was the only one besides Webern who didn't join in the conversations about Dr. Show's incarceration. One morning, over an early breakfast of remaindered bacon and toast made from hot dog buns, Webern found himself alone at the campfire with her and Al.

"The con up yet?" Al took his seat on the muddied cloth of his former hammock. He stretched, knocking Webern in the head with a gargantuan elbow. "Whoops."

"He's probably in there, working." Webern offered the skillet to him. "When he takes us back out on the road again, you're all going to have egg on your face."

"Yeah, right." Al observed the remaining scraps of bacon with disappointment. "I been with him longer than the rest of you. He's a goner this time. We're too broke."

"Being broke doesn't make you a criminal."

"It does if you don't like being broke." Al squashed the last three hot dog buns together in his hand, then rubbed them vigorously in the bacon grease. Webern didn't know how Al managed. Webern never got full himself on their rations, and he was less than half the giant's size. "And he don't like it."

"By that standard, we are all criminals, Alfred." Both men turned to look at Brunhilde. She reached for the empty hot dog bun bag. "Who would choose this life?"

"Well, I would." Webern poured himself some more coffee, but it was from the bottom of the pot and mostly sludge. "I did."

"Did you choose this life, Webern?" Brunhilde chuckled. She shook out the crumbs, then started filling up the hot dog bun bag with little pictures she'd cut out of her magazines. They showed through the wrinkled plastic: tanks, flags, a coach drawn by horses on fire. "I suppose you also chose the colour of your eyes."

"What's that supposed to mean?"

Brunhilde didn't say any more. She hummed loudly to herself. Webern dumped the coffee out of his mug and went back to the tent he shared with Al.

Pretending that no one would notice them leaving together, Webern and Nepenthe spent their afternoons exploring the woods that sprang up so near their muddy field. They found trails there, badly maintained—one could only be identified by the slashes of blue paint that marked the trunks of certain trees. Nepenthe often got far ahead of Webern on these excursions, and he struggled to keep up, watching her curls bounce as she slunk away, walking like it was an inconvenience to her.

Each day, they walked until they found the stream they nicknamed Beer Can Creek. On its banks, Webern peeled off Nepenthe's gloves and veil—she never volunteered to take off any more than that—and they lay down on the blanket they brought with them to have a picnic. They used the word "picnic" very loosely. On the first day, Nepenthe brought a smushed peanut butter sandwich for them to share; after that, a bag of chips, then a donut. Webern brought a bottle of Coke, then a couple of Rheingold beers, then a half-empty bottle of hard cider. It didn't matter much; mostly they were occupied with each other. Dead leaves crackled beneath the blanket as they rolled and grappled like wrestlers. And, just when things got to the point that Webern could barely stand it anymore, Nepenthe always extricated herself from him and started telling stories.

She obviously missed having a psychoanalyst. Lying on the blanket, arms folded beneath her head, peach pit rolling on her tongue, Nepenthe described her parents: her father, a company president, always staying in the city overnight for meetings; her mother, whose afternoons began and ended with the death-rattle of the cocktail shaker. She talked about her home in Connecticut, the cruel life of an all-girls' boarding school, her longstanding aversion to horses (she'd once been bitten on the knee), ballet (she called tutus "an affront to women's sexuality"), and tennis ("Swatting at those goddamn balls reminds me of killing yellow jackets at our summer house").

Webern also found out that her deformity, which he'd assumed she'd been born with, was more recent than his own. Although Nepenthe's scales had made brief appearances on her knees and elbows for as long as she could remember, her full-blown freakishness had not begun to take hold until 7th grade, when she'd started at the Appleton Academy. Even then, it had seemed containable for awhile—first it was just the legs—then the arms—then the back and shoulders. By the time it spread to the torso, neck, and face, she had already begun her visits to a vast array of Manhattan's finest dermatologists. On weekends and holiday afternoons, when other girls went shopping in town or dressed up for mixers, her mother had driven the lurching, champagne-coloured Mercedes up the gravel drive to collect Nepenthe for her doctor's appointments. But though the dermatologists charged plenty, they only made matters worse.

With every word Nepenthe spoke, Webern's claim on her seemed to retreat to a smaller and smaller region of her heart. Sometimes it terrified him so much that he pulled her back down on top of him and kissed her fiercely on the mouth, even while she tried to keep on talking.

The clown, dressed like an organ-grinder's monkey in a red suit and fez, stands on an overturned drum, frozen. He holds a pair of golden cymbals. A large silver key sticks out of his back. It glints in the spotlight.

A young girl happens along, wearing ribbons in her hair. She sees the clown, stops, and ponders him. She walks around him slowly, pokes him in the ribs, even kicks his shin. No response. She pouts, then sees the key in his back and suddenly understands. She twists it all the way around, then steps back to watch.

The clown bangs his cymbals together three times, drops them, then jumps down off the drum and runs offstage. He returns riding a unicycle. He circles the drum once, then hops off, rolls his 'cycle offstage, and, with a herky-jerk waddle, approaches the girl. He pulls a daisy from his pocket and offers it to her, then leans in, puckering up. But just as he is about to kiss her, he lurches forward and freezes again. Wound down.

The girl thinks this is a scream. Giggling, she lifts the clown up and puts him back atop the drum. She straightens him up, puts the cymbals back in his hands, then walks around him again. She twists his key—this time with some effort—in two full revolutions.

The clown bangs the cymbals together six times—faster now—then exits and comes back riding the unicycle. He circles the drum once, twice, then leaps off. In a sped-up waddle, he goes up to the girl, holds out two daisies, then leans in for a kiss. But just as before, he lurches to a stop, a wide ape's grin still stretched desperately across his face.

Laughing, slapping her thighs, the girl tries to recover, but for a moment can't. Finally, she lifts the clown up onto the drum, puts the cymbals back in his hands, and exits stage right, still chuckling.

For a long moment, the clown stands alone on his drum. Though his expression is the same, something seems different now—his eyes? His posture? It's as though freezing pains him. Seconds tick by. Then, from stage right, the girl returns with a sailor. She points to the clown, and her companion examines him, walking slowly around the drum. His short sleeves reveal nautical symbols tattooed on bulging muscles. With a show of strength, he easily cranks the key in the clown's back, not once, not twice, but three times all the way around.

Crash, crash, crash, crash, crash, crash, crash, crash, crash! go the cymbals. *Squeak, squeak, squeak!* sings the unicycle's wheel. The clown holds out the bouquet, leans forward—but this time the machinery in him is still turning and he presses his puckered lips against the girl's cheek in a kiss. As he grinds to a stop, though, the sailor's fist comes out of nowhere and sets him spinning once again.

Webern opened his eyes. He was lying on his sleeping bag, and, except for the king-sized snores rolling in from Al's side of the tent, it was utterly silent. Other places they'd stayed, Webern had woken up to the sound of cars humming along highways, waves crashing, or carnival rides whooshing down their tracks. But Lynchville was different.

Still, Webern couldn't get back to sleep. He felt awake, really *awake,* for the first time since they'd arrived in this awful town. The palms of his hands itched, and his toes wiggled in his socks. He kept thinking about the dream, about little details of the performance he'd seen— the silver key, the daisies, the unicycling. It was performable, maybe, with a few minor changes. Maybe Eng could dress in drag to play the girl. Of course, he could think about it again in the morning. In the morning, in the morning. But he was thinking about it now.

Webern kicked away his blankets, shoved his glasses on his face and, in the dark, tried a herky-jerk waddle across the grassy floor of the tent. He moved his arms the way he'd seen wind up toys do, even made a quiet buzzing sound in the back of his throat to mimic the grinding of the gears. It was all about repetition, really, and that sort of odd clockwork jerkiness . . . he thought of clock hands in elementary school, how they always moved backward slightly before clanking forward—a new minute, a new hour, lunchtime. He tried moving his arms this way until he could tell without being able to see that he'd gotten it right, and then a familiar thrill seized him. He knew he wasn't getting back to sleep now. He had a new act.

Webern groped through the darkness over to his suitcase, then popped it open and rummaged around until he found his flashlight. In the rippled circle of its light, he watched his hands pull out a marbled composition book and a school box full of stubby pencils and worn-down crayons.

The pages of the notebook crackled as he turned them, as if they gave off a kind of electricity all their own. Webern had bought the book at a stationary store just outside Dolphin River the day after he left with the circus, and ever since he'd been filling it with plans for clown acts. Here was the clown learning to dance the Charleston. Here was the clown running from an escaped tiger. Here was the clown as an inept barber, an inept matador, an inept snake charmer. Here was the clown floating in a hot air balloon whose movements he couldn't control. Here was the clown and a rain cloud that followed him everywhere, even under the shelter of his umbrella—that one he hadn't figured out how to do onstage yet.

Webern's drawings, some painstakingly cross-hatched and coloured in, others scratched out with angry slashes, lay on the pages alongside his run-on paragraphs of excited description and technical how-to instructions. He had tried out some of the acts in the show already (his favourite had been the matador: Eng made a very convincing bull, and the kids seemed to love it), but even at the best of times his performances fell short of his expectations. His costumes were always too big or too small—children's clothes never fit quite right over his hump, but sleeves made for adults hung down to the ground—and especially with their recent near-escapes, his props were always getting broken or lost. The acts that excited him the most he hadn't even bothered to attempt. If he couldn't perform them the way he wanted to, what was the point? He was designing routines for a professional here, not for a sideshow errand boy, and in his darker moments he considered throwing the whole book out the Cadillac's window. But he knew he never would. Despite his fears, Webern kept filling in the pages. He couldn't help himself.

Holding the flashlight in his left hand, the pencil in his right, Webern began to draw the clown with the wind-up key in his back. The act began to change as soon as he set it down on paper, which always seemed to happen; sometimes it distressed him, but tonight it felt good, like he was still dreaming, but able to control his dream this time. Little mistakes of his pen—the young girl acquired a parasol, the drum the clown stood on became a shipping crate, which Webern labelled "WIND-UP SPARE PARTS"—became part of the plan.

Webern worked steadily for an hour, drawing and colouring his drawing with crayons from the school box. He scribbled annotations in the margins. Finally, he looked over what he'd done, brushing crayon wax and eraser dust from the page. Now he knew it was performable, and a second impulse seized him, almost as strong as the impulse to get his dream down on paper in the first place; he wanted to go tell Dr. Show.

Switching off the flashlight, Webern crept to the flap of his tent and quietly let himself out. It was very late, or very early, but he saw that in Dr. Schoenberg's tent—farthest away from the others—a light was still burning. Tucking his notebook under his arm, Webern set off towards it.

CHAPTER SEVEN

DR. SCHOENBERG STOOD AT HIS EASEL, PAINTING. In one hand, he held his ebony cigarette holder; in the other, his long-handled brush. An Arabian lamp burned on top of his trunk, and a half circle of citronella candles glowed on the ground at his feet like a theatre's footlights. For a long moment, he paused to scrutinize the canvas with careful eyes. He lifted his paintbrush—hesitated, lowered it—slowly raised his cigarette holder—lowered it also. Then, in a flash of inspiration, he confused the two and plunged his cigarette into a daub of yellow on his palette. The burning end sizzled and released an acrid smell. Dr. Show tossed the ruined butt on the ground, then snapped. A new one, already lit, appeared between his fingers.

"*Voilà*," he murmured with a private smile. He was fitting it into his ebony holder when he heard scratching at the canvas wall behind him.

"Enter," he called over his shoulder.

Unlike the other performers' tents, which had zippered flaps for doors, Dr. Show's had a pair of velvet curtains, which hung suspended over the entrance on a wooden dowel. These curtains could be parted dramatically upon entering or exiting, but Webern didn't bother opening them all the way when he sidled in.

"Hey, Dr. Show." He glanced down at the candles. "I saw the lights—hope I'm not interrupting you or anything."

"No, no, on the contrary. I've slept poorly these past few nights, and my art helps pass the time. What can I do for you?"

Dr. Schoenberg unfolded his director's chair and gestured for Webern to sit down. Webern looked at the seat. The gash from Mars

Boulder's sword was painstakingly stitched shut, but he could still see it, raised like a scar.

"I just came up with a new idea for my act." Webern climbed into the chair and ran his hand over the cover of the marbled notebook. "I figured if you weren't too busy, maybe we could talk about it."

"Let's see it, then."

Webern flipped the notebook open to the page he'd just finished and handed it to Dr. Schoenberg, who sat down on his cot to examine the pictures. Webern shifted in the director's chair. His feet didn't touch the ground, and it was hard to keep from kicking his legs.

"Hmm. Yes. This business with the sailor is hackneyed, of course, but the wind-up idea is rather inspired." Schoenberg skimmed a finger across the page. "Is there a way to keep the key turning on your back? That would lend greatly to the verisimilitude."

"Sure, probably, I'll figure it out. Anyway, this got me thinking, maybe I can do a whole series of acts where I'm different toys." Schoenberg started to flip back to earlier pages in the notebook: the clown with the mermaid, the ill-fated high wire act. "Don't look at those, they're not finished yet, they're stupid."

"They look quite spirited, to my eyes. This one in particular—"

"But Dr. Show, listen." Webern grabbed the notebook back and shut it. "Listen. I can be a tin soldier, a marionette, a rag doll, one of those birds who dunks his head into a water glass. Or other stuff even—a suit of armour, a mannequin. I mean, there's so much I never thought of before—and the sets can be simple, the whole thing's so simple really—I can do a different one every week—"

"One thing at a time, my boy, one thing at a time!" Dr. Schoenberg laughed.

"Sorry, boss. It just gets so—I mean, I just have so many ideas." Webern's voice squeaked on the last word, and he coughed loudly, embarrassed. Sometimes his brain felt like a little German car, with clowns packed inside so tightly he couldn't tell if he could ever get them all out. He thought of the crowd at the last show, the woman in the front row who kept checking her watch. "Sorry, Dr. Show." He forced a smile. "I'm crazy, right?"

"Perhaps. I'm not the one to judge." Dr. Show wiped the corners of his eyes. "Ah, I remember the days when it seemed that even the darkest of illusions would soon come within my grasp." He got up and took a bottle of bourbon and two glasses out from behind his trunk.

"Care for a nightcap?"

"Okay, sure. Why did you quit being a magician, anyway? I mean, you still know all the tricks and stuff." The first time Webern met him, Dr. Show had unscrewed the top of a saltshaker and pulled out a white handkerchief with a handful of gold glitter inside. Webern had kept the handkerchief—it was tucked away in his suitcase now—and he still hadn't blown his nose on it. Small and precious, it reminded him of the tiny envelopes he used to get under his pillow from the tooth fairy before his mother died. "I bet you were great at it."

Schoenberg handed him a glass of bourbon and sat back down on his cot.

"You flatter me, Bernie. I was exemplary, perhaps, gifted, sharp, and subtle, but try as I might, I always fell just short of true greatness." He gazed into his drink thoughtfully. "No, my real skill is in orchestrating the feats of others. I have an eye for talent, you know. And, I daresay, a flair for formal composition."

He nodded at the canvas, and for the first time, Webern noticed what Dr. Show had been painting. It was a self-portrait. In it, Schoenberg cut a dashing figure. His cape blew out behind him, its red satin lining rippling in the wind, and his glossy moustache reflected the light of an unseen moon. He stood against a background of rich, midnight blue, reaching out toward the viewer with one elegant hand. Above his outstretched fingers, a red rose bloomed out of the air. A mist obscured his feet, and all over the painting, the colours, dreamy clouds, bled into one another. Though the artist's intent was not altogether clear, Webern had the impression that the ringmaster was supposed to be gazing down from the velvety realm of the night sky.

"Lovely, isn't it," Schoenberg observed. He sipped his bourbon. "I believe it's one of my best. At first I thought I might add some constellations, but I concluded that would detract too much from the focus."

Webern nodded. Dr. Show was always painting self-portraits, and it cracked Nepenthe up. He thought of their afternoon on the banks of Beer Can Creek, the quick rasp of her hands like pumice stone on his back, and wondered how soon she would be awake.

". . . most serendipitous," Dr. Show was saying. "You were just the man I wanted to see."

"That's nice. What about?" Webern drank some more bourbon. It tasted different than usual—less like gasoline. It occurred to him that this was a bottle from Dr. Show's private stash.

Schoenberg stirred his drink with one languid finger. "Do you think I'm—liked in our little company? Well respected, all that?"

"Sure, Dr. Show."

"Yes. Hmm." Schoenberg discovered a fleck of paint on his cuff and rubbed it away thoughtfully. "I thank you for the reassurance, Bernie. But, speaking quite confidentially, I must admit I've noticed a change in the manner of your fellow performers since Paradise Beach. Brunhilde has long made her displeasure known, but I fear her low spirits have begun to affect some of the others. The other day, I overheard Al, of all people, expressing his doubts that I even intend to plan a new itinerary. As you might imagine, upon hearing that I felt greatly—exasperated."

Dr. Schoenberg pressed a forefinger to his temple and fell silent. Webern looked down at his notebook. The black and white blotches on its marbled cover made shapes like bad weather: tornados, mushroom clouds, a falling star.

"Greatly exasperated. You understand, I'm certain."

"I'm sure that Al didn't mean it the way it sounded."

"No, no. I quite understand his concern. I need to regain my performers' trust. That's why I wished to speak with you—I think you may be able to lend some assistance."

"Do you know why I chose this town, Bernie, rather than any other?"

The Cadillac bounced down the lumpy dirt road. A discarded mattress lay in the ditch, along with a deflated inner tube and what looked like the sorry remains of an ancient Christmas tree. A skinny cat darted out from a patch of scrub pine, and Schoenberg braked to let it pass.

"Um—well, because—we were supposed to go to South Carolina . . ." Webern cranked down the passenger side window an inch. Dr. Schoenberg was still smoking energetically from his cigarette holder, and along with the two bourbons he'd had back at the tent, the thick cloud made Webern feel drowsy, almost hypnotized.

"Yes, that's true. But do you know why I chose Lynchville in particular?"

"I didn't know there was a more particular reason than that." Webern stretched, then looked at his wrist. He wasn't wearing a watch. "I hate to change the subject, Dr. Show, but do you think you could maybe tell me where we're going? It's getting kind of late, and I . . ."

"Truer words were never spoken, my boy. But though the eleventh hour has come and gone, you may find I still have a trick or two left up my sleeve." Dr. Show touched the cigarette holder again to his lips. "Have you ever heard of a man named Kingsley Golden, by any chance?"

"It sounds familiar." Webern smothered a yawn as the car rumbled over a set of train tracks. "Was he some kind of businessman or something?"

"Ah." Dr. Schoenberg smiled ruefully. "How quickly they forget. When I was a boy, Kingsley Golden was a household name. The newsmen dubbed him King Midas, because his every enterprise prospered so gloriously. But alas, the fall of '29 brought his empire to its knees. I had the luck of experiencing his greatest achievement some half-dozen years before it vanished for good.

"It may interest you that Kingsley Golden began his career as an inventor of mechanical toys." The Cadillac breezed past a stop sign. "Golden possessed a peculiar sensitivity toward the workings of machinery. In his youth—or so I have read—he would steal away from his bed in the small hours to dissect his family's clocks. Clocks, Bernie! The child was mad. And his obsession only grew more intense with age. As a young man, he rose rapidly in the ranks of the Knickknack Toy Company, but soon the small innovations that delighted his employers no longer interested him. He decided to go into business for himself, and thus Golden Toys was born."

"Golden Toys?" Webern's sleepiness evaporated. Again, he saw those dusty toy store shelves, the glossy hues of painted metal, the delicate machinery that buzzed and trembled like something alive. Alive, but miniature. Manmade. "You're kidding. I used to play with them all the time when I was a kid. Wind-up toys, right? Like in my new act."

"The company lives on to this day, manufacturing race cars and other forgettable trinkets of cheap metal and paint. But these sorry imitations cannot compare with the glories of Golden Toys in their heyday. I possessed only one myself, a pair of clockwork pool players who took their shots at the turn of a key. But there were dozens even more ingenious that I glimpsed in the windows of shops and the grubby paws of my less austere playmates. Meanwhile, Golden was earning a reputation as an exacting tyrant who ran his workers ragged." Schoenberg exhaled a plume of smoke thoughtfully. "I must admit, he served as an inspiration for me in those days."

"I'm still not exactly sure where you're taking me, Dr. Show."

"Patience, my boy, patience! All in good time.

"As his company prospered, Golden again longed for a new challenge, a project that could wholly consume his tireless genius. Before, he had absorbed himself in the delicate machinery of the miniature, but now his mind turned toward the monumental. Genius often takes this turn; I have seen it in myself. No great man wants to leave the world without some grand notice of his passing, some Colossus to stand long after, crying, 'He did live!' I presume our circus will survive me, and continue to bear my name. Likewise, Kingsley Golden began work on an enterprise that he then believed would last into the ages. But it was not to be.

"Goldenland, the world's first wholly mechanical amusement park—I remember it well. Its doors first opened on June 1, 1920. Though I did not pay my visit there 'til three years later, I observed the advertisements with much interest. In fact, one picture, which I tore from the local newspaper, took a prominent space on my bedroom wall, alongside the portraits of great magicians and my own early artistic efforts. I'm glad to say I still have it now."

Schoenberg allowed the car to crunch to a stop and reached into the inside pocket of his tuxedo jacket. Webern peered out the windshield. Purple-dark clouds clotted the sky—it was starting to drizzle. Schoenberg unfolded a brittle piece of newsprint, then smoothed it on the dashboard before he handed it to Webern.

In the dim light of the car, Webern could barely make out the faded lines and shadings that marked the yellowed page. Faintly, he glimpsed the stripes of a wrought-iron gate, and behind that, the curving spine of a roller coaster track. He brought the paper close to his eye. Thunder rolled in the distance.

"I can't believe you kept this all these years," he said.

"Not so odd, really. Goldenland worked a curious enchantment on my youthful mind. When I left home at seventeen, it was the first stop on my journey. And this—"

He tapped the paper.

"—was my map."

Webern stared down at the picture, at the small caption along the bottom. Lightning cracked across the sky, and, in the white flash, he could read the words written there: *The Goldenland Amusement Park,*

Lynchville, West Virginia. A car door slammed. Webern looked up—
"Hey, wait a min . . ." —but Dr. Show was already outside, disappearing
into the night and the rain.

The amusement park, as it turned out, had not been torn down, altered,
or indeed entered since its final closing. But years of exposure to the
elements had taken a toll. Much to Webern's surprise, Goldenland's
padlock crushed to rusty dust beneath Mars Boulder's sword, and its
wrought-iron gate swung open easily, though with an awful scream.
Inside, the grounds looked dark and jungly, grown high with spindly
weeds. A ticket booth loomed like an elephant's gravestone. When
Schoenberg strode inside, Webern, against his better judgement,
found himself following just behind.

Flashes of lightning illuminated the sky, and the rain began
to fall more heavily, but still Dr. Show continued on. His plan, he
explained, hacking his blade through the grasses like a machete,
was to take a relic from the park—a dancing automaton, perhaps,
or maybe a mechanical car—and feature it in his circus. It was not
theft, but an homage to the grand master Golden, whose work had
inspired him since childhood. And now, Golden's work would inspire
others, bring new life to the show; even Brunhilde would have to
admit that. Webern tried to listen, but it was difficult to concentrate.
Raindrops rolled down his glasses, and brambles clawed his pant legs.
Schoenberg pointed out attractions as they passed: the world's largest
cuckoo clock, a nightmare of doors and rotting shingles; miniature
gondolas beached in stagnant water; a child-sized train frozen on a
bend in the track; a clockwork Punch and Judy, motionless behind the
ragged curtains of a long-deserted puppet theatre. As Webern walked
through the ruined park, the sights he had seen in Lynchville began
to make more sense to him. How could the descendants of laid-off
amusement park workers learn to love a circus, when their own palace
of delights had so thoroughly betrayed them?

Schoenberg finally settled on a merry-go-round. It was a small one,
with only four steeds—a unicorn, a rabbit, a squirrel, and an ostrich—
and its base stood conveniently mounted on wheels. Schoenberg
remembered it moving to different parts of the park throughout the
day, and to see if it would still roll, he gave it a mighty shove. The
wheels ground the gravel, and he jumped back in delight.

"Ah, this—this is what I came for," Schoenberg cried. "Bernie, to the Cadillac! We must hitch this to the back somehow."

Webern stared at the squirrel's face, its orange tears of rust, the hollow where one glass eye was missing. For the first time, he allowed himself to wonder if Schoenberg really was crazy.

"Do you think this thing's worth it, boss? It might not even work."

"This is a mechanical marvel, my boy. A dab of grease, a cog or two, and it will run smoothly once more." Schoenberg slapped the rabbit's thigh. "Ah, and I thought I would never return. Perhaps one day, with the proceeds from our show, I could get this park up and running again. You should have seen the crowds back then—the vendors of balloons and cotton candy—the children—and I still nearly one myself. To think how the world spilled out for me, that day. All my life ahead . . . I thought I would possess it all, I truly did. Foolish, perhaps, but I had such ambition, with my deck of cards and my cage of doves. . . . I remember my hands in those days, so nimble, so deft. My mother called them a pianist's hands, a pianist's or a surgeon's, but I knew better. She never understood. I had a magician's hands."

Something strange had come into Schoenberg's voice, and Webern could feel it filling his own chest, too. It was as though he and the ringmaster had disappeared into that faded newsprint picture, as though they might never come out. Nepenthe, lying in her kiddy pool, seemed very far away. Dr. Show cleared his throat, and Webern looked up sharply, blinking fast.

Dr. Show manoeuvred the Cadillac carefully between the ticket booths and concession stands, and they lashed the merry-go-round to its back bumper with the tightrope he kept in the trunk. But when they went to get back in the car, he stopped at the driver's side door and lightly drummed the roof. A strange expression still lingered on his face, and he looked at Webern almost pleadingly, as though he expected his young accomplice to dissolve into nothing at any moment and was trying, through sheer willpower, to keep him from vanishing.

"Bernie," he said. He spun his keys around one finger. "You *are* sixteen now. Wouldn't you like to drive?"

CHAPTER EIGHT

SLOW CHILDREN AT PLAY. Webern grimaced at the warning sign and the decapitated Barbie that lay on the ground beneath it. He could swear he'd seen them before. Maybe he was driving in circles. In the dark, all of Lynchville looked the same. Not that he had the greatest view. Even sitting on Schoenberg's copy of the collected Shakespeare, he could barely see over the steering column.

At three foot ten he wasn't really tall enough to drive, but he hadn't been able to protest when Dr. Show asked him. After all, the Cadillac *was* Schoenberg, as inseparable from him as his curling moustache or his pale, winglike magician's hands. And it was true that there, in the faint drizzle of the amusement park, Schoenberg had looked haggard, feeble even—certainly in no condition to operate heavy machinery. Getting behind the wheel Webern had felt like he had the morning of his mother's funeral, when his father loaned him a tie and showed him how to tie it: though he'd wanted nothing more than to run away, he knew he had a duty to stay and let the knot tighten around his neck. Now he already rued the moment he slammed the car door shut. A bottle of rye whiskey filled the gap between his foot and the gas pedal, and he could hear it slosh as he pressed down on it, carefully accelerating. If he was going to keep this up, he'd have to invest in a pair of elevator shoes.

"Dr. Show—" He bit his lip. "—do you know where we're supposed to turn?"

"Hmmph." Schoenberg wrestled a road map down onto the dashboard. "Allow me to get my bearings. Which direction are we headed now, may I ask?"

"I don't know." A thin icy sweat had started all over Webern's body. He glanced in the rearview mirror, but of course he couldn't see anything past the merry-go-round. It had seemed small back there in Goldenland, but here, out on the road, it might as well be a parade float. At least the rain was letting up. "I guess I don't have a very good sense of direction."

"Hmm." Schoenberg traced his finger down a blue-green squiggle. His map was torn at the creases.

Webern was sure now: he heard another car behind them. Its engine made a different sound than the Cadillac's, a kind of quiet coughing. He glanced over his shoulder, then quickly back out at the road. The important thing was not to panic, not to act suspicious, not to speed or slam on the brakes or break the traffic laws. The traffic laws? What were they, anyway? What did you do at a four-way stop? And which meant no passing—solid or dotted lines?

No—better just concentrate on the road ahead. Don't speed, that was the main thing. But what if the car behind got fed up with him creeping along like a snail? What if the other driver got mad and tried to run him off the road? It wouldn't be hard to do, not with that damn dog and pony show trailing off the back. Or what if the other driver suspected something and called the police? In all the stories they'd told about Schoenberg getting hauled off to jail, the other circus players had never predicted Webern would be locked up in there along with him. Webern saw himself in prison, speaking to Nepenthe through telephones separated by a pane of glass. He'd touched her breast that afternoon, or rather the fabric of the dress above the fabric of the undergarment that cupped and concealed her breast. Now he would never touch it again. He felt the rough scales curving against his hand like living stone, like the black, crackled surface of lava, and for an instant he allowed himself to imagine Nepenthe weeping for him, weeping for him and maybe later helping him escape—a metal file baked in a cake, a rope thrown up to his barred window. But then the truth occurred to him: she'd be furious. Nepenthe didn't have much patience for Schoenberg's crazy schemes. The other day, down at Beer Can Creek, they'd been talking about Brunhilde and all the complaints she'd made over the last few months about the circus. Webern had said he believed Dr. Show was planning a new itinerary, booking locations even—hadn't he made some phone calls from the gas station the other day?—and that soon Brunhilde and the others would be sorry they ever doubted him at all. Nepenthe had just laughed.

"If you believe that, the old guy might as well pull a nickel out of your ear," she'd said.

Webern had glanced around nervously, half expecting Schoenberg to spring from the bushes with a gallant retort, but he hadn't, he hadn't appeared at all, and Webern had felt the strange shame he always felt when he watched one of his fellow players flub a performance onstage. Now he felt a different shame: the shame of imminent disaster. He just needed to calm down, that was all. Most likely the other car would just pass him as soon as the road opened up.

A red light flashed behind the monumental silhouette of the carousel, and a siren wailed. Schoenberg jumped in his seat; his hands flew up from the map as if it had just bitten him. Webern felt a sudden, sharp headache pierce the front lobe of his brain, and his hands fell limp on the steering wheel. He struggled to keep them there.

"Should I pull over, Boss?" His voice squeaked into falsetto.

"Don't be a fool, Bernie! Drive!"

Webern pressed the gas pedal to the floor and prepared himself for the rush of speed that he associated with car chases in late-night movies on TV. But a luxury car pulling a hunk of rusty steel couldn't accelerate quite the way he was hoping. With a high pitched whine, the Cadillac lurched forward half-heartedly. The needle of the speedometer crept up to forty-five and hovered there, quivering.

"What do I do now?" Webern honked the horn for no reason. He glanced back at the merry-go-round, then desperately at the road. A four-way stop lay just ahead. "Tell me what to do!"

"Turn!"

"Which way?"

"Does it matter?"

Webern jerked the wheel abruptly right. The Cadillac cleared the stop sign by inches. The merry-go-round didn't. The one-eyed mechanical squirrel crashed into the sign's steel pole and, with a terrible ripping sound, wrenched loose from its mooring in the carousel floor. It fell onto the street behind them like a piece of giant metallic roadkill. As the cop slammed on his brakes, his growly voice filled a bullhorn: "Stop immediately! Please remain in the vehicle!"

But it was too late for Webern to obey even if he wanted to. He was still flooring the gas pedal, and the Cadillac was flying down a steep hill in the dark. The weight of the carousel fell on the side of motion, and as they sped down the road, it loomed larger and larger in the back windshield, until it slammed into the bumper with an awful thud.

Webern's hands went white on the steering wheel, and his eyes squeezed shut. A too-familiar memory flashed through his head: his parents' Studebaker, smoke pouring from its crumpled hood; his mother's purse spilled on the asphalt. He'd feared cars for years afterwards. What the hell was he doing here?

"My good man, come to your senses!"

Still gripping the wheel with aching hands, Webern opened his eyes a narrow slit, then wider. Before him, the road was flattening out; more incredibly, they had come to a street he recognized, only a block or so from the campsite. Behind a chain link fence, a pack of Rottweilers bayed.

"You've done it, my boy!" Schoenberg clutched Webern's forearm. His dark eyes gleamed. "We are delivered!"

"Oh, jeez, Dr. Show." Webern's heart still thumped in his ears. A whip-poor-will crooned in the distance. The night closed around them again, soft as wings.

Webern turned the Cadillac left, up the final hill before they reached the campsite. So many hills—at least they were going up one this time. They passed a lone streetlight and the engine of a tractor. As they climbed, the road narrowed until branches scratched the windows. No one would come looking for them up here. The carousel rolled back; now it was trailing the car at a safe distance. Webern's hands finally relaxed, and he leaned back in the seat as far as he was able. Cars weren't so bad after all, not once you knew how to drive them. And he was a quick study. Maybe one day he'd have a little Italian sports car, small enough to fit him to a tee. He'd wear elevator shoes and Nepenthe would have on big sunglasses and a scarf to hold her hair down, just like the President's wife. In the road ahead, one of the feral cats stood hissing. No problemo. Pressing his hand down on the horn, Webern avoided it with a slow, leisurely swerve. It was at this particular moment that the Cadillac spurted forward and the carousel disappeared from the rearview mirror.

This time, Dr. Show didn't have to tell him what to do. Webern pulled onto the shoulder in a hurry, splattering mud everywhere, and he and Schoenberg jumped out of the car. The tightrope still hung from the back bumper, Webern saw, worn clean through, but the merry-go-round was bump-bump-bumping its way down the long dark hill. As it picked up speed, some long unstirred gears began to clank inside it, and Webern saw the three remaining figures— unicorn, rabbit, and swan—move eerily through the motions of their final dance. But it didn't last for long. At the bottom of the hill, the carousel rolled like a tank over a patch of scrub pine and slammed straight into a thunderstruck oak. *RRRRSCREEEcrunch!* One cog, the size of a dinner plate, rolled back out into the road and clattered onto its side.

The air hung heavy with silence for a full minute as the two men stared down the hill at the clockwork carnage. Then Schoenberg began to laugh. He bent at the waist, his shoulders rising and falling, his mouth stretched in an open grin. He chortled and snorted. He clutched himself across the chest, as if to hold it inside, but the laughter still bubbled up. He rocked. He gasped and punched himself in the knee. Webern smiled uneasily as the laughter grew louder, more theatrical. Schoenberg laughed until he cried.

Nepenthe lay in the back seat of the Cadillac on top of a pile of sleeping bags. She rested her head on the concertina, grimaced, and reached beneath her back to remove a boutonniere of Dr. Show's: a squashed paper rose, its stem a crooked green wire. Slowly, she shredded its crepe petals with her hard grey fingertips.

Webern, shotgun, watched her in the rearview mirror. When he'd woken her up, explaining in a frantic whisper what had happened, she'd told him he and Schoenberg both needed psychiatric help: "It's not a diagnosis, it's a verdict: criminal insanity." Since then, she hadn't spoken a word to him. It was hard to tell if she was sleepy or disgusted. Now she stretched out across the seats, everyone's bedding crammed and pillowed beneath her. They hadn't had long to make their escape.

"Is it really safe to keep driving this car, Dr. Show?" Webern asked. "What if the cops recognize it?"

"Don't be foolish. The carousel obscured our vehicle entirely." Schoenberg brushed a bit of rust from his sleeve. "Besides, we'll cross state lines well before dawn."

The Cadillac's headlights briefly illuminated a billboard of an angelic girl advertising bread. With her sun-kissed hair and rosy smile, she could have been from another world. Webern thought of the boys at his school who claimed they could tell time by the sun, the inevitable retort: "What'll you do when it's dark outside?" He knew the answer now. Nights like this, time just didn't pass.

Dr. Show forced a faint smile. "We mustn't allow ourselves to be too dispirited, my boy." Insects pelted the windshield, and he switched on the wipers to smear them. "Our quest was ill-advised, perhaps, but the old saw is true: nothing ventured, nothing gained."

In the backseat, Nepenthe smirked and shredded another petal on the rose. Dr. Show cleared his throat.

"Besides, such a large apparatus would no doubt encumber us needlessly. A true showman cannot be weighed down by his accoutrements, however spectacular they may be. He can only thrive when his imagination and skills are given free reign." Schoenberg's expression darkened. "I have seen too many promising artists crippled by their dependence on majestic arenas, elaborate devices that spewed electricity and altered time, exotic beasts, and tantalizing assistants. Though the temptation has been great, at times, I have taken care in my career not to make that same mistake."

Webern wished Dr. Show would stop talking. All he wanted to do was sleep, preferably somewhere dry. He stared out the window at a barbed wire fence. It was starting to drizzle again.

"The life of a performer is hard, perhaps, but true mastery is its own reward." Dr. Schoenberg's wet tuxedo jacket was releasing ghostly steam. "Wouldn't you agree, Bernie?"

"I don't know, Dr. Show." Webern rubbed a mosquito bite his ankle. He felt like he was delivering lines from a play written for Nepenthe's benefit, a play entitled, *I'm Not as Crazy as This Guy*, or *None of It Was My Idea*. "I mean, I don't think I'm exactly a master yet."

"Ah. Well, all in good time, all in good time." Schoenberg glanced over his shoulder. "I apologize if our conversation is keeping you awake, my dear."

"Don't worry about it." Nepenthe tossed the ruined flower on the floor and rolled over on her side. "I don't think I could sleep in here anyway."

An hour or so later, they made camp in an abandoned barn. Dr. Show claimed it belonged to an acquaintance of his. No one really believed him, but they were too exhausted to argue. Sheets of rain blew in through the wide front doors that none of them could manage to shut. After parking the Cadillac and the jalopy inside, Schoenberg decided that the company should sleep up top, in a hayloft accessible only by a splintery ladder. Al ascended first, carrying a flashlight, and when he called down that it seemed safe enough, if none too clean, the other players scaled the rungs one by one.

Webern held his breath until he reached the very top. When he stepped onto the dry boards above, his knees continued to shake. Even with the flashlight switched on and positioned at the centre of the floor, it was very dark. The sloping planes of the roof hung low above his head; beneath his feet, the floor felt tilted and unstable, with nail heads poking out of the planks. A bat swooped down, squeaking, and he screamed. Vlad and Fydor, who had already unrolled their sleeping bag, murmured something in Russian; one of them chuckled. Nepenthe flopped down on a blanket; she fanned herself with one hand. Then from below, they heard Brunhilde's voice.

"I will not sleep here, Schoenberg. I will not sleep where animals feed."

"My dear Brunhilde, I assure you these accommodations are temporary in the extreme."

"Just the same, I refuse. Pay me what you owe. I want no part of this *Albtraum*, this circus."

"My lark, please reconsider. You may sleep in the Cadillac, if you like."

"I will not reconsider. Pay me what you owe. One month's back salary. The cashbox, if you please."

The hayloft looked out on the lower part of the barn. Al, Eng, and Nepenthe gathered at the edge to peer down.

"Bernie, come see this," Nepenthe hissed. Webern shook his head. "Come *on*."

Webern stepped forward hesitantly. Between two boards, he could see a chink of light. "I'm scared of heights."

Nepenthe rolled her eyes. From down below, he heard the Cadillac door open, then the sound of metal against metal—tinny and faint.

"One dime? This is all you have saved?"

"Ah. Er, if you'll allow me to—I have some small bills, I believe— perhaps a personal cheque?"

The ladder creaked. After a long moment, Brunhilde hefted herself up to the hayloft floor. She strode up to the edge, tossed her silk pillow on the ground, and lowered herself onto it with grave dignity. She ran her fingers through her beard.

Webern unfolded his sleeping bag in one corner of the hayloft, as far as he could get from the ladder and the edge. Husks of grain crunched beneath him as he curled up. After a moment, Al switched off the flashlight. The others began to breathe slowly and deeply—Al started to snore. Webern rolled over. A small leak from the ceiling dripped onto his nose. He heard cautious footsteps, and Nepenthe's rough hand touched his.

"Some digs, huh?" Her long curls brushed his face. He could hardly see her in the darkness. "Hey. I'm sorry you're afraid of heights."

"It's okay."

"And I'm sorry Dr. Show made you crash that thing into a tree."

"Don't worry about it."

"You're just such a dope sometimes."

"I thought it was criminal insanity."

"That, too. Plus paranoia, acrophobia, teratophilia, an Oedipal complex . . ."

"What's teratophilia?"

"Trust me, I've done my research, and you have it." She poked his chest. "You've got a whole system of pathologies. It'll take years to sort them all out."

Webern ran his finger in the grooves between the scales on her wrist. "Lots of years?"

Nepenthe kissed him on the forehead. "Consider yourself involuntarily committed."

She padded back to her blanket. Webern savoured the warm feeling that lingered where her lips had touched him. But he still couldn't get to sleep properly. Every time he started to doze off, he jerked awake again, convinced that he was falling.

In reality, Webern hadn't fallen since his sixth birthday, the day of his accident, when he had climbed up into his new treehouse and refused to come down again until the magician arrived. Up in the tree, Webern had stared down, owlish and blinking through his round, thick eyeglasses, while in the yard below his mother folded card tables, setting each one with brightly coloured napkins and orange paper plates. Webern wore a pink dress shirt that day, as well as blue velveteen shorts and a yellow conical party hat. His eyes were red from crying.

Webern had been suffering ever since he started first grade, some weeks earlier. He'd gone in eagerly, with a new bow tie and an apple for the teacher, and he'd come out, bedraggled and speechless, the victim of a violent funhouse. Webern didn't like the loud jangling bells, the dark catacombs of the coatroom, or the grime that collected under his nails by the day's end—crayon wax and eraser dust. He hated the little boys, who sharpened their pencils into spears and threw them at his neck, and the little girls, who snared him in their jump ropes and tittered behind the backs of their hands. He hated story time because, sitting in a circle with the other children, he couldn't get up close to the picture book illustrations the way he could at home with his mother, and he hated lunch—cold tater tots and limp green beans and sloppy joes that seemed to bleed when he bit into them. But, above all else, he hated recess. That first day on the playground, he fell down and scraped his knee on the rough asphalt. When, much to his surprise, no one rushed to pick him up, he wiped his eyes and looked into his stinging wound. In it, little grains of sand, stone, and glass sparkled, and for a terrifying moment, Webern imagined that he'd exposed a second skin, inhuman, metallic, and glittering, just beneath his own.

Webern missed waking up in his empty house and padding through hallways already warm with late morning light. He missed wearing his red robe and slippers, and napping in the afternoons. Most of all, he missed sitting in the kitchen and telling his mother about his dreams. But he couldn't find a way to bring them up at now-crowded breakfasts, with his father rustling through the newspaper, his mother swaying at the sizzling stove, and his sisters, holding hands, cackling at private jokes, and smashing their knees into the table's underside whenever anything displeased them.

So Webern tried to hold onto his dreams all day long. But it wasn't easy. Despite his best efforts, the dreams grew thin and brittle with little holes in them, like peppermints sucked for too long, and most days, by mid-afternoon, Webern had begun to wonder if he'd ever dreamed at all. The sandcastle cities, the marshmallow pillows, the smiling man in the moon—these dreamscapes dissolved and melted into one another till they left nothing but shiny rainbow puddles, pooled on the floor of his mind. So Webern started keeping his dreams to himself, though he could already see the sadness growing in his mother's eyes.

Webern had seen the magician advertised on a poster tacked to the wall of the grocery store. Amidst a flurry of business cards and clipped coupons for haircuts and shoe repair stores, the blood red letters of his sign stood out. "WOTAN THE IRASCIBLE," it screamed.

"ILLUSIONIST FOR HIRE." In smaller letters, the poster alluded to the magician's dark powers, and his availability for weddings, birthdays, and other family gatherings. But Webern, who was just learning to read, didn't trouble himself with these superfluous details. His eyes lingered on the portrait that gazed out of the glossy paper with hooded eyes. The magician, a tall gaunt man with hair black as ink, held a thin black wand with an inch of white at its tip like ash on a cigarette. On his head, he wore a top hat, so tall and black it seemed to be concealing something. Webern stared at this picture for a long time, puzzling over a feeling he couldn't quite articulate. Somehow, this somber, mustachioed gentleman seemed to know the answers to lonesome questions Webern was just starting to ask himself.

When Webern begged for the magician to perform at his birthday party, his mother enthusiastically agreed, and not just because her love for Webern was big enough to burst a smaller heart. No; she knew that Webern didn't want to have a party in the first place, and she hoped that Wotan could sweeten the bitter medicine, at least a little.

Shirley understood her son's dislike of parties. When she had been a child herself, she had also preferred afternoons alone, reading fairy tales or helping her mother out in the kitchen, and it seemed to her that much of what had happened since those peaceful days ended had been a very big mistake. One part of her wanted to shelter Webern forever, to hide him away from the world like a little prince in a tower. But the other part of her suspected that it was her duty to nudge him along. It was this part of Shirley that guided her hand as she addressed the small, bright invitations, as she squeezed ribbons of frosting from a tube, and as she bought bunches of balloons that tugged and bumped at the ends of their strings, trying to float away.

Webern had gone along with all of this, grudgingly but without complaint, until the day of the party when Shirley, arranging candles on his cake, had looked out of the kitchen window to see the rope ladder of her son's new treehouse slither up into the high branches of the backyard oak and disappear.

The treehouse was a gift from Webern's father, Raymond, who'd built it loudly and stubbornly, without consulting anyone. A couple of weeks earlier, on a Saturday afternoon, he had declared that he was heading out to run a few errands, and Webern and Shirley had both looked up in surprise. Raymond never ran errands. He was a burly, slouching man, with skin leathery-rough as a catcher's mitt, and a pugnacious underbite; except for his timid, darting eyes, he looked like a retired prizefighter. Raymond needed his solitude, so he stayed at home, preferably by himself, whenever possible. He spent most weekends stretched out on the couch with a gin and tonic in his red lumberjack's hand, staring at a spot on the wallpaper just to the left of the picture window. Sometimes he let out a short, wild cry, like the unexpected squawk of a seagull. On weekends, if Webern ran out into the living room to look for a lost toy or a storybook, his mother always cautioned, "Don't disturb your father. He's thinking."

"Thinking about what?" Webern once asked. His mother hesitated. "The war, I suppose."

Perhaps that afternoon in the hardware store, Raymond was thinking of the war again, because he returned home with enough planks, nails, and shingles to build a fortress.

"The boy needs some place to go," he explained over dinner, "to get away from this house full of women."

Willow and Billow smashed their knees into the table's underside. The mashed potatoes jumped. The Jell-O salad trembled.

The first week after the treehouse was finished, Webern only climbed up in it once, to hang the gingham curtains that his mother had picked out for the windows. His father seemed disgusted, but Webern didn't care. The treehouse scared him. Webern had expected it to look more like a bird's nest, with soft feathered walls that would hold him gently in the air, like a cupped hand. This treehouse, square and heavy with a hole in the floor, more closely resembled a cardboard box, which might unceremoniously dump him out at any moment. On the morning of the party, though, it seemed to be his only refuge.

Up in the treehouse, yellow, orange, and green light streamed in the open windows, filtered through changing leaves. Webern sat Indian-style on the floor, carefully peeling the wrapper from one of his birthday cupcakes. He took a bite and squeezed his eyes shut, trying to savour it, before he swallowed. He put the rest of the cupcake back in its paper skin. He might have to stay up here a long time—better ration out supplies.

Webern licked pink icing off his fingers, then dared himself to peek out one of the windows. Although he knew he could fall, he could also imagine climbing out the window and walking around at this height, as if on a pair of enormous stilts. He was bracing himself for the wobbly bliss of vertigo when he looked up from his cupcake and realized that he wasn't alone. A little boy with golden hair sat opposite him, smiling impishly. He wore lederhosen, knee socks, and heavy German shoes.

Although Webern hadn't seen him for exactly two years, he recognized him right away.

"Wags Verder!" Webern gasped.

"At your service," said the intruder. He tipped his leather cap. "Happy birthday, by the way." He sized Webern up. "You're growing up fast."

"But you're almost as big as me," said Webern. Wags was; looking at him was like looking into a magic mirror. His gold hair glinted in the sunshine. "How did you get so big?"

"Trick of the light, pal, trick of the light." Wags winked. "Look out that window and you'll see what I mean."

Webern reached for the curtain, then hesitated. "Oh, I don't know."

"Don't be a 'fraidy cat."

Sucking in his breath, Webern pulled back the gingham curtain and peered outside. Down below, Mom had finished setting up the card tables. Party favours—paper hats, kazoos, and Chinese finger traps—waited on each folding chair for the guests. A glass pitcher of pink lemonade glistened in the centre of one tabletop; on another, a lone red tulip drooped in a vase. From Webern's perch in the treehouse, it all looked tiny—a world in miniature. The brightly coloured paper plates resembled bingo chips, and, squinting his eyes a little, Webern could see confetti sprinkled here and there on the tablecloths, as finely ground as fairy dust.

"See?" said Wags. "I didn't get big. The world got small."

"Oh." Webern stared down. He couldn't tear his eyes away. It looked like the backyard of a dollhouse, and for the first time, it occurred to him that maybe God wasn't an old man with a beard, but just a spoiled child.

Before Webern could finish his thought, the screen door banged shut. Willow and Billow had burst through, and they now moved across the lawn jerkily. Willow's long stringy hair veiled her face, even as her bony hands smoothed it back. Billow licked her sausage fingers; chocolate smeared around her mouth. Their white nightshirts looked even dirtier than usual: in addition to the amorphous patches of brown, fresh splatters of black and green soiled the pale cotton. The girls seemed purposeful, excited. About halfway across the lawn, they stopped, clasped hands, and looked up at Webern.

"Bernie Bee, Bernie Bee!"

"Way up in the honey tree!"

"We're locked out, where is the key?"

"Open up your door for me!"

They gazed up at him expectantly, as if they wanted him to finish their nursery rhyme. Standing there in the yard, draped in fluttery white cloth, they seemed like a pair of ghosts that Webern could dispel with the right incantation. But he didn't know what it was. He glanced at Wags, who only shrugged.

"No girls allowed," Webern finally called down. He knew immediately that it was the wrong thing to say, but it was too late. Smugly nodding to each other, the girls produced, seemingly from midair, a pair of monster masks.

When he saw the masks, made of construction paper and paint and dirt and glue, a shock of terror surged through Webern—the same shock he felt when, during a nightmare, he saw a little boy with glass doll eyes or a lunchbox with teeth—the shock of something familiar, yet horribly wrong. Webern had made masks plenty of times, for Halloween and for little plays he performed for his mother in the afternoons. But he'd never made masks like these.

Willow's mask, assembled from branches and mud and dead leaves, was a tree come to life—a tree with a knobby, jutting nose, hooked in like a finger beckoning. Billow's, a perfect circle of white, had a single grotesque feature: a mouth like a crater, a hole, a wound, with ragged edges and inside, only blackness. Webern had to close his eyes. A child's face, eclipsed by ugliness, is a most terrible thing.

"*Presto chango*," Wags observed. "Your sisters aren't very pretty girls. 'Course, they never were."

"Why're you here, Wags?" Webern asked, with his eyes still closed. "How come you were gone so long, and then you came back?" The insides of his lids throbbed neon red from the sunshine.

"Bernie Bee, Bernie Bee!"

"Nowhere to hide, nowhere to flee!"

"Just a little show-n-tell session, pal. The world is very small," said Wags. "It breaks easy, no two ways about that. Thought you should be prepared."

"Mommy said you were my guardian angel," said Webern. "She said you might not come back 'til I needed you. Is that why you're here? Because I need you? What should I do, Wags?"

"You'll come down, just wait and see!"

"You'll meet ol' Mr. Gravity!"

"What should I do?"

"What can you do?

"What can I do?"

"Jump."

"Wags? *Wags?*"

Webern opened his eyes. Wags was gone. Down below, his sisters had started to climb the tree. As they swung through the lower branches, their rhymes dissolved into sounds, not doggerel, not even words, but speeded-up gibberish, like the nonsense that rushed through Webern's mind when he woke from nightmares and even the darkness seemed to move.

"Wags!" Webern yelled again. "Mommy!"

Once, Webern went to a movie matinee with his mother, and on the wide silver screen, he saw a man jump off a bridge. As the man fell, images from his life flashed before his eyes—his wife kissing him at the altar, his first day on the job, the SOLD sign on his little white house—each one more nostalgic than the last. Webern sat in the theatre, legs dangling above the sticky floor, teeth aching from the box of Sugar Daddies he'd just consumed, and wondered what a kid would think of, falling like that; if a kid would have enough memories to fill a slow-motion descent.

But Webern needn't have worried. As he fell toward the leaves that lay like crumpled orange and red construction paper on the ground, his memories rose up to meet him, and they were enough for a lifetime of regret. Webern remembered the baby blue sky outside his bedroom window, with clouds still pink from dawn floating in it; he remembered bath time and the beards he made from bubbles. He remembered walking through the park with his mother, swinging on the swing as she pushed him, her hands light and swift against his back. He remembered Christmas, a symphony of red paper tearing, of tissue crinkling in boxes. And Easter: the hollow eggs, green and pink and yellow, fragile as living things in his cupped hands. He remembered marbles, like tiny shiny planets, and little wax bottles with rainbow elixirs in them, and the tongue of a kitten who'd kissed him once—pink and rough, like a piece of chewing gum dropped in a sandbox. He remembered lying on his back and pretending to walk on the ceiling; he remembered the loneliness, scary as any bad dream, of nights when he couldn't sleep, when the dark house whispered secrets and his parents snored loudly, like a king and a queen under an enchanter's evil spell. Webern remembered snow angels and snow suits, sunshowers and galoshes, jack-o-lanterns and costumes— one year, he had been a bumblebee. He remembered storybooks and building blocks and funny jokes and cartoons and the doll hospital. But most of all, he remembered learning how to swim, how he'd tilted his head back trustingly and felt the water holding him up. As he fell, he did the same thing—he tilted backward into the air and trusted it to hold him up. But when for some reason, it didn't, when it dropped him, sank him like a stone, his one hope was that, somewhere down there at the bottom, mermaids would be waiting to welcome him.

CHAPTER NINE

IN THE WEEKS THAT FOLLOWED THEIR ESCAPE FROM LYNCHVILLE, Webern and Nepenthe took their first hesitant steps toward becoming lovers. It started as soon as they crossed state lines and found a place to camp for the night. Nepenthe and Webern sat side by side during dinner, drinking whiskey from the same toy trumpet as the other players stirred their lukewarm plates of tinned spaghetti. When she rose to go afterwards, Nepenthe took Webern's hand, and almost without thinking, he followed her. In her tent he felt shy for the first time in days: as a silhouette against green canvas still dimly lit with firelight, Nepenthe could have been any young girl. He couldn't say the same for his own misshapen form. He stared at her until he could see, dimly, the ridges of her scales.

"Do you want me to stay here tonight?"

"You'd like that, huh?" There was a laugh in her voice that Webern couldn't stand. He grabbed her hands and tugged on them. He could never kiss her standing up—she was too tall. She would always have to bend down to kiss him. Nepenthe pulled her hands away and moved toward her trunk on the other side of the tent. She lit a citronella candle, then sat down on the floor. She crossed her long legs at the ankles.

"I usually read for awhile before I go to bed," she said. "Have you got a book?"

Webern stretched out atop the sleeping bag with all his clothes still on, even his shoes, and Nepenthe lay next to him, smoking, the red tip of her clove glowing in the darkness. When he woke up, sometime in the early hours of the morning, he saw that she'd gotten into her kiddy pool where she curled in her pyjamas, a waterlogged blanket pulled up to her chin. He reached into the water to pull it back, but Nepenthe, asleep or pretending to be, rolled over with a splash.

In the mornings, Nepenthe made Webern turn his back while she changed into her clothes; in the evenings, she made him turn his back while she changed into her pyjamas. And at night, she lay awake until he finally, unwillingly dropped off, at which point she climbed into her tub and slept. Sometimes they kissed passionately, rolling around the floor as they had at Beer Can Creek, but Nepenthe pushed Webern away when he fumbled with her buttons or the zipper at the back of her dress. Then it was even more terrible for him to stretch out beside her, still in his clothes, feverish, the taste of peach pit burning on his lips. One night when she pushed him away, Webern couldn't get himself to lie still. He sat up, his glasses still fogged with her breath, his hands shaking.

"Jeez, Nepenthe." He rubbed his hump. "Am I really so bad? You knew what I looked like when you met me."

Nepenthe gazed up through a haze of clove smoke. She crossed her legs at the ankles. "Bernie, don't be ridiculous."

"I'm not." Webern tugged at his knotted shoelaces. He thought of the clown from his dream, the laughing girl, the wind-up key freezing him in place. "I want to touch you."

She was silent for awhile. "I know," she finally said.

"Then why—why won't you—"

Nepenthe breathed deeply, then exhaled.

"Can you imagine what our kids would look like?" she asked.

Webern went to the drugstore one dusty afternoon in Starkville, Mississippi. The store was empty as he pushed in the door; bells jingled. He glanced around, but the place looked just as deserted as he had hoped. An old man drowsed at an ancient cash register, and three empty stools stood along a soda counter piled high with bundled newspapers and dog-eared back issues of the Saturday Evening Post. A few flies buzzed at the store's single grimy window. Webern slipped down one of the aisles toward the back of the store. He passed the Band-Aids and cotton swabs, the toothpaste and the ear plugs. His pockets, heavy with change and wadded bills, felt heavy. He had no idea what this was going to cost.

In the back of the store, Webern found them, lined up in brightly coloured tins the size of cigarette packs. Dean's Peacocks—Merry Widows—Romeos—Seal Tite—Le Transparent. Who knew there were so many different brands? And what could the differences between them possibly be? Were there different colours? Shapes? Sizes? Webern stared at the label for the Sheik of Araby, which pictured a turbaned man riding a horse across a windblown desert, and the 3 Pirates, which proudly bore the image of a cutlass in its sheath. For the prevention of disease. Shadows: as thin as a shadow, as strong as an ox!

Webern began to reach for a tin, then glanced furtively behind him. His hand slipped up to rub his hump instead. The Tiger Skin Rubber Company. Blood rose to his face. He lingered on Mermaid Brand (perfection maid!) for a long moment, then grabbed a box at random and strode back toward the front of the store. He reminded himself he'd never come back to this place again.

The nearer he got to the counter, the slower Webern walked. The metal container warmed in his hand, and he stared down at his feet, watching the floor boards. When he placed the tin on the counter, the humiliation roared over him in a wave. The old storekeeper started awake, and he and Webern read the brand name on the package at the same time: Napoleons.

"Could you ring me up, please?"

Webern reached into his pocket for the money. He pulled out a dollar, and a hail of change rained to the ground. As he scrambled around, stomping on dimes and quarters, the storekeeper reached into the pocket of his wrinkled shirt to withdraw a corncob pipe and a pack of matches. By the time Webern finally had his money together, the storekeeper was puffing away, his wrinkled lips working around the amber stem. His rheumy eyes moved slowly from the tin to Webern, then back again.

"You're not from around here, are ya boy?"

Webern stared at the tin as the storekeeper's claws closed around it. "Listen, I'm kind of in a hur—"

"Well, if you *were* from around here, you'd know I don't sell sailor caps to whippersnappers." The tin disappeared beneath the counter. "Shame on you, boy. What would your mama think?"

"I'm not a child," he said. The words came out as a squeak.

"Oh, come on there, sonny." The storekeeper smiled slyly. "You can't be much more than three foot tall."

"I live on my own."

"Oh, you do then? What's your address?"

"I don't have an address, I'm with the circus. We're just passing through. Now please—" Webern gestured at the counter, then glanced over his shoulder nervously.

"With the circus, are you now? You got any identiformation that says so?"

"Just look at me!"

"You look like a boy, from where I'm sitting."

Webern rubbed the toe of his shoe against the tile floor. He couldn't go back to camp empty-handed. Webern looked up at the storekeeper, who in turn grinned down at him. His wizened face reminded Webern of a shrunken head Dr. Show had almost bought just outside of Tuscaloosa.

"Okay," Webern finally said, "how can I prove it to you?"

"What is it you're supposed to do in this 'circus,' sonny?"

"I'm a clown."

"Well then—" The storekeeper slapped the Napoleons back down on the counter. "—better get clowning."

The storekeeper removed a little envelope from the tin and handed it to Webern. His old bones creaked as he leaned back contentedly.

"You know how to do up all them balloon animals?" The storekeeper tapped his pipe against his single front tooth. "Make mine a poodle."

Webern looked down at the little envelope in his hand. TEAR HERE. He looked up again. The cashier blew a smoke ring into his face.

Webern slowly unfurled the Napoleon. He'd expected it to feel dry and powdery, like the rubber gloves doctors had always snapped on before sawing off his body cast or aligning his spine. But this rubber was slick, greasy, even. Webern wiped his fingers on his jeans, took a deep breath, and inflated the tube. Even he was surprised at how obscene it looked: milky white with a nipple-shaped protuberance at the tip.

Lubricant left dark patches on the wooden countertop; the Napoleon kept slipping out of his hands. Webern cursed, holding the reservoir tip down with one elbow as he struggled to twist the poodle's legs.

"Havin' a little trouble, there, are ya, boy?" The cashier slid a candy jar toward him. "Maybe you'd ruther have a bit-o-honey instead."

"I'm good, thanks." The rubber squeaked as Webern squeezed the air out of the poodle's tail. He knotted the latex into bubble-paws. Somewhere a bell jingled.

"I reckon you've proved it well enough," the cashier continued, a little uneasily. "You're with the circus, sure."

"Oh, no, I'm just getting started." Webern twisted the poodle's neck.

"Why don't you just take your farmerceuticals and get along, then? Compliments of the house."

"I never leave the stage in the middle of a performance." It sounded like something Dr. Show would say. Webern double-knotted the balloon poodle's nose, and, with a flourish, presented it to the cashier. "Now, good sir, I believe an apology is in order," he intoned.

"Mister, what's that funny little man doing?"

Webern turned around. Two little girls in party dresses stood in the doorway of the drug store, eating Fudgsicles and watching him. Webern looked from the poodle to the oily splotches on the counter to the cashier. He grabbed the tin of Napoleons and sprinted out of the store.

Brunhilde knelt at her collapsible dressing table, trimming her golden beard. The scissors moved swiftly around her chin, her sideburns, even the nape of her neck. They whispered as they snipped. But, when the hair fell, not a single strand escaped her. She pinched the trimmings in a single tuft between the thumb and forefinger of her left hand, and, as soon as she finished, swiftly wrapped tiny locks—only three or four hairs each—around equally tiny cards. Printed with her name and the date, these cards proclaimed the samples "GENUINE LADY WHISKERS." Her task completed, Brunhilde shut the shears and slid them back into the triangular holster she wore on the belt of her dressing gown. Then she placed the hair cards in a small brown envelope. At the next show, she would offer them for sale.

Once, not so long ago, Brunhilde would never have considered hawking her wares in such a disgraceful manner. But that time was over now. She had lost the crowds that would pay any price to see her long ago, in the firebombing. She had also lost her glockenspiel and her teacher's metronome, the stages on which she'd danced—the Grimms' Tales and the cuckoo clock, the kid gloves and the dainty suede boots, the thick carved headboard of her childhood bed with its scenes of villagers sleeping. She had lost her home, her parents, and their bodies, of course.

After that terrifying night of screams and fires, when she'd huddled against a low stone wall and prayed for the last time, she'd passed several years sleeping in the ruined mansions of her parents' friends, relying on the hospitality of near-strangers. She knew all along it couldn't last. So when her married cousin offered her a place to stay in New Jersey, the offer seemed too good to be true. She knew now that it had been.

Brunhilde had disliked the little house from the start, with its small, high windows and its artifacts of American kitsch—tea cozies sewn to resemble calico cats, a tiny wooden outhouse in which rolls of toilet paper were stored. She spent her mornings idly circling job advertisements in the paper. When Cousin Lisle and her husband left for the workday—he was a bond man, she a substitute teacher—Brunhilde wallowed on the sofa until they returned. At night, she lay awake in the trundle bed beneath a comforter stitched with tiny sheep in slippers, craving knackwurst and her native tongue, or thrashed with nightmares, seeing again the ruins of her home: a shattered window, a blackened tablecloth, her mother's bloodied glove. Then, out one afternoon in the town's drab park, she had met Schoenberg, bent over a miniature easel.

"Say you'll pose for me. You must allow me to sketch you, at the very least," he insisted. "I'll have you know, it's a high honour indeed. As a rule, I only paint self-portraits."

He'd offered her fame, fortune, a return to her former standing, and what's more, his undying dedication to her career. He even tried to address her in his pitiful German until she begged him to stop. She was only the second member to join his little troupe—Al had already signed on—but when Schoenberg spoke of the future, her heart had lifted. Such promises! Silken tents filled up with pillows, performances on the stage, a journey back to Europe in a few years, when, he hinted, she might find her homeland miraculously restored. Of course, now that she saw him for what he was, an escapist so deluded that perhaps even he believed the wild fantasies he spun like straw into gold, she wondered how she could have been so naive. Yet it was impossible to hate him. Once, and only once, the two of them had wandered together through the corridors of a funhouse until they came to a place where their own reflections surrounded them, elongated and rubbery, bulbous and distended. In that room, Schoenberg had kissed her, and before she regained her sense enough to slap him away, a feeling had overcome her, a dizzying sickness, as though, against her own will, she had passed beyond those mirrors into a land of marvellous impossibilities. It was in this realm, she suspected, that Schoenberg dwelled at every moment of his life.

Brunhilde smoothed her neatly barbered beard and reached under the dressing table for her Dresden suitcase. Opening it up, she ran a reverent hand over the photographs she had shellacked inside, then removed a tube of depilatory cream from the tangle of clothes and squeezed a dollop out onto her finger. Slowly, tenderly, she massaged it into the hollow between her breasts. In Germany, she had been the Girl

Esau, but in America, the customers liked their bearded ladies smooth and feminine everywhere but the face. She rubbed a bit more cream onto her forearms and the knuckles of her hands, then considered the tube for a moment. Enrique had stayed behind in Lynchville. Would Dr. Schoenberg finally call his circus *kaput* if another act—say the animal taming—also fell to tatters? Would he finally perform a disappearing act of his own?

Brunhilde imagined tiger fur in the sawdust, Hank's resignation—the last straw. In her mind, Schoenberg stood over a burnt-out campfire, wet logs and char, while the remaining circus players slept in their tents. He unlocked the yellow Cadillac, and drove away to a new city where he would live alone under a new name, a new set of pretenses, a place where no one could track him for payment of any kind. He would have to see the necessity of it, deluded though he was. He would finally have to understand. Only a child would choose a warped mirror over one that showed him the truth.

Had it not been for the distractions of love, Webern couldn't have stood what was happening to the circus. The day after the revelation of the empty cashbox, the players had gone about their business as usual. They rolled up sleeping bags, cleaned out the tiger cages, slurped bad coffee, and burned their fingers smoking cigarettes down to the last puffs. They drove five hours, set up camp in a new town, ate, threw their paper plates in the fire, and slept uneasily amid the drone of the cicadas, the woolly darkness that muffled their dreams. The next morning, Webern went to the main street to tack up advertisements, and when he came back his heart lifted at last: Al, Eng, and Vlad and Fydor were hoisting the orange canvas up the big top's centre pole, and the fabric, filthy though it was, gave off a kind of radiance that warmed him like hope.

The show there drew a decent crowd, and by the end of the evening the cashbox wasn't empty anymore. But something had changed. The players didn't debate the merits of a late night visit to the liquor store versus a local moonshine till, and they didn't loudly argue about what had drawn the biggest laughs or who upstaged whom. Instead, they scattered as soon as the show was done, as if the fact they were still putting out the effort embarrassed them. Webern took Nepenthe to a malt shop in town, but it was already closed. He folded a flower for her from a piece of red cellophane he found blowing in the street.

Lately, Schoenberg had more or less retired to his tent, only emerging for performances or when they packed up to leave town. He'd given up driving the Cadillac, preferring instead the company of the tiger cubs, Fred and Ginger, and the high-piled supplies that bounced along in the red trailer behind the Jeep. He made a strange sight when they opened the door, invariably slouched against one metal wall like a broken doll or a prisoner. Webern couldn't understand why he'd prefer it in there, with the dismantled bleachers and rolled-up posters, the air thick with the smell of the cats' straw, but Schoenberg said it helped him think, that he required solitude to draw his plans.

If solitude was all he really wanted, then Schoenberg was a lucky guy, because he was by himself nearly all the time now. He almost never talked to Webern around the fire, and he didn't even give him orders much anymore. Webern missed the hours he'd spent trudging off to the grocery store with a list written in that unmistakable flourishing hand, the afternoons he'd wasted raking the sand in the ring while Dr. Show looked on, calling instructions into a bullhorn.

Webern had always thought that if he could get away, just for a few hours, he would come up with clown acts that would take the shapes of his dreams, that he would rival even the greats whose feats he'd read about in library books: Joey Grimaldi, Weary Willie, the Fratellini Brothers, Otto Griebling. But now that he had the time, he didn't use it. Instead, he whiled it away with Nepenthe, bringing her lime popsicles and thumbing through the books she carried in her trunk when she didn't feel like talking. Though Freud and the poets featured in the heavy volume *Modernism and You* weren't much like the fairy tales of his childhood, it was comforting to lie by the side of Nepenthe's kiddy pool, surrounded by pages open like friendly wings. Sometimes, though, he had to look up at her, slouched there in the icy water, a peach pit rolling on her tongue, and wonder just what exactly she was thinking.

Dear Bo-Bo,
I've never been happier than I am right now, and I'm still pretty sad. It's just like you always used to say: "Every rose has thorns, every burger's got bones." This postcard is from Medicine Lodge, Kansas. Hope you are well.

Love, Bernie.

Webern stamped the postcard and turned it over. On the front was a picture of an old lady waving a hatchet, standing in a splatter of broken glass. Definitely the kind of thing his grandma would appreciate. He leaned his head against the Cadillac's window and watched the fields fly by. A barn drifted past, its skeleton visible through the chinks in its boards. Beside him, Vlad controlled the steering wheel while Fydor inspected a map. The Cadillac felt wrong, all wrong, without Dr. Show driving it.

Although they never discussed it, Nepenthe and Webern both knew that things had changed once he bought the condoms. As if it were a joke, they started to imitate a married couple. For awhile, she stopped calling him "kiddo" and used "honey" instead; he started kissing her on the cheek when he came home. One afternoon, he even came back to discover her washing his clothes in her kiddy pool.

"You take such good care of me," he said tenderly.

"I found a flea," she retorted. "I figured it was probably yours."

Webern still turned his back when she changed, but he did it willingly now, without waiting for her to insist. He knew it was only a matter of time.

But still, the night they finally lost their virginity, Webern wasn't prepared at all. As usual, he fell asleep beside Nepenthe on top of the sleeping bag, and sometime later he half-heard her splash into the icy waters of her kiddy pool. Webern moved through vague, dim dreams that floated like clove smoke around his head until sometime around five in the morning, when he woke to Nepenthe's kisses.

"Hey," she whispered. Wet tendrils of her hair dangled in his face, but she was dressed in her pink chenille robe, and the thick fabric felt warm and dry beneath his hands. Webern kissed her back, and soon she lay beneath him on the floor of the tent. He reached for the tie of her robe. Nepenthe stared up at him, the beginnings of a scowl showing in the cracks around her eyes. But she didn't push him away as he loosened the knot. He thought it was sweat he tasted, then realized it was tears.

"It's all right," he told her.

"Oh, sure, all right for you maybe."

"What?"

"Forget it. Just do it quick, like a Band-Aid."

Webern undressed her. Nepenthe didn't move. She lay stiffly on her open robe, her arms at her sides. Webern looked down at her body. The scales, flat and silvery-pale, caught the early morning light like plates of mica. In the show, Nepenthe appeared onstage naked except for a loin cloth, stitched from green leather to resemble a swamp leaf, but she always lay on her stomach. Now Webern saw her breasts for the first time. The nipples, wrinkled pink, reminded him of dried rose petals. He leaned down to kiss her hip and noticed the initials ER embroidered on her underpants.

"What's this?" he asked, touching the letters.

"Nothing. Doesn't matter. Maybe I got them in a hospital or something."

Webern scrambled across the floor to his suitcase, then returned with the Napoleons. He kicked off his jeans, then crawled back toward Nepenthe.

"Oh, no you don't. If I'm naked, you're naked, too."

Webern took a deep breath, then pulled off the shirt. Nepenthe touched his hump, feeling the jagged scar there.

"Where did you get this?"

"Maybe I got it in a hospital or something."

"Okay, okay, explain it later." She put her fingers in his mouth.

Afterwards, he did explain, about the accident, how they rushed him to the hospital after the fall and stuck him back together the best they knew how. About how they saved his spinal cord, but made some mistakes; with his back, of course, but maybe also with his growing, because they never figured out exactly why he stopped at three foot ten and just stayed there. He told her about how he'd been a mess of blood and splintered bone; how he'd hit the ground flat on his back, and woke up in a body cast covered with the signatures of strangers. He tried to show Nepenthe the star-shaped scar at the base of his skull, faded now but still visible beneath the crew cut, but then he realized she was asleep, for the first time asleep right there beside him. At the time, he felt happy, but later, much later, he would wonder if she heard his story, if she understood he had been normal once—if she knew that like her, he'd never expected to turn out this way.

The clown stands in the centre of the ring, awash in the white glow of the spotlight. He wears his checkered harlequin suit with the soft silk collar, and beneath one eye hovers a single bright blue tear. As the clown stands there, waiting, romantic music begins to play, lovely but warped and strangely distant. It is a waltz, but a waltz echoing faintly from a faraway window, a waltz played on a child's piano left to dust in an attic.

Before too long, the dance partner arrives. She is seven feet tall, hirsute, lumbering on paws that thump like great overturned tom-toms, but this bear is gentle, and she embraces the clown softly, almost demurely. As the two move together, always in the washed-out glow of the spotlight, the audience does not gasp at the danger, nor do they laugh at the unlikely pair, one towering, the other hunched. Rather, they watch with tenderness, nostalgia even, remembering, perhaps, an improbable dance that they once shared, awash in the softening glow of moonbeam white.

Clown and bear part ways at last, slowly; the harlequin bows deep to his lady as she leaves. But still the distant music waltzes on, and, there in the ring alone, the clown does, too. Arms raised to embrace an invisible partner, his feet slide—hesitantly at first, then with confidence—through the half-forgotten, too-familiar steps.

CHAPTER TEN

THE FIRST NIGHT THEY SPENT IN LEMON CITY, CALIFORNIA, Webern couldn't get to sleep. He finally got up and left Nepenthe's tent a little before five in the morning. He'd always thought of California as a bright and sunny place, but in the half-dawn light, this beach was misty and dank, with hollow green-black crab shells littered everywhere he looked. Webern started walking over toward the big top. He might as well start building the bleachers while it was still cool outside.

On his way up the beach, he heard a sound and looked back over his shoulder at the campsite. Al was coming out of Dr. Show's tent, and he carried a black suitcase the size of a coffin. Webern looked away immediately and kept moving quickly toward the big top, trying not to let Al know he'd seen him. He wished he hadn't.

The bleachers consisted of long wooden slats and metal supports, and Webern usually hated the loud sweaty work of fitting the swinging, clattering parts together. It suited him today, though; it felt like slamming dozens of doors shut.

Webern worked for about an hour. All around him, the orange canvas filled with sunset-coloured light. Finally he sat down on one of the benches he'd built and looked down at the ring, marked by a rope laid in the sand. Webern stared at it, trying to see the clown acts he'd performed there, Nepenthe pale green and writhing, Schoenberg directing the spotlight with an elegant motion of his hand, but all he could see was how small it was. It seemed to shrink before his eyes, tightening like the loop of a noose. He shook his head and went to get some breakfast.

When Webern got to the campfire, only a few of the others were up. Nepenthe, still in pyjamas but wearing a bandana around the lower half of her face like a cowgirl, sat on a hunk of driftwood, gazing out at the crashing waves. Explorer Hank was morosely stroking Ginger, who'd developed a patchy rash on her stomach, and Eng was moving slowly through the exercises he'd taken to doing each morning, a kind of full-body meditation that made him look like he was karate-chopping ghosts. Webern slunk over to Nepenthe. She didn't notice him until he sat down right next to her.

"Hey, you snuck up on me, kiddo." Their married-couple phase had ended a few days earlier. "Isn't this ocean incredible? I was going to write a poem about it, but the whole subject's riddled with clichés."

Webern laid his head against her shoulder. The waves were bigger here than they'd been at Paradise Beach—bigger and colder, too. The colour of iron.

"Al quit," he murmured.

"Really? How do you know?"

"Saw him. It was his turn for spotlights tonight, too, the jerk. Ten bucks says I'll wind up having to do them tonight."

Nepenthe lifted her bandana to sip thoughtfully from a chipped Donald Duck mug. "Well, I can't say I blame him. Maybe he got a better offer. If I had someplace else to go, I sure as hell wouldn't be eating cat food out of cans Dr. Show found on the beach."

"It was tuna."

"So he said. It was kind of hard to know for sure with the labels all peeled off like that." The water reflected metallic in Nepenthe's eyes. "You know, Brunhilde's been saying we should unionize. It probably wouldn't make that much difference, but I know what she means. Things can't go on like this for much longer. It's not healthy." She took a peach pit out of her pouch and held it up to the light. "I can't even remember the last time I had one of these with fruit on it."

Hank scratched Ginger under the chin.

"What the heck's going on, baby girl? You've lost a whisker now," he said to the cat. "And that isn't good, oh no. You need your whiskers the way lil' Bernie there needs his glasses. So you've gotta stop pulling your hair out, oh yes you do."

Webern took Nepenthe's hand in both of his and kissed the softer part, between the fingers. Some distance out from shore, a white sail billowed in the wind.

Webern pushed and elbowed and sidled his way to an empty seat in the middle of the most crowded row of bleachers. His floppy shoes slapped the ground, and his loosened tie swung wildly to and fro. He held an enormous bucket of popcorn with both hands; with every step he took, he managed to douse the audience with another fistful of kernels. By the time he reached his seat, the bucket was completely empty; in lieu of discarding it, he turned it upside down and dropped it over the head of a middle-aged man sitting directly in front of him. Inside, he breathed a sigh of relief. He'd been using this same batch of popcorn for over a week, and it was getting incredibly stale. Now he was finally out.

Instead of performing his whole routine, Webern had agreed to warm up the crowd before the evening's show began, but except for a few titters here and there, he wasn't sure he was making too much of an impression. The middle aged man pulled the bucket off his head and tossed it away without so much as glancing at him. Somewhere behind him, Webern heard the unmistakable, and terrifying, sound of a child's yawn. He turned around and, rubbing his eyes sleepily, yawned right back. Time to make himself comfortable. He pulled off his floppy shoes, revealing a pair of red and white striped socks with a noticeable holes in the toe, then stretched his legs as far as he could and smacked the middle-aged man with his heel. Served him right. Scowling, the guy turned around—finally!—and, murmuring gravely, Webern mimed elaborate apologies. He removed his oversized, limp-brimmed fedora. Beneath that was a straw porkpie hat, a piece of wheat stuck jauntily in its red, white, and blue band. Webern shook his head, continuing to murmur, and with a flourish removed the second hat. Beneath that was a baby's bonnet.

A high pitched whistle trilled offstage. Webern pulled on his shoes and hats and, with deep bows to the crowd, sidled his way back out of the bleachers, leading with his hump. He made a show of moving unsteadily, clumsily, down to the ground, but as soon as he was out of sight, he scrambled to his post at the top of the ladder. It was just as he'd predicted: tonight he was working the lights.

The splintery wood creaked beneath him as he carefully took his seat on the narrow top rung. He tried to keep his mind off the twelve feet between him and the hard dirt ground—more than triple his height. Perched there, high above the top row of bleachers, he had a god's view of the audience, but there wasn't much to see this evening. Two tow-headed boys took turns snapping each other with a broken rubber band; a sad looking old lady knitted a shawl that was already unraveling around her narrow shoulders. The middle-aged man, who Webern now noticed wore some vaguely institutional coveralls, still sat speckled with popcorn kernels. Webern couldn't imagine how they felt, squirming on the hard benches he'd helped to build; he couldn't guess what had brought them there. He snapped off the houselights and waited a long moment in the smoky dark.

Finally, he switched on the spotlight and swung its beam in a slow arc to Dr. Schoenberg, who had just entered the ring through the flaps at the opposite end of the tent. The big top wasn't big enough to conceal the performers offstage, so the troupe stood just outside, huddled near the makeshift entrance, whispering to each other and listening for their cues. In the first few weeks after he had joined the circus, Webern had liked those times best, had savored the anticipation, the tenseness he felt before unicycling or tumbling or dancing into the light. Those moments had a kind of ritual significance to him, as though, when he stepped through the dirty canvas, he would come out transformed, painted a shade too resplendent for even him to imagine. And, despite their grumbling and gossip, their yawns and last minute smokes, he had always suspected that deep down, the other performers felt the same. Now he wasn't so sure. It was better to be up here, with the hot metal of the bulbs' casing burning his hands, than out there in the night, surrounded by a crew of players who, come morning, might well disappear down the road, making their short journey back to the land of strangers.

"Ladies and gentlemen," Schoenberg intoned, "boys and girls, tonight I present for your approval a wondrous exhibition. In my travels around the globe, I have assembled a collection of human oddities which reveal the darker side of our Maker's genius. This evening, for your elucidation, I will introduce the malformed, the twisted, the shrunken, contorted, gifted and strange—anomalies that lie beyond the understanding of medical science, creatures whose existence may lead you to question the very tenets of your cherished philosophy. Once visited by these spectres, you may find yourself forever changed, haunted by what no man was meant to see with waking eyes. I urge you to turn back now—make your way to the exits—for the horrors that lie ahead are not for the faint of heart. But a single word of warning: should you choose to stay, please remain seated for the duration of the performance. Once brought before you, some of my creatures become petulant—and difficult to restrain."

An explosion of blue-white smoke engulfed Dr. Show, and Webern snapped the spotlight off—too abruptly, probably. He'd only done the lighting a couple of times before; up until Lynchville it had been Enrique's job, and the others had taken turns covering for him while he was onstage. Tonight, though, it wasn't just inexperience that made Webern switch off the beam so soon. Dr. Show had looked terrible out there, his eyes sleepless and hooded, his bow tie crooked and drooping. He almost did look like a man haunted by the things he'd seen. Webern quickly fitted the first coloured gel onto the light—yellow—then snapped the bulb back on.

Eng's act was first, and he was already out there, clad in his leotard, waiting, when the spotlight hit him. Quickly, with a dexterity that still made Webern flinch, Eng stood on his hands, bent his legs over his back until his feet rested on his shoulder blades, and began to dart around the ring. He was out of sorts, though, a bit too perfunctory and quick, and the audience clapped dully, unamazed. Only later, if at all, would they realize the impossibility of what they'd seen. Eng sprang back to his feet and twisted around at the waist till facing almost backwards. His pained smile showed the strain. Over the coughs and crackling candy wrappers of the audience, Webern heard Eng's vertebrae pop.

Vlad and Fydor had taken the night off, complaining of not one but two debilitating headaches, so Webern was thankfully spared their hokey patter. Instead, Brunhilde was next. Webern fixed a pink gel on the light. Brunhilde always complained that it made her look tawdry; in fact, it lent her a feminine softness, accentuating the suppleness of her strong bare arms, the smoothness of her towering pillar-like legs. But tonight, as Webern turned the beam back on, he realized that Brunhilde's appearance was beyond salvaging. Ignoring the advice of the other performers, who always urged her to let her long gold hair go free, she'd done it up in two braids that hung, heavy and unappealing as coils of rope, down to her ample bosom. Worse yet, she'd managed to find her Viking horn helmet—Webern would have sworn he'd hidden it deep in the Cadillac's trunk somewhere. The result was that she looked more like a Wagnerian transvestite than a bearded lady. As she opened her lips to sing the first lines of a German folk song, peals of laughter predictably silenced her. For a moment, Webern wondered if she had intentionally sabotaged her own performance, but Brunhilde's gaze to the audience, a dagger of pure hatred, was enough to set him straight. The fact was, she still believed after everything that she looked better that way.

After Brunhilde, it was generally Al's turn to go. Privately, Webern never thought the big guy had been used quite right in the show. If Webern had been planning things, he would have capitalized on the otherworldly quality of giants. He might have dressed Al in animal skins and given him a rock to sit on, perhaps even powdered his face and hands and tried to pass him off as a creature who lived, solitary and thoughtful, deep in an ice cave at the very top of the world. Al's enormous hands, long and bony and double-jointed, his stretched-out funhouse face, fascinated people, made them shiver: Webern had seen it happen. But instead of casting Al as a Norse God, Dr. Show had made a gaffed strongman out of him. Al lifted barbells made out of balloons and flexed the negligible muscles in his spindly arms, and his strength had convinced no one. Maybe it was the meagre applause that had finally driven him back out onto the road.

Dr. Show returned to the stage. Webern could tell by the way he moved that he'd had a few swigs of something since he last appeared; he gestured grandly but less precisely now, swinging his arm back toward the entrance that no one was supposed to see, his voice rich with the kind of merriment that leads easily to tears.

"Such horrifying visions! But now, I offer some respite. This next performance will warm the cockles of your hearts, my beloved audience. In it, you will see the lion lie down with the lamb, as it were; the amity of man and ferocious beast. Oh yes, for there is still tenderness in this world. Despite appearances to the contrary. . . . Yes indeed, oh yes indeed. At any rate, I present, Explorer Hank and his jungle cats!"

Chuckling, Schoenberg wandered offstage. Webern switched the gel to orange and counted to one hundred before turning the lights back on. Explorer Hank took a few minutes to set up, and the clangs and thuds of his equipment filled the dark big top. Normally, Schoenberg played his concertina at this point to cover the noise, but apparently this time he'd forgotten.

Explorer Hank was a favourite of audiences, or at least of children, who cooed with wonder anytime the baby tigers came onstage. Once, at a particularly successful performance, a little girl had bravely slipped from the front row when Hank's back was turned to stroke Ginger's humming throat, her flicking toylike tail. They had all felt the danger that night, huddled outside the tent's back door—though small, Ginger still had teeth and claws far fiercer than an ordinary kitten's—but the audience had trusted her completely, had even rippled the bleachers with spontaneous applause.

Now, though, that had all changed. Fred, perched on the bottom of an upside-down trash can, looked half-grown and feral, despite the bow tied around his neck; when the lights came up he was bent double, one leg in the air, licking himself. Ginger, still small as a bobcat, was a patchwork of thinning fur and angry, irritated areas of skin. The light caught Explorer Hank still setting up a steel hoop between the cats, and he looked out at the audience blinking in surprise for several seconds before he spoke.

"Well, hi there guys and gals, let me start out by saying that me and Ginger and Freddy here're real glad you all came out for the show tonight. Before we came on stage, the kids were saying to me, 'Boy, we sure hope that we get to show off our tricks tonight, Hank!' and I was saying, 'Gee, I do too, because otherwise I'm out of a job!' Ha ha. We like to joke a little, the kids and me. But anyhoo, how many of you have seen a real live tiger before?"

Whenever Explorer Hank came onstage, some part of Webern shrivelled inside. Hank was folksy, ingratiating, but he was also desperate for approval, and the need shone on his face like sweat. He was struggling now, losing ground. The two cats, trained to bat a beach ball back and forth, balked tonight; Hank tossed it at Fred, who batted it off stage, hopped down from his trash can, and slunk away in the opposite direction. As Hank ran to scoop up Fred and return him to his post, Ginger jumped down from hers and began rubbing the abraded skin of her back on the tent's dirt floor. All the while, Hank kept up a stream of patter that sank from self-deprecation to apology to muttering to himself: "There you go, now stay, if I can just get these guys to stay put a minute—oh no you don't—okay, then I'll—" By the time he finally got the two cats ensconced again, the crowd was so restless he had to raise his voice to be heard.

"Well, since you folks've been so patient, let me go ahead and skip to the big finale," Hank announced, his smile a slice of pain cut from his face. He lit a match and held it to the steel hoop, which suddenly blazed. "The kids just love to show this one off, let me tell you." Hank positioned himself on the side of the hoop by Ginger, looking over at Freddy through the ring of fire. "First, Freddy, you jump through. I'll be here to catch you." Hank reached out his arms. "Come here, big guy. You can do it."

Freddy yawned and stretched, then made to jump down to the ground again.

"No. Through the hoop, buster."

If Webern hadn't known better, he would have sworn he saw Freddy shake his head. The cat yawned a second time, then curled into a donut of orange fur and closed his eyes. Hank, arms still outstretched, stood flabbergasted.

"Boys will be boys," he finally said. He walked around the ring of fire and poked Freddy, who released a guttural snore. "But Ginger, you'll show the nice people what you can do, huh? Baby girl?"

Ginger, staring through the fire at him, began to stiffen; her patchy fur bristled, and her lips parted to reveal teeth in a nervous snarl. She batted at her face with one paw. Webern tried to imagine leaping through the hoop without his glasses on. He wondered how many whiskers she had shed, but Hank had forgotten, or else no longer cared.

"Ginger girl, don't leave Daddy waiting." Hank held his arms out. "You can do it. You've done it a million times."

Ginger's eyes opened wide. Finally, hissing, she drew away from the fire. This time, Explorer Hank didn't apologize or explain. He drew out his whip from the belt of his khakis and cracked it in the air. Still, Ginger didn't move. She kept her head turned away. Hank cracked the whip again, and again, but she wouldn't look at him, nor would Freddy stir. Explorer Hank's smile shrank to a scowl, and he lowered the brim of the pith helmet to shade his eyes.

"Funny thing about kids," he said. "You can love 'em all you want, but they test you. Yes they do. So you have to show them who's boss. I'm doing this for your own good, Gingie."

Hank strode over to Ginger, picked her up by the scruff of the neck, and threw her through the hoop. The cub hit the dirt floor like a sack of flour. She did not land on her feet, and she limped a little as she scampered, whimpering, out the back entrance.

That night, Webern and Nepenthe made love with the last of the circus's citronella candles burning in the darkness. Nepenthe crouched over him, the blanket draped around her shoulders like another tent, one just big enough for the two of them. In the flickering light, the sight of her scales, ash-coloured and earthy smelling with sweat, reassured him. Even with everything else in shambles, at least they still had each other to hold onto.

Afterwards, Nepenthe yawned, "Nice lay, Bell boy," shut her eyes and fell, abruptly, to sleep. Webern was getting used to it: every night she turned her back to him, made herself very small, and with a whimper or two, disappeared into a land of dreams he could only imagine. He lay awake for a few minutes; a luna moth spiraled closer and closer to one of the citronella candles. When its wing finally caught aflame, Webern stood up, pulled on his jeans, and stepped out into the night.

He walked out onto the beach, down toward the water, feeling the salt spray on his face. The beach in Delaware had soothed him with its lapping waves, but California's ocean pummelled the sand, gulping and sucking whatever it could. Mermaids here would know better than to come near the shore.

Webern rubbed his hump and continued out. His bare feet smooshed the wet sand and gluey seaweed—low tide. He didn't know why he felt so lousy. He had a girl who liked him, who loved him, probably, and, if Schoenberg's circus really did dissolve, he and Nepenthe were free to do anything they wanted together. They could travel—work odd jobs—maybe even buy a house and settle down someday. But for some reason, that thought didn't comfort him either.

Webern thought of Dr. Show as a little boy, his walls covered with pictures of magicians and amusement parks, and then of his own room back home, the unicycle leaning in one corner beside the wrenches and the tire pump. He thought of his clown notebook, its pages spilling out with acts, and for the first time, it occurred to him that he wasn't entirely free. The circus had staked its claim on him. Even if a surgeon could fix his spine, Webern knew he was beyond saving now.

A steely wave smashed down a few yards away; cold slivers of froth reached Webern's feet, and he shivered. It almost sounded like the wind was calling a woman's name, forlornly, over and over. Then he saw where the voice was coming from. Some yards away, Explorer Hank stood, swatting the surf with his riding crop, bawling, "Ginger! Ginger! Ginger!"

"Hank?" The animal tamer didn't respond until Webern tapped the sleeve of his safari jacket. Then he shuddered.

"Have you seen Ginger?" Hank asked. He didn't look at Webern; the brim of his pith helmet shadowed his face. His voice was hoarse from shouting. "You haven't seen her, have you?"

"No, Hank, I guess I haven't."

"I let them out of their cages—for one minute, one ever-loving minute, so I could change the newspapers. You'd've thought she was a cheetah, she ran so fast." Hank waded out farther. The churning foam gave him no reflection. "Ginger!"

"Cats hate water. I'm sure she'll come back when she's ready."

"Of course she will. I know that." Hank sounded angry. "I'm just a worrier, that's all."

"You want to walk back up to camp together?"

"I'll be there in a minute." Water swirled around the tops of Hank's boots. For a moment, he held perfectly still—he looked almost peaceful. Then he hurled his riding crop into the waves and pulled his revolver out of one pocket. He fired a blank with each wild cry: "Ginger! Ginger! Ginger!"

Webern turned away from the ocean and jogged back up the beach. Suddenly, he felt afraid that when he returned to the tent, Nepenthe would be gone, too. But she was still there, sleeping soundly as before. He blew out the citronella candles, all three, then took off his jeans and lay down beside her. In the darkness, he touched her back beneath the blanket. Muscles moved under her craggy skin like tectonic plates shifting stone.

CHAPTER ELEVEN

THE LIVING ROOM IS ONLY MISSING ONE THING: its fourth wall. In the centre of the ring, it sits displayed for all to see, like the parlour of an enormous dollhouse. Inside, an overstuffed sofa and an easy chair face each other, separated by a small table bearing a plate of cookies and a mug of warm drink. A furry rug spreads across the floor. A fire roars in the fireplace. Books line the walls. The room exudes warmth and comfort. Over the mantle hangs a portrait of the ringmaster. His eyes look curiously alive.

The clown, dressed as a hobo, enters from a door stage right. At first, still holding closed the lapels of his ragged coat, he's suspicious and ill at ease, but as he takes in his surroundings, he relaxes. His red mouth spreads into a goofy grin, and he pulls off his hat to reveal a scraggly grey wig with a noticeable bald patch. He kicks off his shoes and wiggles his toes. Finally, he swaggers over to the fire, warms his hands, then turns around and bends to warm his backside.

Ouch! The fire flares and the clown jumps a foot in the air. He hops on one foot and rubs the seat of his pants. Singed. But he's known worse. Unfazed, he saunters over to the easy chair and sinks into it. Now this is the life. He takes a cookie from the plate beside him and licks his lips. He opens his mouth wide, then chomps down hard.

The clown throws the cookie across the room; he works his jaw to make sure it isn't busted. He picks up a second cookie and strikes it against the tabletop. *Thunk, thunk, thunk.* It might as well be a glob of cement. The clown shoves the plate away in disgust, then settles back in the chair and closes his eyes. At least he can get a little rest. And look, the chair even reclines. The clown leans back, back, back, until, with a *crack!* the chair snaps upright again, popping him in the head and making his eyes cross.

Still a little dizzy, the clown gets up and staggers to the sofa. Much better: here he can stretch out. Yawning, he lies down on the cushions as if getting into bed. He puts on his hobo hat and pulls it down over his eyes.

Sproing! The clown leaps to his feet; a scowl spreads across his face. He points accusingly at the quivering spring that pokes up between two sofa cushions. Does he break everything he touches? Or is the room conspiring against him? He looks up angrily at the portrait of the ringmaster, shakes his hat in its direction, then paces back and forth. He gestures wildly, as if delivering a stream of insults. The portrait's eyes follow him wherever he goes.

The clown puts his floppy shoes back on, fixes his hat squarely on his head, then strides over to the door he entered through. He grasps the knob and tugs, but it just comes off in his hand. An expression of panic spreads across his face. Trapped!

He cannot hear the laughter coming through the missing wall. He can only see one way out. He pounds on the door, to no avail. He kicks and punches it. He rams it with his hump. Then, just when he's finally given up, the whole thing comes off its hinges and falls straight down, knocking him flat.

Webern woke that morning to the smell of elephant dung. It wasn't too hard to guess where it was coming from. The mound stood two dozen yards away from their camp, lumpy, brown, and steaming.

Webern glanced around the campsite, but it was deserted. For the second day in a row, he was the first one up, and for the second day in a row, he wished he were still in bed. Al leaving had upset him, but this was just gross.

They were camped near a two-lane side road that twisted along Lemon City's shore. In the past, they'd avoided such locations for fear that a police cruiser would happen along to evict them. But lately they'd gotten careless. Now, the dung brimmed out of a deep ditch that ran alongside the road's shoulder, where the pavement met the beach's sand.

Webern walked up to the road. He tried to keep upwind of the hill
of shit, but he ended up having to hold his breath anyway. He stood

in the middle of the asphalt and looked first in one direction, then the other.

It was the big top he saw first—the Other big top. Yellow and red striped, it dominated the landscape even from a distance. Alongside it stretched a long black train of the romantic old-fashioned kind. Puffs of steam rose from its engine, and even this far away Webern could see swarms of people milling around the boxcars. Trucks and wagons parked willy-nilly around the periphery of this scene, and to one side milled the elephants themselves, grey and cumulous as low-hanging storm clouds.

Of course, it was bound to happen eventually: they'd crossed paths with one of the bigger outfits—the Mulligan Bros., maybe, or Scarsdale & Lowe. Schoenberg's original travelling schedule had avoided the routes followed by train shows, but now, zigzagging willy-nilly across the country, they'd finally bumped into one of their rivals. Now, it would be an embarrassment, a hassle; they'd have to leave town in a hurry, this morning even, maybe. Another day wasted. And yet . . .

Webern's eyes lingered on the Other Circus. The more he looked at it, the harder it was to look away. Even from this distance, the colours seemed too bright, the action too frenetic, to be real. This big top especially looked like something from one of his dreams. He wished he had a pair of binoculars. As much as he wanted the Other Circus to disappear, he also wanted to see straight into its centre ring: the high wire, the roving spotlights, the giant balls for bears to balance on, the hay strewn here and there for horses.

Webern shook his head. He turned around and went back to Nepenthe's tent. Inside, she lay sprawled on the dirt floor, sleepily reading obituaries from a newspaper she'd bought in the last town.

"I can't believe it. That director Tod Browning just dropped dead. There goes my movie career, I guess." Nepenthe stretched, then wrinkled her nose. "Jesus God, something stinks out there."

Webern went over to his suitcase and pulled out a fresh T-shirt and a bar of soap. It did stink. Just smelling it made him feel disgusting. "Nepenthe?"

She was reading an advice column. "Mmm-hmm?"

He hesitated. "Something weird happened, is all."

"Weird how?" The newsprint crinkled beneath her elbows.

"Come outside and see."

Out on the road, Nepenthe looked from the elephant dung to the Other big top and slowly shook her head.

"We have the worst luck," she said through her pinched-up nose.

Heat rippled the distant forms, and Webern thought of mirages.

"It's really there, isn't it? It's not just an illusion or something?"

"Isn't that proof enough for you?" She jerked her head toward the elephant dung. "Ugh. Why did they have to empty their toilets right here?"

"Maybe to drive us off?"

"Oh, yeah, I bet they saw our tent and got really intimidated."

Webern looked down at the puny white T-shirt in his hand. He tried to imagine the Other clowns. Lithe, athletic figures mimed and tumbled across a sawdust floor.

"What are we going to do?" he asked.

Nepenthe snorted. "Well, I guess a little competition can't be a bad thing."

The circus players loitered around the campfire all day, always with the backdrop of the Other Circus hanging in the distance. There was no purpose to staying in Lemon City another day, not with a real circus in town, but the matter remained unspoken. Their own big top, dingy and stunted, remained up like a parody, and their fire, without new wood to feed it, grew pale and whispery. No one moved to disassemble the bleachers, or to make a trek to town. But for all the apparent indolence, the players burned with a restlessness that flushed their skins like fever. Vlad and Fydor paced, Eng flexed and rotated his arms around and around in their sockets, Hank busily cleaned Freddie's ears with rubbing alcohol, and Nepenthe smoked cloves and rolled her eyes at the slightest provocation. Brunhilde twisted the chain of her locket tight around her neck.

Webern speared a hot dog and held it over the flames until it split and bubbled. He wasn't hungry. He had thought that his curiosity might fade with time, but the longer he sat here, the more he wanted to go explore the Other Circus. Only Dr. Show, who never emerged from his tent, seemed immune to the strange pull of the wagons and rattling boxcars out across the rolling sand.

The circus players watched as giraffes stilted from train to tent, casting long shadows. Their eyes followed a jouncing fire truck and a dozen ponies trussed up in gilded saddles. When a line of shining pale cars began to move along the highway from town toward the Other Circus, Explorer Hank threw down his packet of cotton swabs and pushed Freddie off his lap. His face had changed since Ginger's disappearance; there was no softness in it now.

"All right," he announced, "let's go already."

So they went. Hank detached the red trailer from the jalopy and those who couldn't fit in the cab piled into the bed of the truck. But when Webern started to hop up among the others, who sat on old costumes and blankets folded like seat cushions, a parallel image flashed vividly to mind. Again, Webern saw the yellow Cadillac, angled there on the street before his house, its passenger door agape, a box of Mexican jumping beans jittering in the backseat—the moment he'd stepped into his current life.

"Did anyone ask Dr. Show to come?" he asked, poised to hoist himself up.

Vlad and Fydor exchanged glances, and Eng shrugged. Nepenthe folded her legs Indian-style. She'd wrapped a white scarf around her head so only her eyes were showing.

"I think we all expected you to do it," she said. "You're his right hand man, you know." The cloth muffled her voice, and Webern couldn't even guess at her expression. Not for the first time, it occurred to him that she might be making fun of him. He stared up at her for a long moment, then, when she dropped her eyes, dashed over to the drawn curtains at the entrance to Schoenberg's tent and stopped there, panting.

"Dr. Show?" Webern called. No response. "Dr. Show, you in there?"

He touched the curtain, then glanced back over his shoulder. Someone honked the horn of the jalopy. Webern bit his lip. He gave the velvet one more shake.

"We'll be back, okay?" Webern turned around and ran back to join the others.

On the way over, the players sat tensely in the back of the truck, their heads turned to the wind. Out here in the dunes, Nepenthe looked like an Arabian princess with eczema around her eyes. She took Webern's arm, and he felt the cool satin of her glove slip against his skin. She said something to him through the scarf, an apology or a joke, but Webern couldn't hear it and he just nodded.

Dust rose up from wheel ruts and hoofprints; the midway choked with it, and Webern blinked in the sandy-coloured haze. Concession stands bearing tanks of green and pink lemonade, castles built from Cracker

Jack boxes, and drippy ice cream rose up on all sides. A giant neon thermometer (flashing "Strong—Stronger—STRONGEST!") took a beating from a blond boy with a red rubber mallet. A novelty stand fluttered with pennants and parasols. A strange old woman sat in a booth by herself, surrounded by writhing chameleons safety-pinned to the walls by their tails. Webern clutched Nepenthe's hand as they pressed through the crowd. Slowly, he grew aware of a feeling he hadn't experienced in years. Here were normal people, hundreds of them. But no one was looking at him—no one was pointing at him—no one was paying any attention to him at all.

Webern and Nepenthe had lost the others back at the ticket counter, but they'd most likely all meet up again in the sideshow. He and Nepenthe were inching closer to it by the minute. At least he thought they were. As they passed several wagons circled round in an impromptu petting zoo, Webern craned his neck to look. Llamas paced and nickered inside, and children stuck hands wrist-deep into their fur. Right after that came a hillbilly band—washboard, tub, and saw—and then more concession stands: onion rings, chicken, corn on the cob. A calliope whistled and children threw softballs at barrels and a man with a sewing machine hurriedly stitched initials onto piles and piles of green Robin Hood hats. They were already inside the sideshow's maw when Webern got his bearings. THE PARLIAMENT OF FREAKS, read the gilded sign.

This low, rectangular tent looked simple enough from the outside, but inside it became a dim labyrinth of platforms and partitions. Human oddities crouched at every turn, each positioned behind a different curtain. Venus de Milo, the armless girl, played a ukulele with her toes, while the Human Torso rolled and lit a cigarette using only his lips. The Elastic Man pulled the flesh of his neck up to his chin like a turtleneck sweater. The barker stuck knives into the box where Miss Twisto balled up like a fist, and Madame Butterfly, a disembodied winged head, batted her eerily long lashes from behind a pane of glass. The fat lady sold rings the size of napkin holders, the Southern preacher-dwarf hawked miniature Bibles, and the Blockhead offered handfuls of oversized nails freshly pulled from his cranium.

The Ossified Man, the Pygmy Princess, the Pinheads and their goat... as the barker guided the audience along to each performer's tiny stage, Webern appreciated the little touches more and more: the ebony combs in the albino girl's long hair, the jungle plants surrounding the snake charmer. He wondered just what made the crowd draw nearer instead of recoiling in disgust, as they so often did at Schoenberg's circus. It could have been the costumes: even the tawdry elements—the armless girl's negligee, the Human Skeleton's rakish, pencil-thin moustache—seemed high quality.

Or maybe it was how clean the freaks looked here, how posed. Gazing at the fat lady, whose skin glowed with rosy health, Webern grew aware of the dirt under his own fingernails, the grey tinge to his skin. He imagined traveling the country in style, reclining in a train cabin with Nepenthe as snowy fields rolled by in the moonlight. He would have a trunk of costumes, made of silk and velvet, and a paint box full of makeup, glitter, powder, and paint. They would go to cities and sleep in hotels, where they would drink candy-coloured liqueurs from tiny bottles and order hot toast from room service. And he would take a bath every single day. These freaks were so lucky. Going to work here would be like going to sleep. As they left the snake charmer's booth, Nepenthe stopped to peer at the brittle skins Serpentina had for sale. Webern reached for his wallet and bought her one with his last dollar bill.

"Wow, Bernie. Thanks, I guess. Although more scales are literally the last thing I need." Nepenthe wrapped the snakeskin around her neck loosely, like a second scarf. "What do you think? Does it lend a certain—*je ne sais quoi*?"

"It suits you." Serpentina stroked the head of one of her pythons with a lacquered green talon. The other audience members were making their way toward the "Egress," and, along with a leering patron in a straw hat, Nepenthe and Webern were the last ones left in this little booth. Serpentina leaned low over the footlights to get a better look at them. "I don't think we've met. Are you in the show?"

"Not exactly," said Webern. His self-consciousness rushed back as she scrutinized his hump. He wondered if the other freaks had noticed him as he passed. Maybe they'd even been hurt or angry that he didn't stop to speak to them, to acknowledge he was one of their kind. He felt vaguely embarrassed, like there was an etiquette here he'd breached, and, looking down, he dug a toe in the sawdust. "We're just visiting. You've got a neat set-up."

"How'd you get your job here, anyway?" asked Nepenthe.

"Practice, practice, practice." There was something oddly fang-like about Serpentina's smile. She stepped down from her platform and, without shyness or the least hesitation, did what Webern never would have dared. With one deft movement, she reached her long manicured nails toward Nepenthe's face and pulled loose her linen scarf. It fluttered down around her shoulders.

"Hey!" Nepenthe's hands flew to cover her face.

"Leave her alone!" Webern tried to help Nepenthe put her scarf back on; she slapped his hands away.

But Serpentina had already seen and she stood back, appraising.

"What do you think, Frank?" she asked the man in the straw hat.

"Very nice, very nice," said the leering man, stepping out of the shadows. The skin around his mouth had wrinkles shaped like quotation marks, as if he was always grinning. He even grinned while he spoke. "You live up to expectations, hon, and that's no joke. Your friends told us all about you."

"My friends?" Nepenthe turned away from him as she struggled with the folds of linen. "You don't know my friends."

"Sure I do. What were their names?" Frank snapped, as if he'd just summoned the memory back up. "Your lovely lady friend, Brunhilde. And of course the twins. Vlad and Fydor, isn't that right?"

"What did they say?" Nepenthe stopped trying to wrap the scarf around her head. She looked suspiciously through splayed fingers, her hands pressed to her face.

"They told us you were extraordinary," said the snake charmer.

"What's going on here, anyway?" Webern looked back and forth between them. "How did you meet our friends?"

"How could we miss them?" asked Frank. He turned back to Nepenthe and reached into his jacket pocket. "Here, take my card, and feel free to stop by my office after the performance. If you and your little companion are interested, I'm sure we could all do some beautiful acts together."

When they emerged, blinking, from the dark tunnel of the sideshow, Webern thought of a picture book of Greek myths his mother used to read to him when he was small. He remembered pictures of strange creatures—half-man, half-bull, a boy with wings—and the ornate splendor of the Underworld. Once you ate the food there, you were destined always to return.

"Bernie?" Nepenthe waved a wax paper bag in front of his face. She'd wrapped her scarf back around her head, but looser this time.

Webern could glimpse some grey scales through the eyeholes. "You in there, kiddo?"

Webern took a handful of peanuts, still warm and greasy from the machine. "Sorry, I'm just thinking."

"Oh, I bet you are."

"What does that mean?"

"Nothing."

"What?"

"I just think it's cute, that's all."

"What are you talking about?"

"That you're jealous."

Blood rose from his neck. "I am not."

"I knew it."

"Nepenthe, cut it out. I'm not jealous. What would I be jealous of?"

"Hey, don't snap at me. I guess there's no joking with you today, is there?"

"You can joke. Just don't say things that aren't true."

"Okay, okay. But listen, there's nothing wrong with being jealous. I was a little jealous too, when we saw that girl with the legs."

"With the legs?"

"Or without the arms, rather. Don't pretend you didn't notice. She was giving you the eye." He could tell from her voice that she was smiling. "Bet you never thought we'd be in such big demand, huh?"

Webern followed Nepenthe into the big top. They scanned the crowd for their friends and when they didn't find them, he followed her to a pair of empty seats deep in the heart of a curving row of spectators. But though she spoke to him, he could hardly hear her over the noise of the audience.

"I think Hank's up that way. There's some guy in a pith helmet, anyway." Nepenthe squinted. "I had no idea this place was so huge, did you?"

Webern glanced around. Huge was an understatement. In the centre of the arena hung a tangle of nets, loose-woven and ropey as the rigging of a ship, and dozens of slender metallic poles spiked out of the ground, leaning beneath the weight of canvas. An unseen generator rumbled beneath the seats, and everywhere he looked, white-suited candymen moved industriously through the aisles. Finally, Webern and Nepenthe took a seat by a little girl who had just gotten cat whiskers painted on her face. The child's mother glared at them, moved herself and the child down one seat, then returned to her conversation with a bouffant-headed schoolmarm in the row ahead of her. They didn't stop chattering until the lights went down.

The show began with a woman dressed as Cleopatra riding an elephant, closely followed by three medieval knights. Nepenthe leaned forward in her seat. A painted lady gyrated at the end of a rope she held by her teeth; a man leapt from the back of a pure white horse. A tightrope walker strolled high above, champagne flutes balanced on the palm of each hand; down below, a pyramid of lithe acrobats tumbled, then re-formed. And even with Frank still eerily grinning in the back of his mind, Webern had to admit it was all perfect, perfect, perfect. Dr. Show always declared that circuses like this one had sold out, that they allowed money and success to soil their glittering dreams with reality, but watching this, Webern thought of Fred and Ginger, with their patchy hair, the single spotlight's quivering beam, Vlad and Fydor forgetting their lines in the middle of a performance, his own stale popcorn and smudgy face. He let himself admit the truth: Schoenberg's circus was actually the flawed one, the one that allowed grim fact to taint and limit it.

A man juggled torches in the dark, Roman chariots came and went, springboards creaked, a bear rode a tricycle. By the time the clowns came out to perform their hapless fire brigade, Webern was only half-watching the action in the ring. The circus worked on him like a drug. As the buffoons smacked each another with rubber axes and squirted hoses full of seltzer down one another's pants, he let his eyes drift shut, dreaming. In his mind, the ring filled with clowns dressed as spacemen, quack doctors, toy soldiers, Indian chiefs, racecar drivers, mad scientists, tuba players, horse-shy cowboys, Napoleon Bonapartes. It was only when he felt Nepenthe touching his arm that he looked up and realized the performance was over.

CHAPTER TWELVE

DR. SCHOENBERG SAT ON THE EDGE OF HIS COT, SMOKING. His black cigarette holder looked like a magician's wand, but it didn't conjure much, just vague, grey forms that hung in the air a second before disappearing. He refilled his glass with bourbon, then dropped the empty bottle and kicked it across the floor. It rolled to a stop beside the painting that lay facedown at the base of his easel.

After his players had left him that afternoon, Schoenberg had come out from his tent and stared in the direction of the Other Circus for what seemed like hours. The sunlight made his eyes water, as they did so often these days, but still he stood there looking for as long as he could stand it. He could think of a million names to curse the performers, a million words to describe their perfidy and betrayal, but he couldn't think of a single condemnation that didn't also apply to himself. In the end, he'd been a fool, and that was far worse than being a villain. At least villains delivered fine speeches now and then, and their death scenes were always memorable.

He removed the cigarette end from his holder and crushed it beneath his shoe, then took a long sip from his drink. The corners of his moustache dragged in the bourbon, but he didn't care. Once, years ago, he'd had a moustache cup, a teacup with a ledge of porcelain inside the rim to keep one's whiskers dry, but it had met its untimely end when a spiteful baggage handler in Marseilles dropped his suitcase down a flight of stairs. No matter. It wasn't as though he'd be receiving visitors tonight, or indeed any time soon. The performers were gone. They'd already returned to camp—though they'd tried to sneak back on foot, his sense of hearing was keener than an ordinary man's—

and left again, off to join that obscene spectacle, no doubt. He'd heard every suitcase click shut, every tent flap zip and unzip, and though he had not gone back outside since nightfall, he could see the deserted camp vividly inside his mind: tent stakes still stuck in the ground here and there, a pair of three-legged pants rumpled in the dirt, an empty tub of Nepenthe's skin lotion, lidless, collecting rain. For though it was not raining outside, a dry sky just felt ill-suited to the scene. He stirred a finger slowly in his drink. How could they have done such a thing? He had not been the best of masters, it was true—he still recalled with shame the incident of Brunhilde and the cashbox, and he would be the first to admit his grooming had been abominable the last several days—but really, such treachery was beyond the pale of his experience.

"That was the unkindest cut of all," he murmured, thinking of Webern. Just then, as if on cue, he heard a quiet scrabbling outside of his tent.

"Who goes there?" he called.

"It's just me." Webern peeked between the curtains. "Did I wake you up?"

Dr. Show scrutinized him. Webern could hold no secrets in his face—it was this transparency that made him so appealing as a clown—but tonight his expression had a strangeness about it that Schoenberg couldn't place. Around the mouth, Webern looked cautious, reserved, but his eyes danced with light, as they only did on evenings when he came up with a new routine for the show.

"What troubles you, my boy?"

"Oh, nothing. I just wanted to talk to you, that's all."

"Ah. Well, let's hope it isn't about your salary." Schoenberg reached under his cot and pulled out a brand new bottle of green Chartreuse. "In that case, I'd be forced to confess a slight misappropriation of funds. Care for a glass?"

Webern nodded and sat down on the floor. Schoenberg gave Webern the glass he'd used for bourbon; he poured his own Chartreuse into a clean cup. For a while the two men drank in silence. Webern wrinkled his forehead after each small sip; he couldn't figure out exactly what he tasted. Dr. Show drank deeply, inhaling at the same time, like a man underwater trying to drown. Finally he spoke.

"Did you know," he asked, "that the recipe for Chartreuse is nearly seven hundred years old? It was concocted by an order of Carthusian monks. They persist into the present age, a mad anachronism, dedicating their lives to solitude and contemplation. They spend their days crouched in wooden huts, listening for the voice of God, deep in the Desert of Chartreuse. They chew herbs by the mouthful. And at night, they see terrible visions."

He chuckled.

"Only two monks know the recipe, and they are sworn to secrecy. They sign oaths written in blood and holy water. But before they die, they must pass their formula on, lest it be lost forever, like so much ash upon the wind."

Dr. Show ran a finger around the rim of his glass, and for a moment Webern saw the slope of his own father's disappointed shoulders, the sag of his loosened tie. He found himself wondering where the old man was tonight—slumped in front of the TV, maybe, or at the Barrel Head, drinking alone and eating peanuts for dinner. He looked down at his drink. "I've never had Chartreuse before."

"You can have the bottle when I'm through." Schoenberg lifted it thoughtfully; green liquid sloshed inside. "It will make a lovely vase."

For some reason, this made both men laugh, Schoenberg with a loud theatrical booming, Webern bent forward as if trying to hold it inside.

"Bernie, have I ever told you about my voyage to the Old World?"

"Not really."

"I was just a youth at the time, but the experiences I had there were to forever change my art."

"Yeah?"

"Yes, Europeans have a flair for spectacle, you see. When I arrived, my notions of theatre came primarily from the vaudeville houses of my youth. But in Europe, theatre is everywhere. Mimes perform on street corners, puppet theatres dot the marketplace, and Shakespeare's words echo in the public square." Dr. Show swallowed some more Chartreuse. "I must admit, sometimes I wish I'd stayed.

"I first visited London and the British Isles, then traveled onto the continent. In the Basque country, I joined a clan of gypsies, posing as a marriageable suitor for their daughter. But though she was a lovely creature, I had given my heart to showmanship long before. From her father, I learned the secrets of legerdemain; with her mother, I studied the reading of cards and the telling of riddles. Her cousin kept the accounts; her two brothers were acrobats, who spent the days oiling their golden bodies and wrestling the lions they had tamed from infancy. In the Old Country, the circus is not a shrine of commerce, beholden to the forces of market and the highest bidder—no. It is a sacrament, a tradition, passed down with tender care from one generation to the next. A family, bound not by money but by blood.

"I slept in the wagon they kept filled with holy relics, some thousands of years old: the fingerbone of John the Baptist, a lock of Mary Magdalene's hair. And older remnants still: a point of Neptune's trident, a drop from Bacchus' cup, a shard of the eggshell from which Helen hatched. Sometimes Molara would join me there. Molara." He savoured the word. "I believe that was her name."

"So why did you leave?"

"Oh, you know how these things go, my boy. No matter how idyllic it may seem at first, it always turns sour in the end. Nothing gold can stay." He tossed off the rest of his drink in a single angry swallow, then refilled his glass. "Allow me tell you something, Bernie. Something I have not yet revealed to another living soul." With one trembling finger, he pointed at the crossed blades that hung against the wall of his tent. "Do you know how I came to own those swords?"

"Sure. You got them from Mars Boulder, right?"

"In a way."

"What do you mean?" Webern sipped his Chartreuse. He thought of the monks, bent over their cauldron, secrets passing between them in the bubbling steam.

"The gypsies' performances were a banquet of sensory delights—delicately prepared but hastily displayed. One element, however, never failed to enthrall the humble villagers who came to pay us homage: Molara's sword dance." Dr. Schoenberg's lips now shone with a pale green gloss, as if he was succumbing bit by bit to a subtle poison. "The family owned an ancient blade, a gypsy sword that had once slain cruel noblemen and honoured bandit kings. In her dance, Molara writhed as though in ecstasy, swinging it by its hilt, balancing it on the delicate flesh of her forearms, cradling it like a lover. Though the sword was old, it still shone with an otherworldly light; its edge cut easily through swaths of falling silk.

"Even in my earliest days with the gypsies, I knew that I would one day return to America to launch a production of my own. As I journeyed with them across the continent, I came to believe that Molara's sword—or one of its equal—would transform any performance into a timeless work of art. But knowing how precious the blade was to them—the most cherished of all their possessions—I did not want to cause undue concern. And so, one night, I slipped from Molara's bedchamber with the bejeweled scimitar in my hand.

"I found an ironsmith who promised he would forge me a new sword, identical in every way to the one of ancient beauty that I presented to him—identical, but new. Indeed, it was more than I had dared to hope, except for one stipulation: he needed to retain the ancient sword until the new sword was forged, to copy the original in every detail.

"The gypsies greeted me with suspicion when I returned to camp; they already knew their sword was gone. I told them that I had tracked the thieves for miles, but had finally lost the scent. Molara's cousin doubted me, but the others took me at my word. I was their daughter's betrothed, after all, and an ardent student of their craft. Only to Molara did I reveal the truth. She returned with me to reclaim the swords when his work was complete." Schoenberg's moustache drooped. "But the ironsmith refused to deliver them to me. I have rarely seen such malevolence. He declared I never paid him for his work." Schoenberg glanced at Webern sharply. "But I did."

"Sure," Webern said. But as he gazed at the swords, he thought of Brunhilde—the incident with the cashbox—the expensive bottle of Chartreuse. "I believe you, Dr. Show."

"I paid him in advance, every penny that I had," Schoenberg said bitterly. He reached into his jacket pocket and withdrew a tattered paper, small and faded, with deep creases like a map's. "And if anyone doubts me, you can tell them I showed you this."

He handed it to Webern. The receipt's words were foreign and the numbers just a scrawl, but Webern looked at it for a long time. He traced one finger over an ancient rusty thumbprint.

"He claimed it was merely a deposit, that I owed double the amount. Perhaps there was some misunderstanding—I spoke little of his language, and he none of mine. Perhaps I thought that with some negotiation ... well, it's difficult to recall. At any rate, he demanded from Molara payment of another kind." Schoenberg took back the receipt. "Her charms were quite apparent, you see. I thought it unseemly, of course, but she couldn't bear to return to the camp empty-handed. Her cousin had been questioning the locals; no one knew anything of the bandits I'd so vividly described. Even her brothers had begun to look at me askance. I imagine Molara thought, without the sword, her family wouldn't allow me to continue accompanying them on their travels. And as for what he asked—it wasn't as though she was unschooled in such matters. She was a dancer, after all."

"You—sold her to him?"

Dr. Show folded the receipt and put it back into his pocket. "I wouldn't characterize it quite that way, but . . . I suppose. Temporarily."

"Wow." Webern held the taste of Chartreuse in his mouth; the herbs burned there like medicine.

"We returned to camp with sword in hand—the duplicate I kept concealed beneath my cloak—and celebrated the bandits' defeat with feasting and revelry. All had been restored, or so I believed.

"But after that day, Molara's manner toward me changed. She read the basest motives into my every gesture, demanded assurances, wept freely at all hours of the night. Even her dancing suffered. She felt, I suppose, that I saw her as a common prostitute, rather than a bride. Of course, to me she was neither. No tie bound us other than the force of our passion, and when that faded, I said adieu. Or rather, I left under the cover of darkness, to spare us both an unpleasant scene. I of course planned to take the sword the ironsmith had crafted for me, but the night of my departure, I reconsidered. I saw myself reflected in that blade, and it disconcerted me. The likeness I saw there bore no resemblance to the man in my self-portraits. Perhaps it was the unflattering light.

"In the years that followed, though, I thought of that sword often. In it, my own vision had, for once, melded with something even greater than itself, something which I grasped but dimly at the time: tradition, resilience, the honour of a birthright. I should have known that no good could come of leaving such a weapon behind."

"So, what happened then?"

"Pardon?"

"What happened? To Molara, and the gypsies? Did you ever see them again?"

"No, no." Dr. Show poured himself a few more inches of Chartreuse. "They scattered to the four winds after my departure, as gypsies are wont to do."

"What did Mars Boulder have to do with them? How'd he get the swords?"

"Molara's cousin, the keeper of accounts—he never cared much for me. Jealousy, I suppose. He and Molara had been inseparable since childhood. By some hopelessly jejune logic, he concluded that made her his own. Some years later, he voyaged to America, bringing with him what few relics remained from his days with the caravan. When he saw our circus advertised, he decided to exact his revenge. He sent me a letter, offering the swords at a discount—well, you know the rest."

"Her cousin is Mars Boulder?"

"That's what he calls himself now. It's quite dramatic, really. He seems to think that I brought about the downfall of his family, and crushed the fragile spirit of his only love."

"Jeez. What a nutcase."

"Oh, I suppose there's some truth to what he says. It's hard to remember properly. I was young, you see. And no one delights in recollecting his own villainy." Schoenberg's eyebrows knit together. "Boulder's made my downfall his profession. A popular career, it seems. He has some fierce competitors."

"Don't say that. Nobody wants—"

"Tell me, what did the others say to you before their defection?"

Webern took off his glasses and carefully wiped them on his shirt. "Actually, I wanted to talk to you about that, Boss."

"Oh?"

"Yeah. Since everybody else's going to try and get jobs over there . . ."

"Yes?"

"I guess I was just wondering what you were planning to do." Webern put his glasses back on. "If you were going to, you know, go on with your circus, or—"

Dr. Show looked affronted. He plucked at his bow tie.

"This is not the first time my vision has been tested, and it will not be the last. If you're suggesting that I might despair over a slight such as this, you know little of the strength of my character." He twisted one end of his moustache defiantly.

"No, no, that's not what I meant. I know you'll be all right and everything. I just was wondering where you were going to go, what you were planning to do. You know, for a job."

"Ah. Well, I have my skills. Perhaps I'll return to the continent. As I said, sometimes I wish I'd stayed." Schoenberg moved his pale fingers dexterously, manipulating invisible cards. Then a new thought occurred to him. His face climbed through what seemed like a preordained series of expressions, like notes on a musical scale, until finally he lifted his head and looked at Webern with a devilish gleam in his eye.

"My boy, have *you* ever visited Europe?"

Webern looked down at the drink in his hands.

"I can't say I have."

"But you must! To truly understand clowning, you must visit its very roots. Oh, the things I could show you, Bernie! On the continent, you'll see the grand halls of kings, where jesters once plied their merry trade, and the cobblestone roads once traveled by wandering minstrels all the way to Rome. The circus there is like Chartreuse: the recipe is ancient, but known to few. You and I will learn its secrets. Perhaps we'll even find Molara's family and make amends. I could return the swords, at least. As I recall, her brothers used to perform a comic mime in utter silence, accompanied only by their sister's flute—it was quite your sort of thing. What do you say, my boy? Shall we stow away on a steamer?" He glanced around, then laughed wildly. "After all, you said it yourself—there's no going on like this."

"Dr. Show . . ." Webern looked away from Schoenberg, over at the two swords that hung crossed above the trunk. One still shone; the other, opaque and battle-scarred, half-blocked its glancing light. "I'm sorry, but I can't."

"Oh, nonsense, of course you can." Dr. Show waved his hand dismissively. "At your size, we can pack you in a crate quite easily."

"That's not what I mean. You see, Nepenthe . . ." Webern finished his drink in a gulp, then said the rest in a single breath. "Nepenthe got a job with the Other Circus's freak show—she's there right now, fixing up our bunk—and they wanted her so much they agreed to take me on, too—just doing odd jobs at first, but if I learn fast—well, they'll let me clown." In fact, Frank had offered him a job with the Parliament of Freaks up front, but Webern turned it down categorically; he didn't want to perform anywhere but the big top. "They've got a great set-up over there and . . ."

Schoenberg rose slowly to his feet until he towered over Webern. He cast his glass down. It bounced on the dirt floor without breaking.

"*Et tu, Brute*? Why did you come back here, may I ask? To soothe your conscience? To drink my fine liqueur? Or merely to torment me?"

"Please don't yell at me, Dr. Show."

"I'll do as I like, you ungrateful—"

"Stop it, stop it, stop it! You're the one being ungrateful. I've worked so hard for you! I went along with every—and I've never complained or called you—crazy or—or—and didn't you notice, I'm the only one who came back?"

Dr. Show's expression changed again. As the anger drained away, his face took on the quality of a well-wrung sponge. He stood there idly for a moment, then reached into his sleeve for a handkerchief. Three emerged, red, green, and yellow, knotted together at the ends. He used them to mop his brow. As Schoenberg sank back onto the cot and bent to retrieve his glass from the ground, Webern felt a strange emptiness where his insides used to be. It was almost as though he might float away.

"Dr. Show," he said, "I didn't mean—"

"No, Bernie, you are entirely in the right. I do apologize." Schoenberg pressed the handkerchiefs to his eyes. "I don't know what came over me."

"It's just, Nepenthe and I can be happy, I think. She said—she wants me to come. And anyway," Webern went on, surprising himself with every word, "it's what I want, too. You really should see it for yourself. Then you'd know. I mean, it's beautiful. The acrobats and the trapeze artists . . ." He trailed off. Schoenberg sat motionless, his head still in his hands. This wasn't going the way Webern had hoped at all. "I didn't come here to torment you."

"I know, my boy."

"No, but really. I want you to come with us. I came to convince you. They're always hiring people, over at Barker & Smart, that's what Frank said, and I know that if you wanted to you could—"

"And what would I do in this Other Circus, may I ask? Allow me to repeat what I told you long ago: I cannot juggle, I do not throw knives. I ride bareback only when necessity demands it. I am a ringmaster, Bernie. That is my only skill."

"That's not true. You're a magician."

"Ha."

"No, really. You're great at it. I've seen you—"

"Tonight is the night for unpleasant confessions, it seems. Bernie, despite my—I failed on the vaudeville circuit. Before I changed careers, I was reduced to performing at bar mitzvahs and children's birthday parties."

"That's not so bad."

Schoenberg smiled wanly. "Spoken by a man who's never found himself upstaged by cake."

Webern forced himself to smile back, but Schoenberg turned away. He placed another cigarette in his holder and lit it.

"Leave me now, Bernie. I'll make my decision in the morning."

"Are you really okay?"

"I am fine, my boy, quite fine."

Webern stood up, walked to the curtains, then stopped.

"At least let me help you put this stuff away."

Webern went back and picked up the two empty glasses, as well as the empty bourbon bottle. For a moment, he looked around, as if trying to find somewhere to wash them. Then, impulsively, he threw all three objects in the air and began to juggle.

Webern bent, dipped, and scuttled around the tent, as if the juggling was next to impossible for him. He slid onto his knees, grabbing one cup at the last minute, and spun around on one heel to keep the bottle from falling to the ground behind him. As he performed, his expression kept changing: he grinned with foolish triumph after a near save, grimaced with exaggerated concentration, and opened his mouth in a perfect "O" of surprise when a glass struck the tent's centre pole and rang it like a bell. Then, slowly but surely, his juggling fell into a measured tempo, as if he had just gained his footing at long last. He smiled with lazy contentment as the objects spun round him, seemingly of their own accord, like spokes on a wheel. Just as he appeared completely confident and in control, all three rained down and hit him on the head—cup, cup, bottle. *Plunk, plunk, plunk!* Webern stuck out his tongue drunkenly, crossed his eyes, and fell over backwards.

It was a perfect performance, but as he got up and dusted himself off, he noticed that Dr. Show wasn't laughing. In fact, Schoenberg's eyes looked misty as he stared down at his shoes, watching the dark reflections there.

Webern felt stupider than he ever had in his life.

"I'm sorry, Dr. Show. I thought I could cheer you up," he said.

"No, that was splendid. Splendid. Thank you. I truly appreciated it."

"I hope you aren't mad at me."

"No, I understand your situation all too well. And I'll think over what you proposed. It was quite kind of you, to come and see me like this."

"All right."

"Bernie?"

"Yeah, boss?"

"You asked me once if I had any children." Schoenberg smoothed the colourful handkerchiefs draped over his knee. "After I left the Old Country, apparently Molara confessed herself to be pregnant. By myself or the ironsmith, she couldn't say. Her cousin offered to marry her, but she refused. She chose instead to fall upon the very sword whose creation she believed had ruined her. At least that's the story Mars Boulder told to me." He idly touched the tip of his cigarette; its fire had gone out. "I wonder now, what he'd have been like. That gypsy son."

Webern didn't know what he wanted to say, and he didn't know the words to say it. He looked at Dr. Show for a long time, but it was as if the ringmaster was sitting on the deck of a ship that had already set sail. The distance between them was opening wider and wider. "All right. I'll come back in the morning, boss."

After Webern disappeared through the curtains, Schoenberg untied his shoelaces and removed his tuxedo jacket. Beneath it, he wore only a dickey and suspenders. He hung the jacket on a notch in the tent pole, then pulled out his wallet from his pants pocket and opened it. It contained a single crumpled dollar and one weathered photograph. He pulled this picture out and smoothed it with his hand.

It was a snapshot of himself, taken after a talent contest when he was sixteen, shortly before he left home for good. In it, he sported white gloves and a cape. His first moustache, a source of real pride at the time, was impeccably waxed and turned up at the corners. Beside him was a cardboard sign, painted in gold and crimson, he recalled, though the black and white photograph coloured it grey. It read, "Watch Gilderoy the Great Make Himself Disappear!"

Schoenberg put the photograph away and looked over at the two swords that hung, crossed, against the tent's canvas wall. He stepped over and lifted down the older one by its jeweled hilt. In his hands, it felt cold and heavy. He stared down at the cobwebs of scratches dulling its once-bright surface. Then he ran a finger along its edge. To his surprise, it still cut him easily.

His mind turned again to Molara (or was it Moirae?), and the first time he'd seen her dance. He remembered vividly the village square, the way her ankle bells had jingled as her feet stamped the cobblestones, the brown hens that pecked, indifferent, at the dirt, even as the crowd filled the air with their raucous cheers. But even when he closed his eyes, he could no longer see her face. Perhaps because he'd hardly seen it at the time. In those days, women's faces stayed with him no longer than their names.

It seemed to him now that his youth had passed behind a painted screen of his own creation, a screen that passion and vice had served to illuminate but never to pierce. Upon the screen shone images of the glorious path his life would one day follow: marvelous illusions, daring escapes, intrigue, adventure, and above all, unquestionable genius, all evoked in the most brilliant of hues. Only now, in his old age, his "obsolescence"—he muttered the word out loud, like a curse—had that barrier finally been slashed to tatters.

Dr. Show hefted the sword up onto his shoulder and held it there, as though knighting himself. He felt its edge touch the skin just above his collar and felt the blue-green vein pulsing there. He wondered how Molara had felt dancing with the sword, if she had ever feared the sharpness of its blade. She might have believed that any misstep she took would bring her only the pain that she deserved. Any true artist would hold himself to the same standard.

"*Acta est fabula, plaudite*," Schoenberg intoned.

He held still for a moment and watched as his breath fogged the aged metal. Then, carelessly, he let the sword clatter to the ground, turned around, and hobbled back to his cot.

"You old fool," he murmured.

Because, after all, wasn't this the final delusion, the final shred of the screen that had once shielded him—that he still had an audience now, after all these years? That he was a failure, true, but that somewhere one-time admirers looked on, mourning amongst themselves of how far he had fallen, how he had squandered his youthful promise?

There were no lookers-on now, if indeed there ever had been. The world was not waiting for his next act. Even Bernie had forsaken him: Bernie, who had once committed grand larceny on his behalf, whose standards were so low he saw no shame in performing alongside a sick pony in a child's backyard. Bernie, who he'd thought would be there until the end.

Schoenberg felt his chest constrict tighter than before, and then all at once release—as if, stepping outside for the first time in years, he was at last able to exhale and breathe in fresh air. The world was not waiting for his next act. Fans were not thronging at his door. No one in Europe remembered him; there was nothing to return to, there. What he did now mattered to no one except himself.

How had it taken him so long to see? He could adopt a new name, a new set of tricks—he could leave behind the Cadillac, with its sticky scent of spilled dried rum, and the swords that had caused so much sorrow and made a madman track him across the world. He could leave behind the circus that bore his name, the cobbled-together tents, the ridiculous red trailer and filthy cages. He could leave behind his debts. Again, he saw the clockwork carousel roll down the hill, faster and faster, its ancient gears grinding as it thundered toward vanishing, and again he laughed out loud, but this time with real joy—with relief. What freedom it gave him, what sudden exhilarating freedom it gave him, now in his obsolescence, to begin again!

In his mind he saw the crowds. Every night the other circus would draw them by the hundreds, and every night, he would work his way through the rows, one among many with the candy men and the peanut sellers, performing simple tricks. He would call himself Caerus the Wise. He would have a dove again, silk scarves, a pack of cards, a new top hat; he saw himself delighting a simple child who, grabbing for the hat, would demand, "Where did it go?" only to feel the bird alight on her own small shoulder. So what if the vendor of funnel cakes or salt water taffy drew her attention away the next instant? He owed Bernie an apology—no, he owed him thanks. There were far worse fates for an old man than making a child smile.

It was then he saw the shadow Mars Boulder made as he filled the doorway of the tent. Schoenberg leapt to his feet. He bent to seize the sword from the dusty ground and held it out with both hands—an offering.

"Please," he said. "I've wronged you, I confess. Take this, with my compliments—take anything at all. I won't protest, I assure you. There's so little that I need."

CHAPTER THIRTEEN

THE BLOOD, PURPLE-BLACK AND EVERYWHERE, didn't resemble blood, even though it was leaking out of Schoenberg's side. Webern held two paper cups of steaming coffee as he stood in the tent's entrance, unable to step inside or to turn away. At first he thought that the liquid was paint, and that the stabbed body lying before him wasn't Schoenberg but merely one of his self-portraits.

The detectives sat Webern under a naked light bulb and offered him a cigarette. It seemed like they might have a firing squad waiting just outside. They asked him for his relationship to the deceased. They asked him how come he'd found the body. They asked what kind of a show they'd been running anyway, who would come out to see a bunch of bums playacting like they were the Ringling Brothers. They asked if Schoenberg was a pervert, a fairy, a pimp, a thief, a con man, a drunk. They showed him a telephone book. They asked if he knew Schoenberg's record was as thick as a telephone book. They asked him to go through his story from the beginning. They asked what he was hiding. They asked how come his fingerprints were all over the crime scene. They asked him why he was crying. They asked him for his relationship to the deceased. Webern sat on a metal folding chair and looked at himself in the two-way mirror. His face started to change the way it had before, on his birthday, when he'd seen his reflection in the sword. They asked him for his relationship to the deceased.

They shut the door of the holding pen. Through the single, high window, Webern could see a square of sky with bars on it. He imagined a little clown floating across it, holding onto a bunch of balloons. He gave the balloons names. One was Kiddo. One was Ma. One was Gram-

Gram. One was Pops. One was Boss. When the door of the holding pen opened again, Mars Boulder was standing on the other side. He had on handcuffs and leg cuffs and a leash around his neck. He looked deader than Schoenberg had. He'd already confessed.

"You stay here," one detective told Webern. "We'll have your paperwork through in a jiff."

Mars Boulder stepped inside. The door clanged shut behind him. His leash hung down his front like a joke, a giant leather necktie. Experimentally, Webern stepped up the man and punched him as hard as he could in the chest.

"Monster," Webern said. His voice came out low, Dr. Show's tenor. He punched him again. Boulder's chest felt hard, a shield of bone. "You—you—you're not even human, are you." He punched him again, in the abdomen this time.

Mars Boulder coughed. He bent at the waist. Webern stared up at him defiantly. Then Mars shuffled toward one of the cell's two wooden benches. Webern watched the leg irons drag across the concrete floor. Mars Boulder sat down heavily and folded his cuffed hands.

"I understand," he said. His voice was thickly accented. The metal links of the handcuffs dangled between his wrists, almost delicate, like jewelry. "You were his apprentice."

"Yes. I was."

"It is a hard thing." Mars Boulder pitched forward. He coughed again. The bench groaned beneath his weight. "You are your own master now."

"They're going to give you the electric chair." Webern hardly knew what he was saying. "They're going to make you eat rat poison. They're going to light you on fire."

"Still, you have your trade. You must never forget that." Mars pressed his face into his sleeves. His next words came out indistinct, muffled by the fabric.

"What?"

Mars Boulder lifted his head.

"Without your trade you are master of no one," he said.

The two men sat across from each other for an hour, the cage full of their silence. Then the detectives sent Webern to the morgue to identify the body. Schoenberg was in an ice-cold room full of people-sized drawers. He lay on a table beneath a white sheet. A beautiful lady with thick black hair removed it with a flourish, like the conclusion of a magic trick.

"His lovely assistant," Webern said.

She smiled. "How's that?"

The beautiful lady gave Webern a box that held the contents of Schoenberg's pockets, along with his watch. She'd cleaned the blood off the band herself. She told Webern she'd taken a liking to Dr. Show, that it was a shame what had happened.

"I've never seen such elegant hands. Not even on a woman," she told him.

The two detectives were waiting outside the morgue. Now that they had the killer, they looked sheepish.

"I guess you're free to go," said one.

"But don't cross state lines," the other warned him. "We'll need you to testify."

Webern nodded. The minute their squad car drove around a corner, he stole a child's bike off the street and rode it to the Other Circus. By the time he got there, they were already pulling up stakes. He felt dizzy from pedaling so fast. He wandered into the sideshow, where Nepenthe and Serpentina were helping to pack up the armless girl's booth. Nepenthe dropped the box she was holding and looked at him without saying anything for almost a whole minute, and then picked him up and carried him to their bunk.

"I'm so sorry," she whispered as she pulled the blankets up to his chin. He closed his eyes. When he opened them again, they were passing just south of Tucson, Arizona.

The days that followed passed in a sickness. Webern lay in the bunk he shared with Nepenthe, unable to think or talk or eat. Occasionally he forgot to breathe until the air came to him in a wrenching gasp like a sob. Sometimes Webern thought he was in his body cast again. It was the same feeling: alive but mummified. Other times, he thought he was dead and that the pain he felt came from Mars Boulder's swords piercing the very core of him.

Nepenthe came and went from the bed. She pressed herself close; her arms constricted his chest, her hot wet face scraped his hump. She tugged at him and pulled on his hands and cursed and rocked him back and forth. She spooned lukewarm chicken-flavoured water into his mouth and talked, soothing words that faded to nonsense by the time they reached his ears. She slid ice cubes along her scales by the dozens;

one night she used a bag of ice as a pillow, and when it burst and melted she tried to change the dripping sheets, but Webern still wouldn't move.

Webern closed his eyes and didn't sleep; he opened them and didn't wake up. Inside he felt hollow. The outline was there, but with nothing inside. He was a clown-shaped hole.

One night was very dark; the train made chopping sounds as it moved along the tracks. Webern lay bunched up against the wall. In the distance, a little golden figure was moving toward him. He got bigger and bigger as he approached: the size of a thumb, the size of doll, the size of a child, the size of an angel. A boy with golden hair, laughing; a boy almost big enough to fill the space Webern had left.

"Jesus God, please wake up, Bernie," Nepenthe whispered in his ear. "You stubborn fucking fool. Don't you know I love you?"

The golden boy waved. He turned around and retreated back the way he came: small, smaller, smallest.

The next morning, the train had stopped. Webern climbed out of the bunk and, on shaky legs, wandered outside. The air smelled mossy; all around him, trees wept their branches to the ground. Nepenthe was sitting on a blanket, smoking a clove and reading the *Encyclopedia of Psychiatric Disorders*. A few yards away, two pinheads took turns shoving each other into a mud puddle. Mosquitoes swarmed in itchy clouds. Nepenthe noticed him with a little start. She pinched out the lit end of her clove before she spoke.

"Well, it's about time you got up. Hank quit, Brunhilde's dead, and one of the elephants just stampeded into the swamp. It's probably been eaten by gators by now. We lizards, you know, we don't miss a beat." She put the clove back in her cigarette case. Her hands were trembling. "Regular heaven on earth, right? Vacation Wonderland, that's what the sign said a few miles ago. I swear to God, Bernie, if you've gone crazy too I'm going to leave this place and never come back. Even my parents weren't this fucked up."

Webern sat down next to her on the blanket and tilted his head against her shoulder. After a long moment, she kissed the top of his hump.

On the night that she died, Brunhilde unfolded the Lemon City Gazette and turned to the second page, where the murders were listed. It had been a busy week for the small town: there had been four. The first three were of local interest. The manager of the five and dime, in a jealous rage, had slain his wife and twin sons who, the article tacitly implied, might not have been his own. The other murder happened between circus people just passing through and would not have been of interest to anyone at all, had it not been for one deciding factor: the paper's photographer had snapped a picture during the suspect's arrest, just as the victim's body was removed from the scene.

The image, however sensational in its subject matter, was off-kilter in its composition and captured an instant after the real drama had effectively ceased. In the foreground, slightly out of focus, the suspect, balding and grizzled, doubled over the hood of a squad car as one officer cuffed him; the other waved a night stick, wand-like, above his massive back. In the background, a stretcher floated toward an unnecessary ambulance, draped in a sheet of ghostly white. Beneath the cloth, the vague silhouette of a man presented itself. It could have been anyone, a hero or a scoundrel, a matinee idol or a tired old man. But it was Schoenberg.

On the night that she died, Brunhilde sat in the circus's pie car and sipped a mug of hot weak tea as she gazed at this image. She stared for so long that the microscopic dots that composed it began to shimmer and dance on the newspaper. Then she removed her beard trimming scissors from their holster and carefully snipped the picture from its place between two columns of smudgy text. She rose and, leaving the Gazette where it lay on the table, walked back to the boxcar she now shared with Tiny Tina and Rhonda, the two fat ladies from the Parliament of Freaks.

The circus train was not traveling that night, and the desert air felt warm and dry as she walked alongside the tracks. A breeze, scented lightly with night-blooming cactus flowers and the needles of the spiny trees—cypress—that seemed to flourish here, ruffled the long, unkempt curls of her beard.

Inside her boxcar, Brunhilde carefully lifted her only suitcase from its hiding place on her upper berth. She flipped it open and unceremoniously dumped its contents onto the floor. Bending, she retrieved a small jar of paste from where it lay amidst the jumble of her clothing and trinkets, then sat down on Rhonda's concave mattress. Every inch of the suitcase's lining was shellacked with images of the burned or burning city, and it took a moment for her to find the perfect position for her new clipping in the collage. She finally fit it inside the lid, in one corner just beside a row of smoking bodies and the Zwinger

Palace in flames. After pasting it in place, she shut the empty suitcase and walked outside.

Brunhilde often doubted that it was the same sun that shone on her here as it had been during her girlhood in Dresden, that the same moon that once had floated in the sky like a white paper lantern was the one that now, here in America, shone as yellow and glaring as a neon sign. But tonight, the stars emerging from the darkening sky looked oddly familiar, landmarks on the way to somewhere she once knew.

Brunhilde paused surreptitiously near where the roustabouts tugged and shouted at one another across the expanse of brightly coloured canvas that, come morning, would rise into the towering dome of the big top. A toolbox, a mallet, a pair of iron spikes lay on the dusty earth. Brunhilde leaned forward to grasp a coil of rope that rested beside them, then continued on her way. The empty suitcase swung lightly in her hand.

The boxcar where Webern slept with Nepenthe was packed with bunks, floor to ceiling; between eight and ten other new circus people slept there at night, depending on who was sleeping alone. A big sliding door opened out onto the night air, and sometimes it got so hot one of the roustabouts pulled it open with a gravelly screech while the train was in motion, filling the car with a rushing wind that pulled loose blankets. It was all men and freaks in the boxcar, with the exception of a lady sword-swallower who hated the double entendres associated with her profession, who drank with the strongest of them, and who rolled out the open boxcar door one night when the train was crossing the Florida panhandle, never to be heard from again.

It didn't take Webern long to realize that there were two circuses. One circus faced the parking lot; it was the circus of midway games and steam calliopes, ticket booths, smiles and prizes. This circus was the dream of the real circus, which lay facing the railroad tracks.

At the real circus, Webern stepped over craters left by elephant feet, ducked through underwear that hung on crooked clotheslines. He stood at the window of the pie car, watching men drop quarters from their wages into a slot machine with one broken reel. He washed himself under a spigot in the open-air showers and helped Nepenthe into the costume they had her wear, a ruffled iguana head that left her hair sweaty and limp, plastered to her scalp.

There were no children here. These performers got divorced, cashed their paycheques, talked about joining the army or quitting the sauce or going back to school. They visited the doctor, an old man who'd once botched a nose job and now worked out of a seedy bunk with a 1958 calendar on the wall and a trash can full of bloody gauze; they went to the funeral for the guy from the motorcycle cage, who'd died not from a burst tire but from diabetes. Even on sunny days, walking around this circus gave Webern the feeling of being inside a thin grey cloud.

When he saw Vlad and Fydor, or Eng, as he seldom did those days, a look passed between them that was the opposite of recognition, as though whatever they'd endured together was rapidly being erased. Vlad and Fydor were big stars in the Parliament, glamorous and removed; they wore a sequined jumpsuit with a red lightning bolt that zigzagged between them and rarely spoke in English, or to anyone besides each other. A few months later, when a talent agent from Hollywood cast them in a Red Menace episode called "Sideshow Spies," no one was surprised that they never came back. As for Eng, he disappeared into his new troupe of contortionists, who formed M. C. Escher patterns with their bodies on brightly coloured gym mats during slow points in the show.

Webern didn't start working right away. He needed time to think. He felt like he was searching, but he didn't know for what. When Nepenthe was performing, he wandered all over, from the gilded gates at the midway's entrance to the Parliament barker's tilted stage, from the Laff House corridors, all glass and tinted mirrors, to the bales of hay in the elephant corral. He lingered in Clown Alley, where the jokers all bunked together, and strained to eavesdrop on plans for acts, rehearsal strategies, but usually he only overheard pinochle games and the occasional dirty joke.

It was as though the barrier between reality and dreams, breached during his illness, could never fully be restored. Webern passed from the real circus to the dreamed one by hopping a ditch of mud and sugar water, or by sidestepping a barrel of trash, or by walking from the back of the dart toss, where the game operator's wife lounged on a three-legged lawn chair with her swollen feet in a bucket, to the dazzling neon bull's eye at the booth's front.

Sometimes he even stopped at the boxcar where Brunhilde had hanged herself, looking for something—a clue, maybe, as to what had gone wrong. She'd ended it in a supply car, loaded with barrels and splintery crates, a real mess; it seemed like nothing of her fastidious self could remain in there. The rope, the suitcase she'd kicked out from under her, the note she'd left crumpled on the ground: it had all gone out with the trash long before he'd come looking. But one afternoon, amid the abandoned cellophane wrappers and uncooked spaghetti noodles, Webern finally saw something she'd left behind—a golden strand, glinting on the dusty floor. He stooped to pick it up, and the minute he did, he realized what it was: the locket Brunhilde never took off. The clasp was broken, and he spent a minute fiddling with it. Then he opened the locket itself.

Inside was a family portrait. The man wore a pince-nez very like the one Brunhilde had carried in her pocket, and the woman wore her blonde hair short and oiled like a man's. The little girl was lovely, perhaps twelve years old and wearing a pinafore; her only surprising feature was a pale Van Dyke beard, pointed sharply from her chin. Webern thought of the Dresden suitcase, all those images of destruction. Yet this was the picture Brunhilde had worn over her heart. Perhaps Brunhilde hadn't been as hard-bitten, as realistic as she seemed. Perhaps it was the memory of this shimmering moment, rather than of everything that came after, that had haunted her the most.

The first day of Webern's new job, his boss handed him an axe and directed him to the dead horse in front of the tiger cages. The second day, he handed Webern a shovel.

PART TWO

LITTLE
FALLS

1967

CHAPTER FOURTEEN

WEBERN WAS PRETTY STONED, but not stoned enough to start fooling around with Venus de Milo, so when she started licking the banana cream pie off his face, he had no choice but to push her away. It was tougher than he expected, especially since she had him backed up against the sofa. He had to tear some spangles off the neckline of her costume before he finally got free. "Jesus Christ," he mumbled to himself. He wiped pie from around his eyes and groped around on the floor for his glasses.

It was just like Venus to pounce on him, especially after her third flagon of homemade jam jar wine. She treated lovemaking like it was tackle football, or at least it seemed that way to Webern— he didn't know from personal experience, thank God. Venus was an angular, fast-talking girl, forever tapping her foot or cracking her gum, and if she had arms they would have been perpetually crossed in impatience. She spoke with a frank Brooklyn accent about menstruation and female ejaculation, even in Webern's presence, since she considered him "practically a broad himself," and, with pounds of blue-black hair in a lacquered, tornado-shaped bouffant, she looked nothing like the placid statue she imitated as the Armless Wonder in the Parliament of Freaks. In his more annoyed moments, Webern thought that Venus de Milo might have been better off in secretarial school, even if she did have to sit with her feet up on the typewriter. It was beyond him why she and Nepenthe spent so much time together.

"What's the trouble, shortcake?" she asked him now. With a deft motion of her left foot, she pulled off her rhinestoned cat's-eye glasses and touched the earpiece to her lips mischievously. "Don't want to cheat on your girl?"

Webern sat up. He was lying on the floor of his cabin, half a train car he and Nepenthe shared back toward the caboose. He'd done pretty well for himself the past few years, and the place almost looked like a home, with the little bed covered in a Mexican blanket and a scarred grey desk made of indestructible metal. Nepenthe had taken to growing rock candy in an aquarium on the windowsill, and he looked through the crystals into the dark night. The floor vibrated slightly. He pictured the railroad ties passing beneath them, but the thought just nauseated him.

"That's right," he said, cleaning his face on his T-shirt. He thought of pulling it off and tossing it in the direction of the laundry basket, but Venus might take that as further encouragement. "'Til death do us part."

"What did I miss?" Nepenthe stood swaying in the open doorway. She wore a tiger mask and held a plate of cold bacon—probably the only thing she could dig up from the cookhouse this time of night. "You two carrying on your torrid affair?"

Venus swiped a dot of banana from her nose with one big toe. "Men, who needs 'em? I'm through."

Webern rolled his eyes. Even if she hadn't just jumped on him, he wouldn't believe it for a second. Venus was forever railing about men—it was always plural, even though she usually just meant Zeus Masters, the company strongman. Sometimes she offered Webern the backhanded addendum, "Present company excluded."

"Um-hmm." Nepenthe discarded her mask. Her face was hot, the scales glistening. She crunched on a piece of fatback.

"Lemme have some." In addition to the two jays he'd shared with Nepenthe, Webern had drunk a few beers at a bull session with the other clowns after tonight's performance; now, he stumbled to his feet. Nepenthe grabbed him by the hump and guided him to the sofa.

"To the conquering hero," she said. She raised a piece of bacon as if making a toast. Webern opened his mouth, but she bit into it herself. "Oh, God, this is good."

Tonight's festivities celebrated Webern's most original show yet. Dressed in a suit of tinfoil and pie plates, his skin painted an unearthly green, he'd descended on invisible ropes and spent the better part of fifteen minutes inspecting common "Earthling" wares as an alien might. He'd washed his face in a can of paint, greeted a fire hydrant as he would a living creature (even extending his hand for it to shake), and hungrily stuffed his mouth full of marbles before spitting them out—*ptooee! ptooee!*—machine-gun fast in the direction of the ducking, shrieking audience. Most of the other clowns weren't sure what to make of it yet—the idea still seemed a little conceptual to them, and they weren't sure the younger kids would catch on—but Webern felt certain they'd come around in time. Punchy Joe and Silly Billy had already come up to Webern after the performance and agreed to play "Earthlings" in the next act, and after they signed on to a project the others were sure to follow.

"You'll be the first clown on the fucking moon." Nepenthe lit a clove. She still rolled them in green paper but now they shared space in her cigarette case with the yellow joints she nicknamed "banana sticks."

"That's right. I'm a tin man superhero." Webern chewed on a piece of bacon. He could feel the individual grains of salt like constellations on his tongue. "Think I'll get a raise?"

"He's a card, hon," said Venus, stretching, cat-like, onto the rug. She scratched one knee with the other. "He's goin' places. Better hold onto him."

Nepenthe leaned over her portable record player.

"Oh, please don't." Webern pressed his hands to his ears until he heard the underwater roar of the inside of his head. "Can't we listen to something fun for once?"

Every night for the last week, Nepenthe had played her new Galactic Vibrations album, which Webern detested, especially when he was stoned. Their long spiraling guitar solos reminded him of the endless flights of stairs he had to go up and down all through elementary school, slowed by his stunted legs and twisted back. He preferred his old Spike Jones records; those songs, full of gunshots, slide whistles, and breaking glass, turned into cartoons the moment they burst into his ears. But Nepenthe loved the Vibrations, or at least considered them "important."

"There's a war on, kiddo," she said now. She turned up the volume, then shouted over it, "You can't just laugh your life away."

"I'd rather die from laughing than from boredom."

Nepenthe pointed to her ear, to indicate she couldn't hear him, then yelled, "Everything's political, when you come down to it."

Webern braced himself against the dull music. He'd told Nepenthe before that they would probably draft the Jolly Green Giant before they touched him, but to her that was beside the point. Not knowing any able-bodied young men could hardly stop her from worrying about them. Sometimes she made Webern a little jealous, scratching away at letters to her Congressman (how did she even know which one to write to? She lived on a train, for Chrissake) or tie-dyeing her veils in buckets on the floor while he lay in bed, naked and waiting for her to join him.

One night, as she slouched against the pillows, eyelids low, high and drowsy and picking at her scales, she told him that she had dreamt of a young draftee throwing himself onto a grenade for her, and after that she felt indebted to help stop the war. Webern didn't know how to respond. It was a lot to compete with, especially since his own body was already broken. After she fell asleep, he lay beside her, imagining himself in another body with muscles and tattoos, or a college education and a decent haircut, or even as a rage-faced, pony-tailed amputee—with a hollow pant-leg, sure, but with large square shoulders and a chiseled jaw. These were the guys from the news, ducking explosions or soberly arguing that after what they'd seen "over there," the draft should stop at once, and watching them Webern felt confused, not knowing whether he was lucky not to be with them or jealous that he couldn't be.

The soldier in Nepenthe's dream continued to bother Webern until, sleepless, he finally consoled himself in the cruelest way he knew how. He pulled back the sheet and looked down at the grey-white shell of Nepenthe's skin, and as the scales rose and fell with the rhythm of her breathing, he reminded himself that the soldiers would never choose her. Even men who saw death overseas wanted pretty girls when they came back home. As soon as Webern let himself think it, though, the spiteful thought boomeranged right back. Was that why she'd stayed with him all these years? Because she couldn't get anybody else?

Now, Webern pressed the sole of his sneaker into the soft flesh between Venus de Milo's shoulder blades, until she rolled over onto her back and gave him a wicked grin. Her body was a perfect hourglass, without any elbows to interrupt it. Nepenthe wasn't paying any attention, though; her eyes, half-shut, looked faraway as she grooved to the Vibrations' strains. Would it kill her to act a little jealous? Webern looked down at Venus's feet. Her toes were painted with images of tiny monarch butterflies, and it occurred to him that she'd probably always longed for a manicure. In another life, she would have had talony, clacking nails and rings on several fingers. Somehow this thought made him very sad.

"Listen, listen," Nepenthe whispered, although the record was turned up so loud they didn't have much choice. "This is the best part."

"He lives in a flat
In a flat little town
He thinks he's a king
But he ain't got a crown
He thinks he can sing
But he don't make a sound
Ohh
He's Eustace Ordinary . . ."

"I've never met a single person named Eustace in my entire life," Webern protested. "If he's so ordinary, shouldn't he be named 'Bill' or something?" He wished that Nepenthe would turn off the record and kick Venus de Milo out. This whole scene was getting him down.

"Jesus God, Bernie, it's a metaphor. Eustace stands in for all the normal people. You know, the squares."

"I don't think anybody is normal. Not Eustace, anyway. Even his name is weird. Eustace. Eustace." The more he repeated it, the funnier it sounded. "Eustace Eustace Eustace. They at least should have named him Eustace Useless."

"You're missing the point."

But now he was cracking himself up: "Eustace Gooseless. Eustace Moosejuice. Eustace Moontooth. Eustace Loomfruits."

Nepenthe rolled her eyes and tucked her feet up underneath her. "Someday you're going to realize there's more to life than making fun of everything you don't understand."

"Aww, it's good for a guy to have a sense of humour," Venus offered. "Especially if he's funny-looking."

Webern didn't dignify that with a response. Instead he lost himself, as he often did at such times, in daydreamy contemplation. Nepenthe was wearing her ancient pink bathrobe, which had fallen open at the neck to reveal a triangular wedge of grey scales. Webern thought of her body, its strange comforts, the way her skin had a crust like the Earth's. Then, as he continued to stare at her, a disorienting transformation took place: the pink robe became his grandmother's burgundy smoking jacket, dark plaid and open at the throat, revealing the high, wrinkled neck of a Mother Goose nightgown. He'd barely thought of Bo-Bo in ages—he'd stopped writing her postcards years ago—and later, he would take the sudden, vivid recollection of her as a premonition of what was to come.

The first day he performed in the clown troupe—at long last, and as an alternate—Webern had nearly come to blows with a swarthy dwarf, who claimed that Webern had "stolen his face." What he meant was that Webern's mask of greasepaint and eyebrow pencil too closely resembled his own. But his words echoed in Webern's head still. This grand new show could influence him, sure, but to steal someone else's face would be to lose his own, and he couldn't stand the thought of that. So he worked tirelessly to be original, even in the slightest practical details, and his relentlessly imaginative antics onstage had gained him a reputation as something of an eccentric.

Webern was one of the highest-paid clowns now, but though he'd won the respect of the others over the years, his intensity held them at a distance. He found himself missing Dr. Show more, not less, as the years went by, and sometimes he still woke up in the middle of the night bursting to tell his old mentor about his latest bright idea. For awhile, Webern had even started talking to the Great Vermicelli, an eerily lifelike ventriloquist's dummy he'd won in a card game with a fire eater—Vermicelli's eyes, glossy and button-black, brought to mind Dr. Show's, and hearing his own voice helped Webern put his thoughts in order, even if no one was listening. But when Nepenthe declared the puppet creepy and threatened to throw it off the train, Webern sighed and relegated the little doppelganger to a drawer.

Webern's job was stressful: one laughless night, one clumsy pratfall or poorly thought-out costume change could topple him from the position he'd worked so hard to reach. It didn't help that the circus was always changing around him, and usually in ways he didn't like. Barker & Smart had one of the last traditional big top circuses in the country; most of the other large outfits had switched to stadiums and arenas, and some of them had also stopped traveling by train, preferring the cheaper and less romantic semi-truck to house livestock, while the performers jostled along in trailers behind. Barker & Smart stuck to the old ways, but for commercial rather than nostalgic reasons—not much else set them apart from the likes of the Mulligan Bros.—and as a result, they were always cutting corners everywhere else. More than once, Webern had requested, say, the red VW, only to arrive under the tent and find a green go-cart in its place, accompanied by a grease monkey grunting something about transmissions. He hated having to scramble to adjust his act at the last minute. He sometimes found himself missing the time he'd spent with Dr. Schoenberg's circus, when he'd had no one to depend on for his routines but himself.

That night, after Venus de Milo finally sashayed back toward the cabin she shared with five other girls from the Parliament, Webern lay in bed with Nepenthe. He watched the lights of the little towns swim by their window. Heat lightning flickered in the June sky, brightening the storm clouds into enormous purple balloons. They were in Illinois, probably not too far from Dolphin River. In all his travels, he still hadn't been back since that evening, many years ago now, when his old ringmaster had first stepped out of the Cadillac under the streetlight, dressed all in black like a darker slice of night. That memory and the town were inseparable now. When Webern squeezed his eyes shut, Dr. Show's skin, always so immaculately pale, took on a greenish tint, as though Webern were seeing him through the bottom of a glass of chartreuse.

"Bernie? You still awake?" Nepenthe whispered from inside the spoon their bodies made.

"Yeah."

"You really did do a good job in the show tonight. I was watching."

"Really?" Since the Parliament of Freaks was on the midway, not under the big top, Nepenthe had to make a special trip to see Webern's act. Most of the time she just went home instead. More than once, he'd hurried back with his makeup still on to find her already asleep on the couch, a satirical limerick about Robert McNamara half-finished and forgotten in her lap.

"Uh-huh. I liked it. That thing you've been practicing? Using the fork as a backscratcher? You did it exactly right."

"Oh. Thanks." Webern didn't know quite what to say. He felt obscurely embarrassed, as if somehow he should have known she was there. He imagined Nepenthe lurking in the shadows, the child's tiger mask covering her face, as he dunked his hands in pink paint up to the elbows and stuck marshmallows in his ears. He kissed the back of her neck. The dry scales smoothed under his tongue.

"Venus attacked me tonight," he told her. "But don't worry, I resisted."

"Really?"

"Yeah. Right after I showed her the pie routine. How can you stand having her around? She's such a floozy."

"I trust you. Besides, everyone's got a fetish." Nepenthe rolled over to face him and rubbed her knuckles against his hump. "Guess what mine is?"

If Webern had gotten more focused and intense over the years, Nepenthe had softened; she went without her gloves and veil inside the Parliament tent even between shows, and cried more easily—a movie, a song, a hangnail could set her off. But Webern couldn't tell if she'd gotten more used to her life as a freak, or started to despair because of it. There were some things they still didn't talk about.

Some mornings, Webern woke up to the sound of her hiccupping into a tissue, but when he tried to rub her shoulders, she just turned away and pressed an ice pack to her brow. She was always hot, too hot, but she didn't bother with the kiddy pool anymore. She didn't bother with much of anything that might make her feel better, unless she could light it or drink it. It hurt Webern that he couldn't console her. In the months after Dr. Show's death, Webern had wanted her to hold him all the time, to crush the sadness out of him if she had to. But Nepenthe wasn't mourning someone, and she didn't want comfort. So, as much as he hated it, Webern had grown used to listening to her cry.

The morning after he performed the Martian routine, though, Webern woke up to utter silence and stillness in the boxcar room. With an unpleasant lurch, he realized he hadn't dreamt. He tried to cling to any strands of fantasy still cobwebbing his head, but it was too late. If they had been there at all, they were gone now.

Webern carefully climbed over Nepenthe and out of the bed. He hated nights when he didn't dream, and they happened much more than they used to. It scared him a little, going through life without dreams would be like being dead half the time. And onstage he would be just as dull as Happy Herbert, whose entire oeuvre consisted of sticking a whoopee cushion down the back of his pants.

Webern went to his trunk, swung back the lid, and pulled out a pair of fresh boxer shorts, then went over to the couch, where he found his eyeglasses jammed between two cushions. They were smudged and sticky from the pie. He put them on and scratched his hump thoughtfully. He noticed the train had stopped moving; outside, wagons clattered, and farther away canvasmen cursed at each other as they raised the big top. That meant it was probably after nine o'clock, maybe later. By now all the good donuts would be gone from the cookhouse.

As Webern stood there in his boxers, idly wondering if he should bother getting dressed before suiting up for the one o'clock rehearsal, he heard an unfamiliar sound: a knock, one-two-three, on the outside door of his cabin. No one ever came by performers' rooms this early, and a chill of nervousness shivered through him. Maybe the Martian act hadn't gone as well as he thought—it had been a little far out, to use a favourite phrase of Nepenthe's. He imagined a tough-looking messenger standing on the doorstep, holding a pink slip. Or maybe it was just a bunch of the other clowns, sent over to pie him into submission.

"Um—just a minute," Webern called, hurrying back over to his trunk for a T-shirt. Pulling it on, he gave the room a quick once-over. Nepenthe stirred in bed; one naked thigh slithered over the blankets. An empty baking tin, surrounded by creamy splatters, half-hid under the couch. An ashtray shaped like a sombrero balanced precariously on a stack of Nepenthe's LPs, its ceramic hat-brim crowded with green and yellow butts. An overturned jam-jar lay in a dried purple-brown puddle, and a box of Napoleons lay open between two wide-toed, red patent leather squeaker shoes. The knock came again: one-two-three. Hesitantly, Webern went over to the door. Housekeeping didn't matter much anyway. It wasn't likely to be a health inspector.

Webern unlatched the door and opened it. The man stood there in the sunlight, blinking. In his grey, worn suit and fedora, he looked for a moment like a Fuller Brush salesman, or an agent from an insurance company, but he didn't offer his hand for Webern to shake. His face looked ruddy and ill-used, and his nose massed with split capillaries, nearly as red as a clown's. Webern couldn't speak at first, and when he finally did, the one word he croaked out seemed nearly false to his still disbelieving ears.

CHAPTER FIFTEEN

WEBERN'S FATHER WAS SIX FEET TALL, with large watery eyes and a cardboard briefcase. His crew cut sparkled silver; his skin was so red it looked boiled. Webern had almost forgotten the stiff, slow way he moved, the strange whistling sighs his breath made. The old man dolefully removed a Porky Pig Pez dispenser from the cushion of the sofa, then sat down and turned the plastic device over in his hands, snapping it open and shut. His motions were deliberate and methodical, but perfectly inconsequential. He looked like an extra in one of the clown acts, doing stage business in the background that no one would remember.

Nepenthe bustled around the train car, the tie of her bathrobe cinched tight around her waist, and Webern watched his father's eyes follow her as she moved to and fro. She dropped the pie plate, flecks of bacon, and the contents of ashtrays into a greasy brown paper bag, then picked up a can of soda from the floor and popped the tab. It exploded in her face.

"God fucking damnit!" she screamed. Irritated, she violently scratched her arms, then raked more hair down over her eyes. Webern's father folded his large rough hands and gazed up at the ceiling. Between his shoes and pant cuff, threadbare socks showed.

"Your great uncle was in a wild west show," he said. "He died on a wagon train. I guess it's time you knew, you have Cherokee blood. Or maybe Italian."

Webern stared at the old man, who slumped on the couch like his back was crooked too, and a memory returned to him, of the weeks after his parents' car accident, when his father still limped slightly from an injury he'd sustained. People had taken their flaws for a family resemblance, when in fact it was only bad luck, separate, undeserved, and excruciating. That was when Webern first realized he didn't want to be mistaken for a smaller version of his father. He handed the old man a cup of coffee and sat down on a pillow on the floor. The rug stretched out between them. This was as far away as he could get.

"Is there anything I can get you, Mr. Bell?" Nepenthe yelled, using a blow-dryer to blast splashed Moxie from the curtains. As the liquid dried, pale, continent-shaped stains remained.

"You can call me Raymond!" his father shouted back.

"Ray Gun?"

"No, Raymond!"

"What?"

"RAYMOND!" his father yelled just as Nepenthe switched off the blow-dryer. His roar hung in the air for a moment before he coughed and returned his gaze to the ceiling.

"You can't be very comfortable down there," he finally said to Webern. He made his first darting pass at eye contact.

"Did you come all the way here just to tell me about Sitting Bull?" asked Webern. His voice sounded angrier than he expected.

Raymond took off his hat and handled it gently—flexed the brim. "Ha." He changed his tack: "It's been too long, son, too long."

"Yeah, well, I've been busy."

Raymond glanced around. His eyes lingered on an empty bottle of rum, adorned with a wreath of Silly String. "I can see that."

If the old man was trying to make him feel guilty, it wasn't going to work. Webern remembered more than one occasion after his mother's death when Willow and Billow had disappeared for days at a time, and their absence had neither cheered nor disheartened Raymond, whose sports games had continued to echo uninterrupted from a living room stinking of gin.

"So, why did you come find me now?" Webern asked. He emphasized the last word a little.

"Well, it's like this, son," said Raymond. He squeezed his fedora between his palms. "Your grandma Bo-Bo is failing."

"Failing? She's sick?"

"I'd say it's worse than that."

Nepenthe, who had been streaking the train car's window with a damp blackboard eraser, stopped to look over her shoulder for Webern's reaction. Webern stared down at his knee, pudgy and misshapen, half-covered by the hem of his boxer shorts. An image of Bo-Bo, not half so vivid as the previous night's, hovered before him, and he saw her pipe—her eye patch—her monkey—in a quick impressionistic swirl. Then, just as quickly, she was gone.

Webern had lived with Bo-Bo for some months after his mother's death, but though he had come to rely on their daily chess games and the comforting taste of the raccoon meat she roasted each night, the time they had spent together blurred in his memory. No one image stayed seared in his mind the way his mother's every gesture seemed to, even though Bo-Bo was still alive. Alive—but failing. He hadn't seen her for almost six years.

"I don't understand," he said now. "What's going on?"

"Well, we're none of us getting any younger, son."

"I know that, I'm not an idiot." Webern was trying to get his father on a technicality. "But did you talk to the doctor?"

"He says it doesn't look good. And your Bo-Bo, well, she more or less asked me to take you to her. So, when I saw this—" Raymond pulled a folded poster from his jacket pocket and smoothed out the creases with his hand. Webern recognized it immediately. In the picture, an artist's rendering, a hunchbacked clown waved a red cloth at a charging rhino. The clown's face, a wide-eyed caricature of terror, bore little resemblance to Webern's, and the hump was on the wrong side, a fact he still registered with annoyance. His one poster, and they'd done it all wrong.

"When I saw this, I knew it was you," Raymond continued. He tapped a finger triumphantly on the hump. "I said to your Bo-Bo, I'll bring him to you."

"Bring me there? But Dad—" Webern struggled to lower his voice below squeaking range. "Dad, I can't just leave my job."

Sometimes, the old man still had the bewildered, wide-eyed gaze of a boy. He blinked at Webern, then shook his head slowly. "She'll be very disappointed to hear that. You know, when your mother died, your Bo-Bo didn't have a thought for herself. Bring him here, she said. I'll take care of him."

It hadn't gone like that at all. Little Webern, hovering near a doorway in his pyjamas, had overhead that conversation. He had been eight, but even now he could still play back every cadence in his mind. Raymond had blamed Webern for his grief and drinking, saying, "He's like a weight on me" over and over until Bo-Bo finally replied, in her deliberate, gravelly voice, "If that's how you really feel, you never should have had a son." Now, when he spoke, Webern tried to keep his voice as even and rational as hers had been.

"It's the middle of the season. You wouldn't have seen my picture on that poster if they didn't need me for the show. Now maybe in a few weeks—" Webern glanced over at Nepenthe for help, but she still stood at the window with her back to him. She'd stopped cleaning. Webern tried to imagine how he must sound: like a prima donna, probably, putting his act before an old lady's dying wish. *The show can't go on without me.* As if that were true. He hated himself. He hated everyone: Bo-Bo, his father, Nepenthe, the circus. He looked back up at Raymond. It was funny how normal it was to see him, even after all these years—how nothing had really changed.

"Okay," said Webern. "Okay. I'll try to figure something out."

By the time Webern left his train car, the hired hands had already spread the canvas and unloaded most of the animals. Since Nepenthe was a freak, they didn't live in Clown Alley, and it was a bit of a trek down the length of the train to the cars where the other clowns—mostly single, all of them men—bunked together and rehearsed. As he walked, Webern sidestepped the burly men hefting trunks and the nefarious claws of the big cats, which swiped through the bars of the occasional unattended cage. He nodded toward Jerry, the Wild Man of the Congo, who touched the bone stuck through his nose in salute before returning to his mystery novel, and Celine, a long-legged tightrope walker who did not return his greeting. This was the time of the day Webern disliked the most—all hubbub and disaster—and he was glad when he reached a cabin that he thought of as Clown HQ, knocked on the door, and let himself inside.

Four of his fellow players were already there: Silly Billy, the unofficial head of the troupe, a lanky bald guy with a rubber face and a knack for tumbling; Professor Shim Sham, who wore his trademark white lab coat even now, over a wifebeater and a pair of pyjama pants; Pipsqueak, an irritating kid who'd joined the company three weeks earlier and constantly talked about his aspirations for "serious acting;" and Happy Herbert, the crudest clown that Webern knew, and the only other little person in the troupe. Webern hated it when people confused them. Webern's clown name was Bump Chuckles.

"Heya, Bump," Silly Billy said now, peering over the tops of the little half-glasses he wore offstage. From the look of the room, the clowns had had a late night, too. Several empty wine bottles lay beside the lower bunk, and the four men sat at a table littered with empty glasses and playing cards still sticky with fermented juice. "You look spic and span. What's the occasion?"

Webern pulled up a chair. He was wearing his clean jeans and a collared shirt he'd begged off a girl from wardrobe.

"Listen, I need some time off the show."

Pipsqueak whistled, a confused bird twitter. Professor Shim Sham raised his woolly eyebrows.

"You get the gator girl knocked up or something?" Happy Herbert asked.

"Nothing like that," Webern said. He picked up a joker from the table and turned it in his hands. Two laughing faces mirrored each other across a divide, one right side up, one upside down. "My grandma's dying, I guess."

"How soon you have to leave?" asked Silly Billy.

"Soon as possible. Today."

"And how long till you'll be back?"

"Not long, it doesn't sound like." Webern wiped his glasses on his shirt. "A week, tops. Not even. I could probably meet you guys in Little Falls. You think anybody in management'll notice if I'm gone?"

"Notice?" Pipsqueak asked. "Jeez, Bump, you're the whole show."

"Kid, you're forgetting. Management never *watches* the show. We could go out there, high on glue and dressed as ladies, they'd never know the difference. As long as they sell their peanuts, they're happy." Silly Billy cleaned his nails with a penknife, then gestured at Webern with the blade. "Tell you what. We'll cover for you in the acts. If payroll comes around asking, we'll tell them you're sick, but my guess is they won't."

"You sure?"

"Don't worry about it." Silly Billy nodded across the table. "We'll put Herb in your spot."

"That's right. Huh huh." Happy Herbert's laugh sounded like rusty plumbing; even before makeup, his lips were fat and red. "Nobody'll even miss you."

Webern wanted to smack him. Too bad he wouldn't be around to do it in the show tonight.

"All right," Webern said finally. "See you in Iowa, then."

When Webern came back to the boxcar, he found Nepenthe lying on the bed, reading the back of a record sleeve. On the cover, a suburban house blasted off into the night sky.

"So you talked to the guys?" she asked. "You're definitely going?"

"Uh-huh."

"I hope you have a good time. Without me."

"It's not exactly a pleasure trip. You heard my dad. She's dying."

"Supposedly."

"Are you *mad* at me?"

"Nah." She hid her hands in her robe sleeves. "I don't know what I'm worried about. I just feel like something terrible's going to happen if you leave."

"It's not like I want to go."

"But you will."

"You would, too." Webern went over and sat down on the bed. "I'll be back before you know it."

Nepenthe reached into the windowsill aquarium and broke off a piece of rock candy. She folded Webern's hand around it.

"To remember me by," she said.

Webern looked at the green crystals. He and Nepenthe had never been apart for more than a day before. Being with her now was almost like old times, when they were first together—he filled up with sad, sweet longing, knowing they wouldn't sleep in the same bed that night.

"I'll be finished with it by the time we're out of the parking lot."

"Guess that shows what you think about me."

Webern set the rock candy on a stack of LPs, then rolled Nepenthe over on her back and untied her robe. He scratched the scales on her belly the way she liked him to, until thin grey moons of her dry skin started forming under his nails.

"Shh, what are you doing," Nepenthe whispered. "Your dad's prowling around outside."

"He's in the car." Webern climbed on top of her. Nepenthe turned her head to one side, and he kissed the crackles in her neck. "I'm going to miss you."

"Yeah, right. You're going to take one look at all those normal girls and never come back."

"I don't want a normal girl. I want you."

"Jerk." Nepenthe grabbed him around the waist and easily pinned him down onto the mattress. Webern laughed and squirmed beneath her. "You little shit. Take it back."

"What was I supposed to say?" Webern protested. He tried to slap her hands away as she tickled him. He could hardly breathe. "C'mon, what was I supposed to say?"

"Not that."

"But it's true."

Afterwards, Webern picked up his rock candy and gathered a handful of spilled pocket change from the floor. He felt woozy and wished he'd had a decent night's sleep. If he didn't keep moving he'd pass out. Fortunately, he didn't need to bring much of anything along: when he'd run away to join the circus, he'd left most of his clothes at home, and before coming to get him his father had packed him a bag.

Webern cringed to think of what he'd find in there: cardigan sweaters, no doubt, penny loafers, and pale pink collared shirts— probably even his old pyjamas, with tiny images of Roy Rogers printed all over them in patterns. But these clothes would be in better shape than the ratty jeans and armpit-stained T-shirts he wore in his off-time, and it wasn't like Nepenthe would be around to laugh at him and call him a square.

Just before he got into his father's car, she kissed the top of his head, and he hung on to the sleeves of her pink bathrobe for a moment after she released him, trying to take in the texture of her skin, her musty smell, her warm and quick-beating pulse.

"What'll you do when I'm gone?" he asked.

"Don't worry about me, kiddo." She ran a hand over his forehead, then smoothed her veil of hair into place. "Catch you later." She disappeared back inside the boxcar before they drove away.

Webern's father had just gotten a new car, a Chrysler, and Webern spent the first few minutes of the trip feigning interest in the array of dials and knobs that lined the space-age dashboard.

"That's nothing," said Raymond. "Watch this." He pressed a button, and he and Webern both watched the passenger side window roll down.

"Pretty neat." Webern licked his rock candy. He didn't really want to keep eating it, but there was nowhere to put it down—he was surrounded by supple leather upholstery.

Webern's father cleared his throat. "You and her . . . quite a pair."

Where had his father learned to make conversation? Neptune? Rows of corn scrolled past the car windows. Webern's head ached. He needed a cup of coffee soon.

"Yep. We've been together a few years now."

"Does she—work—too?"

"Uh-huh."

"Work like you do?"

"Not quite."

Raymond set his jaw. He squinted at the windshield, which was flecked with tiny dead bugs.

"I don't believe in a woman working outside the home."

"Mmm-hmm."

"But if she has a sort of—talent—I guess she shouldn't waste it."

"I guess not."

"God gives us all our gifts."

"Yeah."

"And it's good to save up. God knows insurance doesn't cover everything."

"Right."

"Some people can't be insured. They're uninsurable."

"That's true."

"You meet her parents yet?"

"Nope."

"It's good to meet a girl's parents. You see how your kids turn out."

"Sure."

"Say the girl's red-haired, but her parents are blonde. Well, there's a blonde baby for you. But if her *parents* are red-haired too—"

"Uh-huh."

"So, why haven't you gone out to meet them?"

"I don't know, Dad, because they netted her in a swamp and sold her to the freak show?"

Raymond didn't say anything. After a moment, he rolled the window back up.

Over the years, Webern had gotten used to the rumbling, halting progress of the train; he hadn't been in a car since leaving Schoenberg's circus, and now it affected him strangely. He wasn't used to seeing the world rushing towards him through the huge clean pane of a windshield. It was like falling forward at a tremendous speed. He could only look for so long before he switched on the radio. A call-in show came on, and Webern found himself listening to a local woman arguing that the "snoot-nosey" draft boards shouldn't "favouritism" college students, but should put them in the front lines for causing all the trouble. It would have sent Nepenthe through the roof, but after a few minutes it started to wear on him, too.

"Is it okay if we listen to some music?" he asked. Raymond shrugged.

Webern flipped through the stations until he found something innocuous and swingy; no reason to start another argument about rock music he didn't even like. Just as he started to relax, though, a terrible thought occurred to him.

"Willow and Billow aren't going to be there, are they? At Bo-Bo's?"

"I wish you wouldn't call them that."

"That's what they call themselves."

"When they were kids, maybe." Raymond shook his head. "Bernie, you know Wanda and Betsy left home years before you did. Your Bo-Bo and me, I guess you could say we're all alone in this world."

"You haven't heard from them at all?"

Raymond sighed. "Well, now that you mention it, they did stop by the house not too long ago. Apparently they've made quite a name for themselves with their dog catching. I never could understand them much, the way they talk, but from what I gathered they were curious about you."

"What? You didn't tell them where I was, did you?"

"Nah. I was tracking you down myself, then."

"I can't believe you saw them. Do they really have jobs? Where do they live?"

Raymond gave him a sidelong glance. "You starting to miss your sisters all of a sudden? From what I remember, you used to lock yourself up in closets to get away from them."

"That's because they threw dead turtles on me when I was in a body cast."

"It's a sad thing, when a man's children don't get along."

"I wouldn't have even *been* in a body cast if it wasn't for them."

"Now, I won't have that. Your sisters aren't perfect, but you can't keep blaming them for everything that goes wrong. You had an accident. People do." Raymond lowered the sun visor. "One of these days they'll be the only family you've got left."

Webern leaned back and shut his eyes. He could see them, even now: Willow and Billow with their halos of smudgy dark, their fingers moving like spiders, like wind, like the scratching, grasping branches of malevolent trees, and always toward his throat.

A long time after he pretended to fall asleep, he actually began to doze. Images from Bo-Bo's house flitted through his mind: pearly teeth smiling in a jelly jar, a bathtub with claws, radiators that leaned against the walls like skinny dogs with all their ribs showing. Going back there would be like opening an old picture book he hadn't seen since childhood. Only it would be stranger, because he wouldn't be able to shut it again so easily.

Raymond decided they would stop for lunch at a place called the Buzzard's Den, and as Webern looked at the menu, he found himself wondering if his father was nostalgic for the subtle flavours of Bo-Bo's cooking. Raccoon was conspicuously absent, but quail, frog, and hare dotted the list, along with the mysteriously named "Meat Stew."

"Guess they're getting easier to catch. Wild animals." Raymond took off his fedora and set it on the table. Beneath it, his scalp shone; an isolated wad of hair squashed down in the front. Almost unconsciously, Webern ran a protective hand over his own short mop. "Lot of construction round here lately. Driving them out of their nests."

"That's a shame." Webern decided to get a burger and shut his menu. He was still a little queasy. Maybe he'd feel better with some food in his stomach.

"Nah. I remember when this was all fields. Flat as a pool table, boring as hell."

Webern thought back to the Dolphin River of his childhood. He'd hated a lot about it, but it sure was easy practicing his unicycle on the flat, wide sidewalks.

"That sounds about right," he said. He read the back of the mustard bottle, then looked at his menu again.

After a few minutes, the waitress came by and took their orders. When she left, Raymond made a great show of unfolding his napkin and setting it in his lap. His hands shook a little. Webern wondered if he'd had a drink yet today.

"Do you think we'll make it to Bo-Bo's tonight?" The waitress put Webern's coffee down in front of him, and he took it gratefully. The mug felt warm and secure, heavy in the familiar way diner mugs always did.

"Oh, I'd say so. We got a pretty early start. We'll probably get up there just after dark sometime."

Webern nodded, gulping his coffee. The car trips to Bo-Bo's had always seemed epic when he was a child, but she was only about five hours north of Dolphin River. Compared to all the travelling he did now, that didn't seem like much.

"What exactly is wrong with Bo-Bo? Just so I can prepare myself."

"Well, if you were a little younger, I'd tell you her ticker's getting tired. But medically, it's more complicated than that."

"Okay."

"Your Bo-Bo liked her suet and her game meats, and a good pat of butter just like the rest of us. She stayed fit and trim, but I guess her veins got blocked up just the same. Including one in her heart. Now, here's the kicker. Where most people would have a heart attack, Bo-Bo grew a whole new vein."

"What?"

"It wraps around her heart, since the blood can't go straight through the middle. Wait, let me draw you a picture." Raymond grabbed a pile of napkins from a dispenser on the table and drew a shaky heart with one line passing through it and a second looped around the outside, like a noose. He tapped the second line. "See? Longer, but it still gets there. A scenic route."

Webern turned the napkin toward himself and studied it. His father always drew everything out—whenever he gave street directions, described new models of cars, or recounted the events of the latest baseball game, he had a pen in hand, and his dinnertime conversations with Webern's mother had come with their own booklets of illustrations. Images came easier to him than words. But even discounting the years they'd been apart, this was the first drawing he'd done for Webern in a long, long time. Webern folded the napkin in half and tucked it in his pocket. "So, what's the problem, then? If the blood's still getting through?"

"Because the new vein doesn't give the heart room to pump. It's squeezing the heart on every beat."

"Bo-Bo's heart is choking itself to death?"

"That's right."

"That doesn't make any sense."

"You're one to talk."

"What's that supposed to mean?"

Their food arrived. Raymond lifted his hands in a little gesture of surrender as the waitress plunked down his chicken-fried muskrat.

"You know a lot of people with . . . conditions. You've got a condition yourself. I remember, when your mother and I took you to the hospital, they'd never seen anything of the kind."

Webern ground his teeth. He thought of Dr. Show, his mother, Bo-Bo, even his little friend Wags. It was ridiculous: of all the people he'd loved in his life, his father was the one he got to keep.

"Bent up like a paper clip, but you could still wiggle your toes. Let's put him in a body cast. Okay."

This day was hell on earth. Maybe at dinner they'd rehash Mom's funeral. Webern bit into his hamburger. The inside was cool and raw as earthworms. His stomach turned.

"I'll be back." Webern threw his napkin on the table.

In the bathroom, Webern splashed cold water on his face and held onto the sink with both hands. For a second he squeezed so hard he felt like he might break the porcelain, and he thought of Zeus Masters, the strongman, bending barbells into figure eights above his head. Nepenthe and Venus were probably watching him practice right now, giggling and nudging each others' hips the way they did. The thought of that made him even madder, but not any stronger, and he finally let go of the sink. Maybe he could work this into a clown act sometime— the weak little harlequin trying to vent his rage—but he doubted it. He couldn't see much humour in the situation yet.

CHAPTER SIXTEEN

As THEY NEARED Bo-Bo's HOUSE, the landscape changed. It reminded Webern of the thorny, overgrown path to Sleeping Beauty's castle: wild rose bushes grew along the roads, their lavender blossoms shedding moth-eaten petals; the naked trunks of birch trees shone like tarnished silver; train tracks thudded beneath the car's wheels, and out of the corner of his eye, Webern saw the hulking shell of an abandoned luxury caboose.

Bo-Bo lived in Tarantula, Illinois. The town's name was pronounced "tare-ann-TOO-lah" by natives; until seeing the sign this trip Webern had never associated it with the venomous spider. Tarantula was a sleepy town, with thin soil the colour of eraser dust; what crops grew here were spindly and frail, propped up by trellises in old ladies' backyards.

Raymond turned the car onto Bo-Bo's street, a narrow lane paved with smooth stones like the bed of a river. He parked in the driveway, and as Webern got out, he saw the place was just as he remembered it. Bo-Bo's house, grown thick with ivy, sprang from a yard full of tall, seedy grasses and steel-jawed raccoon traps. As Webern followed his father up to the door, he was careful to stay on the path. Purple twilight gathered in the house's shadow. Maybe they should have called before showing up like this. Last time he checked, Bo-Bo was pretty trigger-happy with her shotgun.

Webern and his father scaled the uneven steps to Bo-Bo's front door. The porch, a shelf of limestone, glittered dully in the early evening; from its ceiling hung a wooden swing that could seat two on its wind-worn slats. Webern touched the seat and it began creaking back and forth on its chains.

Raymond cleared his throat and looked toward Webern as if he was about to speak. Then he lifted the iron knocker and let it fall. Both men heard the hollow knock echo into the house. After a long moment, a bolt scraped, and the door swung inward on its hinges. A greying chimp glared up at them, her long prehensile fingers still wrapped around the knob.

"Marzipan," said Webern. He could hardly believe she was still alive. He stepped forward to hug her, but she was too quick for him. She turned on her heel and swung on her knuckles into the dark house.

Outside the sky was purpling, but inside it might as well have been the dead of night. The living room was a cavern, with dark green curlicues seething on the wallpaper and a crystal light fixture dangling from the ceiling like a dripping stalactite. In one corner, Webern saw the grand piano, large and black. When he was a child, its curving, wing-shaped body comforted him—it was hunchbacked too, but, as Bo-Bo once explained, the lopsided frame gave its music particular loveliness. She used to play in the evenings, after her Scotch but before her pipe. Now the piano grinned to no one; its yellow teeth collected cobwebs in the gloom.

Marzipan left the living room and climbed the ancient stairs to the second floor. Beneath the faded red and gold carpet, boards groaned. Webern looked at the photographs that lined the walls as they passed. Some were daguerreotypes of people he'd never known: an angular woman in a tuxedo and top hat, a fleecy-bearded man standing with one arm around a cigar store Indian, a stout, stern baby wearing what appeared to be a wedding dress. When Webern had asked Bo-Bo about these characters, she'd only shook her head and replied, "That was long ago." But as they neared the top of the steps, Webern did recognize some of the faces he saw: first Bo-Bo, young and furious, with one bright eye and a second, even brighter, made of glass; then Raymond with Uncle Eddy, dressed in suits with shorts, each holding a wooden box and a butterfly net. A third photograph showed Bo-Bo with the boys on the porch's steps. In this picture, an additional figure had been razor-bladed out, leaving behind only the jagged shape of a man. Even when he was a child, Webern had known well enough not to ask Bo-Bo about this one.

In the upstairs hallway, it was almost too dark to see. Marzipan's fur brushed along the ancient wallpaper as they walked toward Bo-Bo's room. The cut glass doorknob turned in her rubbery hand.

Bo-Bo lay in bed, under comforters piled so thick that they hid the shape of her body. Only her head protruded. But even this was enough to reveal changes. Her hair, once tightly curled in a blue poodle cut, was now an azure wisp, and next to the black of her eye patch, her skin paled to the fragile white of old Bible pages. She was asleep, and as she dreamed her mouth moved soundlessly. On her nightstand, a set of teeth floated in a highball glass.

Marzipan stretched her lips into an exaggerated pucker and blew the loudest raspberry Webern had ever heard. Bo-Bo stirred. She slowly rose to her elbows. She squinted her one eye at Webern and Raymond. Then she drank the glass of water, teeth and all.

"Well, don't look so frightened, Bernie." Her face formed a new, more familiar shape around the teeth. "I'm not about to sit up and grab you."

Webern walked up to where she was lying and perched on the edge of the bed. Looking at her up close, he could see that her one eye had dimmed considerably. He thought of her antique rifles, the midnight target practice that always woke the neighbours. Bo-Bo, the crack shot, nearly blind.

Bo-Bo reached up and touched his face. Webern closed his eyes, and she touched his eyelids, too. It was like she was sculpting his face with her knotted hands. "Bo-Bo," Webern finally said, "I'm sorry I haven't come to visit."

"Don't start with an apology. That's worse than a weak handshake." She released his face, then reached behind herself to set up the pillows. "I'd ask what you've been doing with your life, but with young people these days, maybe I'd rather not know."

"I joined the circus. I'm a clown now."

"I danced the Charleston once, but I didn't make a career of it." Bo-Bo smiled. Her false teeth shone unnaturally; Webern had forgotten that some of the ones toward the back were silver. "A traveling show. That explains the postcards. What else?"

Webern tried to think. The circus nights swam in his memory. He thought of the way his boxcar looked through the bottom of bottles, Nepenthe's veils strewn all over the place. All the irritations and successes seemed too small to tell.

"I've got a girl," he said.

"I'm glad to hear it. Take care she doesn't break your heart."

Webern looked into her milky eye and saw a ghost of himself reflected there.

"I will."

Bo-Bo nodded. She leaned back in her bed. "Go away now and let me sleep. I just might join you for dinner."

When Webern was a boy, Bo-Bo dined at eleven, shot skeet at midnight, slept four hours and woke with the dawn. Once a week or so, if her traps stayed empty, she skipped the skeet and hunted the raccoons that lived under her house instead. If pickings were slim there, she ventured under the houses of her neighbours. Webern could still remember sneaking into the narrow dark of other people's crawl spaces, holding a shaky flashlight, and bursting into tears when Bo-Bo perforated a bristling 'coon, whose soft dark ears resembled his favourite teddy bear's. Later, in a rare show of tenderness, Bo-Bo rewarded him for his help with a freshly stitched Davy Crockett cap.

"It occurs to me that I've paid little mind to the interests of boys your age," she said, lifting the pelt from the newspapers she'd wrapped it in. "Now, I think it's foolish looking, myself, but the television tells me it's the latest craze."

Though Bo-Bo's neighbours had never pressed charges—Tarantula's raccoon problem had long since spiralled out of control, and they considered Bo-Bo an inexpensive, if noisy, extermination service— now that she was dying they showed her little regard. Since her illness began, she had received only one card, and it offered condolences rather than get-well wishes. It was on the living room mantelpiece when Webern went back downstairs to get his suitcases. "May God Bless You and Keep You," it read. Below the elegant script was a coloured pencil drawing of a well-tended grave.

Webern had just turned eight when his mother died. When his father sent him to stay at Bo-Bo's, she had put him in the room that his father and Uncle Eddy had shared as children. It was scary there at first, amid the dive-bombing balsa wood planes and the shadows of strangely sinister Noah's ark animals, but after a while it started to feel almost like home. Lying on the narrow twin bed closest to the window, Webern stayed up late carrying on long conversations with his tiny friend Wags, who, being only the size of a thumb, slept in the centre of the other bed's pillow, tucked inside a little blue sleeping bag made from a wool sock with a hole in it. Webern piled his Space Ace Grin McCase comic books on the nearly empty shelves, and, towards the end of his stay, even started putting his brightly coloured clothes away in the heavy wooden drawers that always stuck, unless he yanked hard enough to pull them free entirely. Now he went into the room again and slung his suitcase onto the bed. The springs gave a familiar groan under its weight.

Webern unbuttoned the shirt he'd taken from the circus's wardrobe that morning. He suspected it had been worn most recently by Raoul, whose death-defying house cats leapt and clawed the centre ring: Raoul was always dousing those white Persians in talcum powder, and the sickly sweet odour still clung to the shirt's cuffs and collar. Webern popped open the lid of the suitcase his father had brought for him from Dolphin River. It was loaded with things Webern thought he'd left behind when he ran away to join Schoenberg's circus. No wonder it was so heavy.

Webern had forgotten how he used to dress in high school. Just looking at the selection of his old favourites embarrassed him. Webern discarded a red cowboy shirt, with ten-gallon hats embroidered on its lapels, a sweater stitched with reindeer, and a pair of bright blue corduroys, before he finally put on a mint green dress shirt that he used to wear to church on Sundays. Until he took to the road, Webern let his mother's old taste in clothes guide him whenever he bought new ones; although it made him look even more freakish, it had comforted him to think that his colourful get-ups might bring a smile to her face if, by some miracle, she returned. Maybe that was part of the reason why clown costumes still appealed to him.

Beneath a pair of girlish overall shorts, a Hawaiian shirt, and a Jack-o-lantern orange cardigan sweater, Webern glimpsed something else in the bottom of the suitcase. He moved the clothes aside to look.

Inside a miniature model of a Bavarian chalet, two carved figures—a blond-haired girl and a soldier in a helmet with a little gold spike on top—balanced side by side on a tiny strip of wood. Webern took the device out of his suitcase and set it on his lap. The tiny girl drifted out of the house; the soldier stayed inside. Amazing; it still worked.

The weather house was the only souvenir his father had kept from the time he'd spent in Germany at the end of the war. When Webern was growing up, it sat on his father's chest of drawers, along with a pile of change and some gold cufflinks he never wore, collecting dust. On the few occasions when Webern had hoisted himself up on the bed to stare at the tiny carved people, his father had told him to keep his hands off it, until one day just a few months before Webern's accident. It was morning, before Webern's father left for work, and he was knotting his tie at a mirror that hung on the back of his closet door. Webern had come in to tell his father the pancakes were ready downstairs, but instead of leaving right away, he had climbed up on the bed to peer into the tiny German faces. His father saw him from the mirror, but instead of scolding him, he sat down on the bed beside him, and, carefully lifting the weather house from its place on the chest of drawers, had held it in his lap and shown Webern exactly how it worked.

"See this little stick they're standing on? It wobbles like that because it's glued to a strand of catgut. When it's dry outside, that shrinks up, so she swings out like this. When it's wet, well, the catgut loosens up and the soldier comes out his door." The little house had looked so strange in his father's big, chapped hands; Webern had held his breath, for fear it would get crushed by mistake. But his father had been unimaginably gentle. He set it back in place on the dusty bureau, then tousled Webern's hair and sent him back downstairs.

Webern carefully set the weather house on the nightstand and looked down at it. It surprised him that the old man had even remembered. He never thought his father was the sentimental type. Staring at the tiny wood-chip shingles, he wondered what other memories of their family his father lingered on and cherished. Maybe, like Webern, he often recollected the way Webern's mother looked as she stirred cookie batter, the dreamy expression that crossed her face as she tossed in a handful of chocolate chips. Maybe he still saw little Webern sitting at the kitchen table sometimes, his back unbroken, colouring in line drawings of spacemen and explorers.

Webern stepped out into the hall. He shouldn't have let so much of the car ride pass in silence. He'd probably been missing opportunities to talk to his father left and right since the day they'd put his mother in the ground. He saw his father coming up the stairs and stopped to watch him. He looked like the world's shortest giant, stooped and clumsy, leaning on the banister.

"Hey, Dad," he said awkwardly.

"Didn't see you there, ha ha." Raymond slipped something into the pocket of his jacket, and Webern caught a glimpse of glass and silver. The flask. Jesus Christ, it was after five o'clock already. It would be better if they could just have a drink together, without all this sneaking around. Maybe in a day or two, Webern would work up the nerve to suggest it.

"I took your old room," Webern said. "I hope that's okay. If you'd rather I stayed in the guest room . . ."

His father shrugged, his eyes searching the ceiling. "I figure you can stay wherever you want, long as you keep it spic and span."

Raymond tried to slip past Webern, but Webern stood in his way. An awful suspicion cut through him.

"Where are your bags?" Webern demanded. "I didn't see them in the trunk."

"Now, Bernie, don't get all upset."

"I'm not upset, just tell me where your bags are."

"See, it's like this. Your Bo-Bo asked me to bring you to her, and I did. You're the one she really wants to see. And I've got my job to think of—"

Webern was so mad he couldn't even speak. He felt his mouth opening and closing in angry hiccups, but no sound came out.

"Now, I'll be back up for the weekend, but—"

Webern didn't let him finish. He went back into the child's bedroom and slammed the door. He heard his father walk down to Bo-Bo's bedroom and murmur some good-byes. Then the stairs creaked and he was gone.

Webern wished he could call Nepenthe and rant about all this, but he had no way of reaching the circus on the road. So, as his father's new car gunned its engine and sped off, he was left alone in the roomful of ancient toys, fuming.

He should have seen it coming. The last couple years Webern had lived at home, after his sisters had finally fled for good, the old man was forever abandoning him. Webern would cook dinner—hot dog casserole and a Jell-O mold dotted with marshmallows—and Raymond would fill his plate and shuffle off to his recliner while Webern ate alone at the table. Or Raymond would flip sadly through old Polaroids, but turn on the TV when Webern tried to talk to him. For a long time, Webern thought it was grief that did it. Maybe it was.

What made this particular situation even worse was that Raymond had done almost exactly the same thing the first time he'd left Webern at Bo-Bo's. After overhearing the two adults' conversation, Webern had some inkling of what was coming, but he was still surprised and terrified when he woke up to find Marzipan and Bo-Bo standing over

him, like executioners pronouncing a death sentence: "Your father and I discussed it. We think this is best for the time being." They'd presented him with a packet containing raccoon jerky and a new toothbrush; then they'd left him alone. Webern had spent the morning reading books about the moon, wondering if he would be able to live in a plastic-domed bubble there someday. Now he was twenty-one years old, and things had barely changed.

Webern picked up the weather house from the bedside table and balanced it on his knees. Raymond was giving this to him—as an apology? An attempt to erase everything that had happened since? Webern shoved the weather house off his lap. It *thunked* against the floorboards. Webern stared down at it, then stood up and kicked it under the bed. It served his father right for thinking that Webern was still just some kid whose affection could be bought off with toys. It was too late for that now.

Webern collapsed backwards on the mattress. He needed to forget all this, to make himself smile, if only for Bo-Bo's sake. Cracks on the ceiling made a woman's face. It almost looked like it had been drawn there on purpose.

Webern had always felt tiny in Bo-Bo's dining room. Sitting in a looming throne-like chair, his feet dangled high above the ground, and the mahogany expanse of the clothless table stretched out before him in all directions. Even the silverware was huge: his fork and knife, heavy ironware, dwarfed his puny hands. Webern held the spoon up; its bowl was almost as large as his palm. It figured: unlike most everyone else, he would never experience the sensation of returning to a place from his childhood and finding it small and harmless. For him, the past would remain large and terrifying.

Marzipan banged around in the kitchen, so loudly that Webern idly imagined her crashing two frying pans together like a pair of cymbals. In a minute, she would probably come in, perfectly composed, to ladle soup into his waiting bowl. But if Bo-Bo didn't feel well enough to come downstairs, it would be silly for Webern to eat here all by himself. He'd rather just grab a sandwich in the kitchen, or talk to her up in her room. He'd wait five minutes, then go up and check.

The minutes ticked by. Just as Webern started to get up, a horrific sound came from the direction of the stairway—a *thunka-thunka-thunka* that made him leap to his feet.

When Webern ricocheted around the corner into the hallway, though, he didn't find the old lady in a heap at the bottom of the stairs. Instead, an open coffin lay kitty-cornered between the wall and the banister. Someone had attached the soles of several roller skates to the bottom to give it wheels. Bo-Bo lay inside, tranquil, her cloudy eye half shut.

"Don't just stand there, child," she said. "Give an old lady your arm."

"Where did you get this thing?" Webern asked, helping her up. Bo-Bo leaned on him for support as they walked back to the dining room.

"The undertaker. He came calling a few weeks back. A funny little man. Didn't you see his card on the mantle?"

"But why did you buy a coffin?"

"He was hell-bent on selling it—needed the business I expect. I thought, if I'm about to buy one, I might as well get some use out of it first. Marzipan took the trouble to attach the wheels."

"It's . . . nice."

"It's a necessity. I can't get around like I used to." Bo-Bo stopped for a moment and leaned against the wall. "A stitch in my side."

Webern helped Bo-Bo into her chair, then walked down to the other end of the long table. From this distance, she looked so faraway, it was like she was gone already.

CHAPTER SEVENTEEN

BO-BO DIDN'T LIKE TO TALK DURING DINNER. But Webern didn't mind the silence much, especially not tonight. Raymond's silences were dotted with little throat-clearings and half chuckles, surprised expressions and bemused head-scratchings—as awkward as conversation, and just as exhausting. But Bo-Bo's silence was full of doing and quickness, a straightforward silence, meticulous and neat.

As she cut her meat into dark little squares that she ate one at a time, it comforted Webern somehow. He hadn't realized how much he'd missed the stringy raccoon chops, which left redolent grease pooled in the centre of his enormous plate. He tried to put it out of his mind that this might be the last time he'd ever taste them. Instead, he concentrated on Marzipan. Her table manners were almost perfect; she could have instructed debutantes except for the loud slurping sound her rubbery lips made as she inhaled each new spoonful of soup.

After dinner, Webern followed Bo-Bo and Marzipan out to the sunroom, where Bo-Bo took her Scotch and her pipe in the evenings. The sunroom jutted off the back of the house, facing the garden. Windows covered three of its walls, but the only light they ever let in was from the moon or the buzzing tails of fireflies that filled the backyard each summer. During the day, Bo-Bo kept the curtains drawn.

Webern sat down on the weathered sofa that Bo-Bo always called the davenport, while Bo-Bo took her customary place in the rocking chair. Marzipan disappeared, then returned with a bottle of Scotch and glasses. It was just like old times, only now she brought three glasses instead of two.

"I suppose you're of age," Bo-Bo said as Marzipan brought Webern his drink. "It doesn't make much difference to me, anyhow. This was my medicine as a child."

"Thanks." Webern took a glass from the chimp.

"Besides, I have things to tell you. They say that liquor loosens the tongue, and there's no doubt truth in that. It also makes it easier to set quiet and listen." Bo-Bo settled an ancient quilt around her shoulders and closed her eye. "I don't have much time."

"Don't say that."

"I'm no fool. It's the truth. So I won't mince words. Webern, do you know how you came by your name?"

"Dad heard it when he was in Germany, right? And he never wanted to forget about what a great war hero he was, so he pinned the name on me. Like a medal." Webern shrugged and looked into his glass. His own words surprised him. "I dunno, maybe that's not fair. But that's what I always figured, anyway."

"Your father wasn't a war hero." Bo-Bo rocked her chair backwards. Her blue hair caught the light like gas fire. "He was a fry cook in the mess hall."

"What?" Webern pictured his father peeling potatoes like Steamboat Willy. Marzipan, already well into her glass of Scotch, let out a hilarious shriek and slapped her hairy thigh. Bo-Bo shot her a chill look before continuing.

"I'm not telling you this to tear down Raymond in your mind. You already think he's a confounded idiot, and I'm not disagreeing. But I want you to understand him."

"It's not the first time he's lied to me." Raymond used to say he had to swallow his heart during the war, to hide it from the Krauts. For a long time, Webern thought that was why his father never cried. "I understand him fine."

"I don't think you do. You see, over there in Germany, he killed a man."

The Scotch tasted of smoke and leather, with no ice to dilute it. Webern coughed. "With his cooking?"

"Don't make light." Bo-Bo set her glass on an end table and folded her hands in her lap. The veins stood out, thick and green, like the vines on the outside of the house. "Raymond took an assignment with the military police to catch some local toughs, men in the black market. He wanted a story to take home with him, I expect. The war was over then, and I believe your father felt he'd missed his chance. Chance for what, I don't know. He always was a funny child."

Webern kicked off his sneakers. Every day in the newspapers, draftees boarded buses without him. "What happened?"

"From what I understand, he was told to wait outside for trouble. That boy never could handle a weapon. When a stranger walked out, he shot without seeing. The man died on the spot. The worst of it was, though, the man was a professor—wrote music—had nothing to do with the black market at all. Raymond was torn up, of course, but what could he do? He came home a sorry sight—pants on backwards, shoes on the wrong feet. Your mother wouldn't let him in the house. Said she didn't recognize him. She'd only just recovered from some troubles herself, nervous thing that she was. So I took him in for a week or two. He learned to butter his bread, of course, but he never was the same. When you were born, one year to the day after he'd shot the professor, he took it as a sign.

"He named you after the man he'd killed. He believed you were his last chance to make right." Bo-Bo opened her eye slowly, as if waking from a dream. "Sometimes I wonder if that name wasn't a curse on you."

Webern drank. The Scotch went down smoother the second time.

"Why are you telling me all this?" he asked.

"Raymond's just a man, Bernie. He's had some very bad luck." She smiled wryly; toward the back of her mouth, silver flashed. "He had a terrible upbringing, you know."

"Let's not talk about my dad anymore."

"Fair enough." Bo-Bo held out her glass as Marzipan refilled it with Scotch. "There's something I want to give you. Something I haven't used in a very long time."

"Okay."

"Marzipan, get the box."

Marzipan left the room, and Bo-Bo and Webern sat quietly for a long while. With a *clunka-clunka-clunk*, Marzipan dragged the coffin back to the top of the stairs before her footsteps retreated beyond Webern's hearing. Bo-Bo's rocker creaked against the boards. Finally, the chimpanzee returned, holding a little velvety blue box about the size of a jewelry case. She handed it to Webern and he held it for a moment, imagining what could be inside: Bo-Bo's wedding rings? His father's silver rattle, dented with ancient tooth marks? He opened it. Inside stared a pale blue, wide open glass eye.

"After your grandfather left us, I swore I'd never wear it again. I blamed it for drawing him in the first place."

"It's beautiful." Webern picked up her eye from the velvet. It felt like an oblong marble in his hand.

"Don't keep it in a drawer." Bo-Bo finished her second Scotch, took out her teeth, and set them in the glass. Without them, her face looked like a cake fallen in on itself. "Now I'll say goodnight. Marzipan, put some water on these."

Marzipan took the cup of teeth and disappeared. Webern felt a lurch inside. Bo-Bo hadn't even smoked her pipe yet. He stood up to help her out of the rocking chair, but she shook him off. By the time she reached the top of the stairs, she was wheezing, and all colour had drained from her face.

"I should call the doctor," said Webern.

"Nonsense, child." Bo-Bo squeezed his arm with uncanny strength, and for a moment he felt frightened. Already she had taken out one eye and her teeth; he could imagine her nose and ears pulling out just as easily, her blue hair and her tongue, until her head was nothing but a mask of caverns. "Bed rest, bed rest, is all that man ever says. The undertaker took a greater interest in my health."

Webern guided her down the hall to the bedroom, where Bo-Bo turned back her covers and folded herself under them with her old deft precision. It wasn't until she looked back at Webern that her face took on a strange expression, the changeful look of a fading dream.

"Bo-Bo?" Webern felt very far away from her. He tried to make his voice sound manly and sure. "Bo-Bo, I'm calling the doctor right now. Are you all right?"

"I am." Bo-Bo drew the covers up to her chin. "Now take that monkey and get out of my house. I don't want you to see me die."

Webern dressed Marzipan in the pair of old yellow overall shorts from his luggage and led her outside, first carefully through the yard, among the metal jaws, and then down the sidewalk beneath the blooming trees.

It was a beautiful summer night, with a sky so dark blue and glowing it could have been made of stained glass. Marzipan's fur ruffled in the breeze, and Webern thought of how Bo-Bo used to trim it with a pair of rusty, grinding scissors. He wondered who would do it now, and he felt a pressure in his chest so strong that it was like his own heart was choking to death.

Marzipan's feet slapped the pavement as they walked through the night-dark town. Webern played games in his mind: he imagined that he was a little boy, and that Marzipan was his kid sister; he imagined that he lived in a house with Nepenthe, that people came to his own backyard to see his circus shows. He imagined that he was a doctor and that tomorrow he was shipping off to Vietnam, where he'd be made a hero for gathering up all the blown-off limbs of his fellow soldiers and gluing them back into place.

When he got tired of these games, Webern tried to remember the little train-car room he shared with Nepenthe, down to the very last detail. He tried to picture her lying there, her hair a mass of loose curls, her scales drinking in cool moonlight and steaming off heat. He loved her so much it twisted in him; he almost couldn't believe that he would get to go back to her and that woozy train-world, where bottles rolled across the floor and the world slid by endlessly, too big to ever use up.

Webern and Marzipan stopped in an all-night diner, with glossy laminated menus that showed pictures of the food. The fry cook looked askance at Marzipan until she pointed to the Denver omelet. Webern drank a glass of orange juice with ice cubes in it that chattered. Then they walked back to the house and sat on the stoop for a time.

As the light began to grey the sky, Webern was struck by how much Marzipan's wrinkled, malleable face resembled Bo-Bo's. He wanted to warn the chimp that her life was about to change, but he didn't know what words to say. So instead they sat there without speaking, completely silent except for the heavy animal sound of Marzipan's breath. Only after morning came, really and truly, and people started coming out their front doors, did Webern and Marzipan go back inside.

"Bo-Bo?"

Down at the bottom of the stairs, Webern found the coffin again. This time, the lid was shut.

When Webern opened the grave-card on the mantelpiece, he found the undertaker's number inside. He dialed it on the heavy, clanking wheel of Bo-Bo's rotary telephone. The undertaker sounded delighted.

"Your grandmother was a wonderful woman. So kind-hearted to send business my way. Especially at a time like this. With all the ugly rumours that've been circulating about me, I was starting to think I wouldn't break even this year."

"Well," said Webern. He stared at the coffin down the hall. "I'm sure they're unfounded."

"Unfounded?" The undertaker said the word like he'd never heard it before. "Oh, the rumours. Ha ha ha. Unfounded. Of course they are."

The undertaker was still laughing nervously when Webern hung up the receiver and went into the sunroom to wait for the hearse. Marzipan was already there, hanging from the curtain rod by one hand. Webern stopped in the doorway and looked up at her. It was the first time he'd seen her do anything so monkeylike. Marzipan gazed down at him, her face moulded into an exaggerated frown. She let out a single cry—high-pitched, lingering, and forlorn—then dropped to the ground and swung out of the room on her knuckles. Webern turned to watch her go down the hallway. She paused for a moment beside the coffin, unfastened and shucked off her yellow overalls, then draped them over the lid. Naked, she swung on past, around a corner where he couldn't see.

Webern had never been in the house without Bo-Bo. He opened the sunroom drapes and for the first time saw the yard in daylight. It was pitifully small, with scraggly, wheat-headed grasses, shards of skeet, and a lightning struck tree that raised its burnt black arms to the sky. A dying raccoon writhed in one of the steel traps. Webern started to shut the drapes again. As he did, something dark and shapeless fluttered near the trunk of the ruined tree. But when he turned his head to look, whatever it was had disappeared.

Webern sat down on the davenport. He took the blue velvet box out of his pocket and opened it. The glass eye felt cool and heavy in his hand. He wondered how he could contact his father, if their phone number could possibly be the same after all these years. Webern pulled off his shoes. Maybe if he dialled home, he wouldn't reach his father. Instead, another, equally impossible person from his history would answer: his mother, his rhyming sisters, his old friend Wags, his own scrawny, fearful, six-year-old self.

CHAPTER EIGHTEEN

DAMON FAIN, EXCITABLE, PINK, AND PLUMP AS A PORK SAUSAGE, walked with a prancing gait and squeezed his moist hands together whenever he cried out the names of surgical procedures in his high, thin voice. He was first in his class at medical school and had once been the spelling bee champion of the state of Indiana, two facts he never failed to mention in quick succession. The morning after he rubbed a strong-smelling, pale blue cream all over the crackled expanse of Nepenthe's naked body, she woke up feeling itchy, guilty, and more than a little pissed off.

She reflected that she had not been the greatest judge of character in Webern's absence. First she'd gone with Venus de Milo to that party thrown by Killer McVeigh from the motorcycle cage; now she'd allowed a piggy little man from South Bend to touch her all over without so much as asking for his medical license. Jesus God. She could read all the Anaïs Nin she wanted, but obviously that didn't stop her from being naïve as hell. Who was Damon Fain anyway? Not a dermatologist, most likely. Maybe he was some kind of psycho pervert who got off on smearing poison creams on sideshow girls. Later in the day she'd go blind, or crazy. Her brains would liquefy and he'd come back to kidnap her and sign her up for some sex slave ring. Yeah right. She needed to stop flattering herself.

Nepenthe rolled out of bed and groped around on the floor for her cigarette case. She was wearing her pink robe, but, much to her disgust, the inside was now streaked with greyish-blue grease from her skin. She shucked it off and, naked, opened her cigarette case, which promptly slipped from her oily fingers onto the floor. So disgusting.

This was worse than passing out in a frat house and waking up with your hand inside a raw chicken—something that had happened to a cousin of Venus's once, if that tramp was to be believed. Already Nepenthe was blaming Venus for what had happened the night before. She reached for a green clove, then reconsidered and took out a banana stick instead. This was all getting way too weird for her. She needed to mellow out—way out.

Nepenthe sat down on the couch, and, smoking the jay, leafed through the already-yellowing pages of the underground newspaper she'd bought two towns back. It was called *Mindfücke*, and although it wasn't quite as good as *L'Enrage* or *The Druid Free Press*, it still had some pretty trippy poems and an interesting opinions page. Nepenthe started reading a piece about how Lyndon Johnson and his team of hairy-knuckled flunkies had planned to take out JFK with silent air-powered shoe guns until J. Edgar Hoover got to him first, but as she smoked, the article began to merge with the one in the adjacent column, about how drug cops—"the Man's man"—had been digging through Arlo Guthrie's fan mail for leads. Next to that was a political cartoon of an unrecognizably caricatured general hugging a fish. She ended up just staring at the boxcar ceiling to get a sense of reality back. The world was fucked, young men were exploding, and her legs really itched. Maybe she should just go back to bed.

The whole situation with Damon Fain had started the night before, right before the sideshow closed up and the real circus under the big top began. Nepenthe had been terminally bored, as usual; she and Venus de Milo had been drinking Singapore Slings off and on between performances since three o'clock in the afternoon, so she was pretty soused, too. Damon Fain had come in with the last group. He'd stood in the back, but when everyone else cleared out of Nepenthe's partitioned-off stage to go see "Tiny" Tina and Rhonda, the fat ladies next door, he'd lingered behind. Producing a jeweler's eyepiece from the pocket of his seersucker suit, he introduced himself as "Damon Fain, MD," and asked if he could take a closer look at her scales.

"Whatever tickles your pickle," Venus giggled, hopping from behind the curtain that separated their stages with a near-empty pitcher of Slings gripped in one pedicured foot. "We'll brush your teeth for a dollar. And we'll floss 'em for three."

"Can she speak?" asked Damon Fain while he bent over Nepenthe's shoulder blades, magnifier securely in place.

"Of course I can, you fascist quack. Get your filthy shoes off my Spanish moss." Nepenthe had an elaborate set, complete with vines and an enormous artificial alligator made of foam rubber and latex paint. Earlier in the evening, she'd sat on the alligator's back sidesaddle like she was riding a pony, but now she was stretched out on it facedown. She sat up and noticed, with a mixture of satisfaction and irritation, that Damon Fain recoiled when he saw the scales also covered her face. Nepenthe thought of the sharp-tongued heroines from old caper pictures. She added, "And if you try anything funny—I can scream, too."

"Oh. Well—" was all the good doctor could say.

Damon Fain took his time staring at her back; he also looked at her scalp, her legs, and the skin between her toes.

"They aren't webbed, if that's what you're looking for," Nepenthe yawned. "I'm a lizard, not a goddamn mermaid. Venus, can you pour me another drink?"

"How long have you suffered from this?" asked Damon Fain.

"I don't call it suffering as long as I'm getting paid."

"It's hard for a girl to make it in the world." Venus placed a seductive foot on Damon Fain's shoulder.

Nepenthe looked away. If Venus hadn't started turning tricks yet, it wasn't because she was too subtle. Not that Nepenthe could really blame her for her desperation. Since Webern had left, Nepenthe had tried to picture what her own life would be if he never came back, and it looked pretty lonely—days at the sideshow, nights watching local girls do the twist with the motorbike riders—a lot of pineapple-flavoured drinks and a progressively messier boxcar. And now a strange fat finger probing the scales behind her ear. After a few months of this, a sweaty fumble behind the Tilt-a-Whirl wouldn't sound so bad—not that anyone would ask her.

It was funny: before Webern left, she had this idea that he was holding her back, keeping her from being part of the new generation she read about on record sleeves and in the rock-and-roll magazines she sought out on their trips into town. But now that he was gone, she realized that without him in her life, she'd be a total recluse—a virgin in a beekeeper's suit. When the signs for concerts and be-ins said, "FREAKS WELCOME," she wasn't the kind they meant.

"Listen, pal," Nepenthe said, leaning over to take her cigarette case out of the fake alligator's mouth. "Let's cut to the chase. What can we do for you here?"

Damon Fain cleared his throat. "I guess," he said, "I'm more interested—heh heh—in what I can do for you."

"Please. Enlighten us, Herr Doktor."

"I'm an expert in rare conditions of the skin." He pressed his hands together. "Scleredema—Vitiligo—Xeroderma Pigmentosum."

Nepenthe lit a clove. His words reminded her of the abracadabra Dr. Show used to intone before performing one of his magic tricks.

"So which one have I got?" she asked, taking a new Singapore Sling from Venus's outstretched foot. Her friend's long toes uncurled from the glass.

"It looks like lamellar ichthyosis—but not a classic case, especially if you weren't born with it. I wouldn't presume to diagnose without a complete medical workup."

"Well, you're not going to get a—'complete workup.'" Nepenthe exhaled; her smoke broke in waves on Damon's face. Venus giggled. "So I don't see what you can do for me."

"Just because I haven't made a conclusive diagnosis doesn't mean I can't treat the symptoms. Wait." Damon Fain hopped down from the stage and trotted over to a corner of the sideshow tent, where he'd parked an old-fashioned doctor's bag. Jesus God. He had all the accoutrements, that was for sure. Which, if anything, could be more evidence that he was a phony. Nepenthe half expected him to put on an inflatable stethoscope and squeal, "Let's play doctor!" but when he opened the case, she saw it was actually full of jars with prescription labels glued to their lids. All three of them peered inside.

"Got anything in that bag for me, Doc?" asked Venus.

It was then that Damon Fain made his proposition: he'd try Nepenthe on one of his creams, and if she didn't see a change in twenty-four hours, she'd never have to talk to him again. But if it worked, he'd get to use her name and picture in a study he was doing—plus she'd get a lifetime prescription for the medicine that cured her.

"Wait a second. When you do a study, don't you have to use the negative results too? You know, the patients where it doesn't work out?"

"Sure. But we kind of gloss over that part, you know?"

Nepenthe thought of all the dermatologists she'd visited with her mother—the teen fashion magazines in the waiting room filled with toothpaste advertisements and prom dress patterns. Those doctors, used to a parade of shiny-haired princesses whose clogged pores or ingrown hairs were barely visible under a microscope, whose only flaking skin came from a sunburn at the Cape, had waited for her with dread. This one had come looking for her.

"You should do it, Nepenthe," Venus whispered. "He's a rich people's doctor, you can tell by his shoes."

Nepenthe looked down at Fain's feet. He was wearing spats.

So he'd followed her back to the boxcar, she'd shimmied out of her artificial snakeskin miniskirt, and after snapping on some rubber gloves, he'd kneaded her like dough. It had been the most disgusting experience of her entire life. Halfway through, she'd put down some newspapers on the floor because the thick bluish cream kept glopping onto the rug. Damon Fain's hands were hot and alien-feeling inside the latex; he whistled songs from *The Duchess of Idaho* and related anecdotes about the world of competitive spelling while Nepenthe took shots from a whiskey bottle she'd found under the couch. At first she was worried about being alone with Fain, but after awhile she was glad Venus had headed out for her date with Zeus Masters—no witnesses would make this easier to forget. It felt like it took hours. All that Nepenthe could remember now was that it had been well past midnight when she'd finally shoved Fain out the door and barricaded it with a chair behind him. Then she'd wadded up the gooey newspapers from the floor and thrown them out the window at his head.

Fortunately, she still had the one she was reading. Nepenthe blinked—she'd been half-dozing again, but the itching woke her up. She dug her nails into her greasy thigh. Jesus God. What was this crud, anyway? It was coming off in strips.

Nepenthe moved her newspaper off her lap to get a better look, and when she did, she almost passed out. Because it wasn't the medicine she was peeling off. It was her skin.

Webern woke up to the sound of someone rapping at the door. For a long moment, lying there on the couch, he didn't know who it could possibly be. A cartoon image flashed through his mind: Death himself, in a black hood with a heavy, skull-topped walking stick, striking his bony knuckles against the wooden frame. Webern hoisted himself up off the couch, shaking himself awake. Of course it was the undertaker.

He wasn't thinking straight. His arms and legs felt heavy, and in his mouth lingered the sour, cottony taste of nightmares.

"I'm coming!" he yelled in the direction of the foyer.

Lightning bugs hung thickly in the air around the porch, turning the air an eerie, subterranean yellow-green. They blinked like glowing eyes.

"Hi," Webern said.

The undertaker offered a trembling smile. "I'm terribly sorry for the delay," he murmured in a professionally soothing voice. "So many roadblocks in this town. It makes one feel like a criminal, just driving to a client's house."

"That's okay," said Webern. His face felt swollen and bunchy. He'd been crying in his sleep. "You can come in."

Webern led the undertaker through the darkened rooms. Richly patterned rugs, like fast-asleep magic carpets, lay side by side on the cold wood floors; cloudy, warped mirrors showed the world curving and dreamlike; and ancient, delicate teacups that Bo-Bo had once remarked were made from ground-up bones rattled quietly in the cupboards as they passed. Webern wondered if it was possible to pinpoint the moment a house got to be haunted, the moment that a creaking floorboard or a groaning wall became a voice. He thought of his own house in the days and weeks just after his mother died, the way her smells—chamomile, lipstick, fabric softener—had returned at the strangest times, wafting up like ghosts out of the medicine cabinet, a long closed drawer. He had thought she'd linger on forever that way, but after a while the smells had faded, too.

The undertaker stopped in front of the coffin at the base of the stairs. His tongue darted out to moisten his lips.

"She's gotten a head start on me, I see."

Webern shrugged. Just looking at the box made him feel a little sick. He tried to imagine what Bo-Bo had been thinking when she closed that lid on herself, but it was beyond him. Maybe she'd been preparing herself all those nights she'd crept through narrow crawl spaces, hunting raccoons in the dark.

"Do you need help . . . rolling it out to your car, or anything?"

The undertaker cracked his knuckles and sighed deeply. "If you'll excuse me, I thought I might have a look here first. See what I have in store."

"All right." Webern picked up the overalls Marzipan had left on the coffin's lid. Where had she gone? "Let me know when you're . . . done, I guess."

"Oh, I will." The undertaker smiled; his lips clung unnaturally to his teeth.

Webern went out into the kitchen and let the door swing shut behind him. He half-expected to see Marzipan bent over the stove, her wizened faced hidden in a cloud of steam, but, except for a sink full of dishes floating in brackish water, the kitchen was empty. Maybe she was upstairs, stretched out on one of the beds. Or in the dining room, chain-smoking Pall Malls and ashing into a saucer. But somehow Webern didn't think so. Hesitantly, he set the overalls on the counter, then slowly approached the kerosene freezer. Might as well check. Inside, shelves of iced raccoons stared out at him, their eyes black and accusing, their fur dusted with frost. But no Marzipan, thank God.

Webern took a frozen Snickers bar off the top shelf and closed the door again. He sat down on the stepladder Bo-Bo kept to reach the cupboard's highest shelves, carefully unwrapped the chocolate, and took a bite. He looked out the window as he chewed. When he stayed with Bo-Bo before, she'd given him these every so often as a special treat. Webern never liked them much—he preferred candy hearts and wax bottles, pure sugar, and the rock-hard caramel hurt his teeth— but Bo-Bo's manner of doling them out made them seem inestimably precious. Judging from the way this one tasted, she might have had it since the last time he visited. Webern wondered if she'd been expecting him back all these years, if she'd saved this one chocolate bar just in case.

Webern took the blue velvet box out of his pocket and held it in his hand. Don't keep it in a drawer, she'd said. But what was he supposed to do with it? Webern opened the box and held the glass eye up to his. He stared into the pupil, and as he did, he realized that he could see through the murky, shaded glass. There was the window, and past it, the yard, midnight dark but visible. A soot-coloured rosebush hulked in the shadow of the eaves; grasses swayed like a green-black sea. And, just as Webern started to lower the glass eye, a dark figure—or maybe two—darted around the corner of the indistinct garage.

Webern blinked and shoved the eye back into the box, but it— they?—had already disappeared. He tried to open the window, but it was painted shut.

"Hey! Marzipan?" he yelled, rattling the glass. Great. If it was Marzipan, he couldn't just let her wander around in her current state, swinging through trees and scaring the neighbors. But if it wasn't Marzipan . . . Webern got down off the stepladder and went out the back door into the yard. If it wasn't Marzipan, he'd probably just been imagining things.

"Marzipan?" he called again. He stepped carefully through the grass, avoiding raccoon traps. There was a trick to opening them that only Bo-Bo knew. Raccoons were clever animals, intelligent as spies—not many people went to the trouble of outsmarting them. In a way, they'd probably miss Bo-Bo; scheming against her had given their lives spice and meaning. Webern picked up a fallen tree branch and angrily jammed it into the spring release at the heart of the nearest trap. The metal jaws chomped down, splintering the wood in half.

"Marzipan?" Webern shouted so loud his throat felt sore. Dark birds flushed out of a nearby tree. This was ridiculous. He kicked what was left of the stick and went on toward the garage.

Bo-Bo's garage had always been off-limits. Not that Webern had cared too much about it anyway. Ever since his mother's crash, he'd hated cars, hated the smell of them, the intestinal twisting of their engines, the cranks and jacks and lug nuts, the spilled gasoline, puddled like dirty rainbows on dips in the concrete. So it had been just as well that Bo-Bo's garage was boarded up, its doors laden with iron chains and padlocks. Wild rose bushes, the kind he'd only seen in Tarantula, had grown up its walls, even onto the roof. Their ragged lavender blossoms filled the air with a heady sweetness that made Webern think of enchanted sleep.

He rounded the garage's corner, but there was nothing on the other side: only more rose bushes and a few tipped-over garbage cans, their black plastic bags ripped and spilling refuse. Webern sighed and set them back up. He'd been right about the raccoons. Already they'd started eating trash; before long they'd grow fat and lazy and over-numerous, their black paws stained with ketchup and chicken fat, their bellies swinging like overfed house-cats'.

As Webern put the metal lids back on, he glanced up. Just above the garbage cans was a window, small, but big enough to climb through, and its glass was missing—shattered. A branch of roses hung down over it, not quite concealing the gaping hole. Raccoons were smart, but not like this. Half-remembered scents—day-old road kill, bug juice, burnt hair—filled Webern's nostrils, and as his throat tightened, he felt an old, familiar sensation: a strange, tipsy vertigo he hadn't known in years. He gulped and breathed through his mouth, singing inside his head, forget it, forget it, forget it, there isn't the slightest chance, until the words ran together into gibberish. But he had to know for sure. Before he knew what he was doing, he was climbing up on top of the garbage cans, and into the cool dark of the garage.

Webern tumbled down onto a workbench, knocking over what looked like several hatboxes and a pile of expired almanacs. It took a minute for his eyes to adjust to the light. Motes of dust swam in the air, and up among the rafters stretched a wire clothesline; at least a dozen men's suits hung from it, their ancient lapels dotted with flecks of mould. In the centre of the garage was a car he'd never seen—an old Packard from the '20s, midnight blue with a rumble seat. Cobwebs hung from its mirrors, and its convertible ragtop looked cracked and brittle with age. Its tires were completely flat.

Webern got up and dusted himself off. The rosebush branch had scraped his hand, and he licked away the beads of blood that glistened on his skin. The taste made him feel even sicker. He stepped over a Panama hat that lay brim up, on the concrete, and cautiously made his way around the car.

"Hello?" he whispered.

No one answered. Webern ran his hand over the car's hood. His fingers left trails in the dust. He glanced around. A coat tree made of antlers leaned against one wall; a leather armchair sat in the corner, laden with mildewed suitcases. To his left was a large wooden crate with many glossy scraps of paper spread out across it. Webern blew away the dust shrouding them. Each one showed a single, isolated figure, like a paper doll cut from a photograph. It was the same man every time. In some of the pictures, he had a pencil-thin moustache; in others, a single hand tucked between the buttons of his jacket. In the one Webern held up to the light, he leaned jauntily on a lion's head cane. Though Webern had never seen him before, the room was so full of the forgotten man that Webern almost expected him to materialize.

Webern heard a noise behind him and spun around, but it was nothing—only the rosebush branch tapping against the window frame. Biting his lip, he dropped the picture of his grandfather and, rubbing at the grimy windshield with his shirtsleeve, peered into the Packard's dark interior.

The dashboard bore a large black scorch, and empty cat food tins, some singed feathers, and gnawed-clean pigeon bones lay on the front seats, grimy and old. Webern struggled to breathe. And that was before he glimpsed what was in the back.

The masks lay on the backseats, side by side. Time had only deepened their strangeness, their cruel otherness. Billow's mask, stained and discoloured with age, had become as brittle and discoloured as bundled newspapers in a madman's house; Willow's knotty tree-face, thick with dirt and now-brown tree leaves, sprouted a pale spider egg, nestled in one cheek. Webern stared at the masks as if looking into a pair of living faces; their empty eyes gazed steadily back. For a single instant, he felt like he'd fallen out of the world. In his mind, he saw Willow and Billow, the way they must be now: sunburnt, skin cured like leather, with cracked and darkened fingernails; full-grown, with sweat and blood and tooth decay. Dressed in rags and garbage bags, feral, spiteful, crouching. Their room had always smelled like the woods; they had never feared the elements. They could be living here, in this shed. They could be anywhere. Webern heard a familiar laugh—a little boy's—and everything went black.

Webern woke up to find the undertaker standing over him and a faint chemical smell in the air. But for a split second, the man's pallor, his dark suit and darker hair, confused Webern and he saw Dr. Schoenberg instead.

"What's going on?" Webern struggled to sit up. He was on the living room floor. His throat felt raw, and his voice sounded scratchy. He touched his cheekbone gingerly. It felt tender—bruised.

"Search me." The undertaker's voice no longer sounded melodious and consoling. "First the chimp, now you."

"What?"

The undertaker jerked his head toward Marzipan, who was sitting in Bo-Bo's rocking chair, an afghan drawn around her shoulders as she knitted. "That thing wouldn't let me near the coffin. Then you started up out back." He shook his head. "I've almost never heard such screaming."

"I don't understand. How did I get inside?"

"You kept slamming yourself into the back door—like you thought you'd jump straight through. After a minute or two, you knocked yourself out. Then I carried you in here." The undertaker looked at him strangely. "You're sure you don't remember any of this?"

Webern closed his eyes, but his sisters lurked there too: a tangle of limbs, spindly and thick. Eight, like a spider. "Were they really there?"

"You might want to see a grief counsellor." The undertaker handed him a business card. "I'm sorry for your loss."

Webern followed the undertaker to the door and bolted it shut behind him. He watched the hearse drive away. It occurred to him that the girls could be anywhere, even inside the house. He bumped his forehead against the cool window and bit the scratches on his hand.

"Marzipan?" he called. Dutifully, the ape rose from her chair. She followed him down the hall and sat with him as he dialled his father's number on the rotary telephone. When he started shaking uncontrollably, she even draped her blanket around his hump.

CHAPTER NINETEEN

IN THE YARD AROUND THE HOUSE, a fine mist hung in the air. Webern watched it from the front porch swing, huddled under the blanket Marzipan had brought him. A teacup full of Scotch trembled between his cupped palms, and he stared into it. He hadn't slept that night, not for a minute, and his thoughts were jittery and confused. He thought about the coonskin cap Bo-Bo had given him so long ago. She'd cured the hide in her basement; the innards she'd stripped away with an old straight razor. Strange how easily a living thing became a hollow shell.

Webern could hardly believe Bo-Bo was gone; it wouldn't have surprised him if she'd come out the front door, shotgun jauntily balanced on one shoulder. It certainly would have frightened him less than seeing his sisters again. But, despite the fact he'd sat up at the window all night, he hadn't glimpsed them yet.

For a moment, when Webern first saw his father's Chrysler approaching through the mist, he thought it was some sort of mirage. On the phone the night before, the old man had sounded pretty bleary, and Webern hadn't been making too much sense either. Their conversation had been all stops and starts and pauses so long Webern kept thinking they'd been disconnected. Webern didn't even know what he'd said. His words had made no sense to him; they'd come out like gibberish, faster and faster, until he realized he was sobbing too hard to make himself understood. Marzipan had pressed a damp washcloth to his brow to cool his face, and he'd held it there for a long time.

Whatever he'd said had somehow managed to lure his father back, though, because the headlights were real, making two tunnels of cloudy white down the road ahead. He stood up, and the blanket dropped from around his shoulders. Goosebumps rose on his arms; one hand slipped up automatically to cover his hump.

Webern remembered his own mother's funeral, the wreaths of carnations piled around the casket, as if it had come in first in a race, and he remembered walking towards it, slower and slower, the funeral home's plush carpet crushing beneath his shiny black shoes. At that moment he had wanted his mother desperately, needed her more than anything in the world; but at the same time, her body was more frightening to him than even the sound of his sisters rattling his locked door handle in the dead of night. Staring down at his mother's face, waxy and artificial against those sea-foam green pillows, Webern had been consumed with the sensation of falling up, as though his own spirit was rising to meet hers in the cold cathedral of the sky. Today, Webern realized, his own father was feeling the same way. They were both orphans now.

For once, Webern felt like it might actually be possible to talk to Raymond. Maybe his father would even understand about Willow and Billow, would protect him for a change. He swallowed the rest of the Scotch from his teacup and went down the stairs to meet the old man's car.

Raymond parked at an angle on the curb, the left front tire narrowly avoiding the jaws of a raccoon trap. Webern stood for a moment, staring through the windshield. For the second time in two days, he found himself peering into a car's darkened interior with a mixture of horror and disbelief. Because there in the passenger seat sat a woman Webern had never seen before.

She looked like the type of woman who had been called a "cupcake" long ago, but now, as she squeezed herself out of the Chrysler's passenger side, she released a miasma of musky toilet water, corned beef hash, and day-old donuts. She wore tight-fitting black Capri pants and a green-and-black men's bowling shirt, hiked up and tied around her middle, just below her ample breasts. A red bow snarled in her dirty-blond hair, and her pancake makeup, no doubt merry and bright in the neon glow of jukeboxes and beer signs, had the odd effect of flattening her features in the early morning light, so her face looked artificial, painted-on—almost clownish.

"Hon." She minced toward him in a pair of ill-fitting slingbacks, her arms extended. "Hon, Madge is here now. Don't you cry."

"Who *are* you?" Webern whispered. Insanely, he thought: *she's stolen my face.*

Webern's father rolled down the driver's side window. "Bernie, get in the car."

Webern buckled into the backseat as Madge unsteadily mounted the front steps of the porch.

"I should've told you sooner," his father said. He fiddled with some of the buttons on the dashboard. "But I figured you had enough on your plate as it was."

"What's she doing here?"

"Well, I figured, better safe than sorry. There's been some vandals in Tarantula—killing birds, breaking windows, even burned down a kid's playhouse. I figured they might've seen the hearse." He rubbed his eyes. "Madge'll keep a lookout 'til we're back."

"That isn't what I meant."

"A man needs someone to keep him warm at night. Horse doesn't need to be a thoroughbred to pull the cart. Seems you know that well enough."

"I love Nepenthe. I'm not ashamed of her. I wouldn't be with someone I was ashamed of."

"I didn't say I was ashamed."

"That's right. You didn't say anything about her at all."

A loud shriek came from the direction of the house. Seconds later, Marzipan appeared at the door, wearing an eyelet bonnet and carrying two suitcases. She appeared unruffled as she made her way down to the Chrysler and began strapping suitcases to its roof. Then she walked around to the passenger's side and let herself in. She sat shotgun, directly in front of Webern, and in this new space he noticed for the first time her peculiar smell: musty and sweet, like a fur coat stored with sage leaves and rose petals.

"So, are you driving me to Little Falls or not?" Webern asked. "Because I really need to leave. Right now."

"I figured you wouldn't want to stay for the services."

"I figured you wouldn't want to stay with Bo-Bo while she died. And I was right. You left that up to me."

Raymond's breath whistled. "I never thought a son of mine would grow up to be so cruel."

"Maybe I learned it from you, Dad." Webern kicked the back of the passenger seat. His tennis shoe left a scuff.

Webern tried to sleep all the way to Little Falls. But he couldn't stop himself from waking up from time to time, and when he did it was invariably with confusion. Once he thought that Dr. Schoenberg and Nepenthe were in the front seat, navigating the vehicle down the ugly road to Lynchville. Another time, Marzipan's quiet whimper brought to mind Fred and Ginger, growling from their cages in the jalopy. The last time Webern woke up, he thought he was in the old Studebaker with his father and mother side by side in the front seat. Even after this illusion fell away, he kept staring at his father's craggy profile for a long time, trying to get it back.

As the road snaked through green cornfields toward the big top, it started to strike Webern as incredible that he'd lived the life he had for so long. Back in the days he'd spent manacled in a back brace, propped up at a desk in a classroom squeaking with chalk and clicking with overhead projector slides, he'd dreamed of one day travelling to a different world, full of festivals and costumes, exotic sights that could compete with the copies of National Geographic he paged through during study hall. Now here he was, about to step through the door of a boxcar into a magical room filled with forbidden herbs and growing candy, where a girl lay waiting under a Mexican blanket, naked except for her scales. Webern tried to feel relieved to be back, joyful even, but he couldn't shake off a persistent, gnawing ache. It was as though his life at the circus, with all its pleasures and excesses, its gorgeous eccentricities, was a painting he'd never get to climb back into.

"Here we are," said Raymond, turning the car into the patrons' parking lot. White paint, still glistening wet, marked spaces on the dusty ground. Webern started to open his door, but before he could, Raymond cleared his throat. "I hope you get along all right. With your work, and your—lady friend."

"You, too." They still hadn't talked about anything, anything, and knowing his father, they never would. Webern gripped the handle of his bag. "Listen, I know—I know this has to be hard for you, and I didn't mean—"

"Never mind that. It's been good seeing you again. Don't be such a stranger." Raymond hesitated. "I'll be sure to keep an eye out for your posters."

"Well, don't hold your breath. It's not like I'm a high wire act." Webern looked down at his foot and willed it to stop tapping. "Let me know if there's anything else I can do, okay?"

"Come to think of it, son, there is one other thing I've been meaning to ask you." Raymond removed his hat. He glanced significantly at Marzipan.

As the Chrysler pulled away into the warm mid-afternoon, Webern and his inherited chimpanzee walked in the direction of the freak housing, carrying their respective suitcases. Marzipan seemed to take her change in surroundings in stride, hardly glancing up as they passed a team of practicing fire eaters and the elephants getting hosed down with Fat Rhonda. None of them paid any attention to Marzipan either: it wasn't like they'd never seen an ape in a bonnet before.

Webern was marveling at her resilience as he climbed up the steps to his cabin and pushed open the door. But as soon as he stepped inside, all his other thoughts fell away. Because there on the rug stood a beautiful young stranger, wearing only a pair of underpants and a beaded necklace, looking herself up and down in the mirror.

She was standing with one arm outstretched, snapping Polaroids of herself. A pile of shiny photographs in various states of development lay scattered at her feet.

"Bernie," she said, turning to look at him. Her voice sounded light and breathless—the voice of someone who'd just arrived. Before Webern could answer her, the flash snapped again. A permanent likeness of her expression—eyes wide, lips slightly parted—seared itself onto a square of paper. She popped it out of the camera's back and tossed it down to the floor.

"Hi," said Webern. He stared at her skin, pink and unblemished as a mermaid's newly formed legs, and for an instant he knew he had to be in the wrong boxcar. Then a feeling crept over him, a feeling he'd known since childhood, a feeling he thought of as the opposite of recognition. It was the feeling he'd had when he'd woken up in his room back home, then realized he couldn't move because of the body cast; the feeling he'd had when he called his mother's name in the night, then remembered she would never answer him again. It was the feeling that nothing was familiar anymore. Webern thought of the way Nepenthe had looked just before he'd left: naked, sated, her eyes glowing the dim soft green of the ocean floor. The eyes staring at him now were the same, but all wrong.

"So, what do you think?" she asked. "I guess this is what you miss when you leave for a couple days, huh?"

She stepped back, as if that would help him take her in all at once. But the longer Webern looked at her, the more she began breaking into shapes: the hollow of her neck, the knob of her ankle, the curve of her hip, the whorl of her ear. He couldn't hold her together in his mind.

"Bernie, are you okay?"

"I just need to be alone for a minute." He sat down on the floor.

"What're you talking about? You just got home! I've got so much to tell you." Nepenthe walked over to him and unceremoniously yanked him up by the hands. Her palms felt smooth and slightly greasy; once he was on his feet, they slipped away easily. "Look at me!"

Webern tried to, but it was hard to keep his eyes focused. Nepenthe's face floated above him.

"I mean, you haven't even asked me what happened yet!"

Webern picked up a record sleeve from the couch; unreal psychedelic patterns swirled up at him. Count Five, *Cartesian Jetstream*. "Okay, what happened?"

"Thank you. Finally. So, Venus and I met this guy, this dermatologist. A classic oral character, this guy. Anyway, he had this whole bag of lotions and he asked me—"

But Webern wasn't listening anymore. He had dropped the album cover and was staring at the Polaroids on the floor. In them, Nepenthe was mugging for the camera: leaning against the wall, a clove dangling from her lips; lying on the bed wearing nothing but a pair of high heels; sitting cross-legged on the couch with a white feather boa around her shoulders—a boa he'd used in one short-lived sketch where he'd played a chicken learning how to fly. If Nepenthe herself was impossible to take in all at once, these pictures encapsulated her beautifully. She was a voluptuous girl with the pouty, pillowy lips they used to call a Cupid's bow, a girl with the body of a nightclub singer who lies on the piano lid and whispers into a microphone. Her breasts were just big enough to make other girls call her easy without knowing her name. At least, they would have at his high school.

He reached down and peeled back the negative paper from one photograph that still lay shrouded on the floor. In it, Nepenthe leaned over his desk, her bosom pressed against his clown notebook, her soft mouth slightly ajar. He felt a surge of arousal tinged with guilt before he remembered he was looking at a picture of his girl. His girl. She was still talking.

"—but I guess it worked," Nepenthe was saying. "Wait. Let me show you something."

Nepenthe hurried over to the bed and pulled a cardboard box out from underneath. In the open carton, Webern almost expected to find the real Nepenthe, crumpled and folded with dead, glassy eyes. But instead, he saw the box was half-filled with her scales. They looked pitifully small without her body inside them. Webern picked up a scale and held it between his thumb and forefinger. It was already brittle, turning translucent; through it filtered only the palest, most diffuse kind of light.

"Gross, right? But I figured I could sell them at Parliament. Souvenirs, you know? Like Brunhilde used to do with her beard hairs."

Nepenthe grinned. Then she did something Webern had never seen her do before. Her hair was falling into her eyes, and she raked it back, *away* from her face. An unveiling. He'd never noticed it before, but she had a slight widow's peak. Her face was heart-shaped.

"Are you going to stay like this?" Webern asked.

"Fuckin' A! He gave me a lifetime prescription. Weren't you listening?"

Webern sat down on the bed. His mind was racing. As Nepenthe flung herself down beside him, he thought of the first time he'd undressed her, the way she'd yielded, as if he'd been prizing away the last of her secrets. But he hadn't been. Nepenthe had this skin all along, just beneath the scales she'd shown him. Webern felt tricked. He began to remember the old necessity of hiding his body: the lumpy sweaters, the tight-closed blinds. When Nepenthe ran her hand over his hump, he shrank away. She glared at him accusingly. A small line appeared between her eyebrows. She had a tiny mole, a freckle really, high on one temple.

"You're not even happy for me," she said. "The best day of my life, and you're not even happy for me." She held the camera at arm's length and snapped another picture. This time, both of them were in the shot. Nepenthe popped it out of the camera, then flapped it back and forth in the air, to make it develop faster. "The happy couple. Jesus God. Say something, won't you? Don't just sit there like a zombie."

"I'm sorry." Webern covered his face with his hands.

"Hey, how'd that thing get in here?"

Webern looked up. Marzipan had finally come inside, carrying their suitcases.

"Just put them anywhere," Webern told her.

Marzipan dropped them where she stood. She folded her arms.

"Whose is it?" Nepenthe wrinkled her nose. "Wow, it smells like mothballs."

"She's my grandma's. Her name's Marzipan." He plucked at the Mexican blanket. "I guess I'm taking care of her now."

"For real?" Then Nepenthe realized what he meant. "Oh. Shit. I'm sorry, Bernie. No, I really am. I can't believe you didn't tell—well, whatever. I'm a bitch." She paused, as if waiting for his grief to pass. Then she added lightly, "Does it—does she do tricks? Maybe you can use her in your act."

"I don't really think she's that kind of monkey."

"Maybe she is. Look, she's smiling."

Across the room, Marzipan was baring her teeth.

"No, she isn't."

"Yes, she is." Nepenthe spoke with authority: "This is a trained ape."

Webern shut his eyes. Hesitantly, he touched Nepenthe's back. It was smooth, smooth, smooth—except for the one scale she'd missed, a brittle husk still clinging to her left shoulder blade. It came loose as soon as his hand touched it, but Webern held it in place against her skin for a long moment before finally letting it drop.

CHAPTER TWENTY

THE STILT WALKERS MOVED PRECARIOUSLY ABOVE THE MIDWAY. They sidestepped an exotic dancer, a half-dozen tame peacocks, and a little girl carrying a basket of piglets. They teetered by a pair of mechanics who bent over a dissected clown car, fingers blackened with grease, and three equestrians who were washing their tights in a vat of pink lemonade. As they balanced on their stilts, they juggled: one tossed batons, another bowling pins, a third casaba melons. They wore fringed jackets and armbands with fluttering ribbons, and impossibly long seersucker pants, and enormous papier-mâché heads with eyes that moved and mouths that opened and top hats that sprouted real flowers. It was a brand new act. Even some of the vendors stopped pulling taffy or frying corndogs to gawk. But when Webern passed them, he didn't even slow his pace.

When he pushed past the animal trainers and the roustabouts, the strongmen and the acrobats, he saw only one thing: the broad, straight shoulders, the muscles and the height, of the men who worked alongside him in the circus. Webern wondered if Nepenthe had been outside since her transformation, if any of these men, catching a whiff of her perfume, had turned their heads in her direction, if they'd whistled or nudged each other, or, worst of all, stood with mouths ajar in respectful silence until she disappeared. He thought of her, in an angora sweater and a tennis skirt, eating an ice cream on the midway, and the thought struck him as obscene. Now that she'd shed her scales, along with the gloves and scarves she'd worn to conceal them, it was like she was walking around naked for everyone else to see. Smells of hay and excrement, fresh paint and old candy, filled the air as Webern stepped under the big top's awning into the hot, sawdusty shade. The other clowns were there already, practicing in the farthest ring. Webern passed the elephants Stanley and Hortense, who were rehearsing for the daintiest tea party they could manage, and climbed up into the empty stands. As he moved among the bleachers, he looked down, seeing, for the first time in a long while, what the audience saw: the sheer size of the arena, the weathered red and yellow canvas stretching forever upwards like the wind-worn dome of a hot air balloon.

Webern sat down on the bleachers. When he'd left, Nepenthe had been digging through her trunk, searching for the scantiest clothing she could find. Her face had flushed pink with exertion as she tossed muumuus and trench coats over her shoulders. She'd cursed when her clove had burned a hole in a rumpled tie dye T-shirt, but she'd pounded out the flames with a clown shoe and kept on searching for some long-forgotten halter top. Now, here in the dusty ring, Webern felt a kind of relief. At least he still could escape into this.

Even though they weren't in costume, Webern saw right away that the clowns were practicing a version of his Martian act. Happy Herbert, playing the lead, moved stiffly, robotically; he held his arms as straight as rocket launchers and kept his eyes wide and glassy and fixed forward, mechanically swivelling his whole head when he turned to look at something. It was a typical performance for him: at the first sign of strangeness, Herbert always turned his character into a cartoon, an instantly recognizable grotesque that mimicked the minor characters of TV sitcoms. When Herbert played a clown policeman, he became all swagger and billy club; when playing a drunk, he continually stumbled and hiccupped, never colouring his portrait with the various shades of rage, sorrow, and merriment he so vividly displayed most nights at the Clown HQ. Now, as a spaceman, he was no different. The tin soldier walk, the blank expression, had been stolen from a million mediocre sci-fi movies—movies that Herbert had no doubt glimpsed on drive-in screens over the tops of fences Friday nights when he and his hometown buddies rode on the back of a pickup truck to the empty field where they would huff paint thinner and tip over cows.

Much as he wanted to, Webern couldn't look away. It was almost impressive how completely Herbert had missed the point. The Martian was supposed to be like a child, seeing everything on Earth for the first time; his wonder and curiosity were meant to reveal the strangeness of ordinary objects—a telephone, a lamp post, an umbrella. Herbert had only seen the spaceman's strangeness, and had turned him into a figure of ridicule. It made Webern sick, but in a way it was comforting, too. It would have been humiliating to see Herbert outdo him at something.

The other clowns wrapped up the rehearsal with the usual backslaps, friendly insults, and idle horseplay around the scenery. It wasn't until they began to part ways that Pipsqueak spotted Webern in the stands.

"Hey guys, look who's back." Pipsqueak bounded over. Up close, Webern could see he still had on eyeliner from the last night's show. "Heya, Bump! How's tricks?"

Webern tried to smile. Pipsqueak's grin faded.

"My condolences." Silly Billy strode up with his hand extended for Webern to shake. Webern wondered how he had heard about Nepenthe until Billy added, "I lost my grandma a few years back—she keeled over, sitting right next to me in church. Now there's a shocker, I'll tell you. Boy, you shoulda seen my face."

"See, it wasn't that bad. With Bo-Bo, I mean. She was in her coffin with the lid shut when it happened. But I'll probably have nightmares about it anyway, you know?"

Webern realized he was still shaking Silly Billy's hand. Hurriedly, he dropped it and wiped his moist palm on his pants.

"Sounds like you kinda jumped the gun on those funeral arrangements." Pipsqueak exchanged glances with Silly Billy.

"You okay, man? You need a cup of joe or anything?" Silly Billy stepped aside as Happy Herbert blustered up to give his regards. The trio of clowns, all scrutinizing him so closely, reminded Webern of the doctors who once stood over his hospital bed, alternately prodding him and holding X-rays of his hump up to the light. The illusion held until the short, pudgy doctor in the middle suddenly squeezed Webern's hand in his two fists and began to pump it aggressively. Webern blinked and yanked his fingers away from Happy Herbert's.

"Huh, huh. Bump." Happy Herbert undid his belt and attempted to tighten it a notch, then gave up and let the Texas-shaped buckle dangle idly near his crotch. "I've been wanting to thank you."

"For what?" Webern glanced suspiciously at the other two clowns. Silly Billy doodled with his toe in the sawdust; Pipsqueak whistled and looked over his shoulder.

"For the laughs, that's what. For going away and leaving me all your routines. Kids've been eating it up. I owe you one."

Webern nodded slowly.

"We better get going," Silly Billy told Webern. He grabbed Happy Herbert firmly by the shoulder. "You probably need some rest."

"What rest?" Herbert protested. "He just got back from vacation."

Webern watched the clowns walk away; as they passed a trash can, Herbert punched it. The metal lid rolled on its edge for a few feet before finally tipping over. Webern stared down at the ground. An empty Coke bottle lay gleaming in the dust. Then he looked up again sharply. If he hadn't known better, he would have sworn he'd just seen a little boy, no bigger than a mouse, run across the bench just in front of him.

When Webern got back to the boxcar and found it strewn with brassieres but otherwise deserted, he sat down at his desk and covered his face with his hands. This was bad. Even when he held perfectly still, his thoughts kept whirling around and around, like a carousel of intricately carved nightmares. Bo-Bo's coffin, flecked with dirt, rolled by, the lid opening slowly. Nepenthe, smiling and blowing kisses to everyone but him, rode on Happy Herbert's back. Madge, dressed in his mother's apron and heels, pranced alongside his father, who carried his grandfather's lion-head cane. Willow and Billow scuttled by on their many legs, dragging a net of cobwebs and bones. And last of all was Wags, snapping the straps of his lederhosen, playing a merry klezmer song on Dr. Show's concertina.

Webern stood up. His hands were shaking. He crawled under the bed, pushing aside dust bunnies, Napoleon wrappers, and clove ash, until he finally found a half-empty bottle of Campari. It was warm and disgusting and bitter as blood, but he didn't care. He drank the whole thing, then lay down on the floor. Now the room was spinning, but his mind mercifully stopped.

Webern stared up at the ceiling. Everything felt very hard and sharp and clear. Nepenthe would leave him. He thought about it like it was happening to somebody else. Once, a long time ago, she'd said she didn't believe in marriage because it was impossible to promise you wouldn't fall out of love with somebody: "You can promise to stay with them forever, I guess, but that's not the same thing. That's basically just promising to be miserable if your feelings change. This country is a cesspool of repression."

Webern pictured her at a party in an apartment full of beaded curtains and batiked silk tapestries of unicorns, kneeling beside a bong made of swirling coloured glass. "I used to be a circus freak." No one would even know if the story was true until she started to blubber about how guilty she felt for leaving her hunchbacked midget lover. Then they'd all spring to her defense. "No one could go on living that way," a guy with a week-old beard and an Oriental tunic would declare. "You have to think about yourself sometimes, baby. Throw off those shackles, you know?" Then he'd talk about how life is cyclical and about three hours later the two of them would be screwing in the bathroom.

It was so obvious, so inevitable, it was almost funny. But one part of him refused to accept it. That part of him lingered on even now in Nepenthe's old tent, holding his breath, watching her sleep in silvery water for the very first time. That night, so many years ago, Webern had seen her clearly; he had seen her soul, if that was the word for it, written on every inch of her body, from the knee, draped in sodden fabric, that tilted lazily against one wall of the kiddy pool to the grey fingers that skimmed the water's surface. She had seemed like no one in the world but herself—stubborn and funny and haughty and angry and shy. He had felt that if he was very careful he would have the luxury to know her all his life.

Webern's hump ached against the hard floor. He pulled himself to his feet. Unsteadily, he picked his way through Nepenthe's clothing and the Polaroids that still littered the boxcar floor, pausing only to kick the Porky Pig Pez dispenser out of sight under the couch. Then he opened the door and stepped outside. He was going to look for Marzipan.

Webern walked past more stilt-walkers and a few contortionists energetically practicing outside in the noonday sun. Normally, this was the time of day he liked best; between the troupe's rehearsal and that evening's show, he developed his ideas into new acts. Most days, he took a sandwich and wandered down the line of boxcars; he usually nodded to the old fortune teller beating her rugs and the Ossified Man cleaning off dishes with a hose. The squalling voices of the sunbathing dancers and catcalling motorbike riders put him in a kind of trance, and he often found himself moving again through the landscape of a recent dream, perceiving details—a bouncy ball, a squeaky sound effect—that he hadn't recalled upon waking, details that he hastily scribbled in his notebook the moment he got the chance.

Webern jammed his hands in the pockets of his jeans and held his head low as he walked. Today, he just wanted to get away as quickly as possible.

He sidestepped picnic blankets and wagon cages. He passed the hungry crowd outside the cookhouse, where a vat of spaghetti and a vat of paste for hanging posters boiled side by side, mingling scents and steam. He walked on, past the boxcars still loaded with machinery and tarps, past the rumbling light generator wagons and the empty flatbeds and down toward empty tracks that twinned each other all the way to the horizon. After awhile, he reached a tree on the edge of camp. Marzipan was up in its highest branches, picking summer apples and dropping them into the pockets of her apron. When she saw Webern looking up at her, she bit into one and, chewing thoughtfully, began a long, swinging descent down to where he was standing.

As soon as she reached the ground, she tossed away the core of the apple she was eating, pulled out a new one, and gave it to him. Webern stared at it there in his hand. Its skin was deep, deep red, so dark it was almost purple, flecked with tiny white spots that looked like stars in a violet sky. As he watched, the stars began to orbit, forming shifting constellations, until they became the sky of his childhood, a sky he recognized from one autumn night, when he stood at the bedroom window in his pyjamas, looking anywhere but Earth.

Willow and Billow babysat Webern the night his mother died. His parents were going to a costume party, even though it wasn't yet Halloween, and when they came out of their bedroom they were dressed so strangely he almost didn't recognize them. Webern's father wore his old army jacket over a pair of wrinkled khaki pants. When Webern asked him why, his mother cringed, but his father just said, "Because it's the scariest thing I own." His mother was dressed as a mermaid, with a green silk skirt and a bodice made of a million clinking seashells. Her heels, taller than the ones she usually wore, made her unsteady. She moved through the house slowly, moving her arms as though parting ribbons of seaweed. Before they left, she came to Webern's room to kiss him good-bye. She had green glitter in her hair and for days, he kept finding it: on his cheek, his ear lobe, the palms of his hands.

His parents left in such a hurry they forgot to close the garage door. Webern came downstairs and stood at the living room window to watch their Studebaker drive away. This was the first time he'd been alone with Willow and Billow since before his accident. He was still wearing the brace that was meant to straighten his back, and it squeezed him like a vise. When he heard his sisters behind him, he felt it tighten around him even more.

"Bernie Bee, we have a surprise."

"Come to the kitchen, close your eyes."

Webern took a deep breath. His sisters took hold of him: Willow grabbed his shoulder, Billow his hump. He held his eyes shut as they steered him through the darkened rooms. In the kitchen, Webern expected to see a dead squirrel in a pizza box, or a pair of dead man's shoes they'd dredged out of the lake. But nothing could prepare him for what actually greeted him when he opened his eyes.

His sisters had prepared him a feast. Candy corn and watermelon slices, a milkshake dusted with Ovaltine—orange marmalade spread on graham crackers and maraschino cherries dunked in hot fudge.

"Bernie Bee, we make you eat."

"Nothing bitter, always sweet."

Webern turned toward his sisters in disbelief. The twins wore newly dyed black aprons that left smudges on everything they touched. As Billow proffered a peanut butter and marshmallow fluff sandwich, he noticed the dark grease that lined the creases in her palms and knuckles, the undersides of her fingernails. She was taking an auto mechanics class at her high school, and she often came home in the evenings with complex, mimeographed diagrams that she pored over for hours while her sister desiccated cat bones with a hairdryer for biology. Webern thought of the coiled entrails of the Studebaker's engine, Billow's tools laid out on his father's workbench like the scalpels and forceps of a messy operating table, and as the wind howled outside, he imagined dead leaves whispering along the concrete floor.

"I'll be right back," he whispered.

In the garage, pliers and cranks lay scattered everywhere, and in the centre of the room a discarded bolt lay in a puddle of black motor oil. Webern pushed the button on the wall, and the automatic door clanked down, one heavy panel at a time. Later he would remember how dark and empty it had looked, how sealed up, like a walled-off, unheated room that has outlived its original use.

When he came back into the kitchen, Willow and Billow clamped their hands around his arms and steered him to the sofa in front of the black-n-white TV, where they waited on him as he uncomfortably watched cartoons. The twins stood behind the couch, holding hands, breathing down his neck.

"Eat it all—all that you can." Willow poked him with a Pixie stick.

"Here, have another ginger man." Billow nudged him with the tray.

"Thanks," mumbled Webern. On the TV, a cat in a convertible crashed into a barn, leaving a car-shaped hole.

At nine o'clock sharp, Willow and Billow dragged Webern up to bed, then stood over him watchfully as he climbed under the covers with all his clothes on. Cautiously, he folded his glasses and set them on the nightstand, but still the two didn't budge. A long moment passed. Then they linked arms, and, without opening their mouths, began to hum a lullaby. It was more a kind of buzzing through their teeth, but Webern recognized the tune. It was a song his mother had made up for him. He hadn't heard it since he was very small. When they finished, the twins smiled at each other.

"Now go to sleep, our little prince." Billow switched off the lights.

"Or we'll cut your cheeks and make you wince." Willow closed the door.

Webern got out of bed immediately and changed into his pyjamas. Then he lay back down. His teeth felt grainy with sugar, and his hump throbbed in a way it hadn't since just after the accident. He rubbed his hand over it gently.

"Wags?" he called softly. No one answered.

After an hour or two, Webern finally fell asleep reading comic books by flashlight. He dimly heard the storm door slam when the girls slipped out for their usual late-night walk. But a few hours later, he jumped up, wide awake, when he heard the collision outside.

He ran to the window and threw back the curtain. The Studebaker was in the driveway, slammed snout-first into the heavy panels of the closed garage. Smoke poured from its engine, and on the passenger side, his father struggled with the jammed car door. Webern's mother was in clear sight, her head and shoulders and arms extended like a diver's through the hole where the windshield had once been. Her face rested on the crumpled hood of the car. Later, Webern would say the metal had squashed like a Coke can, but in that moment, he saw its rippled surface as waves, and the bits of glass that sparkled around her as diamonds and rubies, ancient treasures or lost cargo that could have been found at the very bottom of the sea.

CHAPTER TWENTY-ONE

WEBERN LAY UNDER THE APPLE TREE, the core of the purple fruit still in his hand. Up above, the leaves whispered in the breeze. He felt empty, as if the wind had been knocked out of him, and for a moment it occurred to him that he could just lay there, under the crisscrossing shadows of the branches, forever. Then Marzipan poked him with her toe. Abruptly, he stood up. She grasped him by the wrist and led him back toward the camp.

Marzipan and Webern walked together, past the donnikers, their antiquated half-moon doors squeaking in the breeze atop a flatbed car, and through the maze of folded lawn chairs, bottles, and discarded cellophane that was the performers' campground. It wasn't until they had passed the fortune teller, who shuffled and muttered to herself amidst several milling cats, that Webern noticed that a line had formed outside his own boxcar.

It was like a freak show in reverse. The Skeleton Dude stood near the front; the delicate calligraphy of his shadow zigzagged on the dusty ground. Behind him, three pinheads carried useless gifts: an empty, flapping cardboard box, a tennis shoe, and what looked like a makeshift doll, styled out of horsehair and a Mrs. Butterworth bottle. The giant came next, in his ten gallon hat; he led the Shetland pony he kept near him at all times to give his audience an exaggerated sense of scale. The others stretched on behind in single file: the albino girl, her pink eyes flashing, her blinding white hair avalanching down her back; the Elastic Man, his distended arm-skin hanging in two drooping folds like fleshy wings; the Missing Link, his thick fur coarse and bristling, tangled with lint and old popcorn kernels.

Sitting on an overturned crate in a one-piece bathing suit, Nepenthe greeted each of them in turn. She hugged the Skeleton Dude and exclaimed over the pinheads' gifts. She stroked the Shetland pony's mane and leapt up to shake the giant's hand. She crossed and uncrossed her legs, her smooth thighs shone in the sun, and when the albino girl leaned toward her to share a confidence, her laughter rang out like the first notes of a melody. She had never seemed so happy, so completely at ease with the other freaks as she did now that medicine had proved she wasn't one of them.

Webern thought of the storybook princess who dropped her golden ball into the mossy well where the frog king made his home, the way her cries had summoned him, malformed and web-footed, into an unwelcoming realm of palaces and light. As the Human Torso poked Nepenthe's shoulder blades with a riding crop he clasped between his teeth, Webern slipped past the crowd unnoticed, up the steps into the boxcar.

For a long time, he lay on the bed, watching rock candy grow in the windowsill aquarium; he squinted his eyes till he believed he saw the crystals forming. He didn't move until Marzipan finally returned from the errand he'd sent her on, with a bottle of Scotch and two Dixie cups. Then they sat on the bed, Indian style, and facing each other proceeded to drink. Marzipan's eyes, large and brown, glowed with a warm amber light that Webern could only identify as understanding. As she poured him another glass, he began to appreciate why Bo-Bo kept her around; she was everything pleasant about a human being, without the mess and confusion of words.

Nepenthe came inside about an hour later, carrying a bottle of cheap champagne and two Mickey Mouse juice cups Webern had sometimes seen the pinheads using. Venus followed close behind, dressed in a slinky red dress with the armholes sewn up, and a pair of strappy sandals that showcased her red, glossy toenails. Venus's eyes were done Elizabeth Taylor Egyptian style, with two small black tails curling away at the corners.

"Hey, Pluto." Nepenthe waggled her Mickey Mouse cup by one of its ears. She flung herself down on the bed between Webern and Marzipan, then made a grab for him, but Webern backed into the pillows at the head of the bed. His legs jackknifed up against his chest.

"So where've you two been?" he asked. The strap of Nepenthe's swimsuit had slipped off one shoulder.

"Haven't you heard? Your girl works for the ball toss now. She just stands there and the dopes all win her prizes." Venus smiled slyly, uncoiling on the sofa.

"Shut up!" Nepenthe shrieked. She laughed a little too loudly. Marzipan got up and, glancing over her shoulder surreptitiously, put the Scotch away in one of Webern's desk drawers. She pulled out the desk chair and sat down. Nepenthe went on, "We were right outside, kiddo. Didn't you see us?"

"I saw some kind of crowd. I dunno, I was tired. I *am* tired." It was true. Right then, there was nothing Webern wanted more than to close his eyes.

"Poor fella." Venus kicked off her shoes and flexed her long toes. "Needed his little naptime, huh?"

Nepenthe ran a careless hand over her knee. The curves of bone moved visibly, languidly beneath her skin. "Well, you should've stayed. It was my retirement party."

At the word "retirement," Webern pulled off his glasses and pressed the heels of his hands to his face.

"What's wrong with him?" Venus asked. Papers crinkled as she paged through one of Nepenthe's underground newspapers with her feet.

Webern felt the springs of the bed quake beneath him as Nepenthe rose.

"Let's put on some records," he heard her say. A minute later, the record player's needle scratched into the well worn grooves of her Question Mark and the Mysterians album. *96 Tears.*

"You know, this guy had a vision that he'd be singing this song in the year ten thousand?" Nepenthe's feet padded across the rug. "I heard him on the radio."

"He's smoking stronger stuff than you, hon," said Venus.

Nepenthe flopped onto the couch. "The weird thing is, he actually sounded happy about it. If I thought I was going to keep living the same thing over and over, I'd probably kill myself. Then again, he also said he came here from Mars back in dinosaur times, so I guess he's already used to it." She raised her voice a little. "Hey Bernie, what do you think? You think Question Mark knows what's up?"

Webern opened his eyes slowly. Nepenthe was stretched over the cushions, her legs crossed at the ankles, her arms folded behind her head, just like a pin-up girl. She knew exactly what she was doing, and Webern hated her for it—for all of it. He hated her for the bathing suit, for the Polaroids, for the box of scales, dead and dried out and sold to strangers. He hated her for letting another man rub her skin, for letting the giant and the skeleton gawk and prod her. But most of all, he hated her for the way she was smiling at him now, as if he were any other rube she'd seen on the midway, some stranger she could test her powers on.

"I think he's stupid," he said. His voice sounded tiny and childish, even to him. "Like all these stupid bands you listen to."

Nepenthe's smile faded; she tossed her hair and drew it loosely into a ponytail, then got up off the sofa. "Start the record over, Venus. I want to dance."

Venus raised an eyebrow, but obediently reached one foot over and moved the needle to the beginning. Nepenthe got up and began to punch the air. Her hips swivelled like a hula hooper's. With a sidelong glance at Webern, Venus joined her, her whole body swaying in lithe, serpentine motions, her feet describing tiny circles on the rug.

"Move around a little, shortcake." Venus jerked her bouffant in his direction. "Might do you some good."

"Aw, Bernie doesn't want to. He hates this band, remember? But you know who just might." Nepenthe turned her back toward him and sashayed toward the desk. Marzipan saw her coming and jumped up on the chair, but Nepenthe grabbed her hands before she could get away. "C'mon and cry, cry, cry, cry," she crooned. She moved Marzipan's shaggy arms up and down through the air. "Let me hear you cry now."

"Stop it!" Webern sat up.

"Mellow out! Look at her. She likes it."

Marzipan glanced desperately at Webern, her rubbery lips stretched back to expose her teeth. She twisted, but Nepenthe held on tight.

"Leave her alone!" Webern jumped up. He grabbed Nepenthe by the elbow and tried to pull her away.

"Let go of me." She shook him off. "You're freaking her out."

Marzipan shrieked; she yanked backward as hard as she could, and Nepenthe let go all at once.

"Damn it!"

The chair fell over, and Marzipan toppled onto the floor.

"What did you do to her?"

"What did *I* do? What the fuck, Bernie! You care more about that goddamn ape than you do about me. She's fine!" Nepenthe stomped her foot. Marzipan got up and rapidly swung on her knuckles out of the boxcar. "See? She's completely fine!"

221

Webern sat down on the desk chair. As much as he tried to hold them back, the tears wouldn't stop; there was a kind of relief in such complete humiliation. Venus glanced back and forth between him and Nepenthe, then followed the chimp outside.

"Come find me later, sweets," she called over one shoulder. It wasn't clear which one of them she was talking to.

For a long time, neither of them spoke. Webern bent over the marbled cover of his clown notebook and held his head in both hands. Finally, Nepenthe put her hand on his hump. He didn't shake her off this time. Her fingers burned there.

"Listen," she said. "Venus and I are going to a party tonight. You can come if you want. I'd like you to come."

Webern flipped open the notebook. He imagined himself cartwheeling and tumbling into the colourful pages, vanishing into a landscape of sawdust and spotlights and painted cardboard towns. He shook his head.

"I didn't mean to ignore you," she told him. "Earlier, I mean, when everyone from the Parliament came by. I just figured I'd let them all get a good look. I owe them that much, at least. It gives them—I don't know—hope or something. If that's not too cliché."

"Sure." Webern thumbed past clowns in fire trucks, clowns sitting in front of malfunctioning typewriters or haywire hair-growing machines.

"You're sure you don't want to come out with us? It might be fun. You could juggle. People love it when you juggle."

"I just got back. I have a lot to do." He stopped at an old drawing— the clown followed by a rain cloud he just couldn't shake. He still hadn't figured out how to make it work onstage. Dry ice? Lighting tricks? Some sort of projection? He traced one finger over the small, stooped figure he'd drawn in for himself. "Have a good time, okay?"

"Okay." Nepenthe let go. "I will."

That night, Webern watched the big top show from the stands. One of the acrobats sprained his wrist during a handspring—Webern saw him later, holding ice against the swelling—and the timing was off all night: the elephants had hardly finished lumbering through their tea party when a team of men wheeled out the motorcycle cage, and a pair of trapeze artists collided in midair with an audible thwack.

Webern dreaded the clowns, but they were even more awful than he expected. Happy Herbert had replaced the Martian's tinfoil suit with a boxy costume that made him look like a walking TV: it was ugly, but even worse, it restricted his movements, so he could only turn at right angles and couldn't even bend his elbows. Webern fixated on that costume. He promised himself that it would be the first thing to go when he started performing with the other clowns again. He pictured himself lighting it ablaze, preferably with Happy Herbert still inside.

He went back to the boxcar by himself. Marzipan sat on the couch, knitting. The window was ajar, and a faint breeze, along with the incredible jumble of clothes, records, clove ash, and magazines strewn on the floor, gave Webern the unpleasant sensation of walking into a home that had just been ransacked. For a minute, as he stood in the doorway, he pretended to himself that he really had been robbed—his girlfriend kidnapped, his fortune stolen!—and that, when he found Nepenthe again, tied to the railroad tracks, maybe, or shackled to a chair, she'd fall into his arms, sobbing with gratitude. But he couldn't make the daydream come into focus: Nepenthe's scales wouldn't stay in place, and she kept stepping back, away from him, to link arms with her captors, a pair of broad-chested radicals whose cause she had recently joined.

Webern shoved a few wrinkled costumes into a scarred trunk and rubbed at a sticky patch of dried Moxie with an old T-shirt until Marzipan grabbed him by the wrist. He was cursing loud enough for his neighbours to hear. It was no good anyway. The place was still a mess. He sank into his chair. After a long moment, he opened the drawer of his desk.

Behind the box that held the Great Vermicelli was a smaller one, with pictures of individually wrapped coffeecakes printed on its top and sides. It was the box he'd gotten almost five years earlier, the day he'd gone to the Lemon City morgue to identify Dr. Show's body. Inside were the contents of Dr. Show's pockets. Webern set the box on his knees and opened the top. He sifted through the ticket stubs, the brightly coloured handkerchiefs, the photographs, until, down at the bottom, he found what he was looking for: Dr. Show's watch.

On its face, an acrobat pointed her cartwheeling arms at the minutes and hours; on the back, the engraved words GOLDENLAND 1923 were almost rubbed away. Webern set the watch by his alarm clock, wound it, and put it on his wrist. It hung there loose and heavy, and he stared at it, thinking of the night when, like him, Dr. Show waited up for performers who were never coming back.

Nine, ten, eleven, midnight. At quarter to one, Webern finally got up and started pacing. Marzipan looked up from her knitting with mild concern.

"Stay," Webern told her. He pointed at the couch.

Marzipan rolled her eyes and went back to work. Webern opened the door and stepped out into the balmy night.

Outside, two of the fat ladies—Rhonda and Tina—staggered around the corner of a wagon, hooting, and Pigalle, the trapeze artist, stood outside her boxcar like a lanky bird with one leg bent, smoothing powder onto a fresh bruise beneath her eye. But most of the boxcar doors were shut. Arguments and laughter and the clinking sound of bottles floated from the windows.

Webern thought about ghosts as he walked: his mother, Schoenberg, Bo-Bo. He wondered if there could be ghosts of people who were still alive. Soon, Nepenthe would be nothing but an apparition—a pink robe, thrown over the back of the chair, glimpsed in the moonlight and mistaken for something else. An empty popcorn bag tumbled along the dusty ground, and Webern froze until it passed.

Maybe Webern himself was a ghost—the spectre of the man his father killed, the man whose name he had inherited. Or he could be the ghost of the perfect child who shattered beneath the treehouse that afternoon. After the accident, when he was still very young, he often looked into mirrors to find his old friend Wags staring back out at him. Something about the way the glass shone, the sharpness of his friend's small face, made Webern wonder if he himself was just the reflection, and Wags was the one being doubled.

Wags had always seemed more alive than Webern. He had popped up everywhere back in those days: in the empty hallway after classes in the elementary school, pratfalling down waxed hallways dusted with chalk; hanging by his knees in the backyard oak long past midnight. He was always performing. It was tough to know what he was thinking, because to him everything was a joke, a hook, a lead into his routine; even his clumsiness was choreographed. The first person Webern knew who was like that in Real Life—funny he felt a need to qualify it that way, "Real Life"—was Dr. Schoenberg. And even with him, the seams sometimes showed: the strain in his smile, his salesman's overeagerness to close. With Wags, there was no difference, no line that separated the character he played from the character he was. There was no Real Him.

"The person in the mirror is me," Webern murmured. The words sounded like nonsense to him. He paused to grip the rusty bars of a wagon cage, just to make sure he could still feel the cool iron against his hands. He hardly noticed the sleeping tiger that lay on the straw inside.

"Say there, fella. Better watch where you're putting them paws."

Webern's lips moved involuntarily. He took a giant step backward and looked up. Sometimes the animal wranglers slept on top of the wagons when they got tired of bunking with the roustabouts. But this didn't sound like an animal wrangler's voice.

"Aren't you gonna say hello?" The tiger stirred in its cage. "What, cat got your tongue?"

Webern shook his head. "I just can't believe it's you."

"Keep trying. It gets easier with practice."

Wags sat down on the edge of the wagon and dangled his legs off the side. His hair shone faintly in the moonlight, like spun gold or fallen stars, and his face was as much like Webern's as ever—maybe even more so. He snapped the straps of his lederhosen and laughed out loud.

"How long have you been sitting there, watching me?"

"Too long. You're a nice guy and all, but I've known figurines with more pep."

"Thanks."

Wags held out his arms like a child asking to be picked up. "Catch me. If anybody knows how to break a fall, it's you."

Webern obediently outstretched his arms, and Wags jumped down. But when he landed he was no taller than a thumb, standing on the palm of Webern's left hand.

"How'd you get so small?" Webern asked.

"Change of perspective, old buddy. It's an art." He danced a little jig. "Always was a particular talent of mine. Remember how I used to run around the clock with the second hand? It was a race against time."

"No, but I do remember when you ran face first into a slingshot."

"I bounced back from that one pretty quick. Hey, remember the time I got trapped inside your family's telephone?"

"That rings a bell."

"Of course, all of that was nothing compared to the day I got thrown in the laundry." He clucked his tongue. "If it hadn't been for the Life Saver in your pants pocket, I would've been all washed up."

"You know, I thought I was going to have to handle this all by myself," Webern said, laughing. He thought of his empty boxcar, the monkey hair on the couch. "But it's just like Mom said. You came back when I needed you."

"Hey, I'm glad to be of service." Wags took a bow. "But don't think I'm just the pit crew here to pull you from a wreck."

"What do you mean?"

"I mean I may be a saviour, but I ain't no angel." Wags grinned; even though his face was the size of a nickel, his smile seemed much larger than that. "Buck up, pal. We're going to have some fun."

CHAPTER TWENTY-TWO

THE ALLEY HOUSE WAS CROOKED-SHAPED to fit the gap between two storefronts. Stairs zigzagged up the side, steep and backless as rungs on tilted ladders: six flights to the top. Wanda and Betsy spoke prayers as they climbed. Each step that squeaked was the alley house's amen.

"Lord Christ please make our bones like thine, clubs upon a sinner's pride."

"Holy Ghost please turn our blood to wine and wake the corpses who have died."

Their landlady was a Christian who forbade fornication and hot pots. Their room was attic-shaped, with tilted eaves, unpainted wood, and cobwebs. Wanda and Betsy didn't mind. They were Christians, too. The home was a vessel for the spirit and if that was pure the home would be also, all appearances aside. Like them, their neighbours below came from the institution, and the grunts and curses that rose up through the vents reminded Wanda and Betsy they were living righteously.

Back when Willow and Billow lived in the treehouse, they had nest-slept, wrapped together in pillows, grey insulation, a tattered coat. In those days, they had woken nights uncertain whose elbow, whose knee, whose fingerbone was whose. It had mattered exactly none, there in the jumble that they made. Now Wanda and Betsy slept in twin beds like dolls in boxes under portraits of the saints. Sometimes, though, they woke in the night under low splintery beams of the alley house, and though their eyes were open they went on dreaming of the treehouse. A trapdoor opened the floor of the attic room; beneath it lay the past. Wanda and Betsy never spoke of it, lying side by side, seeing treehouse in the dark. There was no need. They both still had the same dreams.

They parked their van out front. Gunmetal grey, it had four doors. On its side was written in stenciled letters PROPERTY OF MUNICIPAL ANIMAL IMPOUNDMENT CENTRE. Cages lined the back. Fur tufts and dog shit snagged the bars. It smelled like dogs even when there were no dogs. The van air had a memory.

Wanda was left-handed. Betsy was a lefty, too. When one drove the other shifted gears. Each morning when they drove to report in, the cages shuddered and rattled in the space behind where they sat. Each morning they remembered when a van had come for Willow and Billow. The back of that van had been one dark cage. They lay down there together; Willow lit a match. Later, they learned the sulfur smell of that match had been the reason everyone believed they burned down the treehouse. The van had taken them to the institution, where they lived six years.

The institution wasn't a hospital or a church. It was a Retreat, the doctors said. For Willow and Billow, it was Surrender. They had no weapons there, no bones and stones and snakes to throw. They had no fog to vanish in, no trees to climb, no birds to catch. No wind and storm howled to them. Together at meals, they could not eat; kept separate at night, they could not sleep. What the doctors asked them, they would not tell. Pills made their minds like cool clay. They sat side by side, indifferent.

Nuns crept through the institution from time to time, footless in their hoods of black. They left marks on nothing they touched with their bloodless hands. When they laughed it was with no sound. Willow and Billow began to follow them through the halls. They followed one to chapel. It was there they became schooled in the ways of faith.

Bible study was four to six. Chapel light came through stained glass, barred up like all the windows in the place. There were no Bibles, only pews, and Sister, who spoke in a swaying, uneven voice, like melody. The other patients left right away, but Willow and Billow understood her words. They were sisters, too.

Sister taught them Revelations, and of the demons that would come, of the lamb with seven glittering eyes, and how the Father appeared as cloud and fire. She taught the mysteries of the soul, how the Father marked creatures as his own. Sister didn't feed them pills or ask for them to speak or eat. She called them by their Christian names and told them that on the last day, Lord Christ would do the same.

She taught them charity, piety, perseverance, gratitude. Sister taught them they were two, with different souls in different skins. They were sinners now and as such, condemned. Only with Christ could they be as one, not consigned to separate flames.

Wanda and Betsy became warriors for Christ; they sang anthems for his glory, even while the TV played and others profaned his name. They confessed their sins to a skittish priest, who kept one finger on the NURSE CALL button: they had disobeyed their mother, they had coveted their brother's treehouse, they had huffed glue and pretended to be ghosts. Their necks swung heavy with rosaries; each night they prayed over grey meat and plastic knives. They gave up scratching walls for Lent, then gave it up altogether. One day the doctors declared that they were well, and cast them out into the world.

Sister's brother worked at the pound, so God's provenance found them vocation there. Called to this work, they learned their trade. The Holy Ghost helped them know where the lost dogs hid. Sometimes the Holy Ghost spoke through the men around the oil drum fire.

"There's one back there," the men would say. And the spirit would move them to point at the part of the dump where the tires stood in tall towers, or where the broken refrigerators made blue puddles in the dirt. Wanda and Betsy used their nets.

Wanda and Betsy understood why the dogs got lost. Before they came to know the faith, they too had strayed from yard to street to vacant lot, from the clean sheets of an even bed to the knotted roots of a tree. They had not known that they belonged to God, that their place was in his House; they had not come where they were Called. Wanda and Betsy tried to teach the dogs what Sister had taught them, but the dogs didn't always learn. If they didn't learn, they stayed Lost. Or died.

Wanda and Betsy didn't make many friends at the pound. The other dogcatchers didn't like how they sang songs for Christ, how they committed the dogs' souls to heaven when the injections went in. They sent Betsy out back to fix their vans and watched Wanda nervously over their donuts in the break room as she studied the crucifixes she'd hung on the wall.

In the night, sometimes, Wanda and Betsy went for fog walks as they had in the old days. They moved through dewy grass before the world belonged to dawn. This was the time when the world became a ghost of itself, when all colours faded to grey. The earth grew soft and stuck to their shoes, and even without the Word, they felt they were in just one skin again, with no crooked house built up between them.

Willow and Billow, for a moment only. Then the dawn came and the fog vanished and the feeling vanished too, and they were glad, for it was a testament to their faith.

Wanda and Betsy spoke seldom of their family. It had been God's will, what had passed, and they should not try to understand. Their mother had already made her peace with God, and though she had not loved them they burned votives in her name. She lay beneath the closed trapdoor in the realm of what was done. But when they did speak, they wondered often about their brother, about the soul that hid within that skin. They spoke without anger, again and again, of what he had done, how he had blamed them for his crimes and stood by without confessing. He was a sinner and as such, condemned. How could he find salvation without The Word? How many mysteries did he still not know?

One night, as they parked the van outside the alley house, Willow raised a single, trembling hand and pointed. Billow's hand rose, pointing, too. A circus poster, blistered with fresh glue, shone on a wall between two boarded-up windows.

Nepenthe straggled back to the boxcar around five in the morning. Instead of going inside, she stood on her tiptoes and peeked through the window. She rubbed dust and grit from the glass with one bell-shaped sleeve. Webern wasn't there, but the ape was—tucked into their bed, no less, and wearing an old-fashioned nightcap.

Nepenthe sank down onto the steps in front of the door. It wasn't very often in her life that she knew exactly what she had to do next, and this moment reminded her of the moment, so long ago now, when she climbed out of her dorm room window at the Appleton Academy with only a monogrammed trunk and a thick roll of her mother's fifty dollar bills to call her own. Then, as now, she had been embarking on a new life, sloughing off the old one along with a closet full of navy blue uniform skirts and blouses with Peter Pan collars. She'd felt sick then, too, she reminded herself.

Nepenthe lit a clove and went over it all in her mind again. She tried to imagine auditioning for a new part in the show, one of the gaudy acts the pretty young girls always wound up with. She saw herself teetering on high heels, flinching as knives whizzed by to embed themselves in the turning board behind her limbs and head—some of the girls had nicknamed knife-thrower Leon "the Barber." Nepenthe imagined falling on her ass in the bareback act, getting sawed in half by an inept magician, losing her grip on the trapeze swing and hitting the net so hard it left blue-black welts on her back and legs. No. No. It would never work. And Webern would be the one to suffer when she came home, pissed off and resentful, night after night after night. He would be the one she blamed when she lost her hard-won beauty to something as ordinary and hateful as common old age.

Nepenthe opened her purse—a woven hemp pouch she'd braided together during a particularly dull stretch of shows in the Dakotas the year before—and dug around until she found her notebook, spiral-bound, with the all-seeing eye of the Almighty Dollar emblazoned on the front. Most of its pages were blank, and the others were mostly filled with doodles, song lyrics, and profound thoughts she'd had while she was stoned. But now she felt a poem coming on.

> *In the caboose of a real circus,*
> *I'm sitting, smoking a green*
> > *cigarette in the dewy early.*
>
> *Past the midway, sunlit Adonis,*
> *driving in tent poles,*
> > *sings the blues with grit in his voice,*
>
> *and the midway fortune teller, drunk*
> *already or still, cackles electric*
> > *two cars down, wrapped*
>
> *like a goddess in her dirty sheets.*
> *No drug, no drug*
> *in the world, beats this yellow*
> > *light, landing—here!*
>
> *and here! and here!—*
> *on every pore of my skin.*

> *—July 26, 1967*

Nepenthe squinted through her smoke and nodded approvingly. In fact, the men setting up the tent weren't singing; from what she could hear, they were just yelling the word, "Cunt!" over and over again at each other with varying degrees of irritation. And Yolanda, the fortune teller, wasn't quite laughing either: she was hacking and coughing like it was her intention to projectile vomit her lungs at the wall. Nepenthe wished the old lady really was two cars away, or preferably even farther. Judging by the way she sounded, Yolanda probably had tuberculosis, or emphysema, or some kind of yellow, wet-looking tumors that nested inside her windpipe, just beneath the wrinkled turkey wattles of her neck. Jesus God.

Nepenthe felt depressed all of a sudden. Here she was writing poems; meanwhile, Webern was practically about to be destroyed. Because, not to compliment herself or anything, but wasn't she the best thing that had ever happened to him? He certainly had been for her. He'd been such a comfort all these years—more than that, he'd been a generous lover, gentle and attentive with a female body that would've given most men nightmares. She would take him to San Francisco with her, she really would, but no matter how hard she tried, she couldn't imagine what their life there together would look like. And—this was the part she tried to skim over in her mind, the part she didn't like admitting—she couldn't picture him leaving the circus any more than she could picture herself staying there. He wouldn't give up this life for anyone. Not even for her.

Nepenthe blew out a plume of clove smoke and realized that while she'd been thinking, Webern had materialized right in front of her. In the morning sunlight, his eyes looked hooded with exhaustion; his hump pressed down his left side like it was something he carried. He hugged himself, and Nepenthe's eyes lingered on his little hands, callused like a man's but still the size of a child's.

"Oh, kiddo." She stubbed out her cigarette. "What are we going to do?"

The bus station lay on the outskirts of town, just like the circus, but it was a long walk there through the lonely cornfields. Nepenthe and Webern took turns dragging her trunk, which quickly acquired a halo of dust and the wayward brambles of several dry weeds. As he lugged the enormous box, Webern thought again of the cut-out photos of his grandfather. He wondered what had made the old man leave, what might have made him stay. Nepenthe's hair bounced, her hips swiveled languidly, and Webern tried to forget that this would be the last time he got to watch her walking away like she didn't care if he followed, like it was an inconvenience to her.

Nepenthe and Webern passed a scarecrow farm, with its rows and rows of burlap spectres, and Nepenthe wrested the handle of the trunk from Webern's hand.

"I've got it from here," she said. She'd been picking wildflowers, and Webern saw now that she'd woven them into a garland. She crowned herself with it, turned her back to him, and gave the trunk a tug. Webern didn't know if this was supposed to be his cue to leave, but he mutely followed her anyway. About a minute later, without looking back at him, Nepenthe said, "You know, Bernie, there's something I've been meaning to tell you."

Webern held his breath. A dragonfly paused on his hump, rubbed its wings together, and flew away.

"Just something you should know. In case you want to find me someday, or, you know. If I send you a letter. Anyway, my name's not really Nepenthe. It's Elizabeth. I actually went by Liz, if you can believe that, until my condition started up and I got to be Lizzie the Lizard and tried to drink a bottle of Lysol. Then I became Eliza. Rathbone. Of the shipping Rathbones." The trunk bumped over a rabbit burrow. "I just thought you should know, I guess."

"Are you going back to them?" Webern's mouth felt as dry as the browning stalks of corn that tilted above them. "To your family?"

"If I went back there looking like this I'd probably get gang-raped by the entire Harvard lacrosse team." Nepenthe sighed. The wildflowers were molting already. Petals streamed through her hair. "No. It's just starting to feel like my name again. It's hard to explain why. Though I'm sure my analyst would have plenty to say about it."

They arrived at the bus station in time for Nepenthe to buy a seat for the 8:15 to Des Moines. She determined she could transfer from there to Omaha, and from there on to Ogallala, Cheyenne, and Denver, where all things would be possible, including a transfer to her ultimate destination, San Francisco. Webern stood behind her and tried to ignore the man behind the counter, who inspected him with naked curiosity. Webern gazed at station's one clock instead, frozen in the eternal smile of ten oh five. On his own wrist, Dr. Schoenberg's watch kept on ticking.

"So that's that." Nepenthe tucked the ticket into a pocket of her dress.

The two of them sat down on a wooden bench. Outside the station's windows, a shirtless man with a large red, white, and blue eagle tattoo tinkered with the bus's engine. Webern's stomach tightened as the hood swung down with a *clang*.

An old grandma with a sewing basket, a scraggly boy with acne that looked like grease burns, and a portly man with a tuba case each boarded the bus in turn. Nepenthe's foot began to jiggle. Finally she turned to Webern. Her face had a look on it that he wasn't expecting— blank fear, like temporary amnesia.

"Listen, this is ridiculous. Just come to California with me."

"I can't be a clown in San Francisco."

"There's other stuff you could do. You could be a mime, out on the street. Or, I don't know, maybe you could make balloons for kids' parties or something."

"Upstaged by cake," Webern murmured.

"What? What did you say?"

He didn't say anything. He imagined himself boarding the bus to California, the way she would inch farther from him in her seat with each passing mile. He saw them disembarking and her vanishing instantly into a crowd where she blended in completely.

"Bernie, look at me. Please."

Nepenthe stood over him in a flowing paisley dress, her hair corkscrewing in all directions, dotted here and there with the silky hearts of black-eyed Susans. She looked as perfect and unreachable as a girl in a fashion magazine, and for a second he longed for a pen to draw scales all over her. But then he looked away from her clothes, her body, her face even, into those emerald green eyes, and despite himself, he saw *her* there—a flicker of something familiar and wondrous, like the tip of a mermaid's tail just above the waves.

"I'm not going to forget you, okay?" she told him. She clutched the handle of her trunk. "You ought to know that by now."

The bus mechanic walked by the window. Webern's eyes followed his eagle tattoo. A permanent mark. *If you care so much, why don't you stay? As the tattooed lady, as my wife?* But he already knew the answer. She would never put ink on that skin.

As soon as he walked in, Webern knew it wasn't an ordinary meeting at Clown HQ. The place was too quiet, to start with. The others sat around the table in a half-circle, like they were waiting for him, but even when he closed the door, they didn't speak for a long slow moment. Professor Shim Sham raised a skull and crossbones bottle to his lips; Punchy Joe gnawed beef jerky; Pipsqueak rubbed off lipstick with his thumb; Happy Herbert chuckled, low and constant, the first tremors of an earthquake. They reminded him of jurors, jurors or a firing squad. And that was before Silly Billy started talking.

"Now listen, we know you've had a rough time lately, Bump. And I'd be the last one to discount what you've done here. I mean it. Most of the guys haven't been around to remember, but I do. Before you came, we hadn't had a new routine in years. It was all banana peel gags. Bullshit cribbed from Three Stooges movies. You put us on the map. But now we just want to shake things up a little bit. I'm not gonna lie to you—the crowd loves Herb. No hard feelings, it's just a fact. Between you and me, I was as surprised as the next guy, but there it is. With his mugging and your routines, we're going places. I mean ticket sales. The kids love his Martian. You saw the show last night. Pandemonium. Management's starting to notice. So we've been thinking. Why not make the most of our talent? Your routines—but with Herb front and centre. Just see what happens. We're not scaling you back, just moving everybody around a little. You hear what I'm saying, Bump? Just do some things different. See how it works. Like a trial."

"A trial," Webern repeated.

"That's right," Silly Billy said encouragingly. "A trial."

Webern looked around the room—the empty bottles, the sticky playing cards, the dusty rug, the pile of girly magazines in one corner. It looked the same as always. It didn't look like a trap.

"So what do you want me to do?" he asked.

Silly Billy waved his hand. "The usual. Crowd work. Straight man parts. Playing the double to Herb. We've got a great one we start rehearsing tomorrow—a mirror bit. Kind of a take-off from that painting routine you do. Real funny stuff. It might be good for you. Take it easy, relax. Unhealthy to work as hard as you do."

"Unhealthy."

"That's the spirit." Silly Billy picked up his penknife. He poked Webern's chest with it. "Go home. Sleep on it. We can talk again in the morning if you want. Otherwise, rehearsal at one tomorrow."

Webern stared down at the floor. His sneakers were untied, the laces dotted with burs from his walk home through the fields. A shriveled balloon-poodle lay on the ground by his feet. He realized he was supposed to leave.

"Okay," he said. The other clowns blurred into each other. He opened the door to the boxcar and stepped carefully down to the ground.

Outside, Marzipan was waiting for him. She held out her hand and Webern took it. Her skin was cooler than he expected, her palm hairless. But he never would have mistaken it for a human's. Webern let her lead him home.

Pipsqueak joined Silly Billy at the door of Clown HQ, and they stood there, watching Webern shuffle away.

"Now to me, that's just sad." Pipsqueak applied a pair of tweezers to his eyebrow. "In the theatre, they always taught us, if you have to bow out, do it with style. That way, they remember you for next time."

"The guy thinks he's an artist. He's sensitive." Silly Billy folded up his knife and dropped it into a pocket. "And from what I hear, his main squeeze's shacking up with a motorcycle gang."

From the table, Happy Herbert snorted. "He wants to be an artist, he can move to gay Pair-ee. We like things big and cheesy over here."

CHAPTER TWENTY-THREE

IT WAS THE BEGINNING OF A DARK TIME FOR WEBERN. He thought about his mother more and more—about how years before he was born, she too had faded to a ghost of herself, only to be brought back to life by the volts that arched and crackled through the temples of her skull. As he sat alone in his boxcar, slumped in the red polka-dotted underpants Nepenthe had given him for Valentine's Day, listening for his sisters and drinking his dead grandma's ape under the table, he wondered if there was such a cure in the world for him.

Webern knew that his sisters would come for him now. They had done it before. He remembered peering through their keyhole at glass jars with holes poked in their lids, wings fluttering inside like darkly beating hearts, muddy red handprints cave-painted on the walls. Webern's mother kept the house neat as a pin (her phrase), but she let the door to the twins' room remain shut as she pushed the roaring vacuum past. Once, long before Webern could remember, she had surprised the girls in their play, and Willow had bitten her. She bore the scar, star-shaped, on her palm for the rest of her life. She hid it in her fist with a private shame that Webern couldn't understand.

Willow and Billow frightened Webern when he was small, but in those days the world was full of frightening things: the laundry hamper that opened onto an abyss of black; the oak tree branch that rapped insistently at his windowpane; the garbage men, who came to eat his trash. His sisters were six years older than him; they could leave the house of their own accord, but unlike his parents, they had no stated destinations and they brought no stories when they returned. He believed that one day he would awake knowing why they had brought a squirming red possum runt to die in the living room, or why they kept their costume jewelry buried in a box in the backyard. But he knew now that their lives had always been a mystery to him. Their motives were their own.

Webern put his feet up on his desk. He tilted back in his chair.

"Let 'em come and get me," he muttered.

Nepenthe had left a week earlier, and since she'd gone, the state of the boxcar had taken a definite turn for the worse. The first night, Webern had bundled her newspapers and magazines together with the belt of her forsaken pink robe, but he had become too exhausted and depressed to finish the job, so the pile of papers sat directly in front of the door. Whenever he wanted to go out, he had to kick them aside; *The Druid Free Press* was covered with footprints. Marzipan kept trying to throw them out, but Webern wouldn't let her touch anything that belonged to Nepenthe. The chimp spent her days on the couch, which was shrouded under rumpled blankets and the two or three dirty T-shirts Webern had been wearing the last several days; when she did rise, which was less and less often, she left behind a great number of coarse black hairs and a lingering scent of Scotch. Right now, she stared up at the ceiling vacantly, arms folded behind her head, as the train jolted and stuttered its way through the dark night.

Perhaps the worst part of the mess was overflowing from Webern's desk. Crumpled-up pages lay wadded up everywhere, a riotous garden of paper blossoms. These were Webern's abandoned clown acts. Webern hadn't exactly been inspired of late. The night before, he'd had one brief nightmare—a blurry interlude in which the clown had cried so hard that his glass eye popped out and rolled away—but other than that, his nights had been dreamless, and more often than not, sleepless, too.

Not that it mattered now anyway. With Happy Herbert centre stage, Webern was less than eager to hand over more of his ideas to be plundered, and the other clowns didn't seem particularly interested anyway. Happy Herbert's perspective was simple: if the same gag got the same laughs every night, then what was the point of changing it? Webern could see the logic in this point of view in the same way he could see a car wreck from the windows of the train: just because it was there didn't mean it should be. Webern had always taken for granted that the audience would laugh—people had been laughing at him since he was a kid. What mattered to him was the clarity of the details: the way he bent to smell a daisy just before it squirted a stream of water in his face, or the startled expression he made upon discovering a hole in the bottom of one floppy shoe. Webern longed to make every moment of his clown routine as crystal-clear and unmistakable to his audience as his dreams were to him. He wanted the act to be a dream they dreamed together, a dream that lingered in their minds even after they emerged, blinking, into the midway's garish lights.

Webern had been dreaming his whole life. His mother had taught dreaming to him when she opened the picture books and guided his hands over pages of goblins and unicorns, fairy princesses and dragons. She had dressed him for dreaming in red silk pyjamas with blue and white sailboats stitched on the pockets, in a terrycloth robe the colour of the night sky with constellations embroidered on the sleeves. Now that dreams eluded Webern during sleep, he spent his hours in a half-awake daze, where dreams could appear anywhere—in the sawdust that floated like clouds of gold under the spotlights, in the red and white barns that loomed in the fields they passed. He found himself staring into space as the world around him took on the quality of a vision, the cloudy bright colours of paint spilled through water. Sometimes he looked at his hands and found they had become strange to him. Dreams shimmered on everything he touched, like a glaze. But he couldn't hold them in his mind. He couldn't shape them into acts or mark them down with crayons. He was in them. He was lost in them. He was alone.

Webern opened the drawer that held the Great Vermicelli. The dummy lay inside, his eyes rolled back inside his wooden head, his lacquered skin rouged. His arms lay empty, crossed on his chest, the smooth pale hands supported by wires. Pale hands, like wings. Magician's hands.

Carefully, Webern lifted him out of the drawer. The wood felt strangely warm, pliable—almost alive. Webern set the dummy on his knees, and the eyes opened with a satisfying click. He slid his hand under the Great Vermicelli's tuxedo jacket and touched the talking stick, a grooved spine. The dummy's mouth formed words; a voice came from a dark place at its hollow heart.

"You know, my boy, you would do well to study the great mimes of the Commedia dell'arte. The incomparable Grosseto, in particular, might lend you inspiration. His *pièce de resistance* was a Pantaloon who, convinced by Harlequin that his young wife has been assumed into the heavens, fires arrow after arrow at the sky, only to be pierced with each one upon its descent. Only when he resembles a pincushion does his beloved return from her tryst." Vermicelli chuckled. "In theatrical circles, he has become something of a patron saint for cuckolds."

Webern tipped the dummy back on his lap. The eyes clicked shut again, and the mouth stilled. Webern's hands were shaking as he lifted a crayon and carefully drew an arrow on the clean page of his clown notebook. One arrow, then another, and another, and another.

Webern stood just offstage in a Martian suit made of cardboard boxes. He hated the way the costume restricted his movements; having it on felt more like standing inside a tiny house than like wearing clothes. The big top was full tonight, full to capacity, and the heat of so many bodies filled the air. Sharp cries and laughter thrummed in his ears, and sweat trickled down his hump. Even here in the darkness, he was starting to cook.

Out into the centre ring, amid dry ice explosions and shattered glass, a travesty was taking place. Happy Herbert was many things, but he was not a natural clown; Webern was sure of that. To be a clown, a person had to lose himself in the reality of the act—he had to be perfectly serious, focused completely on the smallest details of his task. He had to move with the disastrous conviction of a sleepwalker or the self-deluded. People always thought the clown and the straight man were two separate roles, but the opposite was true. The clown *was* the straight man, the only one onstage who couldn't see the absurdity of what he did. The clown was a comedy to everyone else but a tragedy to himself. He mourned popped balloons, broken eggs, faithless women. But Happy Herbert wouldn't wipe that smile off his face until someone sprayed mace in his eyes.

Webern grimaced as Happy Herbert cracked the cap off a Coke bottle using an armplate from his Martian suit. Unlike Webern's costume, which was gilded with aluminum foil and staples, Herb's was made from real pressed tin. Out in the audience, the kids shrieked with laughter. Of course.

Webern leaned against one of the tent's poles. He had seen a *real* clown once, just after Dr. Schoenberg found him in Dolphin River. In those first few weeks before he and Nepenthe grew close, he had spent almost every waking hour with the old ringmaster, pouring over ancient playbills and listening to wild stories of the vaudeville days. One night, somewhere in Ohio, Dr. Schoenberg had whisked him away from the camp to see a performer ("An old acquaintance of mine") in the gloomy basement of a defunct jazz club.

In that small, grimy space—which, despite its moist porous walls and low ceiling, still managed to echo—Webern had watched an old man in a threadbare trench coat attempt to put a bicycle together. The room was empty except for him, Dr. Show, and an aging nightclub singer whose baby daughter wore a sequined dress; it was silent except for the buzzing of a fly that rammed its body repeatedly into the spotlight's dim bulb. But Webern was transfixed. The old man's face showed every flicker of disappointment, rage, and elation as he set about his task, and in his hands, the pile of junk and spare parts before him transformed. One bent wheel turned into a hunk of pizza dough; the greasy chain became a bauble of gold. And when the bicycle was at long last completed, it too changed into something glorious: a kind of chariot that its owner could ride into the sky, if he wanted to. That night, Webern finally understood what it was to be a clown, the simple, humble craft of it and the honour, too. But he had forgotten. And now, standing here in the sawdusty shadows, watching Happy Herbert blow raspberries at the audience, that basement room seemed more real than anything that had happened to him since.

Silly Billy blew the whistle, and Webern trotted out to his first position in the ring, careful to stay far from the spotlights. Pipsqueak and Professor Shim Sham wheeled out "the mirror"—really just a huge golden frame with thick screens of black on the sides. The routine played simply enough: Happy Herbert the Martian glimpses his reflection for the first time, and is terrified, then angered by his double, who placidly mimics everything he does.

Behind the black screen on the right side of the frame, Webern tried to compose himself. Heat and alcohol made him woozy, and the cheers of the crowd blended in with the sound of the blood pulsing through his ears.

Happy Herbert began to hum, and, taking a deep breath, Webern stepped out into the light. It was essential that their movements be exactly synchronized, so Herb had devised what he thought was an elaborate system of cues: the tunes he hummed throughout the routine were meant to set the tempo for their movements and actions, as music would for a pair of dancers. Unfortunately, Herb's sense of rhythm was lousy, so Webern continually had to check his motions against Herb without turning his head in the slightest. It was a strain, and as Webern sauntered into the spotlight—easy and casual, just as 241 they'd practiced it—he saw Herb was almost a full step ahead of him. Damn, damn, damn.

Webern slid his feet through the sawdust as he moved into their second position—the surprise pose, when the Martian first glimpsed his reflection. Mouth ajar, head tilted to the side, Webern found himself looking Happy Herbert square in the face for the first time all evening. At this distance, Herb's makeup—light green and slightly metallic—couldn't hide the imperfections of his real face: the stubble, boarish and bristly, already growing in after a five o'clock shave; the low forehead, wrinkled with the strain of thinking. His breath smelled like the hot dog water vendors poured out in parking lots at the end of the day.

But Webern could have borne all this had it not been for one other thing: Happy Herbert was smiling. With his back to the audience, he wasn't bothering to widen his eyes, to narrow his broad mouth to a tiny *o* of shock. Instead, he was smiling—no, leering, really—at Webern. Tough luck, his dim, contented eyes seemed to say. I'm out here, and you're in there, looking back.

Later on, Webern didn't remember making a fist, and he didn't remember winding back to throw the punch. The big top, the sawdust ring, even his own body felt very far away, and his muscles moved of their own accord, as though executing a pantomime he'd practiced a million times before. But he did remember the expression of Happy Herbert's face: the eyes opening wider and wider, the mouth falling open. It was the surprise pose after all.

Happy Herbert reeled backwards; one hand flew up to cup his jaw. He staggered, but didn't fall. Instead he stared at Webern, his wide eyes stretched beyond surprise on into shock, and even terror. Then— unsteadily, clumsily, but at top speed—he turned around and began to run.

Assuming this was all part of the act, the spotlight operator followed him with the beam, serving, like a prison searchlight, to keep him in full view of his pursuer. Which Webern suddenly was. He knew now that one punch just wasn't enough to get his point across. With a blood-curdling roar, he leapt over the gold frame and sprinted at top speed after his doppelganger.

Happy Herbert raced up into the stands. He collided with a peanut vendor and knocked an ice cream out of the hands of a little girl, who let out a siren-like wail. Webern scaled the steps two at a time just behind him. The cardboard of his robot suit ripped at the seams, but he didn't care. Happy Herbert pushed his way through a row of seats, upsetting sodas, buckets of popcorn, and falling, for a moment, into the lap of a tremendously endowed matron in a floral print dress, who shrieked in horrified delight. Then he descended the bleachers on the other side. But Webern was undeterred: he made a U-turn, wheeling around to bound back down the way he'd come. As soon as Webern hit the sawdust ground again he gained on Herb, who was running now like a child in a nightmare: in a zigzag, and always looking back.

Happy Herbert dove beneath the lowest safety net; Webern ducked his head and followed. Bent nearly double, he could barely see where he was going. But as soon as Happy Herbert came out into the open again, Webern knew he had him. Happy Herbert veered toward the lion cages at the other end of the arena, but he was too tired to make it there; his breath came out in high-pitched squeaks and wheezes. With an otherworldly howl, Webern leapt onto his back.

"You're a disgrace! A disgrace!"

"Get your hands off me, you fuckin' psycho!"

The two tiny spacemen rolled around on the ground, screaming obscenities and punching each other in the face. Webern grabbed a handful of Happy Herbert's hair; Happy Herbert kneed him in the groin. Their blood stained the sawdust. They were evenly matched— too evenly. Webern whacked Herb's chin with his hump, and he felt he was finally coming out on top, when Happy Herbert's elbow landed an unexpected blow to his ribs. Gasping for breath, Webern was powerless as the other clown rolled on top of him and grasped his throat in two small grubby hands.

Webern thrashed and slapped and kicked and kneed and elbowed. Happy Herbert's grip only tightened. Black spots swarmed the big top's dome; the roar of the crowd sounded like it was coming from inside Webern's head. It occurred to him that he had been making some very bad decisions lately. Somewhere offstage, an elephant trumpeted.

He was almost unconscious when Happy Herbert began to rise, the pressure of his body lifting from Webern's as though they had entered a realm of zero gravity. When his hands finally, grudgingly, released Webern's neck, Webern sucked in a mouthful of air—sweet clean air—and opened his eyes. Pipsqueak and Professor Shim Sham, in full costume, had come out into the ring to pull them apart. The two clowns now struggled to hold back Happy Herbert, who noisily twisted in their arms, screamed for his rights, and called all of them "cocksmokers." Webern watched for a second, then rolled over on his side and chomped on Happy Herbert's ankle.

"I'll tear you a new one!" Happy Herbert bawled. Webern crawled out of the spotlight. "He's getting away!"

"He's got no place to go," Pipsqueak reassured him.

Webern looked out at the crowd. Utter terror stilled the faces of children, some of whom stared with mouths agape, forgotten cotton candy melted in their sticky hands. Grown men and women bore looks of horror, outrage, and disgust; some covered their eyes; others pushed toward the exits. Only Wags, standing in a distant row, clapped his hands and shook his head and stamped his feet. Only he was laughing.

CHAPTER TWENTY-FOUR

A WOODEN PLATFORM, FIVE FEET BY FIVE FEET, boxed in on three sides with canvas partitions. A single spotlight, trained on the dead centre of the stage. A red vinyl chair, orphaned from a dinette set, with a V-shaped rip in the seat. An unplugged floor lamp, made of tarnished brass. A dustball, a gritty feeling underfoot—sand or the memory of sand.

"It's all yours." Frank, manager of the Parliament, dropped his hand familiarly onto Webern's hump. His straw hat sunk his face in shadows. "It's a step down, I know, but after what happened I'm surprised old Billy could get you this much. Hell, I'm surprised he wanted to, if you don't mind me saying so. Guess the guy felt he owed you something." Frank smiled all the time he said this, but Webern knew it didn't mean anything. Nepenthe had told him a long time ago that the guy couldn't stop even if he wanted to—some kind of muscle damage from the Korean War.

"Tell me what you need, and I'll pass it on to Wardrobe. Can't do much about props, though. For those you're on your own."

"When do I start?" Webern asked.

"Bright and early." Frank patted Webern's hump once, then let it go. As he hopped down from the stage, he called over his shoulder, "Don't take it the wrong way—we're glad to have you. We've been expecting you a long time."

Webern waited until Frank had disappeared. Then he pulled the chair out, straddled it, and sat down, resting his head on the upholstered back. He gazed out at the narrow space where the crowd would file in, where they would stare at him for five minutes before shuffling on to the next attraction. He thought of Nepenthe, coming in here every day for years and years—now it made sense to him why she would want to lie motionless on her rubber alligator, why she didn't bother putting on a show. It took all the energy he could muster just to keep breathing in this place.

Webern took off his glasses and pressed the heels of his hands to his eyes. He could have gone to Europe. He could have gone to San Francisco. He could have made her stay, somehow. Instead he'd chosen this.

The Parliament freaks kept a different schedule than the performers under the big top. Their show started two hours earlier, to catch the midway crowd, and it ended whenever the traffic through their tent slowed to a handful of vulgar old men and bored teenagers looking for somewhere dark and quiet to squeeze each other. As a consequence of this, the freaks put on their costumes in daylight and took them off at night. The giant milled around the cookhouse in his cowboy boots and ten-gallon hat, and Fat Rhonda washed her ruffled skirts as often as her underwear. For the freaks, there was no going into character, or coming out of it either. Except for Jody, the half-man, half-woman, none of them had a face to put on that was different from their own.

Their acts were almost as everyday as the clothes they wore to perform them. Most were simple embellishments on the daily routines the freaks performed every morning before coming to the tent, endless repetitions of the mundane. They spent their days playing solitaire, combing hair, eating, weighing and measuring themselves, as though life had an awful stutter in it, a crack where the needle had lodged. The Skeleton Dude stood on a scale, endlessly munching apples and reading the newspaper. The Elastic Skin Man got up off his cot and stretched, then lay back down again. The Human Torso, who had recently quit smoking, unfolded gum wrappers with his tongue. Only the blockhead and Serpentina, with her drugged snakes, had acquired anything resembling a skill, but their attitude was the same as Happy Herbert's: why bother improving an act that works? Nobody ever comes through this place twice.

Strangely enough, only Venus de Milo seemed to have taken any care with her act. It was simple enough: she styled her hair, painted her lips, all while describing how lonely it was to be a girl like her. But every time Webern had come through the tent, he'd seen little changes, a new double entendre or a shade of toenail polish she'd never worn before. And, in the end, she played the ukulele, her toes deftly plucking strings while her Brooklyn accent raised in the plaintive melody.

"Drop a nickel in, gimme a whirl. Turn my crank, I'm your kinda girl. You wanna catch my number, again and again. I'm your nickelodeon." She sounded like Betty Boop, but at least she was trying.

Once, the prospect of doing the same routine day in and day out would have depressed Webern beyond all reckoning. But that evening, as he walked home from the Parliament with Frank's smile still lingering in his mind, it comforted him that so little was expected. He climbed the stairs to his boxcar and stepped inside. Marzipan glanced at him from where she lay on the couch, then turned her eyes back toward the wall. Webern swung open the lid of his trunk and dug through the wigs and tights until he reached the very bottom. He pulled out his pair of green frogman flippers, kicked off his shoes, and stepped into them. They were old and faded, with a crack along one toe, but they fit him like his own skin. They would have to do for now.

In the mornings, while Fat Rhonda served donut holes on her Christmas plate and the Missing Link—really a kid named Nevis from Tucson, Arizona—brewed coffee in the back of the Parliament tent, the clown who had once been called Bump Chuckles assumed his post as Frog Boy.

The freaks shared their beds as freely as their gin, creating an elaborate and ever-changing network of flirtation and dislike, and they constantly loaned money, argued, and gossiped through the thin swatches of canvas that separated them. But, as he had with the other clowns, Webern held himself apart. Just before they opened, he arrived, dressed in green tights, his flippers, and a white T-shirt. He wasted little time setting up. He spread his lilypad—really just a green tarp—and fitted his lamp with a special green light bulb, just like the ones Nepenthe used to bask under at Dr. Show's circus. Then he stripped to the waist, wadded his T-shirt into a ball, and tossed it to a corner of the stage. In this place, his hump was more performer than he was. It was what people paid to see.

Sometimes, as he sat under the green light, Webern had the feeling he had arrived, a little too late, in the swamp where Nepenthe had been dwelling all these years. He closed his eyes, and marsh gases exploded in the distance, burning their blue fires, while close by cicadas shrilled. He imagined leaping off his lilypad deep into warm, brackish water and opening his eyes to find a trace of her: a single scale, shimmering grey-white in the muck like a sunken treasure. There was so much about her he had never understood.

A hundred times a day, Webern heard Venus perform her ukulele song. "Peek beneath the curtain, get a surprise. I'll sing a lullaby to pull you inside. Grab the brass ring, I'll give you a thrill. I'm your nickelodeon." When he listened closely, the melancholy in her voice surprised him. It comforted him, too. It made him feel less alone. "Are you listenin'? I'm ringing your bell." As he swam through the murky swamp, her song became his underwater jukebox, a sign he was not the first person to visit these depths.

One evening, after work, she came over to his stage. He was rolling up the dusty lilypad, but when he saw her he stopped and pulled on his T-shirt before speaking.

"Hey."

"This was her booth, y'know," Venus said. She snapped her gum.

Webern nodded slowly. "I know."

"Stop moping around, you cretin." She pronounced it "Cretian." "You're not the only one she left. She didn't even say good-bye to me. Miss Hoity-Toity. Like she thought I didn't know. See you in the morning, she says. Where? I says back. The goddamn beauty salon? Some of us still have jobs, y'know. Well, she laughed at that. I knew I wouldn't be seeing her again, not around here, anyways."

She stared at Webern, as though she had just delivered her argument in full and it was up to him to rebut it. Despite the warmth of the night air, she had on a white bunny fur jacket with the sleeves tucked into the pockets. If he hadn't known better, Webern would have thought she had arms in them.

"I did take her to the bus station," he finally admitted.

"Yeah. Figures." Venus jerked her head toward the egress. "Wanna get a bite?"

"What?"

"Get-a-bite. Or have you stopped eating too, ya chump? Christ." She shook her head disapprovingly. "I always told her you were the sensitive type."

Venus and Webern walked out of the Parliament together, out onto the midway.

"Tonight's on me," Venus told him. "My sweetie runs a corndog stand."

"What happened to Zeus?"

"That creep?" Venus glanced at a stand selling monogrammed Peter Pan hats. The green lights reflected in her rhinestone glasses. "He went the way of all flesh. All flesh except mine, seems like. So I called it quits."

"Oh." An old lady and her grandson stood at the shooting game, firing plastic rifles at gophers with glowing eyes. "I'm sorry."

"Don't be. You know what your problem is? You're a romantic. Love's a nice thing, but when it's gone, it's gone. You stay stuck on somebody forever, that's how you go crazy." They arrived at the corndog stand, and Venus sashayed up to the counter. "Hi there, Charlie."

Behind the counter stood a guy in a tank top and jeans sawed off at the knees. His crew cut sparkled with sweat.

"What'll it be, toots?" He crossed his arms over his chest.

"C'mon, Charlie." Venus wiggled. "You know how I like it."

With a sigh, the man yanked a sizzling corndog from the deep fryer and squirted a thick line of mustard down the middle. He held it out. Venus licked her lips and lowered her head. Slowly, the entire corn dog disappeared into her mouth. When she tilted her head back, it was gone, leaving only the wooden stick behind. Webern wondered if she had a gag reflex. Her eyes closed invitingly as she chewed.

"Make it a double." She tilted her head at Webern. "For my friend here."

Charlie squinted at Webern, then back at Venus disbelievingly. "That little guy?"

"Yeah."

Slowly, Charlie drew another corn dog out of the fryer and, with a pained expression, held it out to Webern. Venus grinned slyly. Webern snatched the corndog out of his hand and took a giant step back. Charlie looked relieved.

"Nice to meet you," Webern muttered.

"See ya later, cutie," Venus told Charlie.

Webern ate his corndog as he and Venus continued down the midway. When he finished it, he was still hungry. It occurred to him that he hadn't eaten anything else all day, maybe not the night before either.

"You're a big talker tonight," Venus observed. "What happened, dog burn your tongue?"

"No, it was good. Really." Webern tossed the wooden stick in a garbage can. "Thanks."

"Forget about it. I like having company for a change." They passed a booth where a man arm-wrestled anyone who paid a dollar. Venus flashed him a smile.

"Where'd you learn to play the ukulele?" Webern asked.

Venus shrugged. "My dad, he loved music. Roy Smeck, Cliff Edwards, all those guys. He thought a girl like me should have a skill. Made me practice an hour a day. My girlfriends all thought it was a riot, but I kinda liked it. Old-timey, y'know?" They reached a tent with carved ostrich eggs on display, and Venus turned the corner, off the main drag of the midway. "Don't mind walking a girl home, do ya?"

The sounds of laughter, piped-in music, and buzzing, whirring games faded as the two of them walked toward the train car Venus shared with the albino girl and two trapeze artists. When they reached her door, she stopped. A warm breeze ruffled her bunny fur jacket.

"Y'know, my roomies are out tonight. Went to some roller rink in town. Want to come in for a minute?"

Webern hesitated. "I should go home. I haven't fed Marzipan."

"Suit yourself." She slipped off her shoes and stepped towards him. The sole of one bare foot touched his waist. It struck Webern that for Venus, a hug was wrapping her legs around someone. Her lips brushed against his cheek as she whispered in his ear. "I've always liked you, shortcake. You're a gent."

Webern closed his eyes. It felt good to have someone else touching him; probably no woman in her right mind would come this near him again. Barely anyone had even spoken to him the last couple of weeks. His hand sank into the white fur of Venus's jacket, between the shoulder blades. What difference did it make now, anyway?

Inside Venus's boxcar, two sets of bunk beds stood side by side with a narrow aisle between them. Brassieres, leotards, and stiff tulle skirts dangled from the upper beds, and the air had a ripe sweetness—shampoo and apricots. An open box of chocolates sat on a chest of drawers, the top of each candy pinched, next to a brush tangled with thick, blinding white hair. Carnations wilted in a plastic vase.

Venus sat down on one lower bunk and deftly unbuttoned her jacket with one foot. It fell on the mattress with a wriggle of her shoulders.

"C'mere." She patted the bed with her knee. "Make yourself comfy."

Webern sat next to her, and Venus guided her foot into his hand. He stared at her toenails. Tonight they were painted red, white, and blue, like tiny American flags. He touched the pinky with his thumb.

"You do these yourself?" he asked.

Venus kissed him lightly on the lips. The frames of their glasses tapped each other. She sank back onto her pillows. They were different shapes, hearts, a star, a bright red pair of lips—prizes from the midway.

"I don't think I should be here," Webern said. "I still love Nepenthe."

Venus smiled sadly. Her toes stroked his face, his neck. She was still wearing her negligee from the Parliament of Freaks. "Yeah, but honey. She's not coming back."

The clown floats through the clear blue sky; in one hand he clutches a multicoloured bunch of balloons. Pink cotton candy clouds hang in the air beyond him; he smiles as a warm breeze drifts him to and fro. In the distance, birds chirp. It seems he could go on like this forever.

Two birds—grackles—fly toward the clown's balloons. They duck and circle, their glossy bodies twist and dive. The clown watches them nervously. The birds shriek. They swoop toward the biggest balloon in the bunch—it's aquamarine. One bird pecks with her beak; the other snatches at it with her talons. The balloon explodes, and the birds, frightened, soar off into the sky.

The clown dips a little, but keeps on floating. A worried look darkens his face. He scans the horizon for more invaders. His eyes widen. A whole flock of Canadian geese barrel into him. They jostle his balloons with their wings; they honk and flap, their necks extended, their eyes shiny and desperate. The clown holds on for dear life. Gunshots rend the sky, the birds scatter, and a second balloon, lavender this time, pops.

The clown is down to just three balloons now. He looks toward the ground and feels sick. It's a long way down. But for now he's still airborne. *Plunk. Plunk, plunk.* The clown holds out his free hand, gazes up at the rain clouds. *BOOM!* With a crash of thunder, a sudden downpour engulfs him. The balloons dip and waver in the unceasing monsoon; the clown is drenched. *CRACK!* A bolt of lightning, blue-white, zigzags into his red balloon. It bursts; electricity surges down the string. The clown's bones flash white through his skin. He's left charred sooty black, holding onto just two balloons.

The storm passes; the clown sighs with relief. But something is still amiss. He hangs in the air uncertainly; he sinks bit by tiny bit. Finally, it becomes clear: his white balloon has sprung a slow-but-steady leak. He gazes at it imploringly, makes puppy dog eyes, but still it loses air, deflating steadily until it sputters out its last and drops, small and useless, to the end of a dangling string.

The clown clings to his last balloon: an emerald green one, the loveliest of the collection. He wraps the string tight around his wrist and kisses it for good measure. Then the wind starts to howl. The balloon tosses in one direction; it swings him back in the other. It tugs upward, as though trying to get away. The clown shakes his fist at the balloon; he scowls. Why can't it just stay put? It comes down and bonks him on the head. Finally, he's had enough. He reaches into the deep pocket of his hobo jacket and pulls out a needle, silver and gigantic, gleaming at the tip. He pops the balloon himself.

For one awful moment, the clown stays suspended, knowing what he's done. He goes pale; his mouth shrinks to a horrified *o*. Then, without further ado, he plummets.

Webern opened his eyes. Venus's pink bedspread was twisted around his hips, and the boxcar was very dark. He looked over at the other set of bunks. Up top, the albino girl lay with her hair cascading over the edge of the mattress, a silvery curtain. Pigalle, the trapeze artist, slept beneath her, hands folded under her head like a little girl's. Webern turned to look at Venus, who lay between him and the wall. She was fast asleep on her side with her back to him. Webern pulled the bedspread down an inch. There, protruding from her shoulder, he saw what she never showed even in the Parliament of Freaks: pale fleshy curled things, the beginnings of fingers.

Webern watched himself slide out of bed and grope in the darkness for something (a blanket? a shirt?) to drape around his waist. He watched himself slip past the pinched-in chocolates and the decaying flowers, out into the warm night. Only then, with his bare feet crunching the sun-baked dirt and dry grass, was it safe to go back inside his own skin again.

Webern walked alongside the sleeping train, past windows where monstrous shadows moved, or where dreamy cries wafted out, echoes from another world. It seemed like he might never reach his boxcar.

When he got there, all the lights were on. Webern stood at the threshold and looked slowly around the room. The unwashed Scotch glasses and crumpled papers were nowhere to be seen; Marzipan was setting up Bo-Bo's old wooden chess set on the coffee table. Wags sat in his desk chair, his back to Webern. His golden hair shone as he bent over one of Webern's clown notebooks, scribbling intently. When Webern closed the door, Wags spun around.

"Cheese and crackers! You're finally back. Well, I got started without you—hope you don't mind."

"Started?" Webern asked. He looked down and saw that he was covering himself with the albino girl's satin bloomers.

"Sure. Time's a-wastin'. We've got lots of work to do."

CHAPTER TWENTY-FIVE

WEBERN SAT ON THE BOXCAR FLOOR IN FRONT OF THE MIRROR, parting his freshly bleached hair. In the glass, a familiar boy looked back out at him. His white short-sleeved shirt was buttoned to the very top. His eyes sparkled with mischief. And the straps of his lederhosen were snapped and tightened. When Webern turned his head, so did the boy in the mirror. When he reached for the pot of rouge, the boy in the mirror also extended his hand.

"Cut that out," said Webern.

"You're snippy tonight, compadre." Wags grinned. "Don't worry so much. You're going to break a leg."

"Yeah, probably." Webern adjusted one knee sock. "You're sure I look all right?"

"Would I lie to you? It's perfect."

Webern frowned at the toe of one brown shoe. They had been practicing for a week, but he was still a little nervous. One part of him felt tempted to go to the Parliament dressed as usual in his frog-prince feet, to close his eyes and bask in the dull warm pain of the green-tinged lights, but Wags was so insistent, it was almost impossible not to do what he said.

Webern stood up; Wags did, too. "Would you mind if we ran through the ladder bit one more time?"

"You said it, buster."

Before he went to Tarantula, Webern had not seen Wags, Willow, or Billow since the September when he turned twelve. In those days, Willow and Billow often disappeared for weeks at a time, leaving soiled clothing and moldering furs strewn about in acrid piles until their return. Webern's father hardly seemed to notice their absences—he even left the same amount of lunch money piled on the counter—but Webern always became tense and vigilant, wondering if he was finally safe, if this time they really had left him forever.

Late August of that year, he finally believed that the girls were gone for good. They had been away for five weeks at that point, a record for them, and when he dared peer in through their keyhole, he saw their room was spare and empty: necklaces of animal teeth no longer dangled from the light fixture, and the stolen birds' nests had been emptied of their eggs. Even their collection of lost pet flyers had vanished. He began to let his guard down, just a little; he still locked his bedroom door, but he was no longer afraid to go downstairs for a glass of orange juice in the middle of the night. When he found a squashed iguana in the bottom of his underwear drawer, he even dared to throw it out the window, where it landed beneath the oak tree like some ghastly parody of himself.

A week later, the ghost started to visit him. At first, he thought he was imagining things. Lying in bed, on the brink of dreaming, he sometimes saw the shadows move, or felt invisible snakes slither across his ankles, but when he sat up and turned on the lights, these phantoms always disappeared. However, the footsteps did not.

In the dim glow of his nightlight, a small lamp with the patterns of constellations poked into its black tin shade, Webern concentrated on the sound. It seemed to be coming from directly above his head, and it was slower, more deliberate than regular walking—almost as if someone were imitating footsteps, placing each foot slo-o-owly against the roof tiles: *crrrreeeeak, crrrreeeak.* Webern's breath caught in his throat, and he swung his legs over the edge of the bed. He slid his stocking feet across the floor—sidestepped the toys and open comic books that lay scattered on the carpet. Carefully, he unlatched his window, then sat down on the sill and leaned as far back as he dared to look up at the roof.

He saw the tiles sloping up, the leaves and sticks fallen from the higher branches of the oak that grew close beside the house; he noticed a stranded softball, its white leather gleaming softly in the moonlight. No one was there.

After he switched off the constellation lamp, Webern curled up in bed and squeezed his eyes shut in a semblance of sleep. But it was no use.

The visits continued infrequently over the next week. Sometimes the ghost would fall silent for a day or two at a time. Sometimes its footsteps sounded more like waltzing—one-two *creak*, one-two *creak*. Sometimes Webern felt eyes on him, ones he couldn't see; sometimes he heard a tune, high and faint—a familiar lullaby. But even when he dug an old Ouija board out of the pile of games in his closet, he couldn't get the apparition to appear. One day after school, he decided to write the ghost a letter. He used a blue pen on a clean sheet of notebook paper, and drew a border of tattered roses around the edge.

> *Dear Mom,*
> *I know I'm too old to believe in ghosts. But if you're there, really there, I wish you'd let me see you. I promise I won't be scared. You always told me I was brave. I wasn't then, but I am now.*
> *Love, Bernie.*

Webern speared the letter on a branch of the oak tree that grew right beside his window, where it would be visible from the roof. The paper rustled there like a dry white leaf all afternoon.

That night, he lay on his elbows under the blankets with a flashlight and read all his old picture books. He remembered how the words had sounded in his mother's shy, quiet voice, how her fingernail, pink and smooth as a tiny seashell, had traced across the glossy pages. Footsteps paced back and forth above his head in the rhythm of the words.

When he woke up, Webern found himself surrounded by a half-dozen open picture books; the handle of his flashlight had left a red imprint in the side of his face. Webern climbed out of bed and scrabbled quickly over to the window. He threw back the curtain. His note was gone. Another one hung in its place.

Webern opened the window. The ghost had written with charcoal, and the black marking smeared and rubbed off on his hands as he removed the letter from the tree branch. Webern eagerly smoothed the paper on the window sill and focused on the messy black words.

"Dear Son," the letter read. "I will never leave you. You can see me whenever you want. You just need to close your eyes." Beneath this was a sloppily drawn smiley face: a nose, a mouth, and two large scrawled X's were all they'd bothered to draw in.

The letter was written on a page torn from a book; behind the charcoal writing, Webern saw blocks of printed text. He turned the page over. On the back, he saw a familiar picture. A frail boy and girl walked hand and hand through a dark forest; all around them, menacing yellow eyes peered down from the trees.

Webern slowly turned toward the picture books on his bed. One of them, the book of fairy tales, lay facedown on his comforter. He went to it and turned it over. He ran his finger down the ragged edge where the page had been torn out, then sank down on his bed.

He couldn't make a sound. He couldn't move. He could hardly think. A single thought just repeated in his mind, over and over: *They were here. In my room. They were here. In my room.*

The world was dark, but it was not haunted. There was no ghost— there never had been. When a person died, she stayed dead. He had always known that, but now the knowledge moved through him like a poison. His mother wasn't on the roof. She was in the ground. He lay on his bed, perfectly still, for a long time. In the house below, he heard his father eat breakfast and leave for work. Then he heard the house's stillness.

When Webern got up again, the sun was setting, and his room burned orange-red. His head hurt, and his hands felt limp and sweaty. But he knew what he had to do now. He knew he had to be brave. Webern took off his pyjamas and dressed himself in the darkest clothes he had—his hands shook as he did up the buttons—then went downstairs and sat on the sofa to wait. As soon as twilight had dimmed into night, he went into the garage. He found the gallon jug of gasoline and carried it to the back yard. If Willow and Billow thought they could make a game out of his grief, they were wrong. He would not be haunted like this.

Webern stood in the shadows beneath the oak tree; its branches spread in a dark canopy above him, like India ink spilled on the sky. From where he stood, he could just barely see them crouching up there in the treehouse. In the darkness, the twins' eyes glowed like cats' eyes, sly and golden.

Willow and Billow had been living up there for weeks, amongst cicada shells and rusted nails and rotten knotholes, coming out only at night to move like ghosts through their own house or across its tilted roof. *They were there. In my room.* He imagined them standing over his bed like two bad fairies delivering a curse—saw their spindly fingers moving like insects, like the wind, toward his neck, and he knew what he had to do. He had to drive them out. He didn't care if it was cruel.

Webern moved toward the trunk of the tree and awkwardly, nervously, splashed the bark with gasoline. Up above, he heard the twins stir. Maybe they could smell the diesel. He certainly could.

For a moment after he doused the tree trunk, Webern stood in silence. The empty gasoline jug hung heavy in his hand. His father would be home within the hour. But there was nothing the old man could do to stop him now.

Webern reached into his pocket for the match.

The orange flames whooshed up the oak, and the whole backyard flickered with a hellish red light. Webern backed up. He wanted to run away, but he couldn't take his eyes off what was happening to the treehouse.

He could see Willow and Billow clearly now. They danced in quick circles on the uneven planks, and for a horrible moment, Webern thought that they wouldn't leave the treehouse at all—that they would just swirl faster and faster until they merged with the flames. But then, at the last possible moment, the twins flew out the window; they leapt up onto the roof of the house just as the wooden treehouse walls caught ablaze. The girls tore away like shadows fleeing from the light; they scaled the sloping roof and disappeared over the other side.

Webern turned his eyes back to the treehouse, which now burned with a steady, rushing brilliance, like a comet descending through the sky. As a fire engine's siren wailed in the distance, Webern glimpsed Wags, framed in the treehouse window. For the first time since Webern's sixth birthday party, the little boy in lederhosen was the size of a normal child.

"Wags!" Webern screamed. His heart pounded in his ears. "Wags! *Wags*! Jump!"

But Wags just grinned. He saluted, snapped the straps of his lederhosen, and in a shower of sparks, vanished into the consuming fire.

All of Wags's acts had to do with falling—falling or flying, which were really just two halves of the same thing. Wags had concocted a routine with a stepladder, which Webern fell down *bump bump bump*, hitting his head on each rung, and together they had rigged up an elaborate system of wires and pulleys above his freak show stage, so he could glide, Peter Pan style, up one side and down the other. A swing hung over the little stage now too, and they planned to add a basket, like the ones beneath hot air balloons, that could be raised and lowered with a nearly invisible clothesline.

Wags incorporated Webern's old unicycle in the show, and Webern cleaned the chain and patched the tire, which he hadn't done for years. In one version of the routine, the unicycle bucked forward to throw Webern in a slow motion trajectory (assisted by the pulleys) out over the heads of the audience; in another, he pedaled absentmindedly even as he floated higher and higher above the newly shined seat. Unlike most of his fellow clowns under the big top, Webern had always hated falls, even the ones that sent him thumping onto a padded mat or splashing into a tank of water. But as he trained with Wags, falling unfolded for him, in all its permutations. He learned the classic clown fall—catching one toe behind the other heel—and the best way to dive from a height into a handspring on the ground. He learned to lean too far backwards and circle his outstretched arms in the air—"Whoa, whoa, whoa!"

Webern's skin was dotted with bruises, a harlequin checkerboard of black and blue. But as Wags he was indestructible.

That night, Webern performed perfectly. He split his act into five minute segments, and as the bored crowds filed past his little booth, he took great pride in the startled looks that rippled their unshockable faces. He climbed and tumbled and climbed again and now and then he floated, and even flew. Even after the show under the big top began, people still packed into the space in front of his stage. Their laughs were flabbergasted at first, incredulous—what was this guy supposed to be, the Wingless Soaring Wonder? But as the act went on, the cynicism fell away. The laughs deepened, the crowds stayed longer, despite the barker waving them on. Sometimes a child yelled encouragement, or a lady covered her eyes in disbelief.

At the end of the evening, as he performed one final time, Webern spotted Silly Billy out in the audience, slouched in one corner, smoking a post-show cigarette. Webern knew then that he had outlasted the other clowns, that he was still out on his humble stage as the big top darkened, as the bleachers folded up and the tent poles swooned to the ground. When Webern took a bow, he watched Silly Billy applaud. Then the Parliament cleared out, and almost at once, crewmen started dismantling the tent all around him.

Webern carefully unstrung his ropes and pulleys; he folded up his stepladder and wheeled his unicycle offstage. When he finally glanced up from what he was doing, he saw that Venus de Milo was standing on the sawdust right in front of him. She blew a pink bubble of chewing gum. Then she popped it and pulled it back into her mouth with one deft motion of her tongue.

"So that's what you've been cooking up." She nodded to the pile of ropes and pulleys. "I was starting to worry, seeing a guy like you stringing up ropes all day."

"What do you mean, a guy like me?"

"You know. Heartbroke." Venus took a step toward him and lowered her voice. "A girl doesn't like fellas sneaking out in the middle of the night. Makes her feel cheap. But I'll forgive you this time, on account of what you've been going through."

"Get as mad as you want." Webern coiled the ropes. "I've been busy, but I've never been better, Venus. You don't need to make any exceptions for me."

"Oh, sure. That's why you're dressed up as a Nazi boy scout, throwing yourself around like you want your skull cracked. When was the last time you ate at the cookhouse, Bernie?"

Webern tucked his thumbs in the straps of his lederhosen. "I eat."

"You eat, maybe, but you sure don't talk. Ask how somebody else is doing for a change, why don't you? You might learn something."

Venus's heels left marks in the sawdust behind her, a trail he didn't follow.

Webern walked back to the boxcar by himself. Even now that he was back down on the ground, he still felt weightless, as if he might lift off with his next step or find himself drifting in slow motion down a bottomless well. In the distance, he heard porters shout directions as they loaded animal cages onto the train and lashed tent poles and canvas to the flatbeds at the back. Despite the late hour, the air was hot and dense as steam. The sky was yellow, the eye of a storm.

Webern paused at the door of his boxcar. His hand rested on the knob. He felt an odd impulse to knock. The foreignness of everything— the worn wood of the step, the iron wheels of the train—swept over him in a wave. *I don't live here. I don't live anywhere.* He shook his head and went inside.

The boxcar was spic and span, the cleanest it had been in weeks. Laundry was folded up and put away, his clown notebooks made a tidy file at the back of his desk, and the ragged-edged rug looked like it had taken quite a beating. Marzipan had even set up the chess set on the coffee table. But the most noticeable difference was that every trace of Nepenthe had vanished. Her rock candy aquarium—turned cloudy and overgrown with crystals in her absence—no longer rested on the windowsill, and her stack of newspapers didn't stop the door. Even her pink robe was gone.

Marzipan rose from the sofa and offered him a glass of Scotch. In the mirror, Wags was clapping his hands. He put two fingers in his mouth for a wolf whistle and punched the air victoriously with his fist.

"That was great, old buddy! Just like we practiced. You hit the mark every time. And that bit with the ladder—that was gold."

"Where are they?" Webern asked. "All her things?"

"That old junk? I told Marzipan she could chuck it." Webern looked at Marzipan, who shrugged. Wags's tone grew serious. "I mean, I know you're sentimental and all, but trust me, we need the space. Between the costumes and the equipment we're getting—"

"Equipment?"

"Well, sure. Tricycles, bicycles—fake fruit, toy guns, a pair of rubber arms. Plus a coffin—you know how the kids love Halloween—a Tesla coil too—you name it, we're gonna need it. Boy oh boy. It'll be jam-packed."

Webern started to say something, then hesitated. He took the glass of Scotch from Marzipan. Two ice cubes floated in the amber liquid. He sank down on the couch. It occurred to him that there was no reason he couldn't be happy. He remembered the night he'd walked through Goldenland past dark with Dr. Show, how for the old ringmaster the shadows had restored everything to its former glory. At the time, Webern hadn't understood that he was free to live in his imagination, too. But now he did. This was what it was to be a master—to be king of the clowns. He glanced at his wrist. The acrobat watch had stopped ticking.

"We'll actually have some space for once," Wags was saying. "And time. There's time enough for everything, now—everything we ever wanted to do."

"Yeah." Webern sipped his drink. "Years."

The knock came then: one, two. One, two, three. Webern didn't move from the couch.

"Whoever could that be at this time of the night?" Wags strained theatrically to see around the frame of the mirror.

"I told you they would come," said Webern.

The knock was louder the second time. One, two. One, two, three.

Marzipan got up and answered the door.

Willow and Billow did not look the way that Webern remembered. They wore their dogcatching uniforms, blue denim with cursive names embroidered on the pockets, not stained white shirts, and their hair no longer hung long and tangled with weeds. Billow's bob, short and black, curled tightly as Bo-Bo's once had done, and she stood with her legs wide apart, her short thick arms crossed firmly over her broad chest. Willow moved with the peculiar grace very tall women possess; her neck ducked and swerved, her pale chin-length hair tossed in the light. They were opposites still, as they had ever been, but time had softened this opposition, touched it with a sisterly resemblance. Both had the same Bell nose, small and upturned, and their eyes were wide spaced and pale: the same windows in two different houses.

"Bernie Bee," said Willow. She held a paper bag. She set it on the floor.

"Bernie Bee," said Billow.

Webern finished his drink in one swallow. The half-melted ice cubes slid down his throat.

"What do you want from me?" he asked.

The twins looked at each other. They spoke into each other's eyes.

"We came to bring you salvation," they said.

CHAPTER TWENTY-SIX

THE TRAIN ROLLED LIKE BLACK FOG THROUGH THE NIGHT.

Willow and Billow sat side by side on Webern's bed, picking dog hair off of each other's clothes. They did it without thinking, the way he would scratch his elbow. He remembered the way they had played as children, how they gibbered in a language only they could understand, then shrieked in fits of laughter, how they held tight to each other's hands and spun and spun until their own force tore them apart. But this was not the play of a child mesmerized with the perfect toy of her twin. It was something ragged, something clutched and cherished beyond all reason: a kind of nostalgia, a tragic stubbornness. They stopped their grooming and grasped hands together, a single prayer.

"I'm not scared of you anymore." Webern's words hung in the thick air of the boxcar. *Someday they'll be the only family you've got left.*

"Bernie Bee," said Willow. "God the Father knows what's in your heart."

"Lord Jesus gives a brand-new start," murmured Billow.

Willow turned to him. Her pale eyes, open unnaturally wide, pierced him.

"Will you make a brand new start?" she asked. Billow's lips moved to the rhythm of her words. "Will you drink the blood of Jesus? Will you suck the marrow from his bones?"

"I don't remember that being in the Bible." Webern looked at Marzipan, who sat beside him on the couch. Her hands were folded, but the expression on her long rubbery face was skeptical.

"Will you die on the altar of his Word, and be born again?" Willow drew a cross in the air. They were picking up speed. The train screeched as they rounded a bend in the track.

"Hell's no," Webern said. It sounded like something Nepenthe might say. He said it again. "Hell's no."

Billow stood up. She took a boxcutter from the pocket of her coveralls.

"Lord Jesus didn't fear the cross." Willow shook her head. "The saints didn't fear the lion's jaws."

Billow reached for one of the pillows on the bed. She used the boxcutter to slice a deep gash in the centre of the pillow, then thumped it. White feathers snowed down.

"When you die, your soul falls out, cracks to pieces on the ground." Willow plucked a feather from the air. "Only God can take a million things, piece them into angel's wings."

"You know a lot about things falling down and breaking. What does that make you? The devil?"

"Bernie Bee, tell Lord Jesus what you've done."

Webern put his feet up on the coffee table. He bumped the chess set. Little kings fell to the floor. "Can't He see all that on his magic TV?"

Willow touched her finger to her own lips, then to Billow's. Billow spoke as though her sister had given her voice back to her.

"He wants to hear it from you," she said. Webern had almost forgotten how deep her voice was. It sounded as if she was speaking from inside a drum.

"I haven't done anything."

"Yes, you have."

"Yes, you have."

"Okay, then what? What have I done?"

The wheels churned beneath them like a pulse. Willow raised her voice again.

"Thieving."

"What?"

"You stole grandma's monkey."

Marzipan blinked. Webern snorted.

"Dad gave her to me. If you want to take her, by all means, go ahead. I'd like to see you try."

Marzipan cracked her knuckles. Her lips pulled back in the expression that was anything but a smile. Willow and Billow hesitated. Their linked hands raised a few inches, then dropped heavily onto the Mexican blanket again.

"Confess the burning," Billow said.

The strap of Webern's lederhosen pressed uncomfortably into his hump. He loosened it with one hand.

"Which burning is that? The toast or the eggs?"

"Lord Jesus knows what's in your heart," Willow repeated.

"Then Lord Jesus knows that I'm not sorry. So what's the point of confessing?"

Billow reached for the other pillow on the bed. She held her boxcutter threateningly.

"Go ahead. Hold my bedding hostage. I'm not afraid of you anymore." Webern placed his empty glass on the trembling coffee table. "But I was then. Anyone would've done what I did."

"Bernie Bee, you made us take the blame. For your sin." Willow wagged a finger at him. "You let them catch us, call us insane."

"You *are* insane." The boxcar was so warm, he could almost see the red-hot iron rails through the vibrating floor. "I *wanted* them to take you away. I still can't believe they let you out."

"You bore false witness," said Billow.

"They saw the fire, they drew their own conclusions." Webern leaned over Marzipan. He picked up the bottle of Scotch by the neck. "Everyone thought you were crazy. Even Dad. Especially Dad. Having you in the asylum, that was like heaven for him. Better than sending me to Bo-Bo's, even, since it was paid for by the state."

Willow lay back on his bed. She crossed her arms over her chest like a corpse.

"He is a sinner. You are a sinner," she told the ceiling.

"The last time I checked God didn't accept not guilty by reason of insanity."

"When did we sin against you, Bernie Bee? When did we sin against God?" Billow squeezed the pillow to her chest.

Webern poured himself another glass of Scotch. Some slopped onto the knee of his lederhosen. "You know what you did. You should be the one to confess it. Isn't that what Jesus likes? To hear it from you?"

"What did we do, Bernie?"

"What did we do?"

"You mean before you put me in a body cast? Or after?"

Billow leaned back on the bed. She and Willow silently conferred.

"After," said Billow.

Webern looked at her steadily. Billow used to wear a thick brass ring in one ear, like a pirate; it had appeared there one day after school, in a hole still crusty with blood. The ring was gone now, but the hole was still there, half-healed, asymmetrical. Light shone through it like a sliver of moon.

"You know what you did. To the car." Webern raised his glass. "You killed Mom."

Willow sat up, her arms still crossed against her chest.

"Bernie Bee, you take it back."

"Take it back."

"Take it back."

Webern swallowed all the Scotch in a single gulp. It tasted like sea and fire, mixed together. He wiped his mouth.

"You tell me what happened, then," he said. "You mean you didn't fuck up the car? All those afternoons you elbowed around in there, after auto mechanics class, you didn't snip a wire? Loosen some screws? I saw the grease on your hands, Billow."

"My name is Betsy." She touched the embroidery on the pocket of her coveralls.

"Bernie Bee, accidents happen."

"Funny how they only happen in this family when the two of you are around." Webern stood up unsteadily. His arms described circles in the air. He thought of all the falls he'd practiced that afternoon, how much closer the ground seemed to him now. "I'm sick of you playing innocent. You ruined my life. I want you out of my room."

"Bernie Bee, we know why Mom died." Willow leaned close to Billow—Betsy? Their embroidered names were too blurry to read. Thick black outlines formed around their heads. "We *all* know why Mom died."

Webern tripped over the coffee table. He hit the floor face first. Marzipan sprang up from the couch. She tried to grab Webern's arm. He pushed her away and raised himself up on his elbows. He touched his face. His nose was bleeding.

"Bernie Bee." Willow's voice was gentle, almost kind. "Bernie Bee. You shut the garage door."

Webern pushed aside his glasses. He dug the heels of his hands into his eyes. "Stop lying. I hate how you always lie, how it's always—"

Billow pressed the flat of the boxcutter blade against her hand. She shook her head. "Bernie, Mom died that night because of you."

"And the tantrums that you threw."

"—how it's always two against one with your stupid, stupid lying."

Willow and Billow linked arms. They stood up together.

"That party night, you cried and cried." The girls stepped toward him.

"You said you fell; you wished you'd died. You wouldn't get up to say goodbye."

"She had to go up to your room. We listened outside."

"Your back hurt from the brace. You wouldn't look her in the face."

Drops of blood stained the rug. It felt like Webern's face was melting. "Why won't you leave me alone?"

"She couldn't wait to get away. She drank before she left the house. When she came back, she hit the gas—"

"I *didn't* throw *any* tantrums."

Marzipan leapt onto the mattress, hooting. She jumped up and down. Willow and Billow towered over him. Billow rested her foot on his hump.

"The car hit the garage door and crashed."

"I didn't throw any tantrums." Webern hit the floor with his fists, once for each word. "You break my back, and then you accuse *me* of throwing tantrums?"

"Hooo! Hooooo!" screamed Marzipan.

Willow stooped over him as she whispered. "It started when you had to learn to walk again. They sawed you from your body cast. You yelled and kicked and rolled around—"

"You'd run and hide." Webern squirmed, but Billow's foot pinned him in place. She went on: "Sometimes she'd knock and knock on your door 'til she didn't believe you lived there anymore. She'd drink with dad, or in her room—she'd drink after dinner, but she'd never get mad—"

"Stupid, stupid! Don't you know anything?" Webern finally rolled out from under Billow's boot. He slammed the back of his head against the floor. An almost pleasant ringing filled his ears. "You weren't even paying attention. I never threw a tantrum. It wasn't me—"

"Eeee! Eeee-eeee-oooh-ooh-ah!"

"Bernie Bee, you must make right with God."

"You must confess."

Webern smashed the back of his head into the floor again. He thought of the star-shaped scar at the base of his skull: the pain he felt there scored the insides of his eyelids with a million whirling constellations.

You must confess. But to what? What had he ever done to deserve this? His sisters had terrorized him—he had only been a child. They had been the ones to throw him from the tree; they had set off this whole chain of events.

What can I do?

A voice inside his head answered decisively: *Jump.*

But even if they hadn't pushed him, literally pushed him with their grubby hands through the treehouse window, they had pushed him into jumping with their torment; they had left him no other choice. And wasn't that the thing? They had goaded him into jumping, laughed at him as he nursed his wounds, broken him up and put him back together like some monstrous doll. He still remembered the long days in the body cast, when they'd come and gone from his doorway at odd hours, when he'd been powerless to shut them out. What had they meant, anyway, with their odd combination of malice and tenderness—the daddy long legs they placed on his nose in the morning, the warm milk they spooned him at night? If they were learning the language of affection, they were like deaf children singing, imitating sounds they had never heard.

Bernie Bee, we bring you treat.

Nothing bitter, always sweet.

Maybe they hadn't had the same childhood he had, toy shopping with his mother, or feeling her thin arms grasp him back to safety as he dangled from the monkey bars. Willow and Billow didn't have their so-so report cards taped up to the fridge, or hear their names inserted in familiar songs ("Hush little Bernie, don't say a word, Mommy's gonna buy you a golden bird"). But that was no excuse for how they'd acted, was it? Hadn't they seen how crazy they looked, how frightening, when they came home with their mouths smeared red from what he hoped were berries, when they wiped their noses on the tablecloth? Hadn't they ever learned to see themselves as others would, to sense when what they did was wrong?

Webern had always thought of his mother as long-suffering as she mutely observed the girls digging doll-graves with her silver soup ladle, or thwacking bloated earthworms on the sidewalks with a stolen baseball bat. It had never occurred to him that the kinder and more difficult thing might have been for her to intervene. As his mother's favourite, the girls seemed like animals to him, a destructive force, and the two possible responses to them had always appeared to be pity and repulsion. He had never thought to wonder, without his mother's guidance, how they were supposed to know any better.

His mother had been a delicate woman, nervous and frail; his own earliest memories were of trying to please her, to find the thing that would bring a flitting smile to her pale face. On days when she lay, listless and teary in bed all morning, he made her pancake faces with blueberry eyes and a bacon smile; it had been for her he had learned to juggle, to pinch his mouth into a fish face pucker and cross his eyes. Before Wags even, she had been his audience, the colourful clothes she chose for him the costumes for his acts. But she hadn't expected these things from him; she hadn't grown distant and mournful on the rare occasions when he misbehaved. She hadn't turned to alcohol because of him. Or had she? It was difficult to remember. They had gotten along so well—always—those other occasions had been very rare. And the tantrums—well, that had been Wags—

"Bernie Bee?"

"Bernie Bee?"

Here in the boxcar, Webern felt Willow and Billow's hands—Marzipan's too—patting his face, his wrists and eyelids. He didn't open his eyes.

Yes, the tantrums—those had been Wags. He remembered how it felt to walk in those early days, just after the cast had come off, how stiff and off-balance he'd felt. And how, each time as he approached the mirror, he had been almost relieved to see Wags approaching from the other side. How nice it had been to switch places, to let someone else take over for awhile, even someone who left fist marks in the pillows and Webern's mother in tears. Webern remembered looking at his reflection: sometimes it had taken a moment to see Wags there, but if Webern was patient he always emerged, that smile cutting across his face like a knife.

You said you fell; you wished you'd died.

You wouldn't get up to say goodbye.

Webern had thought these things, but Wags had said them. Webern had just watched from the other side of the mirror, from behind the glass; he had been Wags's reflection, powerless, looking back. He could still remember the way Wags threw himself down on the bed, overacting as usual, kicking his legs and howling, the shape his hunchback made beneath his red robe, the hunchback and the rigid line of the back brace, and the way Webern's mother had tried to comfort Wags but only for a minute, before she left, her hands pressed to her eyes, sobbing down the hall, "Ray, let's go, let's go, let's just go!" Webern remembered now, but that was because he had been there watching, behind the mirror. It had been Wags. . . .

Webern struck his head against the floor again, and the stars orbited once, then disappeared. He was alone in the empty black tunnel of space. There was no Wags; there never had been. He opened his eyes. Willow and Billow—Wanda and Betsy—stared down at him; Marzipan twirled a lock of his hair.

"All right, ladies," he said. His voice was Wags's voice. "I confess."

Wanda doused him with holy water from a thermos while Betsy made the sign of cross. Each twin clasped one of his hands.

"The Holy Ghost will burn your brow."

"You'll live in heaven with us now."

Webern wiped holy water onto his shirt. He struggled to get up, but each twin pinned one hand to the floor.

"I wish you'd let me *go*." He squeaked on the last word.

Betsy produced a rusty railroad spike from the pocket of her coveralls. A piece of yarn was wrapped around the top. "This will remind you of Christ's pain."

"What do you—do with it?" Webern winced, bracing himself. Betsy gently set it by his foot.

Wanda strung many saints' medallions around his neck. "And these of faith through strife and strain."

Webern tugged his hands away and pulled the necklaces off over his head. "Listen, you should save this stuff for somebody else."

"Bernie Bee, these are God tags." She jingled them emphatically. "They show the devil you're not his."

"It's not that I don't appreciate what you're trying to do—" Webern rose unsteadily to his feet. "—but I don't think things are this simple for me."

"But Bernie Bee," Wanda said, "we forgive you. You are saved."

The twins gazed up at him from where they knelt on the floor. Their expressions, frank and plain, rounded and angular, were strangely calm, almost beatific; they glowed with a kind of radiance that sometimes came from old paintings, despite the cracks and wear of years. Webern thought of the masks they'd worn that day, so long ago; how those visions had eclipsed this light. Marzipan squatted beside them, unafraid; she grunted and dragged a knuckle on the rug.

"We are the dogcatchers of the Holy Spirit," Betsy said. "We found you and we brought you home."

"And like I said, I appreciate it. But I don't deserve it. I hope you understand." Webern walked toward the door; almost involuntarily, he glanced back over his hump at the mirror. His face was a mess, blood and tears and holy water—a face nobody would steal. He cracked a smile. "I don't know why I didn't invite you in. I was pretty lonely, up there all by myself."

"Bernie Bee . . . ?"

"Bernie Bee!"

Webern pulled open the boxcar door; outside the ground moved swiftly past. The train was at its fastest now. Dark fields undulated against a darker sky. Behind him, Marzipan howled like something was being torn from her. Webern gulped and leapt headfirst into the night.

It looked a lot like his old bedroom in Dolphin River, Illinois, but as soon as Webern sat up he knew where he was. Two unicycles leaned up against the wall, two copies of the same Space Ace Grin McCase comic sat on two nightstands on opposite sides of the bed, beneath two black tin constellation lamps. Two open boxes of crayons spilled two sets of sixty-four colours on the floor. Webern leaned over the side of the mattress and peeked beneath the dust ruffle. Down under the bed, a left-handed catcher's mitt lay beside a right-handed one, collecting dust. He was on the other side of the mirror.

"You get hit on the head, you're bound to start seeing double," said Wags, stepping out of the closet with two checkered vaudeville jackets slung over his arm.

"That's not funny."

"You want me to be serious? I'll be serious, then." Wags tossed one of the vaudeville jackets to Webern. "I'm beat. You have any idea how exhausting it is, running through your mind day in, day out? You'd think I was in a marathon."

Webern looked past Wags, into the open closet. Identical rows of clothing hung on opposite racks. "So why'd you do it, then?"

"Why? Because I had to get you out of there, old buddy. You didn't belong in that place anymore than I did. And what's the point of being a freak amongst freaks when we've got everything we need right here? There's costumes, there's props, there's a million things to do and a million years to do 'em. And there's the two of us—the wacko and the straight man, the clown and the crowd. Without each other, we're sunk—I'm a notion without a noggin, you're an only twin. But together, we're a team."

Webern slipped on the jacket. The lining felt silky against his arms. It fit perfectly over his hump.

"Something's missing," said Webern.

"Trust me, there's nothing you can't find in here," Wags told him. "Go on. Take a look around."

Webern stood up uneasily; he approached the bureau that stood, as it always had, under the window across from the foot of the bed, and pulled open the top drawer. Two sets of face paint lay amid a sea of jacks. Two red rubber balls rolled to the front of the drawer.

"Mirrorland. This place takes whatever you're thinking of, reflects it right back to you—twice over, and in style. Hey, did you ever hear the one about the mind-reading midget who broke out of jail?"

"Small medium at large," Webern murmured. He opened the second drawer. Two slide whistles, two collapsible top hats. A weather house that housed two little gold-haired men. The jokers from a deck of cards. He knelt to yank the third drawer loose—it always stuck—and one knob popped out and rolled across the room. Inside were mismatched socks. Webern started tossing things out over his head: swimming trunks and boxer shorts, ticket stubs and rolling papers, frogman flippers, Napoleons, album covers, toy trumpets.

"Hey, slow down there, compadre. Where's the fire?"

The drawer was deeper than he'd ever imagined. Pairs and pairs of lederhosen were piled on top of each other. Webern kept throwing them behind him. Leather flopped against leather; their buckles hit the carpet with soft thunks. Finally, Webern felt his hand close around what he'd been looking for. There was only one of these. Webern opened the blue velvet box.

"Now there's a sight for sore eyes," said Wags. His voice was small.

Webern took Bo-Bo's glass eye out and held it in his hand. He thought of how when Bo-Bo's husband left her, she took it out and replaced it with a black patch—how she kept to her house after that, with her mutilated photographs and her dusty chairs, her schedules and routines and her silent piano: a world of her own making. He had been so comforted by her life when he was a child, the order she exerted over things, her unparalleled ability to snip out what pained her, what didn't fit in the pattern of her days. She'd blamed the eye for drawing the man who'd hurt her; she'd taken it out to stop that from happening again. She'd learned that folks could let her down; she caught her own raccoons after that. She'd kept to herself. Then, on her deathbed, she had given this eye to him, with one caveat: *Don't keep it in a drawer.* Yet here in Mirrorland, that was exactly where it was.

The eye had a power: the power to liberate a person, even a miserable one, from that lonely island of her own skull. Or his.

Webern pushed past Wags. He slammed the closet shut. A golden frame hung on the back of the door, where the mirror had been all throughout his childhood. Through it, Webern saw another room, dark and emptied out, reversed: his real bedroom back at home. Webern wound his arm back, the eye squeezed tight in his fist. Wags tried to grasp his shoulder.

"Bernie, pal, hey. You can't do this."

"Just watch me."

"Listen, you don't like this place? We can change it. That's the whole point—it can be anything you want it to be. A stage, a tent, the bottom of the sea—just say the word, and we're there."

"I'm going back."

"And leaving me here by my lonesome? Me—your best friend in the world, your sidekick, your amigo, your blood brother, your strong arm man? Jeez. I'm your buddy—Scout's honour. And I'm the only one who ever really was."

Webern looked at Wags: the pleading, eager expression, the pale skin, the wide-spaced eyes. *The boy in the mirror is me.* He shook his head.

"You're nobody."

Wags let his breath out in a slow *whoosh*. He tucked his thumbs in the straps of his lederhosen and rocked back on his heels.

"Quick to the draw there, pardner—and aimed right at the heart, too. If I didn't know any better, I'd think you were trying to hurt my feelings." He stepped aside. "Okey doke. Be my guest: I can't stop you now. But get one thing through your head first: I'm not nobody. I'm you, Bernie, whether you like it or not. And there's no escaping that." He pointed his hand like a gun; fired once. "See you in your dreams."

Webern threw the eye into the mirror; there was a brilliant flash of silver light. Then everything went black.

Webern Bell woke up facedown outside in the field, arms and legs splayed, as if he'd just been thrown a great distance. He groaned and rolled over onto his back. Prairie grasses bobbed above his head, and cumulous clouds formed enormous shapes in the liquid sky: a dancing bear, a fish, a pillow. His palms were raw, and his head throbbed. He groped around in the dirt for his glasses. He finally found them in the pocket of his lederhosen.

As he pulled them out, he realized he already held something in his hand. He put on his glasses, sat up, and looked into it. It was Bo-Bo's eye. The centre of the pupil was splintered; cracks exploded outward like the rays of a star. He put the eye into his pocket and struggled to his feet.

Webern felt woozy. He stood in the middle of a vast field of rippling weeds. When he touched his forehead, his fingers met a scummy patch of dirt and half-dried blood. Terrific—another injury to add to his collection. He turned around slowly. Some twenty feet away, a set of railroad tracks cut through the prairie, raised on a bed of chalky white rocks. Other than that, nothing stretched in all directions. A lonely black crow swooped down from the sky into the grasses; it reappeared a second later with a squirming field mouse in its beak. It occurred to Webern that he might be sick.

This was what it had all come to, then. After everything he'd lived through, after everything he'd seen, he'd jumped again. What a coward. He thought of how he'd lain there, dreaming, while Nepenthe packed her clothes to leave him; how he stayed hunched over his grubby clown notebooks while she danced around the room—a vortex of terrifying beauty, the only thing that mattered. He had pushed her away, just as he had pushed his mother away, just as he had abandoned Dr. Show. He had been paralyzed and helpless, he had been afraid, he had nursed his wounds. He had retreated into a world of make-believe, just like a stubborn, stupid child. He hadn't understood what he had, all the luck and the chances he'd ultimately squandered.

Webern had seen himself as the boy followed by the black raincloud, the punchline to a joke, cursed by the universe and laughed at for it. But he had never been cursed. He had just been a fool. Now, here he was with nothing, in the middle of nowhere: exactly what he deserved. His sisters were wrong: he would never find salvation. He doubled over and puked into the weeds.

Webern stayed stooped for a long moment. The toes of his polished German shoes reflected the light. He wondered how long he would have to lie here in the field before the crows would come for him, too. The grasses parted, and Marzipan appeared in front of him, her black fur gold-dusted with pollen. Webern stared at her in disbelief. She held out a pail of water.

"Wow." Webern straightened up. He took it from her and carefully set it down on the ground. "Thanks, Marzipan." He knelt in front of it and drank a little, then splashed some on his newest wound. It stung. "There a—farmhouse or something around here?"

Marzipan put her hands on her hips. She wasn't in the mood for conversation. Maybe she'd been looking forward to dumping the whole bucket on his head, and he'd disappointed her by waking up on his own.

He rubbed a little water on his hands. Dr. Show's watch still hung loosely from one bruised wrist. It had started ticking again. Marzipan took her turn drinking from the pail. Then she looked up at him impatiently. It occurred to Webern that she'd gone to some trouble to revive him. She might not take too kindly to his plan to lay down and die where they stood.

"So . . . which way should we go?"

Webern looked around again. He squinted purposelessly into the blinding sky. Somewhere in the distance, he saw what looked like smoke—the kind of haze that humans make. He started walking toward it.

As he pushed through the crackling stalks, he thought of all the places in the world he could go: Venice Beach, Tijuana, Atlantic City, Coney Island. He'd once met a team of dancers from Thailand, who had performed with cowhide shadow puppets; he imagined himself, dimly, learning their ancient trade in a grove of towering bamboo. Or he could always go to Europe. Even without Dr. Show, he might find some gypsies there, aged and irritable from waiting for him all these years.

He turned back. Marzipan was still standing in the same place, hands folded together. Her eyes shone amber brown in the sunlight.

"C'mere, Marzipan," he called. Her rubbery mouth shaped an uncertain frown. He already knew he would go to San Francisco. He saw streets filled with wildflowers and naked women, tie-dyed banners strung up over the roads bearing words in a language too beautiful for him to understand. And Nepenthe—Eliza—swimming in the water beneath a gilded bridge.

He felt his heart beat faster. It was hopeless, of course. So what? A clown's quests always were. He saw the humiliations that were coming— he would sleep in a box on the sidewalk and his shoes would be stolen, he would throw pebbles at the wrong window in her building and awaken the Hell's Angels. He would go to the park to earn a few coins performing mime routines, get swept up in a demonstration, and end up tear-gassed by the police. He would get beat up, held up, pushed down, screwed over, tongue-tied, and heartbroken. He whistled. "C'mon. Let's go."

The chimp hesitated. Webern walked a few more steps. Behind him he heard leaves rustling, feet hitting the ground. Then, all at once, Marzipan jumped onto his hump. She held on tight, her furry arms wrapped around his chest for a piggyback ride. Webern bent under her weight, but he kept walking.

ACKNOWLEDGEMENTS

Writing and publishing a novel can be a long and difficult process, so I've been terrifically fortunate to have the support of so many phenomenal people in my life.

Working with ChiZine Publications has been a thrill; I'm honored to have my book share a shelf with their other marvelous titles. Thanks especially to my editor Samantha Mary Beiko, my publishers Brett Savory and Sandra Kasturi, and my agent Joy Tutela.

I hope I'll never stop learning as a writer. But I was fortunate to have that education get off to an amazing start at Bennington College, under the instruction of wonderful authors like Lucy Grealy, Edward Hoagland, Christopher Miller, and especially the incomparable Rebecca T. Godwin, whose patient, thoughtful attention always went far beyond what my fledging work deserved. Later, studying at Columbia University also enlightened and inspired me; I was particularly lucky to find in Nicholas Christopher a professor who encouraged and nourished my love for the fantastic. And I'd like to thank all the incredible classmates who read the first pieces of this novel in the Columbia MFA program workshops, especially Olena Jennings, Daniel Villarreal, Julia LoFaso, Kat Savino, Vyshali Manivannan, Adam Boretz, Parul Sehgal, Snowden Wright, and so many others. Your insightful comments fueled my imagination, and this book wouldn't be the same without you.

I also owe a debt of gratitude to the brilliant friends who encouraged me to persevere with this project out in the often-lonely world of post-graduate life, especially Valerie Wetlaufer, Courtney Elizabeth Mauk & Eric Wolff, Penn Genthner, Emily Mintz, Stephen Siegel & Nina Stern,

Ryan Joe, David Gerrard, David Redmon & Ashley Sabin, Alex Lindo & Laura Faya, Meredith Dumyahn, and Larry Dague. Eric Taxier, thanks again for never letting me give up.

And I'm glad to have family members who believe in me, including Virginia Sole-Smith & Dan Upham, Laina & Matthew McConnell, and my grandparents.

Last and most importantly, I'd like to thank my parents, Deborah & Dale Smith, whose faith in my work has made every magical thing possible.

ABOUT THE AUTHOR

CHANDLER KLANG SMITH is a graduate of Bennington College and holds an MFA in Creative Writing from Columbia University, where she received a Writing Fellowship. She lives in New York City. Learn more about her on the web at *www.chandlerklangsmith.com*.

EMB
RACE
THE
ODD

THE INNER CITY

KAREN HEULER

Anything is possible: people breed dogs with humans to create a servant class; beneath one great city lies another city, running it surreptitiously; an employee finds that her hair has been stolen by someone intent on getting her job; strange fish fall from trees and birds talk too much; a boy tries to figure out what he can get when the Rapture leaves good stuff behind. Everything is familiar; everything is different. Behind it all, is there some strange kind of design or merely just the chance to adapt? In Karen Heuler's stories, characters cope with the strange without thinking it's strange, sometimes invested in what's going on, sometimes trapped by it, but always finding their own way in.

AVAILABLE FEBRUARY 2013
FROM CHIZINE PUBLICATIONS

978-1-927469-33-0

THE WARRIOR WHO CARRIED LIFE

GEOFF RYMAN

Only men are allowed into the wells of vision. But Cara's mother defies this edict and is killed, but not before reaturning with a vision of terrible and wonderful things that are to come . . . and all because of five-year-old Cara. Years later, evil destroys the rest of Cara's family. In a rage, Cara uses magic to transform herself into a male warrior. But she finds that to defeat her enemies, she must break the cycle of violence, not continue it.

As Cara's mother's vision of destiny is fulfilled, the wonderful follows the terrible, and a quest for revenge becomes a quest for eternal life.

AVAILABLE APRIL 2013
FROM CHIZINE PUBLICATIONS

978-1-927469-38-5

ZOMBIE VERSUS FAIRY FEATURING ALBINOS

JAMES MARSHALL

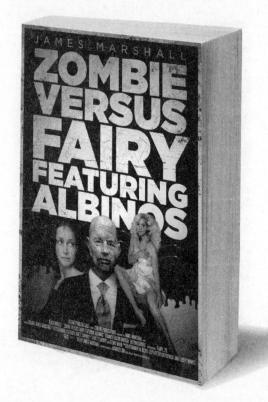

In a PERFECT world where everyone DESTROYS everything and eats HUMAN FLESH, one ZOMBIE has had enough: BUCK BURGER. When he rebels at the natural DISORDER, his marriage starts DETERIORATING and a doctor prescribes him an ANTI-DEPRESSANT. Buck meets a beautiful GREEN-HAIRED pharmacist fairy named FAIRY_26 and quickly becomes a pawn in a COLD WAR between zombies and SUPERNATURAL CREATURES. Does sixteen-year-old SPIRITUAL LEADER and pirate GUY BOY MAN make an appearance? Of course! Are there MIND-CONTROLLING ALBINOS? Obviously! Is there hot ZOMBIE-ON-FAIRY action? Maybe! WHY AREN'T YOU READING THIS YET?

AVAILABLE JUNE 2013
FROM CHIZINE PUBLICATIONS
978-1-77148-141-0

THE MONA LISA SACRIFICE
BOOK ONE OF THE BOOK OF CROSS
PETER ROMAN

For thousands of years, Cross has wandered the earth, a mortal soul trapped in the undying body left behind by Christ. But now he must play the part of reluctant hero, as an angel comes to him for help finding the Mona Lisa—the real Mona Lisa that inspired the painting. Cross's quest takes him into a secret world within our own, populated by characters just as strange and wondrous as he is. He's haunted by memories of Penelope, the only woman he truly loved, and he wants to avenge her death at the hands of his ancient enemy, Judas. The angel promises to deliver Judas to Cross, but nothing is ever what it seems, and when a group of renegade angels looking for a new holy war show up, things truly go to hell.

AVAILABLE JUNE 2013
FROM CHIZINE PUBLICATIONS
978-1-77148-145-8

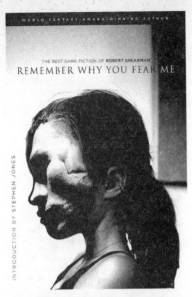

IMAGINARIUM 2012:
THE BEST CANADIAN SPECULATIVE WRITING
EDITED BY SANDRA KASTURI
& HALLI VILLEGAS
978-0-926851-67-9

SWALLOWING A DONKEY'S EYE
PAUL TREMBLAY
978-1-926851-69-3

BULLETTIME
NICK MAMATAS
978-1-926851-71-6

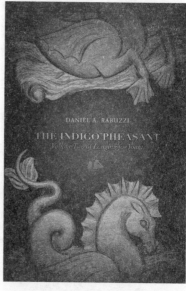

THE INDIGO PHEASANT
DANIEL A. RABUZZI
978-1-927469-09-5

MAJOR KARNAGE
GORD ZAJAC
978-0-9813746-6-6

MONSTROUS AFFECTIONS
DAVID NICKLE
978-0-9812978-3-5

NAPIER'S BONES
DERRYL MURPHY
978-1-926851-09-9

NEXUS: ASCENSION
ROBERT BOYCZUK
978-0-9813746-8-0

NINJAS VERSUS PIRATES FEATURING ZOMBIES
JAMES MARSHALL
978-1-926851-58-7

OBJECTS OF WORSHIP
CLAUDE LALUMIÈRE
978-0-9812978-2-8

THE PATTERN SCARS
CAITLIN SWEET
978-1-926851-43-3

PEOPLE LIVE STILL IN CASHTOWN CORNERS
TONY BURGESS
978-1-926851-04-4

PICKING UP THE GHOST
TONE MILAZZO
978-1-926851-35-8

RASPUTIN'S BASTARDS
DAVID NICKLE
978-1-926851-59-4

A ROPE OF THORNS
VOLUME II OF THE HEXSLINGER SERIES
GEMMA FILES
978-1-926851-14-3

SARAH COURT
CRAIG DAVIDSON
978-1-926851-00-6

SHOEBOX TRAIN WRECK
JOHN MANTOOTH
978-1-926851-54-9

THE STEEL SERAGLIO
MIKE CAREY, LINDA CAREY & LOUISE CAREY
978-1-926851-53-2

THE TEL AVIV DOSSIER
LAVIE TIDHAR AND NIR YANIV
978-0-9809410-5-0

A TREE OF BONES
VOLUME III OF THE HEXSLINGER SERIES
GEMMA FILES
978-1-926851-14-3

WESTLAKE SOUL
RIO YOUERS
978-1-926851-55-6

THE WORLD MORE FULL OF WEEPING
ROBERT J. WIERSEMA
978-0-9809410-9-8

"IF YOUR TASTE IN FICTION RUNS TO THE DISTURBING, DARK, AND AT LEAST PARTIALLY WEIRD, CHANCES ARE YOU'VE HEARD OF CHIZINE PUBLICATIONS—CZP—A YOUNG IMPRINT THAT IS NONETHELESS PRODUCING STARTLINGLY BEAUTIFUL BOOKS OF STARKLY, DARKLY LITERARY QUALITY."

—DAVID MIDDLETON, JANUARY MAGAZINE